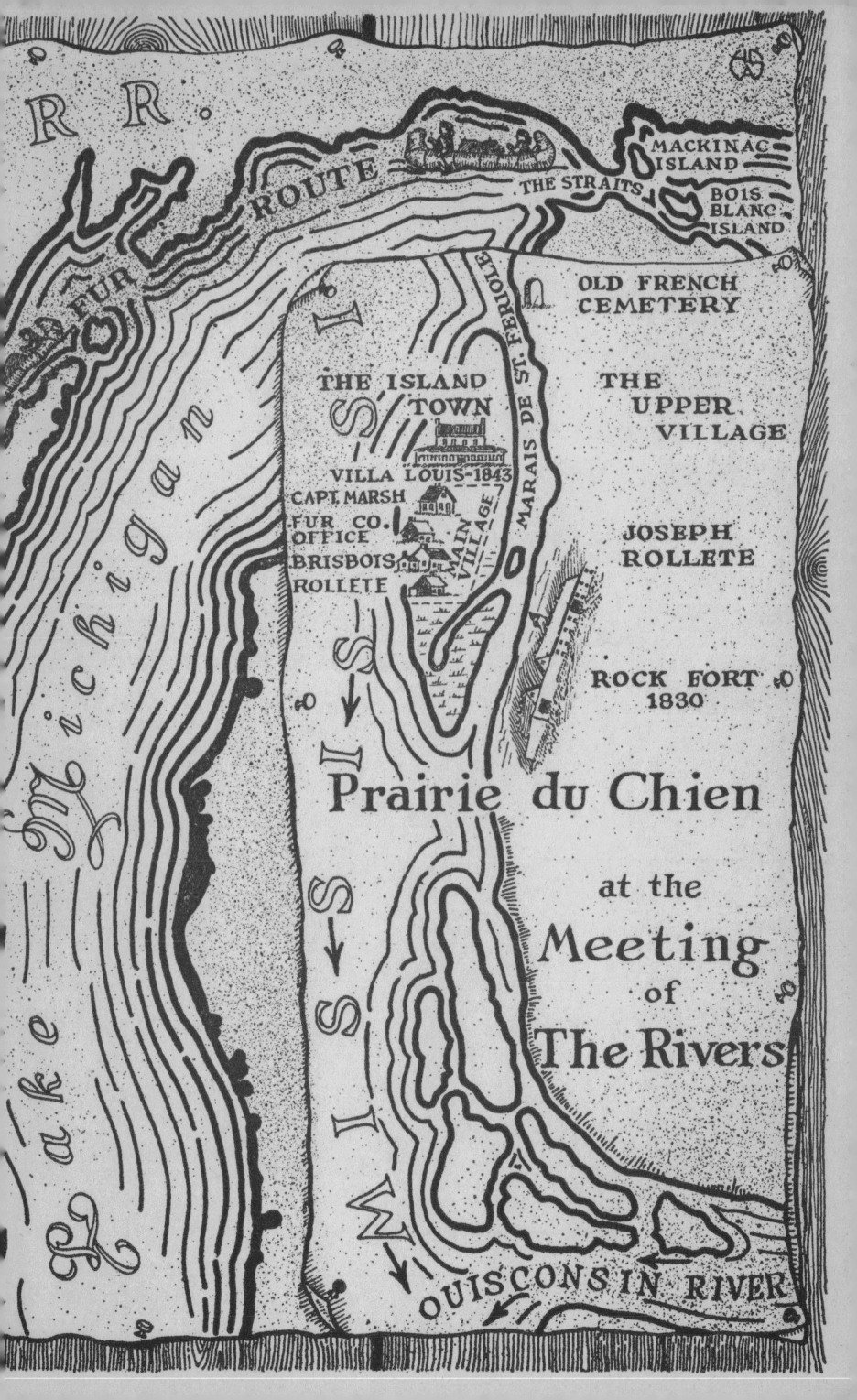

Bright Journey

BY AUGUST DERLETH

Sac Prairie Saga

Prose:

Place of Hawks
Still Is the Summer Night
Wind Over Wisconsin
Any Day Now
Atmosphere of Houses
Restless Is the River
Country Growth
Bright Journey

Poetry:

Hawk on the Wind
Man Track Here
Here on a Darkling Plain

In Preparation:

Still Small Voice:
A Biography of Zona Gale

AUGUST DERLETH

Bright Journey

CHARLES SCRIBNER'S SONS
NEW YORK · · · · 1940

For Hamlin Garland

Contents

While the majority of the characters and incidents in this narrative are historically accurate, apart from such minor changes in time as were thought necessary for greater time-unity in this novel, a certain small percentage of the incidents herein chronicled derive solely from the author's imagination. The life story of Wisconsin's Colonel Hercules Dousman is scattered in the archives of several institutions of learning throughout the United States; its events are told prosaically enough in letters and documents distributed from Missouri to Michigan, from Minnesota to New York. Certain aspects of this life have stirred the author's imagination, and therefore a certain small portion of this narrative must be considered apart from history. I have drawn upon several books for the historical facts herein chronicled as fiction, notably Dr. Grace Lee Nute's "The Voyageur," George D. Lyman's "John Marsh, Pioneer," Gustavus Myers' "History of the Great American Fortunes," and most particularly, from "Prairie du Chien," by that able historian, Dr. Peter Lawrence Scanlan. I owe thanks for generous assistance also to Dr. Louise Phelps Kellogg, Charles E. Brown, Mrs. Ona Earll, Dr. P. L. Scanlan, and especially to Mrs. Virginia Dousman Bigelow, who has throughout the progress of this novel from its inception to its final draft shown a quality of understanding and co-operation seldom encountered.

1.

Shadows Before

1812-1815

THE lake was still with the dying away of wind at dusk, and the air was calm, a little sultry after daylong heat. Gulls flew westward into the afterglow, and the crying of shore birds rose along the water's edge on the north end of Mackinac Island where, in deepening twilight, two boys played almost soundlessly before a stoutly built farmhouse. Mrs. Dousman moved quietly in her kitchen, lit by a small bracket of candles, and from time to time her voice rose, humming a melody.

She came to the door presently to stand at the threshold, her small daughter coming to her side, both looking into the encroaching darkness. She turned her eyes after a while toward the boys.

"Still no sign of papa, Hercules?"

"No, Mama."

Nancy sat down on the stoop and watched bright-eyed.

"Where's papa?" she asked, her voice shrill with determination to draw her brother's attention.

"Out there," he said shortly, waving one hand in an elaborate gesture which described a half circle.

Mrs. Dousman concealed her anxiety and went back to her kitchen. He was late now, very late. She felt herself drawn into a vortex of fear and panic, lest he had been taken by the Indians whose strange avoidance of Mackinac had aroused his curiosity. That he was fleet on the lake, fleeter than most, was no comfort.

At that moment, the gate swung to. The boys saw him first, but he gave them no time to speak.

"Young John, go home and send your father to me at once. Hercules, come inside." His voice was quietly insistent.

3

He strode forward and entered the house, his broad shoulders filling the doorway, his uncovered head briefly aglow with candle-light yellow in his hair. Nancy fluttered before him and his wife came up.

"Michael! At last! Where have you been?"

"On the lake," he replied, smiling wryly. "Wait a few moments. I've sent for John. You'll hear about it."

He brushed his thick dark hair with one rough hand and sat still, his eyes fixed humorlessly upon some point beyond the walls around him, his square jaw set in a firmness that belied the twisted smile on his short-bearded lips. His shirt was open, revealing skin darkened with short, curly hair. In a moment the smile left his mouth; his lips began to twitch a little, his eyes smoldered. One hand clenched slowly.

Mrs. Dousman put food before him, a strong brew of tea giving off an odor to challenge his nostrils. He smiled a little absently and took up the cup of tea.

The gate opened and shut, and in a moment young John Dousman was in the room, breathless, with a few beads of perspiration rimming the hair-line across his forehead.

"Papa's coming. He's right behind me."

Hercules, meanwhile, had taken from his box of stores a carved toy soldier and a flat, shallow container which housed a small turtle, and was sitting on the floor near the wall contemplating both of them with impartial pride in his possession. Young John came to his knees before them. Younger than Hercules by two years, he seized upon the toy soldier.

"Let me have this, Hercules," he said. "And the turtle, too. You don't want them any more."

"Oh, no—they're mine."

"But I want them, too."

Hercules smiled in an aloof fashion, but John clung to the soldier.

"It's a little young for your ten years, Johnny," said Dousman, reaching down to examine it. "But you may have it; Hercules doesn't really want it."

"But, Papa!" cried Hercules.

Dousman smiled, for the first time a genuine smile, without irony. "My boy, you have just got something far more valuable in

return for that painted piece of wood: an elementary knowledge of compromise. Later on, perhaps, you'll learn its usefulness."

The door opened and John Dousman stood there, striking at his legs with a light walking stick. He was a slighter man than his brother, but with the same broad shoulders; apart from this difference in their build, he bore a strong resemblance to Michael. He came in and sat down, blowing a little.

"Damned hot. Hottest July we've had on the island." He looked over at his brother, one eyebrow slightly lifted. "Now then—what's up?"

Michael stroked his nose briefly with an index finger before he replied.

John was impatient. "If you've found a new source of furs, let me hear about it."

Michael laughed shortly. "There are other things. We'll have to forget furs for a little while. And if you've any good packs, you might try to hide them."

"Man! What are you talking about?"

"You know that Aikins and Drew, whom we sent some time ago to trade for furs with the Indians along Lake Superior, have come back to the Sault. But they haven't come back to us. I set out this morning to learn why. I found out. We're at war."

John's eyes widened; his lips half-parted; for a moment he sat so, looking his astonishment. Then he protested. "At war! Michael—with whom?"

"You might know. England, of course."

"Fantastic! As if England hadn't enough with Napoleon!"

"Don't take that attitude!" Michael was sharp. "You'll see soon enough. You'll remember that intelligence we had last month about British impressment of our seamen. This is what it's come to. We've been at war with England since mid-June."

"A month ago!"

"The government, as usual, relied upon the customary channels of information. The British used special messengers. We're accordingly as unprepared as the government itself."

"The country isn't ready for any war."

"Of course not; there are too many War Hawks in Congress, bent on seizing all the land on the continent and justifying them-

selves by any excuse. Any country with adequate preparations for war has also some appreciation of the result of it and refrains from war while some compromise could be effected. This time, at least, Great Britain doesn't want a war."

"There goes the trade!"

"Undoubtedly. The Indians will take sides; I don't like the picture."

"And we'll have to fight."

Michael smiled. "Thanks to the government's laxity, we'll be spared that, at least. We'll take a different role, not inconsistent with the state of war: prisoners of war. Indeed, I was such a prisoner for most of the day."

"Michael!"

"Yes, on the trading vessel *Caledonia,* in possession of Captain Roberts of St. Joseph. We're at this moment besieged by the British and their allies. Our position is quite hopeless, and I wanted only to ask you what you were prepared to do."

"Resist! Resist with every ounce of our powder."

"Nobly said. However, we must not fight, distasteful as this choice seems. There's every reason. I want you to let Doctor Mitchell and Mr. Abbott know; I'm going to see Doctor Day and Mr. Davenport now. Bind them to secrecy; we've no reason to alarm the settlers before we know what the garrison means to do. I was asked not to apprize the garrison, but I have little choice."

"You were asked?"

"I was released on parole, in an attempt to avoid bloodshed. I intend to do so, but I'll do it in my own way." He turned to the boys, who were listening intently. "Now then, Hercules, I have something for you to do. You'll go secretly to the fort and ask for Lieutenant Hanks. See no one else. Ask him to slip out and come to see me."

"Isn't that a little high-handed?" put in John.

"He'll think so, but he'll remember also that I'm Captain of the Militia, and will obey. Go at once, Hercules."

The boy left the room immediately, with only a glance flashed to his mother. Outside, darkness enclosed the island. He stood for a moment on the stoop to accustom himself to the change from the candlelit room to the night beyond. Overhead, the stars shone

brilliantly, released from the yellow glow of the first quarter moon, sinking westward now above the smoldering evening star. From the straits, a loon's eerie cry rose distantly, and an owl called somewhere near by. There was no other sound save for the sullen, almost intangible voice of great waters, moving secretly in the darkness scarcely a mile before him, less than that behind the house, where the lake touched the shores of the island's point.

He realized suddenly that he had forgotten about his turtle, but he was excited now, he did not care, he knew that Cousin John might have the turtle as well as the toy soldier. At twelve, he no longer had any real desire to play with such toys when he might soon take part in the fur trade, he might soon become a man like his father, perhaps even Captain of the Militia. It did not occur to him that there was no need for that office if the British took possession. He set off rapidly down the carriage road leading in a southeasterly direction to Fort Michilimackinac, breaking presently into a run, taking pleasure in the knowledge that in this darkness he could not easily be seen, and certainly not by men on ships off the coast—even if they were that close, which certainly they were not. The moon's wan light fell on the road and made a pale lane of whiter earth to follow among the green fields and pasture. He passed two of his father's cows close to the road, was briefly startled, and veered away a little.

The distance he had to cover was almost two miles, but it was little to him; in a short while he had left the region of woodland and open fields, had passed the cemetery, and was advancing upon the fort. He expected the sentry's challenge momentarily, and abruptly it came from deep within the shadow of the blockhouse looming there, its old walls still faintly aglow with moonlight.

"Who goes there?"

"Hercules Dousman in the service of Michael Dousman, Captain of the Militia," he replied.

"What are you doing here, boy?"

The sentry idled out of the darkness now, his weapon held in woodsman fashion in the crook of his elbow. The moonlight made a silver line along the gun. He stood before Hercules, looking at him with raised eyebrows.

"It's your bedtime, young man. Be off with you."

"I must see Lieutenant Hanks at once, sir. My father sent me."

The sentry was dubious; he looked past Hercules into the darkness, as if in search of something sinister; but in a moment he turned and said gruffly, "Follow me!" striding away into the darkness.

They came to the massive gate, and the sentry struck it with the butt of his gun. A muffled voice answered him immediately from the other side.

"Messenger for Lieutenant Hanks," said the sentry shortly.

After a slight delay, the gate swung outward, and Hercules stepped inside. The sentry turned back to his post, and the soldier at the gate took charge of Hercules. The boy could not at first see what his guide looked like, but after a bit accustomed himself to the flickering candlelight thrown from the holes in the lantern he carried, and saw a heavy-set man with a bushy beard, older than the sentry, certainly, almost forty, thought Hercules. He ran a little to keep up with his guide's long steps.

He was shown into a well-lighted room, where two more soldiers sat at a game of chess, one of them with a shock of startlingly red hair, the other a man with a pointed, graying beard. The red-head looked up inquiringly, fixing sharp keen eyes on Hercules, an air of hostility about his glance.

Hercules quelled a desire to look away; he gazed boldly back and waited for his guide to speak.

"Messenger for Lieutenant Hanks."

"Sit down," said the older of the guards as the guide went out. He made a sudden move on the board. "That does it, I think."

"Look here, Hallett, that's one too many you've got on me," protested the red-head.

"You should watch yourself better, Darrow," retorted his companion. He turned. "Now, whom have we here?"

Hercules, who had taken a seat in one corner, immediately stood up. "Hercules Dousman, sir," he said.

The red-head inquired, "Would that be Captain Dousman's son —or John's?"

"Michael's, I think. Now then, my boy, what is it?"

"I must see Lieutenant Hanks."

"Come, come," said the red-head impatiently. "We can't disturb

Lieutenant Hanks for every boy who comes along. You tell us what it is, and we'll see whether he ought to be interrupted."

Swift, sudden anger rose in Hercules, but he held himself under control. "I'll tell only Lieutenant Hanks."

"Did your father send you?"

"Yes, sir."

The bearded one turned to his companion and nodded slightly. The red-head got up, not without some hostility again for the boy who had disturbed him, and went into an inner room.

"I trust your father's in no trouble."

"I don't know."

Hercules was conscious of the older man's attempt to inform himself, and began to feel a faint pleasure at being able to fence with him. At the same time, however, he began to grow nervous, lest the delay become too great. He looked from the soldier at the chess-board to the door through which the red-head had vanished, and back again, with the fingers of one hand plucking impatiently at his trousers.

The door opened and Lieutenant Hanks came through, slipping into a coat: a tall young man, in his middle thirties, with a round face whose symmetry was broken by a cowlick of hair over his blue eyes, and a well-trimmed moustache above the wide line of his thin-lipped mouth. His hair was tousled, as if he had been lying down. Hercules got up again.

"Hercules Dousman at your service, sir. My father wishes to see you immediately."

"Does he now?" said Lieutenant Hanks, clasping his hands behind his back and fronting Hercules. "What about?"

"Only he can say, sir."

"Indeed. But he knows where I keep myself. I'm not in hiding."

"He was too busy to come. He says to tell you it's most important, it's urgent."

Lieutenant Hanks frowned.

"It would seem," said the red-head behind him, "that the garrison might more fittingly give orders to the militia than the other way round. If you say the word, we can go out and bring Mr. Dousman in."

Hanks answered without turning. "Be still. Dousman's not in the

habit of sending for me without adequate reason. The more so, since he sends his son; and the hour is no longer early. Something's in the wind."

The older man at the table narrowed his eyes suddenly. "Oho! perhaps Dousman has something to tell us about the strange movements of the Indians, this sudden flow of savages into the north, the way they have avoided the island."

"If any one knows, Dousman does," agreed Hanks. "But even he couldn't know what the Indians plan to do from one day to the next. Light a lantern; I'll go."

"Oh, no, sir. My father wouldn't want you to carry a lantern," protested Hercules.

"Well, indeed!" murmured Lieutenant Hanks. "Very well, then, dispense with the lantern; I can find my way with the boy to lead, if that were necessary."

"A horse?" asked the red-head.

"I think we can use a horse. We'll take one of the lanes and come up from the back. There's some method behind this request of Dousman's. We shall at least keep to the spirit of it. Come, boy."

The red-head went out first, shouting orders to some one below. Lieutenant Hanks followed more leisurely, and Hercules came after. The horse was brought around to the front and the fort's commander mounted with ease, reaching down to help Hercules to a position before him. The gate swung open, and they rode out, the sentry snapping to startled attention to see Hercules there. Hercules felt a warm glow of satisfaction at this justification for his confidence.

The moon was now all but gone, low in the west, and great in magnitude; it was more yellow now, and was cradled in a blue-black haze on the rim of earth. The evening star was gone. They rode swiftly, leaving the carriage road near the cemetery for a lane among the fields and wooded places northeast of the fort and the settlement on Mackinac, and in a little while rode through the Dousman pasture, their progress impeded by cattle there. They dismounted at the rear of the house, and Hercules led the way to the front door, which was opened before the sound of their advancing footsteps.

The lieutenant blinked a little and stood near the closed door in-

side. Hercules went back to his corner. His eyes narrowed to the light, Hanks saw Michael Dousman, his brother John, Ambrose Davenport, and Doctor Day, three of them with grim faces; only Michael Dousman kept an imperturbably good-humored smile on his lips.

"Good evening, gentlemen."

"Make yourself at home, Lieutenant Hanks," said Michael, waving toward a chair.

The lieutenant went over and sat down, straddling the chair, so that he might cross his arms upon the back and face them. It was clear that he and Michael were to do what talking must be done; the others gave evidence of this in the way in which they regarded the two of them. He had the conviction that this was no light matter, and, looking from one face to another, his guard went up, he grew wary. He turned to Michael Dousman.

"You sent for me?"

"I did. I'm sorry, Lieutenant, to be the bearer of extremely unwelcome news. My brother and my friends speak their displeasure in their features, as you see. We have no great time for deliberation; so I'll come at once to the point. The fact is, Lieutenant, Mackinac is besieged by the British. We've been at war this day month, and the ordinary channels of information have obviously been shown unfit in our regard, and our government as well, for not only are we not apprized of the war in progress, but no reinforcements have been sent to this garrison."

Whatever the lieutenant had expected, it was not this. It was to his credit that he did not for an instant doubt Dousman's word; he knew the man; he knew that there had been some reason for the mystery of his boy's coming as he did; siege by the British would account for several things, among them, the strange behavior of the Indians, who had failed to enter the island for several days now and were converging in the north, some of them in war paint, and certainly allied to the British.

"Thank you, Dousman." He stood up. "I'll notify the garrison at once and prepare for battle."

"I'm sorry," said Dousman in a grave, measured voice, "but you must not do it. I shall hold these gentlemen to silence, and yourself also. I shall require that you return to the fort and give no warn-

ing. You'll be called upon to surrender in the morning, and I advise you, I entreat you most earnestly to do so without firing a shot."

Lieutenant Hanks kept to his feet, but his eyes took fire. His face reddened, and for a moment he was too angered to speak. But he controlled himself; he swallowed hard and gripped the back of the chair from which he had risen; he glared at Dousman as if suddenly the older man had become an alien invader.

"I can't believe that I've heard you aright, Mr. Dousman," he said coldly, with his anger only thinly veiled. "I shouldn't have suspected you of British sentiments."

"Sit down, Lieutenant Hanks. You're the first to accuse me of British sentiments; you'll not be the last. It's true that the British have chosen me to act as mediator for the time being, and it came about in this way; when I went to learn why my agents Aikins and Drew returned to the Sault but not to us here, I all but lost my life, and would have, had I not had the prudence to permit myself to be taken prisoner by Captain Roberts of Fort St. Joseph, who is commanding the *Caledonia* just off the island. After some difficulty, I persuaded the British that I should be intrusted with the mission to persuade our settlers to retire to a place of safety while the British landed troops to surround the fort. This task is just as distasteful to me as it must seem to you, but I assure you that in this case we have absolutely no alternative."

"Mr. Dousman, we're prepared to fight to the last man," retorted Hanks with spirit.

"In this case, that means fighting to the last woman and child also. I implore you to be reasonable, Lieutenant Hanks. There are a thousand men preparing to invade the island."

"St. Joseph doesn't have a third of that number," answered Hanks.

"You forget the trappers—and those other good friends of the British."

The lieutenant paled suddenly. "You mean, of course, the Indians."

"I mean this: that if we resist the British, they'll not keep the Indians from pillage and slaughter. Women and children will fall to them, you know that. You can't resist with a mere sixty men. No, Lieutenant, you must surrender, however hard this will be for you."

"What are the terms?"

"There are five. First, that the fort shall immediately be surrendered to the British. Second, that the garrison shall march out with the honors of war, lay down their arms, and become prisoners of war, to be sent to the United States of America by His Britannic Majesty, not to serve in this war until regularly exchanged. Third, that all merchant vessels in the harbor, with their cargoes, shall be in possession of their respective owners. Fourth, that private property shall be held sacred so far as in the power of the British forces. And fifth, that all citizens of the United States of America who shall not take the oath of allegiance to His Britannic Majesty shall depart with their property from the island in one month's time."

Lieutenant Hanks groaned and covered his face with his hands.

"Of course, it's not pleasant," said Dousman. "But you must see that we have no alternative. These demands will be made upon you by the British in the morning; for the sake of the island's inhabitants, you must bow to them."

Hanks looked up, his mouth firm, his lower jaw outthrust. "We can hold that fort almost indefinitely."

"Granted. But if you fire one shot in opposition, the British will permit the Indians to go ahead. I need hardly remind you that the women and children have no fort; your fighting will doom them."

"There's always the chance that if we fight to an honorable death, we may be reinforced."

Dousman smiled ironically. "There's no such thing in this instance as an honorable death. Your decision to fight will amount only to murder and suicide. We're hopelessly outnumbered, and if the government was not sensible enough of the importance of Michilimackinac to at least inform us that a state of war existed, let alone to send reinforcements to hold the island against any attack, there's no reason to suppose that there's anything at all honorable in dying to defend it, when the British terms are reasonable enough."

"If they keep them."

"Of course, Lieutenant. You may be sure they'll do their best to keep them, and will probably succeed to some extent. They may break them, but at least they'll not permit slaughter. We have no choice but to accept their terms."

"And you expect me to go back to the fort and pretend to ignorance of this matter?"

"Surely you can see that your only hope of explaining your surrender is to be surprised into it? The military, unfortunately, rarely consider human values in other terms."

"What word do you expect to carry back to the British?"

"Your word to surrender."

Lieutenant Hanks answered without pause. "Mr. Dousman, I cannot give you that word."

"Very well. You must at least promise to observe silence in regard to this conversation."

"I'll follow the course I think best, thank you, Mr. Dousman. And good night."

Dousman got up and held open the door. "Thank you for coming, Lieutenant," he said gravely.

"You were well misunderstood," observed John at his return to his chair.

"I will be more so. But no matter. If only that impetuous young fellow doesn't go and rouse the garrison."

"I don't think he will," said Doctor Day in his quiet voice. "But you have put him into a great soul struggle. You're right, Dousman, unwelcome as the prospect of surrender is. But what do you intend to do?"

Dousman looked speculatively at the clock. "It's ten now—as soon as I can, I'll go to the British and permit them to land on my farm. I believe it quite possible for them to command the mound at the rear of the fort, and, if they can take this in the dark, Hanks will be forced to surrender when he finds a six-pounder looking at him at daybreak."

John Dousman murmured inarticulately.

"What is it, John? Is my plan so treasonable?"

"No, you're right, Michael. But I can't see myself taking any oath to the King of England."

"Nor I, but we'll have to face it. Now, how about you, Mr. Davenport?"

Davenport sighed heavily, his dark face troubled. "I can see you're right, Dousman. But they'll grumble, they won't like it."

"But they'll do it to save their skins, even as we're effecting this

surrender. I'll leave it to you gentlemen to rouse the people and take them to a safe place well away from the fort, in case hostilities should start despite all we've done."

"We might take them to the distillery," suggested Doctor Day.

"A good place. They'll be close enough to intercede with Hanks if he determines to go through with a defense. Go at once, then. I'll make for the coast." He half turned and saw his son watching him intently. "Come along, Hercules. I can use you."

Hercules got up with alacrity and stood ready to go. But his father was not yet ready. He vanished into the bedroom, where his wife was, to take his leave from her, not knowing how or when he might return. Then he came back to the front room, where now the three others had risen and stood ready to go. He shook hands gravely with each of them, saying nothing until they were at the door and he bent to snuff out the candle. Then he spoke only a soft farewell.

They went in opposite directions; the three toward the settlement of low, log houses clustered around the fort; Hercules and his father along the carriage road into the northwest, off toward the island's lonely tip. The moon was entirely gone now; not even a glow of pale yellow lingered in the west to show where the satellite had gone beneath the horizon. In the north a few clouds stood dark against a faint aurora, a pale luminous green low on the rim of earth; overhead, the stars winked and gleamed. A faint wind had begun to blow again from the south, carrying on it the freshness of water, the smell of the lake.

Dousman walked swiftly through the woods now, so swiftly that Hercules lagged behind from time to time, but managed to catch up in little bursts of speed. The water's edge was not far, and, approaching it, Dousman took a footpath over one of his own pastures. Hercules stumbled once or twice on stones in the path. Abruptly they were at the water, and Dousman turned, catching his son by one arm.

"Go up that rock and keep an ear for any sound from the village," he said.

His approach had not been unobserved. There was a secret, whispering sound of paddles in the water. From his place on the rock, Hercules looked out and saw the ship dark against the sky, and be-

yond it, smaller craft, doubtless canoes filled with the Indian allies of the British. A canoe emerged from the darkness and touched shore where Dousman stood. Hercules heard his father's voice.

"Colonel Dickson?"

"Mr. Dousman."

"Where's Captain Roberts?"

"On board the *Caledonia*. He'll see you at once. But you brought some one with you; I heard you speaking to him. Where is he?"

"My son. On the rock behind."

"He'll have to come along, Mr. Dousman."

"Very well. Hercules, come down."

Hercules slipped off the rock and came to where his father stood talking with Colonel Dickson, whose dark-bound red coat was sullenly bright despite the night all around. They got into the canoe, Hercules almost failing to see the Indian at the stern end until he came upon him and, seeing him then, examined him as closely as the night would permit. An Ottawa, Hercules decided presently. The British, as his father had said before, would have many Ottawas and Hurons, some Sioux and Sacs. He was awed now, excited to be in such proximity to the enemy, and apparently in no danger.

The canoe fell away from shore and in a little while came to the *Caledonia*, where a rope ladder, depending from the ship's side, was caught by Colonel Dickson, keeping a balance with difficulty in the canoe. But in a few moments, the canoe was steady, close to the ship's side.

"The boy first, I think," said the colonel.

"All right, Hercules. Up you go."

He went up the rope noiselessly, swiftly, as if he had climbed rope ladders many times before in his life. His father came after, Colonel Dickson last. The canoe sped away into the remote darkness pressing in upon the ship. They were surrounded by dark shapes with white faces glimmering ghostlike all around; low voices spoke to Colonel Dickson; there was the sound of muffled laughter. They moved forward and came to the cabin.

With two lesser officers, Captain Roberts sat at table: a man of middle age, with kindness in his eyes. He looked up from the map which he had been studying, assuring himself first that a minimum of light escaped from the door through which they entered.

The cabin was well lit, but the windows were carefully shielded so that no light might betray the ship's presence to any one on shore.

"Ah, Mr. Dousman," said Roberts, glancing cursorily at Hercules and seeing in him the resemblance that marked him for Dousman's son. "I hope you bring me good news."

"Captain Roberts," said Dousman and sat down in a chair propelled toward him by one of the lieutenants in the cabin. "In regard to the village: the settlers are even now being rounded up to be taken to the distillery, approximately a mile from Fort Michilimackinac, in the south."

"I know where it is," interrupted the captain. "What resistance may we expect from the fort?"

"Unless you proceed according to plan and take a commanding position on the mound north of the fort, I think the garrison will resist. However, I don't think Lieutenant Hanks will have any appetite for battle if he finds a six-pounder commanding the fort at its weakest point."

"He'll surrender, then?"

"I believe so. However, I've instructed my brother and two friends to be at your service in the distillery, if some intercession should prove necessary. Above all, I implore you to withhold the Indians."

"We'll do our best, depend upon that, Mr. Dousman. I'm no more anxious to shed blood needlessly than you are to see it shed."

"You'll find the carriage road quite clear."

Captain Roberts nodded. "Of course, you understand, for the time being it will be necessary to keep you here. And your son, I think, too. I hope it will not cause you too great an inconvenience."

"I don't expect to return until I have done all in my power to prevent bloodshed. Perhaps I can be of some use to you in the morning."

"Perhaps so. If your Lieutenant Hanks is a reasonable man, I see no reason to fear carnage. If he isn't—I'm sorry, but the excitement of battle invariably puts the Indians out of hand."

"We're all sensible of that."

"Very well, then." He turned to the officer nearest him. "Lieutenant Asgood, give the order to invade the island according to plan. We'll proceed as planned down the carriage road and occupy

the height north of the fort. Instruct the Indians to command the fort from both sides, but to harm no one, to engage in no warfare until they are certain that battle has begun. Take the *Caledonia* around at daybreak to command the harbor."

The lieutenant saluted smartly and stepped out of the cabin. Captain Roberts sat looking thoughtfully at Dousman for a long minute, his face expressionless save for the aspect of meditation in his eyes.

"Mr. Dousman, if this venture succeeds, as we have every reason to believe it will, you'll have done us a singular service, and we should in some way repay you," he said presently. "Is there anything I can have done for you?"

"Thank you. My service was to my country, Captain Roberts—a service you would have performed for your own country in similar circumstances, I'm sure. As such, it is its own reward. But there's one thing: if I might be excused from taking the oath of allegiance to His Majesty . . ."

The captain's eyebrows went up. "I would have thought you pro-British, Mr. Dousman."

"No, sir, I'm an American citizen, and I hope to die an American."

Roberts pursed his lips. "I think we can make some arrangement in regard to the oath of allegiance other than those we have provided for remaining recalcitrants. Now, sir, no doubt you'll want to sleep. And the boy, certainly; it's long past his bedtime. I'll have you shown to bunks."

Dousman stood up, and behind him, Hercules rose also. "If possible, I want to be with you during your siege of Fort Michilimackinac."

"I'll wake you in time for you to accompany me, Mr. Dousman."

They were shown to bunks below deck, and there lay to sleep, with the sound of movement on the ship, movement away from the ship in endless sound. Some of his father's withheld unhappiness communicated itself to Hercules, but he fell asleep, tired as he was, in spite of it, and slept for a long while before Dousman's restlessness and helpless bitterness subsided sufficiently for him, too, to sleep.

The night was already more than half gone.

Hercules woke early. It was still dark, though in the east now a faint glowing announced the sun. He sat up, looking into the darkness through a break in the window's covering; he could just make out the dark line of the island, where it lay like a great aquatic creature in the restless waters, the long line of it swelling gradually to shape the Indians' name for it, *The Turtle.* A few rocky prominences shone faintly white, spectral in the growing light, and the high ridge near the center of the island, the Turtle's hump, stood out dark with trees upon the sky. All around brooded a great sentient silence, unbroken even by the monotonous lapping of water against the ship, a watchful silence, that quiet, hushed hour before the dawn stirs to waking the voices of birds, that hour when all earth is still in anticipation of the daily miracle of sunrise. Pale amethyst light fanned upward in the east, beyond the island's rim, and the first touch of old rose came into the morning.

Alert and eager to be about, Hercules climbed down from his bunk to where his father was. Dousman, too, was awake, lying fully clothed as he had gone to bed, with his head supported on elbow and palm. His eyes were fixed on nothing, but he saw Hercules without looking toward him.

"Good morning, Hercules," he said quietly.

Dousman swung his legs out and sat up on the edge of the bunk, stretching a little. "By this time they will have surrounded the fort," he said absently, more to himself than to his son. His lips pushed out and in, he turned his head a little as if the far glance of his eyes might pierce the rough-walled ship and see the island. He looked back at Hercules, a little quizzically, with one finger now ruffling his short beard. "Watch these British well, Hercules. You may learn much to your advantage in the future, when we're again free Americans."

"Will there be a battle, Papa?"

"Perhaps not."

He got up and strode up and down the narrow cabin, his eyes troubled, his hands clasped behind his back. His rough clothing was a comfort to his flesh. He paused and tried the door; it was locked, as he had expected it would be, and he stood contemplatively before it. Light was growing spectrally into the room now.

There was a sound of voices from beyond the cabin, and shortly

after, approaching footsteps. Dousman stepped back from the door
and stood waiting, Hercules moving up to his side. A key rattled in
the lock, the door was thrown open, and Colonel Dickson stood
on the threshold.

"Captain Roberts' compliments, and will you come along?"

He turned abruptly and led the way down the deck to where the
soldiers aboard had disembarked. A canoe was waiting below.
Dousman went over the side without hesitation, Hercules came
after, and Colonel Dickson followed. An Ottawa sat still as stone
in the prow of the light craft; Colonel Dickson took the second
paddle. The canoe shot away from the ship's side into the lake toward the island, which rose singularly beautiful against the great
fan of cerise and saffron that lay against the dome of blue in
the east, and was reflected upon the broken surface of the lake, so
that it was briefly as if the canoe and its occupants were moving
through space toward the island's tangibility. Shore birds flew
in flocks against the morning sky, crying shrilly over the water.
The morning air was warm, but no longer with the heat of the
previous day; the wind idled about the island, and was refreshing
with its water smell, the elusive fragrance of blossoms somewhere.

The hour was still too early for much movement of inhabitants
about the island. But there should be none, in any case; if the plan
had not met with opposition, the inhabitants should by this time
be in the distillery, thought Dousman. They were close enough to
the island now to perceive that the only activity along the carriage
road was an occasional redcoat; of the people themselves, there was
no sign. Dousman looked at his son, who watched with a kind of
eager interest, dividing his attention between the Ottawa and the
face of the island looming now immediately before them. A faint,
distant smile touched Dousman's lips, but his eyes remained grave
and troubled.

The canoe touched the shore, with wading birds in flight before
it; the Indian leapt lightly, gracefully from the canoe and with one
quick, firm motion drew it further up the sand. Two more soldiers
emerged from among the rocks nearby, stepping up to salute Colonel
Dickson.

"Conduct Mr. Dousman and his son to our position above Michilimackinac," said the colonel.

Dousman glanced at the ground of the carriage road; it was clear that some heavy object had been taken over it not long before. A six-pounder, certainly. They had carried through with it, then. He sighed and set out after the two soldiers, a third bringing up the rear. Colonel Dickson stood briefly looking thoughtfully after them before he turned to speak shortly to the Ottawa; then he, too, hurried along the carriage road, catching up to Dousman and Hercules near the Dousman farm.

"I'm sorry, Mr. Dousman—some of our men took possession of a few cattle; I think they belonged to you."

"The fortunes of war," observed Dousman quietly.

Hercules put his hand to his father's arm, holding it tightly in his fingers; he sensed suddenly something of the distance that separated Colonel Dickson and his father, something of the unbroken war that stood between them for all Dousman's good offices in behalf of the British invasion; it was this the boy felt—that his father had not after all done these red-coated soldiers any favor as much as he had done this for some one else, for himself, his family, for the other people in the settlement. He looked out, away from the road, into the east. The sun was not yet up, but the light had now grown so that it was spread over the entire sky, amethyst above, an effulgent salmon and magenta glowing along the eastern sky and for many degrees above the horizon there.

The first rays of the sun slanted across the water and the island when they came to the houses near the cemetery; they were still, deserted, save for animals grazing near by; nowhere was there any sign of human life save for the British—only British all around, their red coats bright against the green grass, the brown log dwellings. They were everywhere, some of them still concealed in places they had sought after their landing in the darkness, some of them boldly in the open along the road. Yet they were all invisible to Fort Michilimackinac.

The six-pounder had been strategically placed upon a little ridge separating a low hollow from the parade ground which looked down upon the fort; the gun was in a commanding position, opposite the weakest approach. Beside the gun stood Captain Roberts, and at his side a tall, thin man whipping at his legs with a cut twig: Colonel Macmillan, whom Dousman had met during his first im-

prisonment the previous afternoon. The colonel still wore the same look of profound cynicism.

Captain Roberts looked over his shoulder, nodding pleasantly, as if it were some casual game upon which he was about to spend his morning.

"Ah, Colonel Dickson. Proceed at once to the distillery with the ten men and take command there. Good morning, Mr. Dousman. We're as yet undiscovered."

The sun was slanting into the town and the stockade around the fort. Dousman came up to Captain Roberts' side and stood looking down. The scene below had the quality of a dream; unaware of any alien presence, Lieutenant Darrow was at the moment crossing toward the outer gates in the company of two men. All around the fort lay the enemy: Indians on two sides, cleverly concealed, as was their custom, in the foliage that grew there; the British on the other two, some of them within Darrow's sight, had he chosen to scan the ridge. He did not; he went out of the gates and down the street toward the distillery, walking unconcernedly among enemies who could have annihilated him and his companions without sound. But he was permitted to proceed unmolested.

Seeing Dousman's fixed glance, Captain Roberts murmured, "Dickson will take them, Mr. Dousman. Let them walk into the distillery."

Dousman could already know what would happen: Darrow and his men would be taken by the British in charge there; even if he managed to return to the fort, it would serve the purpose of the British, for he could emphasize the difficulty of the garrison's position.

"So long as he doesn't shoot," he said quietly.

"We must take that chance," agreed Roberts gravely. He turned to Colonel Macmillan. "Take the flag of truce and get ready to go down, Colonel." He beckoned to the gunners behind them. "Man the gun. Fire a shot off to one side of the fort, and make sure you don't hit any of the Indians over there. Stand back a little, Mr. Dousman. There, thank you. Now then."

The six-pounder belched and roared; in the town's unnatural quiet, the sound rolled and echoed. Lieutenant Darrow and his men had by this time reached the distillery and had gone inside;

no one stirred in the deserted houses. But at the fort the doors were opened, soldiers appeared in position, Lieutenant Hanks came out of the blockhouse into the space enclosed by the stockade, standing to look up.

"All right, Macmillan."

Macmillan started off. Some of the fierce tension that had held Dousman fell away; he sighed, feeling now that Hanks would go through with it, no matter how much it might hurt him to do so. Captain Roberts clasped his hands behind his back and stood with pursed lips watching the scene.

"He will capitulate, I think," he said over his shoulder to Dousman.

"It will surprise me," said Dousman.

"By this time he'll have seen how great the odds are against him," observed Roberts. "Lieutenant Hanks is no fool, Mr. Dousman. Young and impetuous he may be, certainly, but I think he has innate intelligence enough to contemplate the utter futility of resistance in these circumstances." He coughed a little, a forced cough, a sound of satisfaction with himself.

The stockade gates were being opened to admit Colonel Macmillan under the flag of truce. Lieutenant Hanks still stood before the blockhouse, unmoving, his arms folded on his chest. Macmillan went directly up to him and began to talk.

"Yes, yes, it will be all right," said Roberts. "Myself, I dislike bloodshed," he continued conversationally, his voice more at ease now. He put one hand almost boyishly into his pocket and half turned.

Dousman did not look at him; he continued to watch the scene below, still as in a remote place. The dream quality persisted, an aura of unreality; where yesterday life had proceeded normally, without any hint of change, today all was different; the unnatural silence, twice as striking now that the last sound of the single shot had died away, enclosed the scene below in a shell of remoteness. The sound of Macmillan's voice did not come back, so that Dousman saw only movement of hands, of heads; he heard nothing, though he could imagine what was said. Once or twice Lieutenant Hanks' face was turned upward, so that the sun struck across it, turned toward the heights where he stood near Captain Roberts,

and he thought: Is he looking for me? He sighed and dropped his eyes. At his side, Hercules stirred restlessly.

Out in the harbor, the *Caledonia* was moving in.

Now Macmillan started away, and Lieutenant Hanks turned to go back into the blockhouse.

"We'll soon know," said Roberts imperturbably. "What odds do you give me, Mr. Dousman?"

Dousman shook his head. "Hanks has given in, Captain Roberts." Roberts smiled, and stood patiently waiting for Colonel Macmillan.

Macmillan came, saluting; the taut smile on his lips told the story no less than the fire in his eyes. But the cynicism had not wholly left his features.

"The garrison surrenders to our conditions, sir."

Roberts nodded. "Of course. They really had to. Now, then. Colonel Macmillan, detail some men to accompany you and take possession of the blockhouse. Confine the American military to the basement of the blockhouse and to the officers' quarters; we shall presently send to join them such recalcitrants as we may find among the villagers, men and older boys. Mr. Dousman, if you please; we'll repair to the distillery." He turned and beckoned another man to him. "Lieutenant Beach, prepare to take the allegiance of our prisoners."

From the hollow north of the ridge the British soldiers with their trader allies began to form for the march to the blockhouse, their voices rising in laughter and easy jesting, relieved from the fear of battle and death. Captain Roberts swung around, made a small motion to Dousman, and strode away across the parade ground toward the road leading to the distillery.

Colonel Dickson was in charge at the distillery; he himself opened the door to them. Dousman saw with well-concealed disapproval how Captain Roberts strode in to face the company of civilians there with an almost insolent arrogance manifest in his businesslike manner, in the way he took his stand before them and commanded their attention. Unobtrusively but firmly, Dousman walked around Roberts with his son and took his place among his own people, finding his wife easily at Mrs. Davenport's side. She took his arm with what he saw was a defiant air, and, looking around him, he saw on a few faces here and there a definite hostility.

He sighed, but he had expected this. Yet he did not lower his eyes; he sought with patience for the faces of those he knew most intimately; they were all there—his brother, Mr. Davenport, Mr. Abbott, Doctor Day, Doctor Mitchell, Mr. Stone, Mr. Bostwick. Few of them, he knew, would take the oath of allegiance to the King of England.

His wife's fingers plucked at his sleeve, and he glanced down. "They think you brought the British," she whispered angrily.

He patted her hand reassuringly. "The British would have landed without my permission, Jane."

Captain Roberts clapped his hands smartly together, and Dousman was still; every one else had already given the British commander his attention, though not without obvious dislike for him manifest on many faces. But there were those who were indifferent, sensible only of inconvenience to them and the small matters that occupied their days.

Roberts unfolded a paper and read aloud in a firm voice the articles of capitulation, dwelling upon the last of the terms by repetition and amplification. "All citizens of the United States of America who shall not take the oath of allegiance to His Britannic Majesty shall depart with their property from the island in one month's time. We are prepared to take your declarations here and now, so that we shall be able to deal accordingly with you. Those of you who take the oath this morning will be permitted to resume residence of your homes and continue what business, if any, you have." He coughed, as if oblivious to the murmur of protesting conversation that swelled all around.

The captain turned to Colonel Dickson. "Bring up a table, Mr. Dickson."

"Captain Roberts!"

"Mr. Davenport, I believe. At your service, sir. What is it?"

"Captain, I protest this outrage. How can you expect to make English subjects of a people who fought less than forty years ago to free ourselves from the tyranny of a British king?"

"The fortunes of war leave us no choice, my friend," replied Roberts with the imperturbable good humor of a man who knows that his is the whip hand. "If you should elect not to take the oath, we shall be obliged to treat you as a prisoner of war and confine you with the soldiers to the blockhouse, from which you will presently

be released on a basis of exchange of prisoners." He swung his eyes away. "Now, then: come up, please, and let's get this over with."

The movement forward was not long in coming. A long-jawed trapper led the way, and presently, in twos and threes, the small assembly moved toward the table. Dousman stood still; near him, Davenport stood also; in a little while a group had formed around them—the Stones, the Abbotts, John Dousman and his family, the Bostwicks. Both Doctor Day and Doctor Mitchell had gone forward, reluctantly and with glances of inquiry directed at the silent group.

Captain Roberts left the table and came around to them, standing before them with his mouth grim, his hands clasped tautly behind his back, so tautly that his fingers were unnaturally red where his circulation was impeded.

"Mr. Davenport, will you take the oath?"

"No, sir, I will not. I was born in America, and I'm determined at all hazards to live and die an American citizen."

Captain Roberts looked quizzically at him, keeping silent for a moment before he said with an air of regret, "We shall have to confine you to the blockhouse." He went on to Dousman.

"Mr. Dousman, I made you a promise; I intend to keep it, though it's against my rule in like cases. You and your family will return to your farm."

"Thank you," said Dousman dryly. "May I ask—what's to become of the women and children of those men who refuse to take the oath you demand?"

"They'll be permitted to remain here, save for the older boys, whom we shall be obliged to confine together with their fathers."

Dousman made no effort to leave the building. "And to what extent will their movements be restricted?"

"Not at all, sir. Do you think I'm a gaoler by anything save necessity? Of course, any espionage activities will be severely punished, whether carried on by women or children. Mr. Abbott, what's your decision?"

"Mr. Davenport has spoken for me, Captain."

Roberts shrugged helplessly. "The decision is yours, of course, gentlemen. You'll prepare to accompany the soldiers to the block-

house. As for you, Mr. Dousman, I may call upon you at your farm within an hour."

Dousman was dismissed. He suppressed his first inclination to stay, reflecting that to antagonize Roberts at this point would be needlessly stupid, and set out gravely from the building with his small family.

They went in silence up the winding street to the carriage road. It was mid-morning now; time had gone swiftly, too swiftly for any marking of it. The sun was high, its hot light streaming down to the dusty road, bright upon the old logs of the buildings there. No word passed among them until they had reached the road beyond the fort.

"Who spoke against me?" asked Dousman quietly.

"Doctor Mitchell and Mr. Stone," replied his wife.

Dousman nodded thoughtfully. "I couldn't blame them."

They walked on in silence, past the cemetery into the open country where the farms began. Some redcoats and their allies had melted into the settlement behind; the country was calm, with fields showing a little grain here and there, and cattle grazing contentedly in the pastures. Far on the western horizon floated a second British ship, her flag making a distant spot of color in the light wind.

"There will be others, I dare say," Dousman resumed after a while, his eyes fixed immovably on the vanishing point of the road ahead. "Though my motives are certainly not so difficult to understand. Still, no doubt it has a strange look: my movements in the night, my appearance with the British in the morning; their lenience with me." He sighed.

"Never mind, Michael," his wife comforted him.

In a little while they were home. Hercules ran into the house and out again, looking down the way they had come. There was nothing in sight, no man, no cart, not even a cow, though the sound of lowing drifted over a slope from behind the house. He scuffed the ground with one foot, idly, thinking over what he had seen: a living game of soldiers, but no battle—and Indians, whose savagely painted faces came back to him as something insidiously menacing. He went back into the house.

"Do you think Cousin John will come?" he said to his father,

who sat at table now waiting for his wife to put food before him.

Dousman gave him a curious look and said quietly, "Come here and eat something, Hercules." He waited until the boy had slid to his chair, facing the question in his eyes. "Now, then, you had better know at once that it may be that Young John won't come for a while."

"Why?"

"He may need to go with his father."

"Oh." He forebore to ask for any explanation, because it was evident that his father had only begun to speak. He sat still, waiting a little apprehensively, his somber eyes fixed upon Dousman.

"You see, this is no game of toys, Hercules," continued his father gravely, while his wife came and went. "These soldiers are our enemies, and they're only tolerating us. We had to surrender because we were too weak to fight—not our men as men against other men, but our women and children against Indians. Cruelty and rapacity are the inevitable allies of the English. Remember that."

Hercules studied this briefly before he said, "But you let them come."

"Yes, that's true, my son. I let them come because it was infinitely less cruel to do so. Humiliation and imprisonment don't take lives. Let it be another lesson for you, again in compromise. My personal wishes in this matter are nothing; but the welfare of these people is a thing to make concessions for. When you gave Young John that toy soldier, you did it to keep his friendship. What I did to enable the British to take this island, I did to save its people."

"The worst will come if the Americans try to retake it," said Mrs. Dousman.

Dousman nodded. "They will, but not yet. When they do, I'll do everything in my power to help. But first of all, I'll need intelligence of what goes on outside. I must get in touch with Aikins and Drew; I must have some contact with Detroit."

He leaned back, his eyes narrowed, his fingers drumming the edge of the table.

His wife shook her head slowly. "Too dangerous, Michael. Too dangerous. If you were caught——"

He nodded impatiently. "I have an infinite preference to live under the American flag, not the British. My hand may have helped

raise the British flag over Michilimackinac; my hand shall accordingly help to lower it. I'm sensible enough of what danger there is, and I'm not afraid of danger."

She said nothing more, but sat down and broke a piece of bread, watching him with her head turned a little, marking his concentration, knowing that already his shrewdness was pushing to the fore, already some plan was formulating in his mind. Dousman was not unaware of her concern, nor was he unconscious of his son's steady, unwavering gaze, the curiosity in those somber young eyes. The room settled into a kind of mid-day quiet, though it was past the hour of noon. On all the island there was no sound now save the water's almost inaudible murmur, the wind's whispering in the leaves of trees near the house; these grew and invaded the room to mingle with the soft sounds of their eating.

Hercules was trying to understand; it was difficult. He loved his father, he knew he had done right; he could not yet fathom his actions, nor foresee their consequences. At the moment he was occupied with the thought that Young John might not come again for a long while to play with him; this was an immediate thing; it took precedence over everything else. But there was also the clear intimation that his father was somehow, however indirectly, responsible for this. He ate slowly, contemplatively, hunger growing upon him after his long fast. The sunlight lay across one edge of the table, and a fly noised about in it, breaking the room's quiet.

They were still at table when Doctor Day came, his thin, ascetic face having lost none of its grimness, but a little of its color, lending him an unnatural pallor because of the singular darkness of his pointed beard. He came in, carrying his hat in his hand, and was waved wordlessly to a chair near the table.

"Will you have a cup of tea, Doctor Day?"

"None, thank you, Mrs. Dousman. I've no appetite for it."

"Wine, then?"

"Thank you, no. I've been swallowing British arrogance for the hour past and I'm quite devoid of appetite of any kind."

Dousman smiled dryly. "It begins well, I see."

Doctor Day eyed him dubiously, his eyes wavering to and from Dousman's face. His hands fidgetted. Dousman turned and leaned back, smiling a little to put the doctor more at his ease.

"I hope you don't think too ill of my taking the oath," began Doctor Day.

"Certainly not. No doubt you'll be as quick to renounce it when the Americans retake Mackinac."

"Quicker," said Doctor Day hastily, but caught himself and looked around almost as if he might find himself on the instant surrounded by redcoats. He sighed, pulled out a large white handkerchief, and wiped his forehead. "It's a hot day, and the tempo of the morning has been hotter. Both Mitchell and I felt that whatever happened, the people of Mackinac would need physicians."

"Agreed," said Dousman. "Who refused finally to take the oath?"

"Your brother, Mr. Abbott, Mr. Davenport, Mr. Stone, Mr. Bostwick." He paused a moment before he said, with some diffidence, "Word's going around that you were permitted to remain neutral. All the others have been confined to the blockhouse: the men and their sons from the age of ten up. Naturally, your condoned neutrality is causing some comment."

"I should imagine so," agreed Dousman. "I did the British a service in acting as mediator, and they promised me payment; I asked to be permitted not to take oath of allegiance to the king."

Doctor Day grinned. "Do you have free movement, then? Can you resume trade?"

"I hope so."

The doctor's grin held. "Michael, you old fox! You don't deceive me."

Dousman was bland; he said nothing.

Hercules spoke suddenly. "Papa, is Cousin John in gaol?" He had pondered Doctor Day's earlier statement, and had realized suddenly that his cousin was included among those civilians who had elected to remain Americans and were now imprisoned in the blockhouse. His voice betrayed his alarm.

"I believe he is, Hercules," said Dousman quietly.

"What will they do with him?"

Dousman looked to his guest. "Perhaps Doctor Day can tell us?"

"I think they'll ship them to Detroit. That was the talk in the streets."

"When?"

"As soon as possible."

"Can I see him?" asked Hercules.

Dousman looked at him speculatively. "If they'll permit it. You'd better go at once, then."

Mrs. Dousman protested. "But, Michael—the Indians."

"I think they've taken themselves off," interposed Doctor Day.

Dousman nodded privately to Hercules, and the boy was away, running out of the house and down the road, his young mind even more puzzled than before, failing to understand what his cousin had done to deserve imprisonment and exile. The sun was hot now, and he could not run far without becoming too uncomfortable; he settled down to a swift loping walk, impatient with the distance. He had not yet considered the immensity of losing his most favored playmate, for he had no conception of the duration of young John's exile, knowing only that it would be longer than a week, perhaps even a month. Not yet aware of the scale of the occurrences that had taken place that morning, he was nevertheless sensitive to certain sinister implications in what had happened, and he would presently understand.

Rounding a bend in the road he ran full tilt into a company of redcoats led by Captain Roberts, who caught him by one arm. He wrenched himself angrily away, but in a moment listened to some inner sense warning him of danger in imprudence, and masked his features from their inquiry so that they might not see the hostility he held within him.

"Well, well, good afternoon, young Master Dousman. And where might you be off to?" inquired Captain Roberts.

"I'm on my way to see my cousin."

"Oh. Which cousin?"

"The one you put in gaol!"

Captain Roberts turned inquiringly to Colonel Macmillan, whose aloof smile was as if frozen to his lips. "Mr. John Dousman's son, I think," he said tonelessly. "In his eleventh year."

"And what do you want with him?" pressed Roberts.

"I want to say good-bye."

The captain looked at him with one eyebrow cocked, uncertain which course to follow. If the boy carried some message from his father to his uncle, he should not be permitted to go on. If he were, as he said, merely on his way to see his cousin, there was no harm

in permitting him to proceed. I must try not to be needlessly cruel, he thought dispassionately. Abruptly, he stepped aside.

"Very well, boy. Go on. If they try to halt you, say that Captain Roberts has given you permission to enter. Ask for Colonel Dickson."

Hercules could not bring himself to thank him; he walked past the British with a kind of righteous dignity that was comical.

Roberts stood for a few moments looking after him, smiling a little, thinking of his own sons until a warm glow spread inside him. He shrugged and went on, his company after him. They paused at the Dousman gate. Roberts went to the door and knocked, though it stood half open.

"Come in, Captain Roberts."

Dousman stood alone in the front room into which the door opened. His hands were clasped behind his back, his features grave. He indicated a chair.

"Will you sit down, Captain?"

"No, thank you. I came just to tell you that we were setting out for Fort Joseph, but will be back shortly. Colonel Dickson is in charge."

"I wanted to ask you what my neutrality entails. May I expect freedom of action sufficient to go about my fur trade? It will be difficult enough with my brother gone, and one of us should be permitted to carry on."

"At your own risk, of course. You may be shot by Indians, by British who think you American, by Americans who think you British. My advice would be to forget the fur trade for the time being." He shrugged, seeing Dousman's firm jaw. "As you like, sir. I'm not responsible for the actions of a neutral so long as they don't prejudice our position here. I need hardly warn you that any activities directed against us will result in the severest measures I have in my power to impose as punishment."

"I'm sensible of the rules of war, sir."

Captain Roberts inclined his head. "Very well, Mr. Dousman. We understand each other."

He bowed and went out. Dousman stood where he was until his wife came up behind him, uncertainly, and looked past him to the road along which Captain Roberts and his company were moving.

She took his arm, clung to it, her eyes betraying to him her fear, so that she need not have spoken.

"I'm afraid, Michael, afraid of what's to come."

He touched her hand gently. "Not yet, Jane. Wait a little. We have nothing to fear now." He smiled confidently. "Now I must go to see how many of our cattle they took." He bent and kissed her before he went out.

In mid-afternoon Hercules came back. He came running, stumbling now and then, almost falling, but recovering and running again. Seeing him, Dousman hastened across the pasture to the road, where Hercules, catching sight of him, ran over, his young face working, and flung himself upon his father. His impassioned anger brimmed over; he burst into tears.

"Papa, Papa—they're sending John away forever. For all the time. He didn't do anything."

He was sobbing now, with all the despair of a child.

Dousman took him firmly by the arm and sat him down on the roadside bank; he sat down at his side.

"Come, Hercules—it may not be so bad as you think. It may be only a year or so."

It was the same to Hercules: a year or forever; in his wild anger and grief he could not differentiate between them. He looked up suddenly, his tear-streaked face malevolent, with his eyes blazing, his lower lip pushed out.

"I'll kill them all—those damned redcoats. I won't let them take John away because he won't swear an oath to their king."

Dousman smiled bitterly, sadness lying in his eyes now. He put one arm about Hercules' shoulders.

"Not all of them, surely," he said gently. "They might have little boys themselves, Hercules. Have you forgotten to think of them? It's the rule of war they follow. If your Uncle John hadn't been so forthright, if he hadn't been first of all an idealist, he might have spoken these few words, too—it would have done little harm, perhaps. But this was his right; he must take the consequences. Young John must go along; that's the way these things are done. No one of these redcoats is any more responsible than any other, and Captain Roberts least of all."

Hercules' grief was not assuaged; he turned accusing eyes to his father, but said nothing. His lips were trembling still, his eyes rimmed with tears; occasional sobs tore from him, shaking his body.

Dousman shook his head kindly. "My boy, you must learn never to give way so; you must learn to keep these emotions inside you a little more. Tears aren't shameful, no, but never permit them to destroy your power to think for yourself, your ability to reason. Take hold of yourself now; we'll see young John again sometime. I promise you, but it won't be soon."

He got up and stood for a moment watching Hercules fling himself to the grass, his sobs ebbing now, his grief spent. His small fingers were dug into the earth, the grass among them. As from a remote place, he thought: It will not harm him. But he was moved; he reached out and touched the boy gently on the shoulder and, as he turned, gave him his hand.

"Come, Hercules."

The boy rose, obediently enough. Hand in hand they went up the slope toward the house and its mellow, soft brown beautiful against the green earth and blue, cloudless sky behind.

Late in August Drew came under cover of night. A light sleeper, Hercules heard him first. He slept in a low-ceilinged gable loft over the kitchen, and woke to the sound of careful footsteps coming up the slope at the rear of the house, from the island's east shore. He got out of bed and went silently down into the kitchen, where he ran to the window and looked out, his first thought naturally of enemies: Indians come to plunder. In the pale moonlight that lay upon the land, he recognized Drew as one of his father's men, and opened the door to him.

Drew was startled by the apparition of Hercules in his nightgown, but pressed on, ducking gratefully into the house. He pulled his cap from his unkempt hair and peered anxiously around.

"Ye're not alone, boy? Yer pa's here?"

"I'll wake him," said Hercules.

He went quietly to the room where his father and mother slept, and, walking on tiptoe now, paused at his father's side and touched his shoulder at first lightly, then with more insistence, until Dousman woke, starting up in alarm which subsided quickly at sight of Hercules.

"Mr. Drew's here, Papa."

"Go to bed and let me sleep," said Dousman, only half awake. But abruptly he heard what his son had said; he sat upright. "What! The devil you say. Where is he?"

"I let him into the kitchen."

Dousman slid from bed, seizing his trousers to put them over his nightgown. "All right," he murmured. "Go back to bed now, Hercules."

He went out into the kitchen, greeting Drew with quiet joy. Hercules went obediently up the ladder to the loft, but he did not go back to bed; he lay on the floor with his head near the opening and listened to the conversation below, watching the two shadowy figures there, for no light had been lit, and apparently none was to be lit.

"I thought you were taken or killed," said Dousman. "What happened?"

"Never mind that," said Drew, talking swiftly. "We ain't got much time. I'm on Duck Island now—an English citizen. Aye, I took the oath; I've taken a good many in my time; so one more or less don't matter."

"What's going on outside? We've had no news at all, nothing to amount to much. I've had damn' little luck establishing points of contact outside." Dousman was eager and made no attempt to conceal his eagerness.

"If ye mean battlin'—ain't seen any. They got yer brother's place at Fort Howard: Indians burned it out. He's safe enough, though. There's been enough happenin', all right—some of the Chippewas and more Ottawas joined the redcoats. All the men from here have come safe to Detroit, and I got a letter by me from yer brother. I met Aikins on the lake; he wouldn't change; so I get to see him once in a while like that."

"What about General Hull?"

"Don't know," said Drew laconically. "They say he's surrendered, and likely he has; he was just about done for when he heard about Mackinac, figurin' it let all the Indians down on him from the north. And then there's some talk about Tecumseh dickerin' with the redcoats."

Dousman was briefly silent. Hercules edged forward, so that his head stuck out over the floor there; but he could see little more.

The two men were sitting together at the kitchen table, only faintly illumined by the moonlight that streamed into the room through a high window.

"What's goin' on here?" asked Drew. "Is Roberts still in charge?"

"Yes, he is, and likely to stay, too," replied Dousman. "They're putting up a second fort on the height from which they took Michilimackinac; they don't mean to be caught the same way. Fort George, they call it. What news have you from the south?"

"There ain't a damn' thing. Looks like they got their hands full down in Washington and forgot all about us."

Dousman got up and began to pace back and forth, his hands alternately swinging at his sides or clasped behind him. The silence of the house grew, the sound of Dousman's bare feet against the floor was loud as brogans on the boards. Outside, the night was still, save for the brooding sentience of the lake, audible in a secret murmur of movement that went on forever, without wind, the water's deep currents working from end to end of the lake, from one lake to another through the straits. The rough floor boards of the loft began to make themselves felt against Hercules' body, and he moved uneasily from time to time. Presently Dousman's pacing stopped; he came to a pause before Drew, who was still sitting there.

"Are you hungry, Drew?"

"I could eat a little something," admitted Drew. "It was a hard pull."

"It's after midnight; you haven't got long." He went to the cupboard and took out some meat and bread, which he set before Drew. He sat down across the small table from him.

"Now, look here, Drew, we've got to get word to somebody. There's no reason for us to think the British can hold the Michigan Territory for long; they haven't got enough men, especially if we engage them in force in the east. Find out how far south the British have got, and try to get through to Vincennes. What about Dearborn, by the way?"

"No word."

"Captain Heald is still in command there, I think—if the British haven't gone to take it. But that country is filled with Sacs, Sioux, Winnebagos—Indians hostile to both redcoats and Americans; so

that's not likely. No, Vincennes is the best place from which to dispatch word eastward."

"What about the trade?"

Dousman shrugged. "There isn't much left of the trade. I go through the motions, little more."

He sat down again, disconsolate because he recognized the futility of planning without definite information and point of contact from outside. Drew had certainly done his best, but it was not nearly enough.

"Better pack up some of that food and take it along back."

"Oh, I'll make it all right come breakfast time."

He got up, stretching a little.

"I want you to come whenever you have news for me. We must try to learn what goes on outside. The British bring us no intelligence here, though they treat us well enough; we can't complain. As neutrals, we can't expect too much. You said you brought some word from John?"

"Aye. Almost forgot. Here." He took a folded paper from his pocket and gave it to Dousman. "Now I've got to go."

Dousman went to the door with him. Compared to the darkness of the room, the moonlit land outside was bright.

"Lucky ye're far enough away from anybody else—and the fort," muttered Drew. "Good-bye."

Dousman stood there looking after him. Drew ran hunched over, with his arms close to his sides, as if he carried something against his body. In a few moments his dark fleeting shadow was out of sight, retreating down the long, gradual slope to the water's edge where his canoe lay. Dousman turned, closed the door, and went over to the sconce for a candle. He walked catlike across the floor, uncovered the bed of coals in the fireplace, and lit the candle. Holding it in one hand, he sat down at the table and unfolded the letter from John; it was unsealed.

There was little there to be read. John was cautious almost to an annoying degree; he knew no more from this communication than Drew had told him. And yet, in one place John had written cryptically: "We may have to move again!" Did that presage the attack on Detroit, the surrender of General Hull? And again, the fall of Michilimackinac was brought sharply home to him where John

had written: "Hull was defeated at Mackinac, whatever else happens now."

Reading down, he saw that the letter was in three parts; the first part to him from John; the second to Hercules from young John; the third to John's wife from them both. He looked inquiringly up toward the loft and saw Hercules peering down, his small face framed by the yellow, flickering candlelight against the darkness behind.

"Come down, Hercules," he said.

Hercules came down, a little reluctantly, not knowing whether he was to be punished or not. He went over to his father's side. Dousman smoothed out the paper beside the candle, tearing off the lower half and putting it into his trousers' pocket, so that he might take it to his sister-in-law in the morning.

"There's a letter for you, Hercules. From Cousin John." He pointed it out, the three lines, sadly blotched where ink had escaped the quill: a child's letter of commonplaces, echoing his father in part of its substance.

Hercules read it eagerly. "What does he mean, going away?" he asked presently, looking up.

"From the redcoats," said Dousman absently.

"May I keep it?"

"Yes, of course. Show it to mama in the morning."

Hercules folded it carefully and carried it up into the loft. Dousman bent, blew out the candle, and returned to his bed, depressed now with impatience and the conviction that weeks and months must pass before the Americans would move toward Mackinac, time must take its slow progression from the events just past to those which surely must be destined to change them. But deep in his mind was beginning now the faint surging upward of doubt.

His doubt was well founded.

In October, Drew came again. He was caught in a storm over the lake and was delayed, so that it was not until almost dawn that he reached the island; at this time he would not risk discovery by going to Dousman's house, lest he be seen crossing fields and pastures in the growing daylight; so he concealed his canoe among the low pines growing alongshore, and made his way through the

woods to the first of the caves in the rocky eminences northeast of Dousman's farm.

In mid-morning Hercules came upon the canoe. He had crossed the pasture and gone into the woodland toward the far shore of the lake, pursuing his lonely way, restless, solitary, and, tripping over a root, he fell in such a manner that the carefully concealed craft came within his vision. He lay for a moment unmoving, tense with anticipation of sound to warn him of attack; he thought of Indians, he thought of Americans; failing any evidence of the canoe's owner, he thought of Drew. He got up and went over to the canoe; there was no mark of identification upon it. He was convinced that the craft was Drew's. But Drew had not come to the house. Where was he, then?

He was wise for his years in woods lore, taught him not alone by his father, but by Indian boys, young Hurons with whom he had played. He stood quite still, drawing away a little from the canoe, so that he might avoid revealing its presence to any one who might see him. In a little while he reasoned that the storm had prevented Drew from reaching the island in the night; he sought evidence of this, and found it readily enough, in the degree of moisture still lingering in the canoe. He began to walk in a slowly widening circle all around the place where the canoe was, his keen eyes fixed to trees and grass, and presently he came upon Drew's trail: no more than grass bent a little, a leaf turned on an outthrust limb. He followed it, saw quickly that the path led north along the shore, and made directly for the caves less than a mile away.

The morning air was fresh after the night's rain, and the fragrance of pines rose all around, coupled with the deathlike odor of falling leaves from the hard maples, turning red now. The sky was clear, that intense clear blue which always followed storm; not a cloud lay anywhere, and the sound of the waters rushing through the straits came as a distant murmuring. He went swiftly, yet cautiously, his eyes alert for the signs of Drew's passing; these were plentiful now that he knew Drew had gone this way. Emerging on the edge of a narrow strip of field belonging to his father's farm, he was delighted to see his sister Nancy among the cornshocks. He left his trail to run to her and send her for his father. Then he went on, eager as an animal now.

He came to the nearest of the caves and advanced with great caution, looking back toward the island's highest point, searching for signs of redcoats on the Turtle's back. Nothing stirred under the morning's sun; only a muted sound of life rose from the village beyond the high place, invisible from where Hercules stood. He pressed on, dropping silently down from a ledge before the cave's mouth and slipping noiselessly into its darkness, where he stood without movement until suddenly Drew was there.

"Ah, it's you, boy. Ye weren't seen?"

He shook his head. "I sent for papa. I sent for my sister."

The courier's quick alarm was subdued, but his eyes remained narrowed. "How'd ye know I was here, eh?"

Hercules told him without hesitation.

"Ah, ye're a bright lad. Mind now ye keep it to yerself." He paused and listened briefly. "Will he be long, d'ye think?"

"He'll come right away. He's been looking for you."

"That's good—then I can get away this night a-comin'." He grinned. "D'ye suffer much with the British, lad?"

"We're all right."

"Ye're better off than most," he said shortly and was quiet.

In a little while Dousman came, using the same caution which had marked Hercules' approach. He crept into the cave from one side and came gladly to Drew, clasping his hand warmly.

"Drew! I'd almost given up hope of seeing you again. You're a welcome sight."

"It's not welcome news I bring," said Drew glumly, a scowl on his dark face.

"Not defeat?"

"The Northwest is lost. For a month the British have held Detroit. It was true, Hull surrendered. Tecumseh, driven by that fool Harrison, allied the tribes with the British at Malden. When Hull could have smashed them, the damn' fool kept puttin' it off; so there he sat, meek as a lamb, jest waitin'. In the middle of July, he got reinforcements and artillery; he went across to Malden, but he didn't attack. Tecumseh cut off his supplies from Detroit; then he turned around and ambushed the first American force; Hull went back to Detroit. Ye might know what happened."

Dousman groaned. "Will the inefficience of these army men

never cease!" he exclaimed. "The Indians . . ." He left his sentence unfinished, but Drew finished it for him, almost as if with pleasure at the giving of this additional blow.

"They all came in with the British, ye guessed it. Tecumseh said Hull was a coward, and it seems he was. Brock was different; he was a man, and Tecumseh is a man. Why, that Indian not only has all the Shawnees and Hurons and Sacs and Foxes with him, he's got the Creeks to come up against Harrison. They don't like him."

"Harrison has always imagined himself another Frontenac and these peace-loving Shawnees the Iroquois," put in Dousman. "So then Detroit was lost."

"In middle August. Hull saw Tecumseh dropping down from behind, he thought the reinforcements had been cut to pieces, he gave up. Ye'll hear stories of how his men tried for his removal before that time. They could have held them off. As soon as it was done, the word went out." He paused briefly. "There was a massacre at Fort Dearborn; the Indians took it."

"But surely they haven't gone into the Ohio country!"

"Not yet," he answered ominously.

"Fort Meigs?"

"Still ours. But the redcoats aim to attack it. Tecumseh, they say, is wild to do it. But, I ain't so sure." Slyly, he held out a timid hope.

Dousman narrowed his eyes and waited.

"Ye see, Brock's dead. He was a good man, a fighter, like Tecumseh. Proctor's in command now; he's no good, can't make up his mind; he's afraid of his own shadow. I misdoubt he'll do much."

"And what are the Americans doing all this time?"

"General Scott is in the east. Harrison here. He's on the way from Vincennes, but he's not moving fast; he's got to think about the Indians. Tecumseh will strike him time and again; he'll take every chance after Tippecanoe, that mistake of Harrison's."

They sat for a while in silence.

"I see no early relief, then," said Dousman presently. "Harrison will have to retake Detroit, he'll have to destroy Malden, he'll have to deal with Tecumseh . . ." He shook his head. "Mackinac is too far away."

"Aye, so it is. We'll be markin' time."

"But we're not lost, far from it," observed Dousman. "The Mississippi is still ours as long as they've not moved against New Orleans."

"They've not. Or if they have, no word's come north."

"And the West . . ."

"Ye can't hear from them in a week's time," said Drew curtly.

"There," said Dousman, as if he had not heard, "no doubt the British follow their usual methods—stirring up the Indians against the traders and the settlers. They do that well at no great cost."

"If Manuel Lisa can't hold them off, no one can. The British haven't many soldiers to send into the West; so it rests with the Indians. Lisa's been fair with them. Here, ye'll know better than I how Astor has treated them. So they have no love for us; they're easy persuaded, and the British make fine talk."

"Yes, big talk."

"Aye, and they look grand to the Indians, who've a fondness for red."

A kind of restless silence fell between them; they sat quietly looking from the cave to Lake Huron's blueness, rolling now with whitecaps.

"Ye'll be sorry to learn that Lieutenant Hanks was killed on the sixteenth of last month, by a stray shot while he was on parole in Detroit."

"Yes, I *am* sorry to hear that."

"Our Lieutenant Hanks?" demanded Hercules, for the first time taking part in their conversation, to which he had been listening intently.

Dousman nodded.

"But he gave up!" protested Hercules indignantly.

"Yes, yes—it was an accident then," said Dousman impatiently.

Drew smiled broadly. "The boy's thinkin' war is all times fair. Ye'll learn different, lad."

Dousman stood up suddenly. "They'll miss me," he said. "If they come looking, they'll find you. I'll send the boy back with food."

"I'll be needin' it. But take yer time; ye'll not needlessly expose me by comin' back too quick."

Still Dousman hesitated, shifting his weight from one foot to the

other. Hercules had made no move, sensing that his father was not yet ready to go, despite his sudden coming to his feet.

"You'll keep in touch with me, Drew?"

"When I can. Ye'll note, the ice is soon comin'."

"In the spring, then."

"Aye, if I can. But ye can travel, can't ye?"

Dousman nodded jerkily. "When I can get away for the time. I can come to Duck Island, too, in the spring, or the summer. The British treat us well enough, but I can't abide their flag above me."

"But if ye'll be expectin' news of our victories, ye'll bide a good time. Ye know very well how the Indians fight, and there are more Indians than whites in the Northwest—from the Shawnees along the Ohio to the Sacs along the Mississippi and the Winnebagos on the Ouisconsin."

"I know that. But in these times, the trade——"

"Ye'll know the trade's no good as long as the Indians are on the war path. At least, the beaver will increase this while." He smiled mirthlessly.

Dousman turned abruptly and Hercules got to his feet. "Look out, Hercules. See if any one's in sight."

Hercules went obediently to the mouth of the cave, passed out, and looked toward the heart of the island. The pines and maples rose all around and before him, making a pattern of dark green, white rock, and yellow-red leaves broken only by his father's farm between this place along the lake and the knoll in the center of the island, the knoll beyond which lay the new British fort and the village where the old fort was. Nothing stirred but the wind, which keened in the pines, and a calico-bright figure in the yard of his home. Not a redcoat was in sight. He went back into the cave and announced that the way was clear.

Life on Mackinac went on as before, save that the British flag flew over Michilimackinac and the new Fort George, and the trading had changed. There were now no more the great gatherings of Indians and voyageurs along the pebbled beach at the village; there was none of the wild celebration; and the island's social life had ceased save for such few overtures as Captain Roberts made.

In late autumn he sent a private with an invitation for Dousman

to visit the new fort, and have dinner with the command. Dousman sent word that he would be pleased to come, but the private was not yet out of sight before misgivings rose in Jane Dousman.

"Michael, if the others know you've dined at the fort—what will they think then?"

"It will confirm their opinion of me," he said.

"Michael, you can't go. Make some excuse."

He smiled and shook his head. "No, it's my duty to go."

"Your first duty is to our own country."

"We're neutrals, Jane." He laughed. "Besides, it's my duty to examine the fort to discover its weaknesses if there are any."

"Michael, that's dangerous!"

"I've never shrunk from danger, Jane," he answered her quietly.

"I'm going, too," said Hercules.

Dousman turned to him, a smile edging his lips. "Yes, I think you might go, Hercules, if you can remember to keep your ears and eyes open, and your mouth closed."

They walked down in late afternoon. Fort George was constructed on a hill behind the old fort, on that same height from which Captain Roberts had commanded the village during his attack in the summer; he had made certain that the same tactics could not successfully be tried again. It was oblong in shape, its block-house square, and, like its magazine, constructed of great hewn cedar logs. In addition to these buildings, the gateway of the palisades was commanded by two stout lookouts. But there was no connection between these lookouts and the fort, thought Dousman. This was strange, since it was not in keeping with the care manifest in the construction. Passing the gun platforms mounted with iron cannon to cover the lower fort, his sharp eyes detected disturbed earth in lines from the lookouts to the fort, and he thought: There are underground passages. His respect for the British soldiery increased a little. The parapet within the moat was set with three rows of pointed cedar stakes inclined at many angles: a formidable earthwork indeed. It would be almost impossible to scale the parapet, he thought. But he did not permit his eyes to linger anywhere. He was conducted straightway to Captain Roberts, who sat waiting for him.

"Mr. Dousman, forgive me—I'll not rise. I've been unwell."

Indeed, he looked unwell; his face was drawn; his middle-aged look seemed to have given way to an appearance of more advanced years. His eyes were still kind, but fretful now; his mouth was pursed, his lips never still, pushing out and in; his fingers tapped restlessly upon the table before him.

"I'm sorry to hear it," said Dousman gravely.

"Sit down, sit down, both of you. The others will be in directly."

Colonel Macmillan came in even as he spoke, nodded, and sat down at one side of his superior officer. Hercules flashed a glance at him; he was still the same sardonic person, the cold eyes and down-turned mouth manifesting a faint, almost apologetic scorn.

"Do you come as a convert, Mr. Dousman?" he asked distantly.

"I remain a neutral, sir," replied Dousman.

"We're informed you continue the trade."

"There is little."

There was a strained moment; Captain Roberts eyed him fretfully; Colonel Macmillan fixed him with a suspicious gaze, his features immobile until he spoke again.

"We have a report that you had a visitor in the night some time ago."

The moment grew tense. In a second's time Dousman knew the impulse to deny the report, reconsidered with the feeling that the British must have enough evidence to be sure, and made his casual answer.

"One of my men reporting on the condition of the trade."

"We don't expect our neutrals to deal with Americans," said Macmillan stiffly, with a lofty air as if he had settled the matter in his decision.

"You're mistaken, sir," replied Dousman with some asperity. "The man is a subject of His Majesty."

"Then he need not have come at night," retorted Macmillan.

"And would not, had he not been delayed on the lake," replied Dousman.

Captain Roberts coughed. "You see, Macmillan distrusts neutrals. It's a congenital failure. He's good at heart."

Colonel Macmillan stared at his superior with ill-disguised contempt.

Captain Roberts affected not to notice. "I take it, you're not prepared to take the oath, Mr. Dousman?"

"No, sir, I'm not. I shall want to feel free, if I so decide, to enter America at any time in the future."

Colonel Dickson, hurrying in, replied to him. "My dear Mr. Dousman, there may soon be no America, but only a North American England. Indeed," he went on, sitting down on Captain Roberts' other side, and leaning toward Dousman, "even now we have command of the entire Northwest Territory—Fort Detroit, Fort Dearborn . . ."

"Fort Meigs?"

"Ah, that we'll have by spring," he said lightly, as if it were of no consequence.

Dousman smiled. "Your game is well played, Colonel Dickson. But if you've taken Vincennes, you've kept it very quiet, too quiet, to my thinking. And if you've gone into the Ohio country at all, it would seem strange you've not celebrated the event."

Colonel Macmillan fixed Dousman with a cold eye. "Perhaps Mr. Dousman would be so kind as to plan our campaign for us?"

"Thank you, Colonel," replied Dousman. "I'm a fur trader, and Mr. Astor would not like his agent meddling in these matters. Still, if you find yourself at an impasse—perhaps I can make an exception."

Roberts laughed, striking the table with his clenched fist; he laughed until a fit of coughing seized him. Dickson chuckled, his regard for Macmillan evidently touched with dislike.

"Well spoken," said Roberts in a moment. "This wilderness country around us is not so easily taken. You've travelled enough in it to know, eh, Dousman? Now, then, let's eat." He pounded on the table with the flat of his hand until the door opened and a private came in with a platter of food, the aroma of which vied with the pungent fragrance of cedar everywhere.

"You see," continued Roberts, "the American trouble is their retention of old Revolutionary generals in active service. Hull was a good man, but not so any longer. He need not have given up so readily. Indeed, if he'd struck at Fort Malden when he first moved against it, before Tecumseh and his Indians were ready, the thing might have been different. These American woodsmen, the Long Knives—they're fighters, good fighters."

Macmillan made a sound of disgust low in his throat, but said nothing.

The vague, intangible air of tension in the room persisted. Dousman fixed his gaze upon the flickering candles shedding their yellow glowing over the table; a draught animated the flames, but he could not determine its source. He wondered whether he was under observation.

"It would seem you've lost face in the village, Dousman," said Macmillan.

"No doubt of it," replied Dousman. "I should have been surprised if I hadn't. I understand I've even lost face among certain of the British."

Dickson grinned, recognizing the direction of the shaft.

"The fortunes of war," murmured Captain Roberts absently. "Try some of that wine, Mr. Dousman."

"Thank you, I will. I'm fond of dry white wines. I hadn't known there was much of it on the island."

"We brought it over from St. Joseph," informed Roberts. "We shall presently move the greater share of our stores here."

No flicker touched Dousman's face to indicate that he regarded this casual information of importance. Colonel Dickson frowned momentarily; Colonel Macmillan was aghast and angered.

"Perhaps Mr. Dousman would like to learn about the British plan of campaign," he observed sarcastically.

"I'm afraid it would be beyond me," said Dousman. "I'm a simple trader, Colonel Macmillan. While I understand trails easily enough, I've no doubt mass movements would confuse me."

Captain Roberts went on as if unaware of the fencing between his guest and his colonel. "I hope to be relieved of my post here," he said. "My health seems not to improve here, and I trust that by spring it will have proved possible to replace me." His eyes flickered toward Dousman, toward Macmillan; he gave evidence that he had understood the dislike between them well enough. "If I go, I hope to take Colonel Macmillan at least along. He's too valuable a man to keep here."

Colonel Macmillan smiled coldly.

The conversation continued. Captain Roberts spoke about the weather, the imminent freezing of the lakes, the nature of the soil;

from time to time he said something casual about the American navy and the privateers, he rejoiced at the retreat of Napoleon in Russia, at the rout in Spain, he observed repeatedly that it was only a matter of time before the British could swarm in upon the States. He enjoyed talking, though his conversation was broken into occasionally by violent spells of coughing. Meanwhile, Dousman listened with polite attention, never for a moment unaware of Colonel Macmillan watching him. Colonel Dickson took his departure presently, and Dousman was left between the obvious hostility of the colonel and the almost garrulous warmth and friendship of the captain. He glanced at Hercules from time to time, but the boy sat still, his eyes on Captain Roberts.

Intercepting Dousman's glance suddenly, Colonel Macmillan turned upon Hercules.

"Perhaps the boy is ready to take the oath of allegiance to His Majesty?" he wondered with a false smile. "What do you say, boy?"

"I don't like them," said Hercules curtly.

"Ah, indeed! Who is it you don't like?"

Dousman affected not to listen, yet he was acutely aware that Hercules might indict the British. His fingers tightened a little about the arms of his chair, but he betrayed his fear by no other sign, his attention still for Captain Roberts' small talk. He waited for Hercules to answer.

"I don't like soldiers," said Hercules.

"Well, well—why not?" pressed Macmillan.

"Because I'm a trader, and the soldiers hurt the trade."

Captain Roberts recognized the conversation apart from him. "Colonel Macmillan is industrious," he said into the room's sudden stillness, looking neither to Macmillan nor to Dousman. He smiled then at Dousman, as if in apology. "I promised you a tour of inspection, I think. Shall we go?"

His instinct warned Dousman. He was sharply conscious of Colonel Macmillan waiting for him to assent, waiting for him to rise and follow the captain around the fort; the colonel's hostility could be felt in the air.

"I think not, if you'll excuse me, Captain Roberts," he said casually. "I'm tired, and my wife will be waiting for me."

Roberts was astonished, but not as surprised as Macmillan, who

came to his feet with a grunt, bade them an ungracious good-bye, and hastened from the room. "Some other time, then," the captain said.

Dousman agreed. They got to their feet, the captain summoned an orderly, and they were led beyond the fort, their guide taking leave of them beyond the palisades. They went on up the road into the northwest.

Night had fallen darkly now, and stars gleamed frostily in the clear sky. In the north, a faint restless glowing presaged an aurora. The water's ceaseless sound beat upward into the darkness, making a deep monotone of melody in the night-held air. Dousman strode quickly along, looking not once behind him; Hercules ran occasionally to keep up with him, and finally took hold of his hand.

Dousman was preoccupied. His visit had not been in vain—if only he could get word outside. He was not hopeful; with the winter coming on, the waters would soon be frozen, and there was little chance of it. Besides, now that he knew, however obliquely he had gathered it, that St. Joseph Island was all but abandoned, he might be watched the more closely at the instigation of Macmillan. He was not insensible to the menace of Macmillan's hostility; let him once be caught in any questionable act, and Macmillan would have him, despite any protest Captain Roberts might make. He chafed at the restrictions imposed upon him, but he understood the necessity of compromise.

"I don't like the tall one," said Hercules suddenly.

"Hush! Colonel Macmillan is vigilant; that's to his credit. He's about his business as we are about ours."

"But the captain——"

"Say nothing, Hercules. The night wind may have ears."

The boy was obediently silent. But I am too suspicious, Dousman thought. I've caught something of Macmillan's fever. The only fever which possessed him was the urgent desire to establish contact with the American forces advancing upon the British in Canada, and at the moment he knew no one who expected to go to Vincennes or Cincinnati, wherever Harrison now was. He was disheartened.

He went into his house, sent Hercules up to his loft bed, reassured his wife, and spent half the night pacing the floor of the

kitchen in the darkness, listening to the wind's high sound, to the water's monotone, trying to make some plan which could be followed without too great danger. There was nothing left for it but to cross Huron to Duck Island and find Drew.

Even this he could not do at once.

It was a week before he set out for Duck Island, taking Hercules with him. He started after nightfall, but he knew the lake well, and he could paddle as swiftly as any Indian. He had put into his canoe several of the new blanket coats being made for the troops, so that if he were intercepted, he might say that he was transporting them to his men on the smaller island. The wind was not strong, but it was cold, and clouds low in the western sky were ominous; the danger of storm was not small, and he hesitated once or twice, almost determined to turn around, but overcame his fears and pressed on. The island lay behind them soon, retreating into the waters, sinking at the rim of the sky, almost as if it were indeed a turtle drawing back into the water's security. After a while Hercules slept.

The night deepened. Dousman pressed on, a kind of exhilaration in him now, a tonic feeling in his flesh as a reaction against his long inactivity. He had not softened in those months; he was elated and a little proud. The cold belabored him, but he was dressed to resist it.

He was on Duck Island before dawn, and found Drew's secure place without difficulty; it was beside the small station he himself had established some years before to aid in the taking of furs from the Chippewas. Now, if only he's at home, he thought, knocking on the door.

Drew was there. He opened the door suspiciously, surlily demanding who had awakened him; seeing the agent, he threw it wide, his astonishment manifest.

"God bless us! Ye take me by surprise. Come and sit down."

Dousman began without preamble, as if he had seen Drew but an hour past. "I want a man to go into the States," he said. "I'd go myself, but for my family. Can you find me one?"

"Aye. I reckon I can." He narrowed his eyes and waited for Dousman to say more.

"A man who can keep his knowledge to himself."

"Aye, I know such. Ye've discovered something then?"

"Too late for it to do any good this year—but in the spring perhaps. The British are moving supplies from Saint Joseph and Sault St. Marie. Saint Joseph for certain is to be partly disarmed; we can be sure of that." He told how he had learned of this.

Drew made a turn or two about the narrow room. "What does it mean, d'ye think?"

"That the British haven't as many men up here as they could have. They're at Malden, getting ready to go down into the Ohio country. If a force came up the Wisconsin, down the Fox and across Lake Michigan, they could fall upon Mackinac easily enough. They could take Saint Joseph and the Sault, too."

"It would need more men than we've got," said Drew dubiously. "And then, with all the Indians—." He shook his head. "I misdoubt it. But what is it ye propose to do?"

"Some one should carry word to Harrison."

"Harrison!" Drew spat contemptuously. "If it could only be Scott!"

"He's in command; we can't do anything else."

"Aye, that's true enough. Ye might pray we don't rue it. I don't look for Harrison to get this far north. He's a home body, best off among his connections."

By this time light was invading the cabin. Dousman grew impatient. Drew was complacent. He went over, stirred the ashes to reveal red coals on the hearth, and put wood upon them; flames came furtively, licking at the cedar bark, and the sweet smell of burning wood took possession of the room. Dousman loosened his clothing.

"Fetch me your man, Drew. I'll talk with him before he goes."

"Ah, ye've been talkin' to him." Drew grinned. "Ye'll not be thinkin' this a matter I'd trust to some one else? If one knows a secret, he's like to keep it if he means to keep his head. Two is bad enough—but no more."

"But you've taken the oath."

"Ye'll not be sayin' the words stick out on me now?"

Dousman laughed. "Well, no. It wasn't that I meant. I was thinking of myself, left with no one outside except John, and his letters

come too rarely, and say nothing. If you mean to go, I'm glad of it. I'll have no doubts about you."

"Unless I fall in with the Indians and can't talk myself out of it." He turned a chair toward Dousman and straddled it, leaning toward the trader. "Now, then—what is the plan to be? Ye name it."

"Let them take St. Joseph and the Sault supplies. After them, Mackinac."

"They can't do it until they retake Detroit."

"I know it full well. But they can do it easily if they don't wait too long after retaking Detroit."

"Aye, but I'm not the Lord, Mr. Dousman. And ye know that only the Lord moves General Harrison, and I reckon He does it in His reckless moments." He got up once more, walking restlessly back and forth across the room, his hands clasped behind his back, his forehead lined; his shaggy appearance was threatening.

Dousman sat in silence, waiting.

Drew stopped his pacing abruptly. "I'll go this night boldly to Detroit and take my chance of getting on to Harrison after that."

"Take care of yourself."

"Aye, I will that. I think well of this skin of mine. But don't think to hear from me before next April—if then."

Dousman sighed. "I'll exercise my patience."

"Ye'll stay here the day and set out tonight?"

"I think so, yes. You might go down and unload the canoe; I brought along some blanket coats. I'll take your furs if you have any; in that way I have every excuse to go and come on legitimate business."

"What a man chooses to make his business, eh? I can use such a coat, and thank ye for it."

He went out and down toward the beach. Hercules stirred uneasily, drawing Dousman's attention.

"Are you hungry, Hercules?"

"A little."

"We'll eat presently. Be patient. We can sleep, too, after a bit."

He got up and stirred the fire, standing then with his back against it as if for the heat, and looking around him. Drew's cabin was a one-room dwelling only, but had an atmosphere of comfort, so that its crudeness was softened. The walls were rough, of logs; only

one small window broke their expanse. Nails held guns and other weapons to the walls; a solitary braided mat lay near the door; a crucifix hung over the bed against the wall. A small table with a gayly colored spread stood near the fireplace. Hercules, too, looked around him, contrasting this small place with their own home.

Drew came back carrying the blanket coats. He spread one open, examining it judiciously. "That's a fine coat, Mr. Dousman. Aye, ye can be sure I'll find a use for it." He put it aside. "Now then, ye'll be makin' yerself to home. Ye've got the day ahead of you. I'm thinkin' it's no such wait as ye'll have for General Harrison."

He laughed heartily, and Dousman joined him, with an uneasy foreboding that Drew's words were more prophetic than jesting.

It was not difficult to wait through the winter on Mackinac. Winter was a season designed to cultivate patience. Even in time of peace, the island was quiet throughout the snow-held time; now it was doubly so. Ice concealed the waters, locked the lakes; heavy snows all but covered the evergreen groves, the heights of Mackinac, made grotesque the new fort and the shape of the island.

From time to time Dousman was invited down to Fort George. Captain Roberts was more querulous than ever; his illness had grown no better.

"But I cannot complain for lack of variety," he said to Dousman one night. "I have in you a good listener, and here in the fort I have Colonel Dickson, who agrees with everything I say and do, and Colonel Macmillan, who disagrees as readily. As for Macmillan—he's so convinced every one is a spy that he has begun to suspect himself."

In the spring, Captain Roberts was relieved of his command, and Captain Bullock, a florid-faced man who was younger than Roberts, took over. True to his promise, Roberts took Macmillan with him; Dickson stayed behind. Bullock's coming changed nothing on the island save Dousman's visits to the fort. These he hardly missed, since in the winter months the men at the fort knew no more than he himself.

Impatience possessed him from the first day the lakes opened under the sun moving northward. He was fortunate that he had his farm and the remnants of the fur trade to occupy his attention,

so that he had little time to stand on the heights and peer out across Lake Huron for sight of some lonely traveller who might be Drew.

Spring deepened to summer. There was no word from the south; there was no hint of what had taken place in the occurrences at the fort. He grew from impatience into depression; he was convinced that something had happened—that Drew had fallen into the hands of Indians and had been killed.

Almost a year went by in this fashion. Dousman had grown accustomed to his impotence and to his lack of knowledge about the war; he had accepted the idea of Drew's death; he had resigned himself to wait with slowly increasing bitterness, when at last Drew came. Jaunty as ever, he came in an October night, whistling gently as he approached the house. Hercules heard him and slipped down from the loft to open the door.

Dousman, too, heard him. He was incredulous, and reached the kitchen in his nightclothes before Hercules could waken him. The boy stood wide-eyed watching his father embrace the courier.

"Great God, Drew! I'd given you up for dead this long time."

"Aye, and I might well have been."

"We know nothing of the war, nothing at all—if there's still a war."

"There's war still. Ye can be sure of that. But the British are in a bad way, to my mind."

"Ah! It gives me pleasure to hear it. Tell me."

Drew sat down, sighing. "It's a long tale, Mr. Dousman. Malden is burned out, Fort Detroit is ours once more—what's left of it."

"I've maligned Harrison."

"No, ye ain't. 'Twasn't so much our Harrison as the British Proctor. Mark me, if Brock hadn't been killed, likely Harrison would be in Pennsylvania this long time. But Proctor—" He shook his head dolefully. "Down there ye'll hear it told about what Tecumseh said: 'General Brock said, "Tecumseh, *come* fight the Yankees." General Proctor says, "Tecumseh, *go* fight the Yankees!"' And that's how it was, with Proctor willin' and ready for Tecumseh and his Indians to fight. The Indians deserted that woman, as they called Proctor; he hadn't arranged for enough provisions; he abandoned Detroit and burned Malden. Harrison walked in and

took Detroit; he came off Commodore Perry's ships. Then he took out after Proctor and fought him at the Thames River. Proctor was badly beat, and the Americans had a great victory and the British a greater loss. Ye'll know what I mean. Tecumseh was killed."

Dousman sucked in his breath. "And the Indians?"

"Aye, ye guessed it. They scattered, they went back home. With Tecumseh dead, there was no leader among them. Roundhead was too old; Proctor was no man to fight for. So the British have no force worth the name left to take Michigan back. It's ours. Their strongest garrison is right here on Mackinac."

"Then Harrison can take it. You saw him?"

"Aye. I saw him." He clipped his words, and his lips curled upward in ill-concealed contempt. "I spoke with him."

"What did he say?"

"He thought me a spy."

Dousman laughed without amusement. "How canny! What happened?"

"Lieutenant Colonel Grogan listened; so did Major Holmes. They freed me, and ye'll find them in the party when it does come. I had no promise." He was glum, contemptuous. "If I had ten good men, I'd try it myself."

Dousman smiled. "It means more waiting then."

"Aye. The Lord knows how long."

"I'm used to it now," said Dousman. "How does the war go elsewhere?"

"Ye'll have heard about Lake Erie?"

"We've heard nothing," answered Dousman flatly.

"The British were licked there, and good, too. Commodore Perry whipped the fleet under Barclay. It was a good fight, to hear it told. It'll take the British another year to get ready for a second try at invasion—if they've got the heart for it."

"The West?"

"Lisa holds fast. They say Astor is thinking to buy his company, or merge."

"That speaks well. That says a good deal, Drew," said Dousman, satisfaction rising within him. "If Astor means to invest further in the West, he has no doubt the Americans will win the war."

"Aye, by that sign. It doesn't say when."

Drew got up, restless. Dousman stirred. "There's food in the cupboard; help yourself if you've a mind to."

Drew went to the cupboard and took a cold potato. He ate skin and all, standing with his legs spread near the door. "Ye see I've been moving about so much, I'm not fit to sit for long at a time any more."

Dousman apparently did not hear. He was pulling at his ear, his eyes narrowed and thoughtful. "From your own experience, how long would you say we'll have to wait, Drew?"

"They'll not be comin' this winter to be caught in the freeze."

"Clearly not. It's too late. If they had moved at once . . ."

"To give them their due, they'd planned to. They were waiting for two brigs to come up—the *Chippeway* and the *Ohio;* but they went aground. Then the Kentuckians wanted to go home, Harrison wanted to get away—ye know he's a great one for his connections—so there's but a small company under Colonel Cass left. And that's not enough for an attack, ye'll see easy."

"In spring, then?"

Drew shook his head. "It'll take longer than the spring for the soldiers to come together again. Ye'll see."

Dousman's disappointment was manifest. Drew looked away. Both were silent. The room's chill was not dissipated by the faint warmth glowing from the coals on the hearth. The sound of Drew's mastication rose and fell. From above, Hercules looked alertly down, as if expectant of some dramatic action which failed to come; he fixed every detail of the scene in his memory, moved by that strange sense of time passing, the sense that marks off with apparent impartiality great things and small to be remembered.

There was a small sound from outside, like the scuffing of a footstep on the pebbles beyond the door.

Drew grinned slyly. "I brought you pelts," he said casually. "They're down in the boat."

A knock sounded on the door.

"Come in," said Dousman immediately.

A soldier came in, his red coat suddenly bright in the room. He saluted smartly, eyeing them with a touch of belligerence. "Mr. Dousman, there's a canoe concealed along the far shore."

"It belongs to my man Drew, sir," said Dousman.

"We have orders to investigate all strange craft," continued the soldier, his grave eyes hard on Drew.

"Aye, do ye investigate," said Drew easily. "Ye might be so good as to bring my pelts to the house. I'm fair tired from long paddlin'."

The sentry was undecided, but after a moment he stepped back out of the house. His footfalls receded into the northeast.

"That's Bullock's doing," murmured Dousman. "They patrol the island from end to end."

"They've heard about Detroit, then, even if ye had not," observed Drew.

"It would seem so." .

They sat in silence, listening. Presently the sentry returned, pushed the door open, and dropped a pack of furs inside.

"Here they are," he said.

"Thank ye," said Drew. As he walked away, he added with a chuckle, "He's short of breath. They made a load for him."

Drew sat down and Dousman pulled up a chair to sit close to him. They bent their heads together.

"Will you see either Grogan or Holmes again? Or even Harrison?" Dousman asked.

"It might be. Ye'll be sensible of the fact I take pains to avoid Harrison," Drew said, sniffing a little. "I'll see one of the others."

"Now, then, attend me closely, Drew."

"I'm always attendin' ye, Mr. Dousman," interrupted Drew with some indignation manifest in his voice.

"You are, true. But even more than ever now. If you reach either one of them, press upon him the necessity for approaching the island secretly, by night. Tell him to send me word if he can; I'll be on hand at the British Landing place to guide them in, too. As for the new fort—if they listen, they'll need not fear it. Its guns command the village, and there's an underground connection between the gateposts and the fort; if they came up in the night, they could come upon it and get inside before the company knew what had happened."

"Ah," breathed Drew, his eyes gleaming. "Ye reckon they can be surprised despite the fort, eh?"

"I do."

"That should sound good to them. They'll know nothing of the fort, mark me."

"Once they've landed their forces and deployed them, the Americans can keep the upper hand, I'm confident. Especially now that those usual allies of the British are absent—the Indians."

"The Sacs have gone across the Mississippi," put in Drew. "Ye'll see the signs that Tecumseh's confederation died with him. That's one of them. Aye, and they're all scattered, from the Ohio into the Purchase Territory."

"Where do you go now—back to Duck Island, or Detroit?"

"I'll go to Duck Island, and from there to Detroit. I may not go south until after the ice breaks. I don't look with pleasure to another winter spent with the army." He shook his head.

Dousman stood up. "That makes no difference. Just so they'll have word from Mackinac. Just so they get here before the British have time to summon their allies."

Drew laughed. "There are plenty Indians on Mackinac, if ye'll see them."

"Will you rest awhile before you set out again?"

Drew shook his head. "I reckon not. The redcoat might come back. I'll take no chance."

They bade each other good-bye gravely, and Dousman went back to bed, latching the door behind Drew. Hercules lay listening to the courier's fading footfall, until the sound was gone, and all the air was filled with the water's murmuring in the straits. He turned the scene, the words, the actions he had witnessed over and over in his mind. He understood that this was war, and was disappointed; he had imagined something more exciting, more colorful; but apart from the original taking of the lower fort, there had been so far only meetings in the dark. But there was something more to which his thoughts turned: the grain of significance in the men, in their words; this was not lost to him. He pondered these things in the vastness of the dark until he feel asleep.

If Dousman had expected some further inquiry into Drew's presence in the night, it did not come. He settled down to wait for the attack upon Mackinac, where now something of the old life was being resumed. It was the collapse of Tecumseh's dream of an In-

dian Confederation which had released his devoted followers to the trade once more, so that now, as always, the Indians came to Mackinac, to trade their furs for the things they needed and those they did not. But for the British flag flying proudly above Fort George, and the intangible tension among the island's inhabitants, Mackinac might have undergone no change.

Life went on. People died, births occurred, some of the traders took Indian squaws to wife. Captain Bullock went with the spring and was replaced by Colonel McDouall, who was young, energetic, imaginative. Indians brought word that the Americans were constructing a fort at Prairie du Chien, where the Wisconsin met the Mississippi. Forthwith, McDouall sent Captain McKay with a volunteer force down the lake, up the Fox and down the Wisconsin, to capture the post.

There was no word from Drew.

Early in July Doctor Day came to call on Dousman, at work in one of his fields.

"You've heard the Americans have come up the lake, Michael?" he asked casually.

Dousman was bland. "I know nothing."

"They've captured the supplies at the Sault, and they took St. Joseph—burned the British post there."

"They'll likely be on us next, then."

"I would suppose so."

Dousman shrugged, taking off his hat and brushing perspiration from his forehead under the hot sun. "I think perhaps McDouall may hold them off."

"But you're hoping he can't," said the doctor, nodding. "We all are."

Though he did not betray himself, Dousman was filled with excited anticipation. He could hardly wait until Doctor Day had gone before he ran to the house to tell his wife and Hercules. "At last," he said. "I'll expect to hear from them any night now."

"Oh, Michael—if you're caught!" protested Jane anxiously.

He kissed her, undisturbed, soothing her fear.

He heard from his fellow islanders various details of the American assault on St. Joseph and the Sault Ste. Marie; he observed the precautions being taken by the British garrison, not without admira-

tion for the dispatch and decision of Colonel McDouall in his preparation to give battle to any besieging force.

Inexorably, day followed day into the limbo of the past. Dousman grew more and more disturbed. He waited long hours every
night, sitting in the darkness of his home, waiting for word. Where
were the Americans? Where was Drew? He could not understand
this inexplicable silence, this lack of action. It was possible that
something had happened to Drew; once before he had thought so
and had been wrong. This time he might well be right.

But where was the invading force?

A fortnight passed before he had an answer to the question he
had so often asked himself. On the twenty-sixth of that month,
the Americans appeared: seven men-of-war bold in the blue lake
not far off the coast of the island.

Dousman saw them with a mixture of rage and disappointment.
He could not believe his eyes, and stood staring from the heights.
But the flags were unmistakable. They were the ships carrying the
American force, and there they were in broad daylight sailing
around the island as if at some children's game. It was incredible.
Drew could not have reached them, after all; his fears had been well
founded; no soldier would have failed to heed Drew. Yet he was
not entirely convinced. He watched the bold sailing around for a
while as if expecting at any minute that the ships would vanish;
but they went on around and around the island.

He was embittered. He went home and sat disconsolate in the
kitchen. Secretly glad, Jane comforted him.

Hercules was dismayed at his anger.

"Watch this affair carefully, Hercules," Dousman said. "It will
teach you something of the stupidity of men. They come in such
fashion that they give the British ample time to fortify against
their attack, to give their allies time to come together—they're coming already—Indians from all over the wilderness country. Now
they're in such position that they can't even fire upon the fort, with
their inability to tilt their guns enough."

"Maybe Mr. Drew didn't get through," suggested Jane.

"It wouldn't need Drew to teach them common sense," he answered shortly.

He went out from time to time, Hercules with him, going to the

heights from which he could have an uninterrupted view of the lake. The American squadron had divided now, encircling the island as much as possible. He stood looking out to where canoes came on unimpeded to reach the island; his smile was bitter.

"Are they landing?" asked Hercules.

"No, no—those are the Indians coming to help the British."

The ships were too far apart to stop the Indians from coming; this was obvious. Dousman could hardly contain himself. He overflowed, railing against British and Americans alike, Hercules listening gravely.

In the afternoon it began to rain, a sudden heavy shower pouring down; afterward the sun shone briefly again, intensely hot. By evening the heavy lake fog was shrouding the island, the thick whiteness everywhere.

Dousman was more restive than ever. "If only they have a competent guide now," he said. "Now they could land, they could come up, take positions."

"Come to bed, Michael—no one can do anything in this fog," said Jane.

He was persistent. "Yes, the right men can do everything. Wait and see."

He waited, sitting alone in the candle-lit kitchen with Hercules' eyes burning down at him from above.

Close to midnight there was a knock on the door. It was not Drew's knock, but Dousman did not hesitate. He went over and threw it wide. Ambrose Davenport stood there, his beard wet with fog.

"Davenport! By God, you're a welcome sight. Where have you come from? I thought you'd gone to Detroit, been exchanged for. . . . Ah, the ships!"

Davenport come in and sat down. "Close the door tight; I wouldn't want to be caught here. I came from the ships, yes. I'm guiding them."

"It wasn't your doing—this coming to the island by day?" demanded Dousman.

Davenport shook his head. "These men fight by rules and regulations. Mark me, Dousman, I have no word with them; they go as they like, they do what they please. There are some among them

who can understand, but Commodore Sinclair seems to think only a show of might is necessary. We'll not take the fort that way."

"What are they doing now? Surely they're landing under this fog?"

Davenport's lips twisted into a mirthless grin. "Not a bit of it. They're sitting tight and snug where they are. I tried to tell them that now would be the time, now—but they mistrust the fog." He spat angrily into the fireplace.

"Did Drew reach them?"

Davenport frowned. "I've seen nothing of him. He was down in Harrison's country winter before last. Since then, he's not been there." He looked dubiously at Dousman. "You sent him then?"

Dousman nodded. "I thought he could make it once more," he said, sighing. He shrugged as if to put Drew's fate from his mind.

"What message did he carry?"

"Word of the fort's weakness." He told him briefly.

Davenport nodded. "We could have been upon them before they had a chance to defend themselves," he agreed.

"All this bungling is disheartening. A woodsman with a few fellows could do better than all this maneuvering for positions in plain sight of the enemy. You'll go back to them, eh, Davenport?"

"Yes, but I can tell them nothing."

"I had wanted them to come ashore at the British landing, and go from there either by the woods or by the road to the fort." He shrugged. "But it's too late, if the landing isn't effected tonight."

"It won't be."

"Was ever such stupidity manifested!" complained Dousman. "This matter of Mackinac will go down in history as a record for American bungling. It is certainly true that fortune befriends the bold—if it were not, the British would never have set foot on Mackinac, and the Americans would never have forgotten it for so long."

Davenport seemed to recollect himself. "But I didn't come for that. Where are the batteries? Do you know, Dousman?"

"That would seem obvious even from the ships, if they have glasses. Every one knows—there can be no secret about it." He looked up to meet his son's eyes. "Where are they, Hercules?"

"On all the heights—above the distillery, on the height west of

the fort, along the ridge near the village," said Hercules promptly.

Dousman turned back. "You see!"

Davenport brushed irritably at his beard. He said nothing, but his eyes darkened.

"McDouall had so few men here that you might have taken him easily if you'd been bold enough," Dousman went on. "Now that the Indians have come, it won't be easily done—if it's done at all."

Davenport laughed suddenly. "They want to put a battery on Round Island. What do you think of that?"

Dousman shook his head, not trusting himself to speak. He stood with his hands clasped behind his back, frowning, deep in thought. Davenport waited for him to speak again, tapping his fingers on the table, watching Dousman's every move, the expression of his face.

"These men haven't fought a real battle for so long, they've forgotten how," he said, hoping to stir Dousman.

Dousman grimaced. "They can't storm the fort, that's sure," he said presently. "They'll have to effect a landing. It won't do to come as the British did—it's too late for that now. I hope they've seen that."

"They must come as I did."

"On the northeast, perhaps," agreed Dousman dubiously. "But better still, on the southwest, where it's open enough to make fighting difficult for the Indians. The British landing place is impossible with all the undergrowth there—an ideal battleground for the British allies."

Davenport grinned. "They were arguing that point when I left. I gave them my opinion. It wasn't theirs."

"The best advice I should give them is this: go away until the Indians have begun to scatter from Mackinac. Then come back and attack without delay."

"Too late."

Davenport got up.

"Are you going back to the ship?"

"Not yet. I came in great part to see my wife, my family—I mean to see them before I go back."

"You'll be taken!"

"Not in this fog, my friend. I know this island better than the British do."

In three strides he was at the door. He opened it cautiously and slipped out into the fog pressing inward. Dousman stood for a moment looking after him; then he went over and took up the candle on the table.

"Papa, will they fight?"

He had forgotten Hercules. He paused and looked up, smiling ruefully. "I'm afraid they may," he said. "But perhaps I'm not the one to say they should or should not." He shook his head. "At the last, each man can trust only himself; he must stand or fall by his own confidence and beliefs."

Standing there, he had an uncanny conviction that the boy understood him completely, and he looked for a long silent moment into the intent, narrowed eyes, the dark-blue Dousman eyes, and he marked the firm mouth.

"Will I see Cousin John again?"

Dousman had thought Hercules had forgotten. "Not yet, Hercules," he said gently.

"If they fight?"

"Even if they fight, yes." He blew out the candle. "Go to sleep now."

When the fog lifted in mid-morning, the position of the ships had changed. They were standing farther off, and one of them was putting down a boat. Dousman watched them through his glasses, mystified, but in a moment the reason for their activity was manifest. They were pulling toward Round Island, evidently to reconnoiter. He kept them in his glasses, saw them land, watched them disappear into the wooded portion of the smaller island. Then he turned to look toward the British batteries.

What of Colonel McDouall? He would surely have seen the reconnoitering party set out. The British commander was able, resourceful. He had observed the activity aboard the besieging ships even before Dousman; he had, moreover, realized at once that the ships were out of reach of his batteries. They were not, however, out of reach of the Indians. Even as Dousman turned to look toward the fort, scores of birchbark canoes came from the shore

of Mackinac, followed by a few batteaux and other craft, all making directly for Round Island. They could slip past the American ships with ease, their fleetness more than a match for the cumbersome ships.

Hercules stirred uneasily, seeing the Indians go forth. "What is it, Papa? What are they going to do now?"

Dousman told him tersely.

"What are the men on the island doing?"

Dousman spoke without lowering his glasses, which he turned on the reconnoitering party. "They've seen the Indians coming. Mr. Davenport is taking the lead to return to the boat. Some of them are dragging behind. Mr. Davenport's well up near the boat. He has to call back to them, and beckon them. They're delaying about something." He paused abruptly, almost unable to credit his eyes. "Yes," he said in amazement, "they're stopping to pick raspberries!"

"They'll get it," said Hercules sharply.

"That doesn't seem to matter to them nearly as much as the demands of their stomachs," answered Dousman bitterly.

The landing party was delaying inexcusably, but at last Davenport got them all into the boat. They prepared to shove off just as the first of the Indians came up in their canoes; others who had landed appeared suddenly from the encroaching woods and captured the last of the laggards. The boat shoved off, caught on a rock, pivoted, and met the fire of the Indians. Fortunately, no one was hit. The fire was returned from the boat, but no second discharge sounded. The boat cleared the rock and made for the ship. Unused to open battle, the Indians veered away without attacking the boat, and the ship was reached in safety.

"They got one of the party," said Dousman. "This is another lesson in how not to conduct a war, Hercules."

Hercules said nothing, his eyes on the ships, which were now swinging around in preparation for some action. This was the circling of Round Island apparently in an effort to rescue the Indians' captive. All around the *Lawrence,* which was moving now, the Indian craft were returning swiftly to Mackinac Island. A shot was fired after them with no ill effects.

The entire episode had the aspect of a marionette show.

The fog came down again in the night, thick massed vapor descending upon Mackinac and the waters all around. It did not rise until afternoon, and then disclosed the *Lawrence* under the British guns. Alert, as always, Colonel McDouall ordered a vigorous fire upon the American ship, which replied only once before drawing back out of range. The *Lawrence's* guns could not command the fort; the fort's guns were fired with more excitement than accuracy. No shot told.

Scarcely an hour later, the brief sunlight was followed by storm. Clouds had lowered on the horizon for days; now at last the storms came, wind and rain. This weather held day after day. The American ships drew out still farther and thrust at the British where they might with impunity, where their activity would presently take its toll if the siege held out long enough; they took supply ships. Colonel McDouall's letter to the commander of the *Nancy,* out from the Nautawasaga River with supplies, was intercepted, and a portion of the besieging force sent to take the *Nancy*. The Indians fretted; some of them returned into the Michigan Territory south and west of Mackinac, but still others came, from as far away as the Grand Portage.

The comedy of errors became grim when the shortage of flour due on the *Nancy* began to be felt; bread was scarce; certain other supplies were running low. The siege could not be withstood indefinitely. Colonel McDouall sent for Michael Dousman, who came, accompanied by Hercules, who went everywhere with him now.

Colonel McDouall paced the narrow room where often Dousman had sat at table with his predecessor; his young face was aged with grimness, his eyes hard, his jaw firm, stubborn, unyielding.

"Sit down, Mr. Dousman."

Dousman sat down. McDouall continued to stride past him, until he looked at Hercules as if for the first time seeing him. He stopped and stared at Dousman.

"Is it your custom to bring children, Mr. Dousman?" he asked sharply.

"My son accompanies me," answered Dousman quietly. He was alert, seeking to understand the meaning of this summons before McDouall spoke.

Colonel Dickson came in and sat down; he was unshaved, un-

kempt. He betrayed anxiety, but he could still smile at Dousman, shake hands gravely with Hercules. He followed McDouall with his eyes, back and forth, waiting.

McDouall sat down abruptly, facing Dousman. "Mr. Dousman, you're the only adult male neutral on Mackinac, I believe."

"I believe so, yes."

"The fortunes of war put you at our disposal," McDouall continued.

"Say rather my concern for the people of Mackinac," interrupted Dousman gently.

McDouall waved his words away. "As you're aware, the American siege is beginning to tell. We can hold out for a fortnight, I think—at the most. That is, if help does not come."

So they are expecting help, thought Dousman. He said nothing, bending forward in polite attention.

"We'll have to make our position clear to the Americans," McDouall went on. "If they expect us to surrender, they're mistaken. We shall not do so. We've taken Mackinac and we mean to hold it. I need hardly tell you, I distrust the enemy. We're in need of an envoy to convey our ultimatum to them."

"I see. What ultimatum?"

"That if they persist in withholding supplies from us, they may expect the wives of Americans as well as their children remaining here on Mackinac to suffer hunger and starvation. It's our duty to care first for the subjects of His Britannic Majesty. You will understand that."

"I understand only that humanity is the first consideration of every gentleman."

McDouall went an angry red. "You're ready enough with words, Mr. Dousman," he said, scowling at him.

Colonel Dickson interposed soothingly. "Mr. Dousman's comment was well taken. Perhaps it would be best to make it clear to the enemy that we're not contemplating any moves against the civilian American population remaining on the island."

McDouall shrugged. "Will you repair under a flag of truce to the American commander and convey our position to him, Mr. Dousman? We demand his unconditional withdrawal. He cannot storm us, and we'll not surrender. We can maintain the impasse."

Dousman stood up stiffly. "I'm sorry. I can't bear any such message as that. If I'm to suggest by so much as a word that the American women and children remaining on Mackinac will suffer by the American siege, I would be guilty of treason to myself."

"You have the sound of an American, Mr. Dousman," said McDouall, eyeing him sharply, his anger rising again.

"You might expect any gentleman to speak in a like manner."

Colonel Dickson coughed. "We're getting nowhere, please; gentlemen," he said. "Mr. Dousman, please understand our position. We're making no threats; we're hoping to avoid them, hoping as earnestly as we did two years ago when we descended upon Mackinac and you were kind enough to lend us your good offices in effecting the surrender of the post. I want to ask you to reconsider."

Dousman sat down again. "If Colonel McDouall will put his terms on paper, I will consent to convey them to the officer in charge."

McDouall bowed stiffly. "Thank you, Mr. Dousman. We could ask no more. I'll have the note to the American commander ready within half an hour, if you care to wait."

Colonel Dickson got up, smiling, and came across to shake Dousman's hand. McDouall turned to leave the room, his mouth grim, his eyes betraying his withheld anger. Before he reached the door it was flung open and an orderly almost fell into the room.

He came to awkward attention. "Colonel McDouall, sir—the enemy are putting in to the coast on the northwest. They appear to be landing a force."

Instantly McDouall was a changed man. "Ah!" he said. He turned to Dousman. "Thank you, Mr. Dousman. We can dispense with the communication for the enemy. Come, Colonel Dickson. Good day, Mr. Dousman."

He went out of the room bawling orders in a stentorian voice echoed by Colonel Dickson. The fort became a hive of confusion, with voices raised, bugles sounding. In the village below, the alarm bell began to ring. By the time Dousman passed through the palisades, the soldiers were beginning to form for the march across Mackinac to the landing point; the Indians were already filtering swiftly into the woodland beyond the fort. All was activity. He stood for a moment undecided; then he pulled Hercules quickly

after him and set out across the higher ground in the direction of the farm, passing to the right of the redcoats.

The sun was shining. He thought ironically that it must have been this unexpected sunlight emerging after days of storm and bluster which had inspired the American force to this move. And on that side of the island, too! he thought with angry scorn.

He reached the farm with the knowledge of Indians all around him. From the house, he could see them skulking in the woods across the trail that led through the farm to the village.

Jane came in from the barn, alarmed. She, too, had seen the Indians passing like shadows from tree to tree.

"What is it, Michael?"

"Hoh!" he exclaimed in high scorn. "It's war—they mean to fight at last. Where are the twins? And Nancy?"

"The twins are upstairs. Nancy's outside in the barn."

"Fetch her in."

"Where are they fighting, then?"

"If my calculations are correct, just before the house. But for the trees, we might have an unobstructed view of it. As it is, we'll see something of it." He turned and looked from the window into the southeast. "Ah, there's McDouall now, with his redcoats."

The British were moving quickly up the road, no longer in formation, keeping only the rough outlines of a company. Behind them came one of the guns from the fort. A few Hurons danced ridiculous capers about the redcoats, and a body of Shawnees came swiftly from the left, ignoring the soldiers, and disappeared into the woods.

Jane vanished and reappeared, with Nancy behind her; she was anxious, her anxiety obvious in her worried eyes, her apprehensive peering from one window and then another. The twins pushed forward to the windows, watching with big eyes, and talking to each other in a patter used between them, almost unintelligible to any one else.

The redcoats had come through the pasture gate and were taking a position now in Dousman's orchard. The trees at this extremity of the woodland before the house were not so dense that Dousman could not see that a gun was being moved up to command the route the Americans must take to reach the approach to the fort.

Hundreds of Indians lay concealed in the growth of small trees spreading fanwise down toward the landing; a swamp lay before the orchard, beyond it a clearing which the redcoats now commanded; here and there were small clearings, little more than pens. These would serve the Indians well, thought Dousman; they could slaughter the invading force.

The sound of cannonading arose from the direction of the landing. To drive the Indians from the shore, reasoned Dousman. He got up and went outside, standing there to listen for further sounds. On his left, the British were drawn up now, ready for battle. A din of shots and fierce Indian cries rose on the right.

The battle had begun. On the left the British were moving up more guns. Redcoats were at attention around the first gun, ready to fire at the signal. Distantly, through the trees at the right, the American landing party could be seen, flags waving. Desultory Indian fire came from the woods all around.

His view impeded by the trees, Dousman bethought himself of the roof. He hurried into the house, caught up his glasses, and went by ladder up to straddle a gable near the front of the building. His view was improved, as he thought it would be, though here and there massed foliage still shut portions of the battlefield from sight. The American force of several hundred men had now come to one of the small clearings, and were marching steadily forward.

Even Harrison would have known better than that, Dousman thought.

The Americans were in two lines, the militia ahead, but from the right a battalion of regulars was advancing under command of Major Holmes, easily recognizable in the glass. The British line reached from behind a temporary breastwork in the woods, almost directly opposite Dousman's house, along the edge of the wooded tract to the clearing which was evidently to be the battlefield.

Watching Major Holmes with his regulars, it became apparent that the Americans hoped to outflank the redcoats. This was courting disaster. Even as he watched, the Indians opened fire from the nearby woods. Major Holmes pitched forward; Captain Morgan, his second in command, fell backward, but struggled to his feet again, though the major lay still. A few of the soldiers lay wounded and dead. The effect of this fire was to confuse the line where its

need for precision was greatest; leaderless, the men fell out of formation, uncertain whether to advance or retreat, despite the efforts
of Captain Morgan, who strove bravely to direct them, though
he could not long withstand the flow of blood from his side. Hardly
had some semblance of order been gained, when a second fire
cut into the Americans from the woods. The fire was returned, driving the Indians back.

Colonel McDouall gave the order to fire one of the guns, and
the redcoats sprang into action. The gun belched smoke and shell,
roaring into the momentary silence. The Americans' fire was desultory.

Up from the right now came the colonel in command of the
American expedition, shouting commands. A militiaman ran to
his side; his eye fell on Major Holmes lying lifeless near the trunk
of a tree to where some of his men had dragged him. He shouted
further commands, after ascertaining that Holmes was dead.

Slowly, cautiously, the Americans began to retreat. Three men
carried the body of Major Holmes, but presently vanished into the
woods with it, and reappeared empty-handed; this maneuver was
apparently not observed by the pursuing Indians. The redcoats did
not pursue, unwilling to leave their position in the orchard.

Shots came from time to time: the Indians harrying the retreat;
but these diminished when once the Americans reached the less-
wooded ground near the beach. In less than two hours, the action
was over; the Americans had gone back to the ships, and the
ships were again drawing back from the shore. The English were
beginning the march back to the fort. Dousman descended.

"Is it over?" asked Jane.

He nodded. "I'm going back to the fort. Come, Hercules."

The boy presented himself obediently, ready to go.

Jane looked at Dousman. "If the Indians are celebrating—Michael, do you think it best that Hercules go along?"

"I want him to see," he said grimly.

They went back along the road down which they had come
but a few hours before. But they did not go into the fort. People
were standing before the palisades, Colonel McDouall sat in a
chair surrounded by soldiers; before him Indians were grouped.
Dousman drew close enough to see what the savages held tri-

umphantly aloft—heads, hands, feet, legs, hacked from the men who had fallen on the field of battle. Some of the Indian chiefs held proudly to bloody hearts and livers, torn from the dead bodies. Hercules saw; he took Dousman's hand, holding tightly to it. But he did not turn away. He looked from the Indians to McDouall, watching McDouall's approval in nods and gestures to the Indians. Off to one side some of the Indians were doing a victory dance, shouting and yelling bloodthirstily. McDouall sat unmoved, save by his expression of approbation.

When he had satisfied the Indians, he rose and turned toward the fort. Seeing Dousman, he beckoned to him.

"I trust we've not damaged your woods too much, Mr. Dousman," he said. "I'm happy to say that your orchard escaped almost unscathed."

"I saw," said Dousman.

"Ha! Indeed! Well, then—you see how they were served. This is war, and their error is our gain. I daresay they'll think twice before landing on Mackinac again."

"Especially with your allies present," observed Dousman.

McDouall shot him a dark glance, but smiled in a moment, and left him.

Dousman turned and began to walk slowly back toward the farm, drawing gladly away from the cries and bawling of the Indians.

"What was it the Indians had, papa?" asked Hercules.

He told him, explaining that they meant to eat these trophies, thinking in this manner to gain the strength and courage of their enemies slain in battle.

Hercules said nothing, but his silence spoke louder than his words.

"You see, my boy—these are the allies of the British always. They lend themselves easily to incitement by the redcoats."

The boy was quiet for some time, but it was no longer shock and anger that held him. He was bewildered and thoughtful. "Why is it the Indians like to fight with the British?" he asked presently.

"Because the Americans have too often been fools," answered Dousman without hesitation. "Because our government has broken its treaties with the Indians time and again, because our traders have cheated the Indians even at the trading-posts."

"Mr. Astor, too?"

Dousman grimaced. "I'm afraid Mr. Astor has been guilty of similar dealings," he said.

He paused on the heights south of his farm and looked to where the ships were; they had withdrawn beyond Round Island now, but they were still there, retreating no farther. If the attack had failed, the siege had not been given up. Darkness was falling now, and he went wearily into the house to wait for evening and perhaps some word from Davenport, if he dared come ashore again.

There was no word from Davenport, though Dousman waited more than half the night.

In the morning a group of Americans came under a flag of truce and removed the body of Major Holmes, with permission from McDouall. The body would be shipped to Detroit for burial, Colonel McDouall announced. He presented his compliments to Colonel Groghan, and trusted the Americans would now withdraw. This was the word which went around the island.

But the Americans did not withdraw. The ships remained and continued to capture supplies. This harassing action brought the British close to starvation, and made the Indians more restive than ever, causing larger numbers of them to depart. Bread grew steadily more scarce for lack of flour; several of the islanders resorted to making their own flour from grain in storage. It was obvious that the American ships could command the British supply lines for an indefinite time, and several investigating parties revealed the Americans in command of Lake Erie, of Lake Huron, the route from Montreal by way of the Ottawa, Lake Nippising, and French River, and the route from York, through Lake Simcoe and down the Nautawasaga River.

Bread rose to a dollar a loaf; the garrison began to kill horses for meat, and was soon put on rations. McDouall, out of necessity, induced the remaining Indians to return to their homes, safe in the information by a spy that the American troops, save for three companies, had returned to Detroit.

The resourceful McDouall, seeing that nothing but the utmost boldness would keep them from starvation as winter approached, outfitted batteaux to attack the ships *Tigress* and *Scorpion* left to

guard the mouth of the Nautawasaga. They departed at night, and returned in the ships themselves less than a week later. Mackinac once more lay open to supplies from the British posts, and was safe for the winter.

In midwinter Drew came over the ice from Bois Blanc, walking blithely into Dousman's house while they were sitting at supper one evening. Dousman looked at him open-mouthed in astonishment.

"Ye'll have thought me dead, I'll be bound," said Drew, lowering a pack of furs from his broad shoulders.

"Where in God's name were you?"

Drew took off his cap and lowered his touseled head. He found a scar on his scalp and held an index finger to it. "Ye'll see for yerself, Mr. Dousman. I was near enough dead, but not quite. Some Winnebagos took me, meaning to torture me, took my scalp, and were set to have a time at my expense, when another trader came along and talked the old chief out of the idea. Ye can imagine my gratitude. I was wounded, sore hurt; I stayed with him for months, about a year, I reckon."

"You never reached Groghan?"

He shook his head and took the chair Hercules pushed toward him. "I was taken before I reached Detroit. I spent a while on the Maumee after that, and was taken toward the Mississippi. But I heard. Ye'll not be doubtin' me when I tell ye 'twas no surprise to me how it happened."

Dousman shook his head. "It was almost in my front yard, as you might say."

"But 'twasn't the only place, here in Mackinac. A like thing happened in Washington, they say. The British burned part of Washington, would have sacked it all if it hadn't been for rain comin' down too heavy. Redcoats under Pakenham, I heard. They went out and around to New Orleans, and the word's gone around that General Jackson gave them hell down there. They say, too, the war's over, with nobody gainer, nobody loser."

"We've heard nothing of it," said Dousman dubiously.

Drew shrugged. "Ye'll not be needin' to take my word. Aikens told me. He came up from Detroit not long ago, the snow not

bein' too deep. Ye see I've been on Duck Island almost a month now, short some days. I was weak at my comin', and I stayed low to take strength again. Since then, I've been at the traps once more, and I tell ye I enjoy the feel of them, Mr. Dousman."

"I can believe it."

Garrulously, Drew launched into a detailed story of his capture and rescue, fingering the circular scar where a piece of his scalp had been removed. "I reckon this part of me is in some Indian's belt now," he said.

"If the war's ended, why don't they occupy Mackinac again?" said Dousman then. "I'm as anxious as you for the trade to start up once more."

Drew nodded. "Havin' forgot us so long before the war, I reckon they'll forget us a while after. Besides, this winter's not easy for troops to move. They'll likely come up by the lakes." He paused briefly, eyeing a plate of cakes which Dousman handed to him. "By the way, I ran into Mr. Davenport in Detroit on my way back. He said he'd seen you. He spoke of McDouall, saying the colonel had made the women watch the Indians dance with heads and all. How d'ye fare with McDouall?"

"He's a good leader," said Dousman shortly. "I'm not fond of him. But I noticed none of the women at the ceremony."

"Mr. Drew will be hungry," said Jane abruptly. "Draw up your chair, Mr. Drew, and eat with us."

"Thank ye, I will."

Drew moved up, loosening his heavy fur jacket.

"If the war's over, you might stay with us here for a while. We'll need to reorganize the trade," said Dousman. "John will be coming back."

"Aye, but the Indians will need to be met again. They've done with fighting, I reckon, and most of them have gone west of the Mississippi. The post at Prairie du Chien will want growing."

Dousman looked speculatively at Hercules.

"It need not be a large post at first," continued Drew. "It might be well if ye sent some word to Mr. Astor."

"I'll think of it in good time. For the present, Rolette has done well enough, and with Deckson's aid, I don't doubt he can handle the trade."

"They'll be pushing the Indians still further west," went on Drew, taking his food in great gulps.

Around the table the Dousman family sat watching him, listening to him, the twins conversing in whispers, with eyes fixed upon Drew, Nancy demure but alert. Hercules felt himself one of them, a man, too.

"And how'll ye fare when the Americans take the island back, Mr. Dousman?" Drew asked abruptly.

"I see no reason to think that much change will take place here." But he felt a faint apprehension. He got up and stood for a while near the hearth, a light frown settling upon his forehead.

"There are some Americans regard ye as a traitor," observed Drew cautiously.

"And McDouall loses no love for me."

"Aye, ye're caught on both sides." He pushed away from table.

Dousman was undisturbed by any contemplation of the future save only for the trade. "If you've finished," he said, "come into the other room, and we'll talk over what must be done to resume the trade." He paused on the threshold and glanced back to meet Hercules' eyes. "You, too, Hercules—you're fifteen now."

In mid-July the American regulars under Colonel Anthony Butler came to take possession of Mackinac. Colonel McDouall presented his regrets; he was not yet quite ready to vacate the fort; the garrison had not had time to complete fortifications on Drummond Island. Colonel Butler extended his wait for three days, encamping on the beach to await the pleasure of Colonel McDouall. He permitted the American flag to be run up on the lower fort, galling McDouall, who was in any case in a black rage and depression since his information two months before of the terms of the Treaty of Ghent.

On the eighteenth, Colonel Butler and his regulars took possession. He was induced by Captain Morgan to rename the fort in honor of Major Holmes. He sent at once for Michael Dousman, an orderly arriving at the Dousman farm early in the afternoon.

He was casual in his conversation. "You don't seem t' have done much fightin' here," he said. He asked to be shown the battlefield.

Dousman turned at the gate and indicated the British and Ameri-

can positions, showing him where the dead had ultimately been buried, west of the battlefield. The orderly was not hostile; Dousman had a feeling of well-being.

Hercules, coming up from the village, met them going into the fort, and went along.

Colonel Butler was tall, sharp-eyed, a frontier product, though there was nothing in his speech to betray him. He shook hands with Dousman gravely, pointed with a quill to a chair. "The boy?" he asked, eyebrows raised.

"My son," explained Dousman.

"Let him sit, then."

Hercules sat down. The orderly bowed himself casually out. Colonel Butler drew a paper toward him and looked at it with seeming intentness, though there was that in his attitude which said he knew very well what was written there.

"Mr. Dousman, we have information that you served the British here," Butler said. "We are sensible of the facts in this matter—that your service was to the Americans on the island, and we have the depositions of certain fellow citizens who were sent under guard to Detroit in exchange for prisoners. We also learn that you were before the British occupation Captain of the Militia on the island."

He paused and looked at Dousman expectantly.

Dousman nodded and said, "Those things are true."

Colonel Butler smacked his lips, reached beyond the first paper for another and said, "Mr. Dousman, we should like you to resume your post as Captain of the Militia, your duties to begin immediately."

Dousman got up. For a moment he said nothing. Then he inclined his head gravely. "Thank you, Colonel Butler."

Colonel Butler shook hands again. "Good day, sir," he said. He shook hands also with Hercules.

They went out, leaving the commander to his papers, which he made a business of shuffling together, humming a little under his breath.

Dousman strode away, smiling, his gait easy. He had the conviction that nothing had changed at all, that the past three years were but a dream; the trade loomed ahead, years of the trade stretched unendingly away; he foresaw no end, and looked back

to where Hercules dawdled, seeing in him the continuation of his own dreams. He must go to school a little more, he thought— Robinson in New York might take him for a year to teach him accounting after he finishes at Elizabethtown; and then perhaps, in a few years, I can send word to Astor about him.

He turned and called sharply. "Come, Hercules—time is always short."

2.

Where the Rivers Meet

1826

*T*HE apprentice nodded, his attention wandering. His thin-fingered hands were clasped behind his back, his sky-blue eyes seemed not to see Hercules at all, his hair was touseled where he had previously made some attempt at straightening it along his head.

Hercules smiled. "If you tire at this stage, Fauchon, you'll never be a trader. Come, pay attention." He slapped a pile of pelts in the close, aromatic storeroom. "The marten is sometimes called *sable*. It comes in several grades—extra fine dark, number one dark, number two dark, number one fine brown, number two fine brown, number one fine common, number two common, number three common, good, out of season, inferior, damaged, and worthless." He pointed them out as he mentioned them. "We aren't concerned with damaged and worthless pelts—I mention them only because you should know. The only fur comparable to it in value is the silver gray fox, and the otter fur is now gaining in value. There are classifications to all furs, and great variations in the colors. You'll have to watch that, and you must learn your seasons. Muskrat are most common, of course; after them mink, fox, lynx, raccoon, beaver, badger, wolverine . . ." He stopped suddenly, conscious that Fauchon's attention had wandered again.

He brushed past him, patient but feeling his instruction a waste of time. Fauchon turned after him.

"Come along."

He led the way back to his little room in the Astor building, glancing out of the window as if to mark the time by the bright westering sun. The sound of waters in the straits welled into the

room. He glanced briefly at Fauchon and sat down. The youth teetered before him, still with the same absent air.

"What's the matter today, Fauchon?" inquired Hercules persuasively.

The apprentice seemed not to have heard for a moment; then his eyes flickered downward to Dousman's face, a smile touched his lips, and he nodded. "I suppose I am distant today, M. Dousman. You see . . ." He stopped as if catching himself, and his dark skin deepened in color.

"Ah, Mademoiselle Golier, I suppose," Hercules said dryly. He shrugged. "Go to her then, and come back tomorrow—but prepared to learn, Fauchon. I warn you, my patience is long, but it has an end."

"Merci, Monsieur Dousman," said the apprentice, alert on the instant. He flowered into activity, snatched his cap, and ran from the room.

Hercules laughed and took up his quill. In a moment he put it down again, got up, and went to the window, to stand looking down the street where Fauchon ran, pausing every few minutes to wave to some one, and he wondered with a curious interest whether he had ever been like that? Not about a woman, certainly, he thought. But he understood, and he smiled not so much in amusement as in sympathy, filled with the appreciation of the young for the enthusiasms of those younger, recognizing in them the same spirit they had known and still knew.

He folded his arms on the high window sill and looked out, resting his chin on his arms. The street was warm in the sun, filled with a kind of sunshot dust which was not dust, but motes holding sunlight in the quiet air, making a glow which would turn to old rose at evening. Two women stood in conversation a few doors away, and farther still a soldier from the fort leaned idly against a sunlit wall, his blue coat catching the eye. The waters' eternal sound welled and receded in his consciousness; he turned from the window and went back to his desk, where resolutely he looked again to his account book, took up his quill, and set to work.

But he was restless. He put down a few figures and was distracted by the sound of voices in the adjoining room, his father's room, and he heard his name mentioned in a deep rumbling voice not his father's. He sat unmoving, listening.

"As for Hercules," his father was saying. "We shall see. I believe he'll do." There was a sound of movement, and footsteps approached the door. It was opened, and Michael Dousman looked into the room. "Hercules, if you please." He held the door open, his grave eyes fixed on Hercules, who got up and walked past him to face the unspoken inquiry of his father's visitor: a heavy man with a big face and small eyes which gave the impression of great shrewdness.

"Mr. Ramsay Crooks," said Dousman. "You'll have heard me speak of Hercules."

Crooks got up and shook hands a little stiffly. He settled back in his chair and scrutinized Hercules as he might examine an animal, with impartial honesty, his thick lips pushing out and in, his eyes a trifle narrowed. He was bear-like.

"He has a good appearance, Dousman," said Crooks.

Dousman nodded. Hercules said nothing.

"And he looks strong."

"Seldom ill," observed Dousman.

Hercules said dryly, "If I'm on the block, perhaps I should have changed my clothes."

Crooks laughed. "He has spirit, too. Good. Young man, we'll come at once to business, since I see you have as much regard for time as I. You've heard your father speak of Prairie du Chien."

"I've been there."

"Indeed?" Crooks flashed a glance of inquiry at Dousman, his heavy-lidded eyes opening a little and asking, Why haven't you told me this?

"He collected a bill for me there three or four years ago."

"Three," said Hercules without hesitation.

"How did you like it?" asked Crooks, turning to him again.

"I thought it a beautiful site for a village—and for a trading post."

Crooks chuckled. "Yes, yes—the trading post. Mr. Astor has had this in mind. Mr. Rolette—" He looked up. "But you've met him?"

Hercules nodded. "He was just going out at that time."

"Yes, he prefers the going. Deckson's been taking care of the post in his absence. It's a place that needs two men. Now Deckson's gone. So we need some one to replace him. Would you like to assume that responsibility?"

"It would depend upon what status I had," answered Hercules at once.

"You would be responsible to me," said Crooks. "I don't think your father's found me a hard man to deal with. What do you say, Dousman?"

Dousman smiled. "Not at all."

Crooks took up a leather weight and struck the desk a sharp blow. "Of course, the country's wild—wilder than Mackinac, be sure. There are Indians, and where they are, there's unrest, possibly trouble. You may get into it, you may not. In any case . . ."

Hercules broke in gently. "I'll go whenever you think best."

Crooks got up and offered him his hand once more. "Young man, I admire any one who can make decisions without needless delay. We'll get along all right. I hold it against your father that he's kept you locked away here for this time. We need decision and dispatch in the American Fur Company. Come with me."

He walked heavily over to a map tacked to the wall of the room to the right of Dousman's desk. He put his finger on Mackinac, traced silently the course across Lake Michigan into Green Bay to Fort Howard, up the Fox River, across the Portage, down the Wisconsin to Prairie du Chien. There he held his finger, pushed against the wall with such force that a faint white crescent showed under his nail where the blood receded from the tip of his finger.

"The post at Prairie du Chien is the place where the rivers meet, the first of those meetings with the Mississippi," he said musingly. "You'll draw on a large area there—almost all that part of the Michigan Territory west of the lake, the eastern expanse of the Trans-Mississippi country, and for some distance down the Mississippi itself, as well as much of the upper Mississippi Valley. Of course, the country of the Missouri is still under Lisa's men—ours since the merger. There'll be no conflict there. You should have a large trade, if peace prevails."

Hercules smiled. "I suppose you might call it following the trade west, eh?"

Crooks stared at him uncertainly for a moment before he laughed. "Yes, yes—of course, eventually the trade . . ." He shrugged his shoulders. "But all things pass, young man."

He turned to the map once more and placed his hand flat upon it,

so that the place of the rivers' meeting was concealed beneath his palm. "All this is tributary," he said evenly. "There are many pelts there. The American Fur Company has its men throughout this territory, and there are few rivals—even few independents who dare compete with us."

He looked at Hercules sharply, but Hercules said nothing. He had heard tales of what had happened to traders who had pushed the Astor men too far. But he had no knowledge of these matters.

Crooks turned away. "Now, there are two men scheduled to start out tomorrow. If that's too soon for you, I believe they can delay a day or two. Their departure can wait upon your convenience."

"I'll not keep them waiting," said Hercules shortly. "The sooner I reach the post at Prairie du Chien, the sooner I can take up my work there."

Crooks smiled, his satisfaction evident. He settled himself once more in the chair, his eyes almost closed, his smile holding to his heavy face, so that he gave off an aura of great warming comfort.

Dousman, who had gone to a window to look out, turned suddenly and said, "The men are coming at last."

"Drunk?" asked Crooks, without opening his eyes.

"I think not."

The three of them waited until the outer door opened and the men came into the room, one of them short and fat, the other thin, bent, bird-like. Crooks opened his eyes and fixed the men standing before the desk.

"The fat one," he said, "is Lapiage; the thin one is Souligne." He looked at Hercules and added, as if to reassure him, "Both are excellent trappers and woodsmen." He turned to them. "Mr. Dousman is going to Prairie du Chien with you in the morning."

As one, the two men looked at the older Dousman.

"Young Mr. Dousman," said Crooks sharply.

They swung their eyes to Hercules and smiled.

"He'll take Deckson's place at the post there," continued Crooks. "I'll trust you to see to it that he reaches there in good time and with a minimum of discomfort."

"Monsieur Crooks knows he can trust us," said Lapiage, and went on to talk of other matters.

Hercules looked at them. Lapiage had hard dark eyes without the stigma of fear or deference in them; his firm mouth bespoke his domination of the more uncertain Souligne, whose eyes of weak blue with their manifest hesitation and caution betrayed his unsureness. It was Lapiage who took the lead, decided Hercules. I must get to know them better, he thought. Souligne stood a little behind Lapiage, assenting in his opinions, disagreeing when he disagreed, and yet careful not to dare Crooks' anger. Lapiage talked about the trip, speaking of things needed, things to be done before they set out. He turned suddenly upon Hercules.

"We'll leave at dawn, Monsieur Dousman. From the Company's wharf. We try to travel light."

"I'll be there," said Hercules.

Souligne laid a finger against his nose and said, "It may storm."

"I haven't arranged for it," said Crooks with heavy humor.

Lapiage barked polite laughter, made his excuses, and left. Souligne bowed himself out in his wake.

Crooks smiled and took up his stick. He held out his hand to Hercules. "Good luck, my boy. Write to me when you need any advice on policy." He put his hat on and nodded to Michael. "Come, Dousman; join me."

Michael permitted himself a small, satisfied smile for Hercules, and for a moment father and son looked at each other across the room before Dousman came over, clapped him twice affectionately on his shoulder, and went out after Crooks.

He rose well before dawn in the morning. He had put his things together the night before, and now he added to his clothing a small copy of Pascal's *Letters*. He looked around him at his little room, the conviction strong that he would never again lie here. Then he went noiselessly into the kitchen, but his mother was up; she had got breakfast, and stood patiently waiting for him.

"It wasn't necessary you should get up," he said quietly.

"It's a long journey, Hercules," she answered.

He smiled at her and sat down to eat rapidly while his mother stood beside the table, her eyes fixed unmoving on him, speaking her sadness at this parting. He looked up at her from time to time, meeting her grave eyes, and smiling, and he noticed that her face

was still young, though her hair was graying, and her hands betrayed her middle age. But he could not help thinking that with his going, she would have less work. He was sharply conscious of her standing there, with a shawl over her nightgown.

His father came into the room, fully dressed.

"By the time you get to the wharf, it'll be dawn," he said. "Stir yourself, my boy."

"I've finished," he said, and got up.

"Well, then, I'll walk down with you."

Hercules took his pack and slung it over his shoulder. A little shyly, he bent and kissed his mother.

"Take care, Hercules—it's wild country," she said. She gave him food she had packed for his journey.

Dousman had gone outside and stood looking up at the starlit sky. The wind was fresh, but not strong, a restless wind which seemed to have no constant direction. Hercules joined him, and together they began to walk down the road, through the pasture gate toward the heights of the island, and beyond, where lay the village and the wharf. For a while they walked in silence, but Dousman wished to speak, for he looked from time to time at Hercules, yet always drew back. They passed the heights and were approaching the cemetery before any word was spoken between them.

"I need hardly give you advice at this age, Hercules," said Dousman with no lack of direction. "But it may be well to caution you. You know how to conduct yourself in business, you've learned how to deal with men of a political stamp—the late war was a good teacher. But now as for the Company—there are men in it not to be trusted. And there are certain methods. You'll find opposition to all Astor men because of what some of them have done, and escaped doing, thanks to Astor's wealth."

"Father, I mean to be wealthy, too."

Dousman shook his head. "Money is power, true. But much unhappiness lies in its possession. And the evil that men do stems largely from it. They say, and I believe it true, that Mr. Astor has bought judges, representatives, even senators, so that they condone not only theft and robbery, but even murder. You see, there are enemies to a man within as well as outside. Here on Mackinac we know them; it'll take you some time to know them at Prairie du

Chien. But if you have trouble, go to the commander at Fort Crawford there."

Hercules said, "If money is power, Father, it can be a power for good, too, as well as evil."

"Yes, yes—but how seldom!"

They were silent for a while before Hercules said, "You'll not have cause to concern yourself over me, Father."

"I'm sure of it," replied the older man with the quiet firmness of conviction.

They passed by the fort and went silently through the town, where all was still save for one house where a light burned, a dim yellow glowing holding the window. The lake lay sentient before them, the water driving a little under the wind, lapping gently against the shore and the wharf. Into the vast inverted dome of the sky, pale amethyst was coming to dispel the darkness.

Lapiage and Souligne were already there, though they were not immediately in sight. Hearing their approaching footfalls, Lapiage mounted to the wharf, where he stood bowing and pointing into the east in the direction they had come.

"Good morning, good morning—see, just on time. The dawn—she comes."

Dousman nodded. "Are you ready to shove off?"

"This moment," replied Lapiage.

Souligne's head appeared cautiously over the side of the wharf, and he grinned uncertainly. Hercules smiled back at him.

"We'll not delay you then," said Dousman. "Hercules." He put out his hand and it was clasped by Hercules.

"Father, I wanted to tell you about Fauchon," Hercules said rapidly, as if suddenly aware of how quickly time had gone. "Be patient with him. You'll find him absent-minded. I had to send him home yesterday, but he's in love."

"All right, Hercules." He hesitated momentarily. "You'll write to us."

On this casual note they parted. Dousman turned and went up the wharf toward the Astor building; Hercules dropped lightly into the long canoe—one of the large *canots du nord* commonly used by the voyageurs, held steady by Souligne. Lapiage came after him. They cast off, and in a few minutes were advancing into the

straits of Mackinac to cross Lake Michigan and take the route to the Mississippi. Hercules glanced briefly back, his eyes flickering in the dawn from the tall bluffs and rocky promontories so familiar to him, to the pebbled beach and the cluster of buildings that made the village. Then he turned his calm eyes into the south-west. Behind them the dawn flowered in the eastern sky, magenta and cerise invading the retreating night's purple and amethyst before the sun.

Late in the second night they reached Green Bay. Wind and rough water had made their journey more difficult, and Souligne was exhausted. The darkness was deep, but they were accustomed to it. The settlement made dark angular masses upon the sky, and few lights shone: here and there a window, and down the river torches burning dimly at Fort Howard. The night was cool, the mid-spring air still fresh and damp.

"We'll rest a few hours here," said Lapiage. As if in answer to Hercules' unspoken question, he added, "John Lawe knew I was coming through tonight if I could. He'll be waiting for us. We'll need provisions."

They pulled the canoe out of the water and left it high on the shore, partly covered. Lapiage made his way unhesitatingly overland into the settlement; Hercules came after, and Souligne walked last. It was apparent soon that Lapiage was making for one of the buildings from which light streamed and now, as they approached, a voice could be heard, rising and falling, in a kind of sing-song manner, boisterous for a space, and gentle again. Lapiage pushed open a door and entered the general store, where a solitary brace of candles illuminated the large room, casting flickering shadows upon the shelves of trading goods—weapons, blankets, clothing, as well as upon the counter, where the proprietor nodded and a lone customer sat over a half-empty bottle of whiskey, talking. The liquor smell was warm in the air, but not as strong as the fragrance of tobacco, spices, of blankets and coffee and the tartness of vinegar from a barrel off to one side.

The solitary customer was garbed in the typically colorful habit of the voyageur; his short shirt was green, in contrast to his red woolen cap askew on his head; his deerskin leggins, secured to a

belt about his waist, had been loosened a little; he wore a blue capote, and to his yellow sash had attached the inevitable pipe and a beaded pouch. His arms and shoulders had that development which indicated that he had long been in the trade. At their entrance, he fell silent, and turned his shaggy dark face in their direction; his heavy eyebrows made a straight line across his nose, and the flickering light shadowed his eyes, lending his features an expression of evil, which was only momentarily misleading, for a gravely shy smile suddenly lit up his face.

"Lapiage!" he exclaimed. "Now I got an ear to talk into. Lawe's asleep."

Lapiage gave him a cursory glance, but in a moment paused and looked at him again. "Benoit! I thought you were out with Rolette. What's the matter? What happen'? Why are you here?"

Benoit swore fluently. "He go wit'out me. By damn! You know how he is. He go up river an' leave me be!"

Suddenly in his sleep aware that the monotone of Benoit's voice had ceased, Lawe woke up, his mild eyes looking from one to another of them; he licked his lips, as if to take the taste of sleep from his mouth.

"Ah, it's you, Lapiage," he said quietly.

"We're here," said the voyageur shortly. "We need to sleep now. And Souligne's about done in. We had some rough water." He turned and introduced Hercules. Then he turned once more and stared at Benoit.

"They left him sleeping here," said Lawe.

"Forgot him, eh?"

Lawe made a parched sound with his lips and looked bland. Hercules immediately apprehended that Benoit had been left deliberately, possibly to sleep off the effects of liquor.

"There's a boat going up to the Portage in a few days," supplemented Lawe. "He can go back on that."

"No," said Lapiage shortly. "Let Souligne come on that. We can use Benoit."

Souligne nodded quietly, stretching. "I can sleep some," he said. "I don't feel so well."

Lapiage drove his quick eyes toward Hercules. "Benoit's one of our men, Dousman." Without turning, he said over his shoulder,

"Mr. Dousman is taking Deckson's place, Benoit—Mr. Rolette's partner."

Benoit's eyebrows ranged upward and he ducked his head a little, but said nothing.

Lawe came around the corner and led the way to a door almost lost in the room's shadows. He threw it open and waved his arm into the darkness. "You'll find room to sleep in here. What time'll you start?"

"At dawn," answered Lapiage. "If you'll have provisions ready."

"The river's high. With luck, you should reach the Winnebago before nightfall."

Souligne had already gone into the adjoining room, where three low cots were set in a row. Hercules and Lapiage followed. Benoit sat down at a table near the counter and began to talk again, volubly, excitedly, half in French, half in English. Lawe made ready their provisions, put out the candles and left the store. Benoit talked on.

Like many men, Hercules could not sleep well in a strange bed, though he rested. He heard Benoit's voice, distinguished his tall tales told into the darkness, until at last the voyageur slept, too. Souligne had a gentle, wheezing snore which had an apologetic sound, as if secretly he were trying to suppress it, but it came regardless. The smell of the store lay in the room's close air, tantalizing the nostrils. Outside a wind rose and fell, and a shutter banged somewhere for a while.

Hercules remained wakeful. His mind was occupied with a ceaseless shuttling back and forth in time; he stood now on a threshold, before a door opening into his future. He contemplated his coming years with expectant equanimity; he was certain of himself; his dream of wealth and power persisted, strengthened now by his slowly gathered knowledge of people and their frailties. As yet he did not know what he might be enabled to do for the people of his chosen place, but he was confident that wealth might give power for good as well as power for wrongdoing, and, thinking of certain policies darkly practised by the Astor Company, he retreated deeper and deeper into his dream. But he could not sleep, despite his fatigue; he lay quiet, thinking, remembering, his thoughts going slowly back over the past years—past his year with

Robinson in New York, the endless hours of accounting, past his study of the Indian languages at Mackinac, past his schooling in New Jersey, back to that first broad awareness which had come to him ten years and more ago, during the siege and occupation of the island by the British, and, lying there in the silent, close-pressing dark, he could hear again his father's quiet words, the old man's admonitions, warnings, observations printed indelibly on his memory. And before his mind's eye rose his past, torn from his memory by this isolated moment in his time: his father's grim eyes watching the ineptly commanded Americans coming to do battle with the British; the inevitable savage allies of the British well used to bring capitulation under terror; the bitter glances given his father by the Americans for those first years of the British occupation, by the secret British sympathizers afterward.

He turned restlessly, his eyes held to darkness, in his ears no longer the long familiar voice of the waters in the straits, but only the wind's voice eternally keening, the wind blowing up the spring from the direction of that place, the meeting of the rivers, where he went now to make tangible his future. His father's voice still echoed in his memory: *Act with dispatch; think for yourself. . . . If these men had compromised, there would have been no trouble; remember that—compromise, compromise, compromise; if you don't, life will beat you down. . . . No one can tell what will make another man happy, but all life is a seeking for that end, and all of it a compromise between what one would like and what one must take. . . . The British lend themselves to all manner of trickery for the sake of their empire.* Strong in his memory, these admonitions rang and echoed. Before Hercules lay his future; he was eager to stride forward, and yet nostalgically reluctant to leave behind him his pleasant early years. Yet he knew he must, and his anticipation was keener than his looking backward. Filled with his dream, possessed by the strength of his hope for the years coming, he fell asleep at last.

Lapiage, who lay all night like a stone, without movement, got up before dawn and went out into the store. Hercules brushed down his clothes a little and followed. In the faint light that illumined the crowded store, Lapiage prudently removed the bottle of whiskey from Benoit's reach, but as yet made no move to awaken

the giant of a man sprawled asleep upon the table. Turning, he saw Hercules behind him.

"Ah, you're up. We can get started, then." He cuffed Benoit roughly on the head. "Get up, get up! We're off."

Benoit roused himself, shaking his shaggy head, and looked with thick red eyes at Lapiage. Then he came to his feet, knocking the table over, clapped Lapiage on the shoulder and roared, "Lapiage! By God damn! Rolette, he leave me behin'. What you t'ink about dat? Me, Benoit!" He saw Hercules suddenly and said, "I see you before. Lawe! Lawe! By gar! put on de light. Breeng whiskey."

Lapiage disengaged himself firmly, his hard eyes glinting, his precise mouth unmoving. For a moment Benoit stared from one to the other of them, sought the half-dark store for John Lawe; no one moved. Slowly Benoit came back to the previous night, and he remembered.

Lapiage went over to the counter and picked up the provisions Lawe had put up for them. "Come on," he said shortly.

Benoit grinned a little sheepishly at Hercules, who smiled, thinking, So this is one of the men! wondering what all the others might be like.

"Rolette, he weel be down on me jus' lak de Mississip' on a san' bar," Benoit observed.

They went outside into the chill dawn and filed down the slope to the place where they had left the canoe. Alone, Benoit carried the canoe to the Fox and stood waiting while Lapiage and Hercules got in. He pushed off with powerful strokes of the paddle, and they began to move upstream. Fort Howard emerged from the night only to fade into the distance, lingering only in the faint smell of smoke that clung to their nostrils; they passed Green Bay and the rapids and were soon paddling through the flat country beyond, a country of woods and swamps, of low open places bordering the river, and forests coming to the water's edge. Dawn flushed the east, but in the west the waning moon still shone yellowly, and a few stars held briefly to the sky before fading in the advancing light fanning up the eastern heaven. From all sides above the water's sound, the dipping of paddles, came the matins of birds, the caroling of robins and thrushes, the sweet diminuendos of field sparrows, the lyricism of vesper sparrows, the mourning of turtle doves and kill-

deers. Woodcocks and jacksnipes still volleyed down the air, and somewhere an early hawk whickered proudly on the high wind.

Benoit could not be still. He raised his big voice from time to time to draw attention to something along shore: a deer, a muskrat with young paddling after, a flock of teal. And presently he began to talk. Lapiage looked with helpless amusement back to Hercules, as if to express his regret, but Hercules did not mind. Benoit talked about himself and his adventures; he said he had probably been in more scrapes than a dozen men he knew.

"I was for while wit' Pierre Chouteau," he said. "I go wit' Manuel Lisa one trip. By gar! a man could not forgit dat trip. Dat was year of eart'quake: 1811. Dat was tam Astor's brigade he wen' up de Missouri, dat tam Hunt led. De Indians dey make trouble dat year, an' Lisa ask' Hunt to wait, so two brigades could go same tam. But Hunt, he would not do it; he slip' away. Two damn' skonks Lisa sen' away tol' Hunt Lisa was treacherous an' like to turn Sioux on Hunt. Hunt he had eight'-five men and six, seven keels. We had twent'-five men wit' t'ree passengaires. Hunt lef' on twelft' March, an' Lisa on secon' April. Nevaire was a man lak Manuel Lisa for mak' tam; for day an' day w'en we foul' an' snag', we los' tam, but by gar! we catch Hunt, we catch up wit' him June secon', eleven o'clock it was—eleven hundred mile' from St. Charle' to Gran' Detour, sixt'-one days! You can beat dat? No! An' de Missouri—she is no water lak thees. Here you push leetle an' up you go—dere, ten men push." He was briefly loud in Lisa's praise before he changed his subject. He began to talk about a trip he had made with Rolette the previous June. They started out from Green Bay for Mackinac, six boats with furs from Prairie du Chien. At Green Bay they took on passengers: Henry Baird and his young bride, Therese Fisher Baird—Rolette's sister-in-law. "Dat Rolette, he is generous man. He sen' way to St. Louis for food. We had dat tam great plent'—ham, tongue, roas' cheecken, wine, biscuits, crackaires, cheese, tea, coffee, chocolate, brandy, everyt'ing. An' we had eggs, by gar! we had eggs, an' so we have de egg fight. We begin wit' de biscuits one morning; de boats dey come close and de biscuits dey fly. Rolette, he stop' thees. Den dey t'row de eggs. Madame Baird, she get under de tarpaulin, an' de eggs fly. All tam Rolette he try to stop it, but de men dey preten' dey do not hear

heem, an' de eggs mak' pretty in de air. Not so pretty on de clothes. Dat was a trip! Next day, we have anot'er egg battle; dey fly in de air till all de eggs dey gone." He shook his head, laughing, and presently was still.

But he could not be quiet for long; he burst into a boisterous voyageur's song.

C'est un pâté de trois pigeons,
Ha, ha, ha, frit à l'huile,
Assieds-toi et le mangeons,
Fritaine, friton, firtou, poilon,
Ha, ha, ha, frit à l'huile,
Frit au beurre et à l'ognon.

Lapiage looked around once more.

Hercules grinned. "He makes good company," he said. He was not displeased. Benoit's constant talk, his great energy, his booming voice conveyed a feeling of friendly companionship which the hard silence and precise intentness of Lapiage did not.

They were passing through woodland now, and Benoit's voice was thrown back by high trees on both sides of the Fox; here the sound of water rose, water among the roots of trees along the shores, the high spring flowing. They swung out a little, away from the deeps along the bank, lest they strike some obstruction: an unseen rock, a tree washed out from shore. Migrating birds flew from bank to bank, but their songs were muted by the water's constant voice as well as by Benoit's singing.

Benoit stopped presently, contented to hum a little. He chuckled to himself from time to time. "Rolette he weel be surprise'," he said several times. Presently he observed the country through which they were travelling, looked once or twice at the high sun, and said, "We' come to Leetle Kaukalin. Thees tam ol' Grignon get no monee from us."

Lapiage said over his shoulder that Grignon had a trading house there, and his teams took goods and furs while the men took the boats over the rapids.

"What does he get?" asked Hercules curiously.

"Twenty cents for every hundred pounds." He added, as if to reassure Hercules, "We'll have no trouble in the canoe—and the

river's high enough, besides. We'll go right on. We're not far
enough yet, though I guess we can make the Grand Chute, too,
and once in the lakes, we'll make better time."

After a lull which was surprising because it had occurred at all,
Benoit began to talk again, telling tall tales he had heard in the
Mississippi country—stories of superhuman deeds and men, of Indians, western animals and birds. The Blackfeet, he said, could
smell a man on the wind miles away. Indeed, they could tell
whether he was a Frenchman or an American; the Frenchmen, he
said, had a better smell, sweet as a frost-bitten apple. He said the
Arapahoes made rain whenever they wanted it and sent it away
when they didn't. He came back in his monologue to Manuel Lisa
and the Chouteaus; there were never fur traders to equal them.
They were the only ones to hold out against Astor, and they knew
what that meant.

"What does it mean?" asked Hercules abruptly.

"A knife in de rib'!" shouted Benoit. "By gar! I saw men kill'
dat way because dey would not do w'at Astor want' w'en he did
not want indepen's in hees country." But suddenly he was still, he
coughed uneasily, as if he realized that he should not have spoken
so; he changed the subject to talk about the settlers pressing into
the country beyond St. Joseph and St. Charles.

Hercules smiled, but he was nonetheless troubled because he
understood that such was indeed Astor's reputation: murder,
stealth, trickery, lies, deceit. Lapiage's back was eloquent.

Benoit, relieved at Hercules' silence, raised his voice again and
went on with his constant narrative. He had been at New Orleans,
he had been in Santa Fé, and barely got out alive. Damned few
men, he said, had ever been that far west—Indians, some priests,
traders from Mexico, and there were, of course, the Spanish, he
added in a tone evidently meant to suggest that the Spanish were
not properly men at all. For that matter, he went on, the priests
were Spanish, too, small-featured, with sharp eyes—like women in
their long robes. He praised the blue sky, the colors of the mountains in the sunlight and the evening's afterglow. He said he was
with Chouteau's brigade that year, 1817. Locked two months in a
filthy prison in Santa Fé. He thought they would never get out.
There were some men in 1811, he said, who were put to work in

the silver mines—for nine years! It was the silver that drew them down there, and of course, the trade. But they got off after two months, with nothing but their skins—and damned glad to have that much to carry home!

By late afternoon they reached the lakes, first the long blue shallow waters of Lake Winnebago stretching away to the south as far as they could see. They bore over to the western shore and made time going almost half the lake's great length before finding again the place where the Fox flowed through Puckawa and Lac de Bœuf and lesser lakes after them. It was now well after dark, and they made camp along shore, falling asleep at once.

They set out again at dawn, passing through the lesser lakes as rapidly as possible, so that in mid-morning they were back once more in the river, much narrower now, and less turbulent. The character of the country had changed, too; the great flat reaches were seldom come upon now, having given way to undulating ground, and here and there hills, presaging higher hills to come, already visible in the blue haze along the horizon.

They went on. Benoit talked less now. The high, muddy water made their passage easier than it might have been, for the river grew steadily narrower, the current more swift in its channel. Benoit and Lapiage were tenacious; neither would surrender his paddle to Hercules, not, as Hercules realized, to spare him so much as because neither trusted his ability against the river's treacherous strength. The sun drove westward, the purple shadows of dusk crept up the east, and they came out of hill country to a large flat lowland. He recognized it as the place of Pauquette's post, as the *O-ning-ah-hing* of the Winnebagos who had carried his boat there three years before.

"*Le portage,*" said Benoit behind him, expelling his breath in a great gust of relief.

Lapiage looked into the waning daylight and saw the Indians first. "Pah! That committee of welcome," he said. He spat.

The Indians stood in the curve of the bank where the canoe must naturally land, one of them, mounted, standing before the others, three others mounted behind him, and around the horses half a dozen braves on feet. The foremost of them wore the feathered head-dress, scarlet shirt, leg-pieces, and moccasins of a

chieftain; the deference with which his companions stayed behind him gave further evidence of his rank.

"Red Bird," said Benoit. "He's a bad one."

"Winnebagos," observed Hercules. "Let me do the talking. I can talk their language."

They came to shore, and at a guttural command from Red Bird two of the Indians ran forward to draw the canoe to land. Hercules sprang from the canoe and walked over to the chieftain's horse, his arm raised in the traditional gesture of friendship, his eyes fixed upon the immobile face of the Indian before him. He saw the sign of the chieftain's name in the preserved cardinals worn upon his costume as epaulettes. The Indian had a handsome proud head, he thought. He addressed him in the Winnebago language.

"Red Bird, I am Dousman, come to join my partner, Rolette, at the place where the rivers meet. Why are you here?"

"Red Bird goes with his braves to collect tribute at the carrying-place. This place is in the country of the Winnebagos; all those who cross it must pay tribute." His voice was extraordinarily pleasant, his bearing grave and dignified; he was not impressed by Dousman, but he evidently considered that Lapiage and Benoit were less than he, for he never once looked in their direction.

"This was the place of our fathers," continued Red Bird imperturbably.

"If two of your braves will carry the boat to the post, we will pay you," said Dousman.

Red Bird commanded his braves without turning his head. Hercules went back to where Lapiage and Benoit stood waiting and told them that the Winnebagos would portage the canoe. He added that he would pay the required tribute when they had done so. The braves were already taking up the canoe.

"Dat's wrong way," said Benoit. "Don' pay 'em theeng. By damn! we can portage boat. Dat's no way to deal wit' dese red bastards. W'en you mak loud noise enough, dey get out."

Lapiage firmed his mouth and volunteered no advice.

"No," countered Hercules. "All they'll want is some little trinket, which we can easily spare from Pauquette's shelves. The cost is nothing, and we keep their peace." His voice grew sharp. "What

kind of policy would it be to keep the Indians always in anger against us? Benoit, you must learn to think as well as to talk."

Benoit blinked at him, opened his mouth to speak, but only heaved a sigh.

Lapiage grinned furtively.

The three of them fell in behind the Indians, who had begun to move off after the lead of Red Bird. They pursued a winding passage through marshy country for a distance slightly over a mile, a country of long meadow grass where some water stood; but they escaped getting wet because Red Bird chose a course among the higher hummocks and ridges from the Fox River to the broader Wisconsin. He ignored the rough road built there. The sun vanished behind the hills beyond the Wisconsin, a great fan of amethyst, magenta, and lemon held the western sky; the mounted Indians were dark figures moving upon it. All around them birds rose, scattering before them, curlews with piping cries, killdeers wailing shrilly, partridge, whirring out of the tall grass with startling suddenness. The Indians made no sound at all passing before them; but Hercules and his companions made a gentle whispering in the grasses, a soft *swish-swish,* and their feet made occasional sucking sounds in the yielding earth. The smell of smoke rode the air, and in a few moments Pauquette's trading post came into sight, just beyond a small grove of oak trees, on the shore of the Wisconsin.

Hercules led the way into the trading post, caught up a small pile of gaily colored cloth pieces lying loose on the counter, and went out to pay the Indians. With an oath, Pierre Pauquette rose from behind the counter, reaching for a tomahawk swift to his hand. But he recognized Lapiage and Benoit, and drew back.

Hercules came quietly back and tossed a coin to the counter, daring the perplexed frown of Pauquette. The trader stood well over six feet, forcing even Benoit to look up to him; he was well built, muscular and strong; his face was rough, betraying his French and Indian ancestry as well as fearlessness and honesty. He was a man, Michael Dousman had said, of great value to the American Fur Comany.

Lapiage introduced Hercules.

"He have new idee' about de Indian," added Benoit.

"A bad time for to have Indian trouble," said Pauquette. Hercules explained.

"Oh, that eez right, messieurs," he approved, smiling, his eyes lighting up. He began to laugh. "I fail to recognize M. Dousman: I fail to remember he was here two, three year ago." He put out a hand and shook Hercules'. "I know your father. I know your partner. We are American Fur Company, eh?"

Recognizing the uncertainty of his English, Hercules spoke to him in French. "You spoke of trouble, Pauquette?" he asked.

"The Winnebagos, yes. They are restless. Something is in the air. If it weren't for the soldiers in the Territory—if it weren't for that, I say—I think there might be trouble. It's still the old dissatisfaction about the lead mines; they say the white men took them from them; they say the council last summer at Prairie du Chien with Governor Cass was not satisfactory."

"But they signed the peace," objected Lapiage.

Pauquette smiled, but his face darkened. He shrugged. "The white men have signed many treaties," he said softly. The implication of broken faith was obvious.

They talked on, Benoit throwing his big voice into the conversation from time to time. Hercules looked around. The store was much like John Lawe's at Green Bay, with the same smells, the same warmth of candlelight on the log walls. Pauquette said that many of the Indians were calling the white fathers "white feathers," which was not a good sign for continuing peace. Lapiage asked about Red Bird.

"He? He is honest," answered Pauquette. "But he's vain and weak, too. I don't expect trouble from him; he's no great leader. The Winnebagos have no great leader." He took a turn in silence behind the counter. "I'll tell you the man—it's Black Hawk. He's a Sac."

Benoit repeated the name uneasily.

"He's in the Trans-Mississippi now, but he wants to come back," added Pauquette. "The Indians speak often of him. They respect him."

Hercules observed that as long as Black Hawk remained in the Trans-Mississippi country, the settlers of the Michigan Territory need have no fear of him. "The Indians won't fight without their leader," he said.

Pauquette looked at him with interest. "You know much about Indians."

"I know most of the Indian languages in the Territory," he said quietly. "We dealt with all of them at Mackinac—Sacs, Foxes, Hurons, Winnebagos, Chippewas, Ottawas, even a few Shawnees and Sioux."

They talked well into the night, while the store grew darker as the candles guttered, one by one, and went out.

By mid-morning of the next day they were once more well on their way, travelling swiftly now down the widening Wisconsin, fleet among the many islands. The Wisconsin, too, was high with thaw-water, but was not brown with silt as the Fox had been; its water was a clear blue save here and there where sand was swirled up from the shallows to cloud it; it foamed and churned among the islands, swirled around rocks and vine-hung trees along the shores, muttered and roared over fallen boles long half submerged, so that only deft and rapid paddling kept them in the midstream, which swung from one shore to the next and seldom made its course down the center of the foaming wide blue expanse of water.

Benoit was his old self, talking volubly about his exploits throughout the country. He said he had spent a month with Daniel Boone in that same year when Lisa had raced Hunt up the Missouri. Boone had lived on the banks of the river then. He forgot that he had told some of his tales on the previous day, and retold them. He forgot, too, that Hercules had once before been over the Fox-Wisconsin route, or perhaps discounted his earlier trip, and from time to time pointed out places along the way. He promised Hercules such a sight as he would never see again were he to travel past the low marshy places when the lotus blossoms opened. He could go over all the world, it was said, and only in Egypt could he find these flowers. Now the fields were lush and green, beautiful under the sun; but in another month, in the season of heat, they would be wonderfully yellow and white with the lotus flowers. This was one of the reasons why the Winnebagos called this place the chosen spot of Gitchee Manitou, the Great Spirit, because He had planted these blossoms to bring joy to their sight. He praised the catkins of the cottonwoods where in hidden places they still held to the limbs, away from sunlight, or floated on the water with

their thousands of tiny blossoms opening yellow against their dark maroon background. Hercules sat listening gravely, pleased with the joy of living so manifest in Benoit.

When the sun began to swing into the southern sky half way through the morning, they came to the end of the ridge of hills through which the river had foamed on its way into the southwest. The bluffs of the Barribault, Benoit said they were. They drove now around a great paw of land reaching eastward between ridges, the bluffs of the Barribault on the north, a second ridge on the south, twelve to twenty miles between: a lush prairie country cradled in the hills, for a morain ridge rose sharply on the river's east shore, and pale purple along the western sky twelve miles across the prairie stood another range. This was the great prairie of the Sacs, explained Benoit. He added that it was the place where the Sac village had been when Black Hawk was born; he knew an Indian who had told him. You could still see the remains of their burial place and their cornfields.

Hercules expressed the opinion that it would make a good site for a settlement; he asked how long ago it had been that the Sacs had lived there.

Benoit did not know. Fifty years, certainly, because Black Hawk was over fifty.

At this moment Hercules caught a gleam from the high bluff on the southern edge of the prairie; the tree-girt hill grew out of the river's shore and a mass of bottomland trees there, a hill now a fresh bright green with new leaves like a haze cloaking its trees, save for the tall old pines crowning the bluff. Rocks broke the Wisconsin's edge at its base. They were approaching the hill beside a long curved island dividing the river at the lower edge of the prairie. The gleam appeared and vanished again, a quick flashing of sunlight thrown back from glass. Presently, he made out a house, a turreted structure of yellow stone well concealed behind the trees pushing up from all sides. It was not such a house as he might have expected to see in this wilderness, for the country through which they were travelling was, save for a few small prairies dotted with oak and birch groves and wild crabapple trees, heavily wooded, dense along the rivers and the islands.

"Who lives on that hill?" he called out to Lapiage.

"Pierneau!" exclaimed Benoit impulsively. "He's an indepen'. He's friend of dat Black Hawk."

"It's the house of M. le Baron Pierneau," answered Lapiage, with such respect in his voice that Hercules' interest was quickened.

"Long here?" he asked.

"Since before 1800," said Lapiage. "He's old now—and not well," he added regretfully. "And his son's gone—to the east, to school." He was still while the canoe passed around the island's lower tip and the hill's base, going swiftly down the Wisconsin where it curved into the southwest, so that the hill was squarely north of them. "He owns the prairie, or almost all of it. We buy from him when we stop."

"Is he alone there?"

Lapiage shook his head. "No, his wife is with him. And he has three men and another woman. They do a good business in pelts —good pelts, too. He has more always than he and his men could gather, but he says nothing about where he gets them."

He was silent, Hercules asked no more questions, and in a little while Benoit's voice rose again to fill the sun-warmed air with legend and tale, making a colorful pageant of adventure for them to hear above the bird-sound, the water's constant rushing and tearing rising all around. Here in the bottoms along the Wisconsin the wilderness was inhabited by thousands of birds: ducks and geese scattered in flocks at their approach; indigo buntings flashed bluely among the trees, and scarlet tanagers' *chip-churr, chip-churr* rose above the song sparrow's quiet melodies, undisturbed by their passage; trumpeter swans arched their proud necks and wings and defied them; and once a great cloud of passenger pigeons rose out of the woods with a thunderous sound of wings, leaving behind them trees stripped of fresh green foliage. Here and there in open places, the earth was blue with pasque flowers and jacob's ladder, white with anemones, yellow with buttercups and the early grass bloom, blossoms so thick that no grass was visible, and from time to time the fragrance of trees in bloom lay in the air across the water, a tenuous elusive aroma sweet to the nostrils. All the rich beautiful land was sentient with life, and spring filled the day with the stirring, fertile fragrance of growing things, a fragrance com-

pounded of flower perfume, of decaying leaves, of sap rising and earth itself.

The Wisconsin widened to its mouth, and there at last lay the Mississippi. If in that morning the Wisconsin had seemed wide, it was dwarfed now by this stream for so long known only as the Indians' Father of Waters. It seemed, from this vantage point, easily more than a mile in width; it was a deep, intense blue, and lay widely gleaming under the sun, with the distant hills of the opposite shore rising almost unbelievably far upon the sky. Here the tawny waters met, and seeing this expanse, this meeting place of the rivers, Hercules felt surging up within him something of their great, placid strength, the ceaseless, driving force that drove restlessly from the mountains across the prairies and through the valleys to the sea. Soon they entered upon the broader river, high, too, with spring thawing waters from the north, and with here and there great brown clouds of silt not at first visible from the Wisconsin's stream.

They turned to battle their way up along the shore to Prairie du Chien, the settlement at the meeting place of the rivers: a scattering of houses around the military post, Fort Crawford, in the flat land reaching from the Mississippi's edge to the ridge of bluffs not far to eastward. The Mississippi stretched from the western bluffs to the village, running among sloughs on both sides, sloughs in such numbers that it was obvious as they came to the village that certain low places in Prairie du Chien must at times be inundated by the spring waters.

The time was late afternoon; the sun approached the bluffs on the western shore and shed a pale rose glow over the settlement, gleaming from the turbulent water of the Mississippi, flashing from windows in the island part of the village, for Prairie du Chien was divided into two separate settlements together making up the village—the one on the long island strip of land separated from the other, the Town to the east, by the Marais de St. Feriole, a slough which now, as always in high water, made a respectable distance between them. Much of the island was under water, but the buildings of the American Fur Company and its men were on the high part of the island, and in no danger from the river's anger. Apart from the fort, the Astor building, and a small warehouse adjoining, there were less than a dozen habitations for white men; all

around the Town were Indian dwellings, and here and there on the island as well as in the Town were the homes of half-breeds, quarter-breeds, and various individuals whose ancestry was unknown, many of them belonging to the brigades serving the American Fur Company.

A few batteaux, a keel boat, and dozens of canoes lay upon the water along the shore at the landing place where they drew in. Lapiage said that one of the batteaux belonged to the Missouri traders and pointed to a slight difference in the make of it. In the rough street at the water's edge of which they were landing, a small knot of half-naked Indians and *engagés* stood, the Indians tall and bronze, the voyageurs for the most part short, dark, barrel-chested, the red feathers in their caps marking their long service in the brigades. Beyond them stirred only a lone walker apparently setting out for the slough and the Town beyond. The scene was in marked contrast to the incessant bustle and activity at Mackinac.

They stepped to the land. Some of the *engagés* recognized Lapiage and Benoit and called to them.

"I'll see Rolette at once," said Hercules.

"Rolette?" repeated Lapiage uncertainly. "I don't know, M. Dousman. He may not be there. In any case, there's his house. You might go there if you don't find him at the Company office." He pointed to the house not far from the Astor building.

"Thanks. I will." He half turned, but swung back. "When do you go out again, Lapiage?"

"I wait for Souligne now," the voyageur replied. "Two, three days, a week maybe. I don't know, but soon."

"Then I'll see you before you go. We've had a good trip together, and Benoit kept us from falling asleep."

Lapiage beamed, and Benoit threw his cap in the air with boisterous laughter.

With the sound of the big man's laughter ringing in his ears, Hercules set out up the street for the office of the American Fur Company. It was not far distant, but the street was muddier than it appeared; he had to pick his way. He pushed his way into the office and confronted only a sleepy-eyed young half-breed with a week's growth of black whiskers on his face.

"No furs until Mr. Rolette comes back," the clerk said, waving him away.

Hercules grinned. "Where's he gone?"

"God knows—if He does. I don't guess but that Mr. Rolette didn't know either when he set out. He just went. That's all Mr. Rolette ever does—he just goes, and one day he comes back."

"I see," said Hercules. "And you're in charge?"

The clerk nodded, with an expression as if to say that certainly this was obvious.

Hercules was not impressed, but he withheld comment. Doubtless this state of affairs had existed only since Deckson's going. He would have left his belongings, but did not entirely trust the clerk. Still he was not satisfied.

"Has Mr. Rolette left Prairie du Chien?"

The clerk opened his mouth to answer but sat with jaws suspended for a moment while he choked back his answer. Slowly he closed his mouth again and looked thoughtful. "By gar, I don' know. I think maybe—but I don' know." He examined Hercules with renewed interest. "You sell furs?"

"I'm in the business," said Hercules. "But right now, I've none to sell. I want to see Mr. Rolette."

"I don' know," said the clerk doubtfully. "But I tell you—his house . . ." He made as if to get up, but Hercules stopped him.

"I know where his house is. I'll go there."

He set out again, pausing to step back and look into the window; the clerk was still slumped at the table, trying apparently to go to sleep. Hercules half smiled; he shook his head and went on to where the Rolette house stood, within a long stone's throw of the Company's building. The early dusk had come suddenly upon the village at the sun's withdrawal behind the western hills, though sunlight still lay old rose and magenta upon the bluffs beyond Prairie du Chien on the east. A pack of dogs ran snapping and snarling in pursuit of another with a bone in its mouth, almost taking Hercules from his feet. He went up to the house and knocked gently on the door. He was not heard; he knocked again, louder this time, and stood back a little, brushing at his hair.

The door opened very slowly and a face looked out at him cautiously from behind the door: a young woman's face. Dark blue eyes met his inquiringly, a firm mouth looked small with an air of waiting for him to speak. He was momentarily taken aback, not

because he was not expecting a woman to answer the door, but because he had not expected so attractive a woman. She stood revealed to him now: a woman whose dignity of bearing grew out of her nature, whose brown hair was so dark as to seem black, whose fair regular features were as young as her girlish form.

"I'm looking for Mr. Rolette," he said.

"M'sieu' Rolette is not home, sair." Her voice was pleasant, but strongly accented; she pronounced her short *i* as a long *e* save where the influence of the French language she had clearly been taught was manifest.

He bowed. "Will you tell your father that Hercules Dousman is here?"

"My fathaire!" She began to laugh, but caught herself. "Please. Forgive me. M'sieu' Rolette is my husban'. He is expec' you. Please to come in, Mistaire Dousman." She stood aside a little, her dark blue eyes bright with unvoiced laughter.

"I'm sorry," he said, and again, "I'm sorry," with a kind of stolid emphasis. The picture of shaggy Joe Rolette flashed into his mind and stuck there. It was incredible that this beautiful young woman should be Joe Rolette's wife. She was hardly more than a girl, and Rolette was close to fifty. He was conscious of her waiting for him, and stepped into the house, finding himself at once in a small room where Mrs. Rolette had begun to set the table. A baby's voice came in a gusty crying somewhere.

She made as if to relieve him from his burden, but he slid it quickly to the floor and moved it with one foot over against the wall, still somewhat embarrassed.

"Please to sit down," she said. "I must see to the baby."

She vanished into an adjoining room, and he found himself alone. He stood for a moment experiencing the impulse to take up his belongings and slip quietly out, but he quelled this. He sat down.

She came back into the room and sat down. "You mus' stay for dinnaire. M'sieu' Rolette would wish it. We would expec' to have you."

"But Mr. Rolette . . ." he said, hesitating.

"M'sieu' Rolette may come," she answered quietly. "Indeed, I expec' him." She added with a curiously shy little smile, "I am

always expec' M'sieu' Rolette, many times. He is away from home so vair' much."

He smiled in answer. "I suppose I looked my surprise a few moments ago," he said. "I confess, I didn't expect to find in Madame Rolette a woman so young."

"M'sieu' Rolette is older than I am, it is true," she said demurely, and looked down. But in a moment her eyes flashed back to him, a certain eagerness came into her voice, she asked, "Do you have a good trip?"

"Yes, very good, very quick."

"I think maybe M'sieu' Rolette do not expec' you till tomorrow. Yes," she nodded to herself, "it is sairtain, or he would be here."

"I have time now to wait," he said.

She sprang up. "I will put the dinnaire on, if Mistaire Dousman will excuse me. I am sorry I mus' today do this myself, but I have leave my Eugenie go for these few hours to visit her fathaire."

He said a little self-consciously that he would not dream of putting Madame to any trouble.

"It is no trouble," she said. "I assure Mistaire Dousman I am quite capable, even if pairhaps I do not look it."

When he stumbled in his protestations, she laughed and disappeared into the kitchen, managing to hurry without giving the impression of undue haste. She was willowy, he thought, and this contributed to her gracefulness. He heard her voice raised to call from the back door of the house, and presently heard some one come into the house. She began to bring food in to the table, wearing a demure smile, seeming not to notice him. His eyes followed her to and from the room.

In a little while she ushered in a boy of five or six, roughly but cleanly dressed, his pale eyes fixed immovably on Hercules. His resemblance to Mrs. Rolette identified him as her son.

"This is our son Joseph, Mistaire Dousman," she said.

The boy made a little bow and held out his hand. Hercules got up and bowed in reply, took the boy's hand and shook it. Joseph seemed relieved when this ceremony was concluded; he relaxed and took his place at table, forgetting Hercules to examine the food before him. Mrs. Rolette sat down; after her, Hercules took the seat she indicated.

She said grace and they began to eat.

Hercules could not keep his eyes from her. It was absurd, he thought, with growing amazement, but seldom had he seen a woman like this living in the settlements in this western country. Most of them betrayed the rigors of frontier life, most of them looked old before their time. He was possessed of a strong desire to ask Mrs. Rolette her age, her first name, to inquire about a score of trivial details which could be of no use or interest to him. That they were of interest to him was incredible. He watched her as openly as he dared without exceeding the bounds of propriety. He felt that his conversation was stiff, but there was no lessening in the quality of her ease and grace. He began to worry about Rolette, asking from time to time where he might be.

"M'sieu' Rolette have nevaire tell his business to me," she answered at last. "He may have go to Mistaire Marsh." She made a moue of distaste, but her eyes were serene. "He may have go to one of the Indian villages; M'sieu Rolette is vair' friendly with the savages. He may have go with one of the brigades."

"But that would take him away for months!" exclaimed Hercules.

"Sairtain it would," she agreed, unruffled.

He stared at her.

A faint smile edged her lips. She touched her mouth to her tea, and added, "But M'sieu' Rolette knew you were coming. Mistaire Crooks wrote to him. I do not think he would have go vair' far away."

He thought she was laughing at him behind her eyes, and grinned.

The tea was aromatic and strong, pleasant to taste and smell. He asked about it. She said it was a tea made from an herb growing in lowland and upland places around Prairie du Chien. Some people called it "oswego tea," but for herself, she believed the plant to be akin to the red bergamotte. "The English call it bee-balm," she added thoughtfully. "The bees love it, too."

The boy got up and excused himself.

"If you go play with those Indian boys again, change your clothes," Mrs. Rolette said quietly.

"He seems no longer a child," said Hercules. He was fencing for her age again, almost unconsciously.

"Joseph is six," she answered, smiling at him.

He felt himself being examined carefully from beneath her long-lashed lids, and shifted his gaze uneasily to the fine curving lines of her dark eyebrows, to her thick hair, parted in the middle and drawn loosely back to her neck, so that only the tips of her ears were exposed.

"How long will you stay, Mistaire Dousman?" she asked.

"I suppose as long as the American Fur Company wishes me to stay. Or perhaps I had better say as long as Mr. Rolette is satisfied with me."

"That will be vair' nice."

The room was now quite dark. She got up and lit candles at the fireplace, bringing them to the table: three of them. The pale glowing they made on her face pooled in her eyes, marked out the line of her mouth. In the lemon light her hair gave off a faint blue sheen. She sat down again; she seemed grave now.

"Have you arrange' for place to stay, Mistaire Dousman?" she asked.

"No. No, I haven't. I could do that now, and perhaps when I come back Mr. Rolette might be here."

"M'sieu' Rolette would expec' you to stay here, at leas' until you fin' place," she replied. "I am sairtain you will be comfortable here?" She said this with an almost imperceptible air of challenge. "Besides, M'sieu' Rolette is sairtain to come home."

"Then I'll stay, and thank you," he said with decision.

Immediately she got up and began to clear the table. He watched her unmoving for a few moments before he spoke.

"Perhaps I might help Madame?"

She laughed, a gay carefree laugh. "But no, Mistaire Dousman. Thank you. This is woman's work. I would not expec' my husban's partner to do such work. I should have a woman to do it. But today I have promise' Eugenie, and since I have make this promise, I have keep it."

He tried not to watch her, conscious that his gaze might be unwelcome in its rude attention. But since she was the only moving thing in the room, his gaze travelled constantly back to her, his eyes followed her out of the room and waited for her to come back. He grew increasingly uneasy now; the evening was long past; there was yet no sign of Rolette. The boy came in and was

sent to bed, the baby's crying rose again and was hushed, sounds from outside pressed in upon his consciousness: boisterous laughter from the direction of Brunet's tavern, a lone voice singing the voyageur's song—*C'est un pâté de trois pigeons, Ha, ha, ha, frit à l'huile* . . . He seized upon the fancy that it might be Benoit singing. Presently he got up and walked around a little, becoming aware that the room was not after all as small as he had thought it, that it was a little more than most frontier rooms in its furniture and its few hangings, which must have come from Mackinac.

Mrs. Rolette came in and went over to him.

"I'm sorry to have make you wait," she said. "I have do many things I mus' do evair' night for the children."

He murmured his own apologies for making her this extra trouble, but she did not appear to hear him.

"If you will follow me, Mistaire Dousman, I'll show you where you are to sleep."

"If you will, please."

She led him into an adjoining room, and from there into another: a virtual cubby-hole. This was his room, she said. It had a soft bed; she hoped he would be comfortable. But there was no need to retire yet, since M'sieu' Rolette might be home at any moment. It was too bad he had not thought to tell her where he was off to, she said; it would make the waiting easier if he knew how long he had to wait. Nevertheless, they could talk a little yet before they need think of retiring. She led the way back into the dining room and sat down, composing herself with her hands clasped in her lap and her full dress arranged around her so that she made a picture sitting there with her head cocked a little to one side and her eyes bright with interest in anything he might say.

He did not know what to say. Having been little in the company of women, he was fully conscious of everything that must not be said in the presence of ladies. He could think of nothing that would interest Mrs. Rolette.

She came to his assistance, demure as ever. How was life at Mackinac?

He spoke about the island briefly and asked whether she had been there.

She said she had not, not ever.

"Were you brought up here, Madame?" he asked in astonishment.

She nodded. "By my Aunt Domitelle, Madame Brisbois," she said. "Is it so vair' hard to understan'?"

He was confused and tripped over words in explaining himself. He had not thought to find so cultured a woman here in the first place; to discover that she had been brought up at Prairie du Chien was almost fantastic. She must forgive him. It was not usual to find in western outposts anything approaching civilization, only the rough life of rough people accustomed by virtue of their occupation to become hardened against life.

"That was a vair' pretty little speech, Mistaire Dousman. You are a vair' fine talker. M'sieu' Rolette, too," she added loyally.

"Yes," he answered anxiously, gazing toward a clock on a little mantel built especially to hold it against the wall. "He ought to be here."

She agreed dubiously. "M'sieu' Rolette is a vair' busy man," she repeated. "Sometimes it is vair' late when he comes home. But I expec' him any moment. Sometimes I expec' him evair' moment for two, three days."

He looked at her to see if she were laughing at him again; but no, she was apparently serious. To expect her husband momentarily for three days! He forebore to make any comment, but was made no less uneasy.

She came to her feet suddenly. "But I forget myself," she exclaimed. "I am keep' you up. I can see—you are vair' tire'. Yes, yes, it is in your eyes."

He admitted then after his first formal protest that he was tired.

"You mus' go to bed, get some sleep. M'sieu' Rolette have plans for you, I am sairtain. He will have much to have do tomorrow."

He bade her a very stiff good night, bowed to her, and found his way to his cubby-hole. He was shaken with the conviction that he should not stay; he was possessed by qualms about staying in the house without Rolette here; but in a little while the absurdity of these qualms impressed him, and he grew more resigned. He got into bed and lay for a while thinking about the long trip over, the work ahead of him here: and about Madame

Rolette, who looked so much like Joe Rolette's daughter and was his wife. In the close-pressing darkness he could see still her bright laughing eyes, her body's grace, her warm smile; he was amazed at the hold these things had upon his memory, but his amazement did not prevent his sleeping.

When he rose in the morning it was with the certainty that he would see Rolette at last. He came from his room to find that Madame Rolette had breakfast waiting for him. There was but one place at the table. He was staring at it when she came in.

"Good morning, Mistaire Dousman. You have just miss' my husban'. He have go to the office already, and would not wake you."

He was relieved and gazed at her, as if he could now once more be his old self, free of concern about the impropriety of staying at Rolette's home. She was dressed in a cool blue calico with white ruffled fichu, which lent her an additional brightness.

"I'm sorry I overslept," he said.

"You were tire.' You were vair' tire.' Did I not say it? Yes, indeed I did. I could see it in your eyes. Now, please—do not let your breakfas' grow cold. I have had Eugenie do these eggs with bacon for you, and they are not good cold."

Immediately after breakfast, he set out for the Company's office. The morning was sunny, with high white clouds scudding before a wind, no breath of which touched earth; in the village the air was motionless, thick with the sounds of life, rising from the settlement and from the Indians camped outside. Smoke was fragrant in air. The streets were muddy; he dodged nimbly to and fro, from one side of the street to the other, avoiding the mud, which was for that matter already largely occupied by pigs and geese. Approaching the Company's building, he saw that a small brigade had evidently not long before come in.

Rolette had just finished with the bourgeois, who passed Hercules on the way in.

"Ah, Dousman," said Rolette, waving a hand at him as at an old friend rather than a fellow trader whom he had met but once or twice before in his life. "Sorry I couldn't wait for you at the house, but business presses. I assumed you were tired, in any case. Jane told me you had a good visit last night."

"I believe we did," answered Hercules. "So good in fact that I didn't know her name was Jane until you mentioned it just now. My mother's name is Jane."

"There are a lot of things to settle between us," continued Rolette, as if Hercules had said nothing at all. "You'll understand I've a great desire to go out myself, rather than sit here in the office."

"The office work would suit me very well," Hercules said.

"Good, good. Sit down. We'll thresh these matters out."

Hercules sat down. Rolette was no different from his memory of him: the same shaggy appearance, the fine, sharp eyes, the bearded face. His eyes and voice were those of a young man, though here and there a little gray had begun to come into his hair. He spoke rapidly, easily, wasting no words, and managed to be busy with papers before him while he talked. His manifest culture was in whatever he said, though he was dressed as were most of the voyageurs—in leather and a bright red plaid shirt, and he wore an equally bright sash. His trousers were dark, however.

In the first place, explained Rolette, there were the Indians. A great many Indians came to Prairie du Chien to trade; sometimes they camped for weeks outside the village, whole families and tribes.

"I'm used to Indians," said Hercules. "I can speak many of the languages."

Rolette looked sharply and speculatively at him. "That so? That's an asset. Perhaps we can establish something more like influence here."

"I understand you have a strong influence over the Indians," said Hercules.

Rolette shrugged his shoulders in two jerky movements. "Of course, you'll find different Indians here from those you knew at Mackinac. No Ottawas or Hurons. Here you'll find Winnebagos, Sacs, Foxes, Pottawatomis, Menominees—and Sioux," he added dryly. "They prefer to be called Dacotahs. There are Chippewas, too, and you'll find . . . "

He was interrupted by the abrupt bursting into the room of a fine-featured Indian, whose black eyes flashed and burned.

"Ho! Five More," he shouted at Rolette. "Five more—Captain Marsh!"

Rolette groaned. "You leave Marsh to me. *Sacré bleu!* what's he done now?"

"He cheat Indians." The Indian swayed a little; he had been drinking; his eyes grew misty now.

"God damn him to hell!" shouted Rolette, making a wide arc with one hand. "I'll talk to him. Go on, get out now."

The Indian stumbled out, and Hercules turned wondering eyes on Rolette. "Five More?" he repeated.

Rolette grinned. "They call me that out of my habit of settling for five more pelts than they offer."

"Captain Marsh?" pressed Hercules.

"My boy, that fellow needs a barrelful of lead where it'll do him the most good. *Mille tonnerre!* I'm a patient man, I've got influence, I get the Indians settled down to where its livable here, and by God if that man doesn't put his finger in it somewhere and stir them up again. Then there's the devil to pay, and we have to start all over again."

Despite the violence of his speech, Rolette was not in the least stirred up, the expression of his face did not change, he cursed Captain Marsh as expressionlessly as he might make an observation upon the weather.

"Who's Captain Marsh?"

Rolette laughed, a harsh ironic laugh. "He's the Indian agent," he answered. "He's justice of the peace. He married a Wahpeton half-breed, and he's been like something half Indian ever since. He's thick as maple syrup with the Sioux. Now, sir, you'll agree with me that's a combination to try the patience of Job. He knows nothing about law; he couldn't be fair to any Indian unless he were Sioux; he's taken in some of the Sioux' prejudices as his own; he is sly, treacherous . . . " He exploded suddenly. "He's a God damned knave, and Cass ought to have his ass kicked for appointing him."

"I take it you don't like him," observed Hercules dryly.

Rolette barked a short sharp laugh. "My boy, ignore him, but watch out for him. He's not to be trusted. On the other hand, in all justice to him, he has courage. When he was stationed at Fort

Snelling, he undertook to carry the mail during the winter; that's no light trip, and it was dangerous enough. He's got a degree from Harvard, too; he's not an uneducated man, you see. The trouble is, he's heart and soul for the Sioux, and he's too damned friendly with the Winnebagos, especially Red Bird."

Hercules mentioned his meeting with the Winnebago chieftain at the Portage.

Rolette said that Red Bird was seldom known to go so far north in recent months. He shrugged. "But I was talking about the Chippewas. You'll find them easy-going, no trouble to get along with—except for the Sioux; they never did get along with the Sioux. They've had war about their fishing and hunting rights for decades, and Marsh isn't making it any easier to settle that problem." He got up suddenly, scattering his papers, and walked to the window, where he stood with his hands clasped behind his back, looking out into the settlement. For a few moments he was still. "There are great opportunities here," he said presently.

"I realize that," said Hercules.

"Right now the settlement is aroused by the massacre of the Methodes. Methode was a half-breed who with his wife and five children went every spring up to Painted Rock, twelve miles north, to make maple sugar. The Indians killed them all, even the dog—but the dog had managed to nip off a mouthful of red cloth. When Wamangoosgaraha, a bad Winnebago, came to Boilvin to tell him that the Sioux had killed the Methodes, Boilvin noticed that a piece of cloth equivalent to the dog's mouthful was missing from the back of one of the Indian's leggings; so he arrested Wamangoosgaraha and clapped him into jail. He confessed and implicated another, and now both are at the guard-house in the fort. As a result, the Winnebagos, already hopping mad because of what they call the trespassing of white men on their lead lands on the Fever River, are ready to go to war and kill every one at Prairie du Chien. I know for a fact that they've got the aid of Red Wing and Wabashaw, two Sioux chiefs. Wabashaw is a good friend of Marsh's, incidentally. There the matter stands at present."

"Some one should go at once and talk to the chiefs," said Her-

cules. He would have amplified his short statement, but Rolette
gave him no time.

"Eh-eh!" he said as if to himself, peering from the window.
"There goes Marsh into Brunet's. You'll have to meet him sometime; it might as well be now. Come along."

He looked into an inner room and shouted something unintelligible. Then he went outside, Hercules after him, striding rapidly down the street to the tavern, before which Indians were gathered, some of them obviously the worse for drink.

Captain John Marsh was in earnest conversation with Jean
Brunet, the tavern-keeper, whose dark swarthiness compared un-
favorably to Marsh's fair complexion. Marsh was young, of
medium height, slightly stooped, and powerfully built, almost
heavy set, with a face already showing incipient jowls. His mouth
was a straight line, a harsh line, and wide; his nose was thick
and complacent in his face; his forehead was a broad half moon
without a wrinkle, though there were lines about his mouth and
direct blue-gray eyes. His chin was square, determined, and his
manner appeared to be brusque and forbidding. His face was,
while not unhandsome, disfigured by two markedly large wens
low on his right cheek. He was not at this moment a prepossess-
ing man.

Hercules was disappointed. Captain Marsh looked as unlike a
troublemaker as could be. He looked like a settled young trader,
somewhere around his own age, he thought, growing settled in
his rut. He was dressed in a black frock coat and wore a white
shirt, though at the moment no tie of any kind enclosed his neck,
which was heavy and hairy, for, though his fair hair began far
back on his head, it was a thick growth and reached far down.
He had a high, ruddy color, which was not from anything but
excess of exercise.

Rolette went directly up to him, ignoring the conversation being
conducted with the air of secrecy between Brunet and Marsh.

"Good morning, Marsh," he said shortly. "New man in this
morning. Mr. Dousman, meet Captain Marsh."

Marsh turned and offered Dousman his hand. His broad mouth
widened; he smiled; his eyes crinkled in geniality. He was courteous, his manner belying the settled air Hercules thought he had

at first observed. "About time you got some one to hold down your place when you go tearing around the country, Rolette," he observed. "Have a glass of rum, eh?"

Rolette nodded to Brunet, who was unobtrusively watchful, with a fugitive air of getting ready to go somewhere.

Marsh's glance was one of polite interest, coupled with an almost benign air. A man sure of himself, thought Hercules. He was, however, taken aback, not at Marsh's appearance so much as at the lie it apparently gave to Rolette's vehemence. But before this became conviction, he grew cautious; for only an instant he saw a faint sly gleam in Marsh's eyes, and he had the uncomfortable feeling that Captain Marsh was looking at him out of another pair of eyes entirely, looking at him from behind his bland benignity. The impression lasted only a second; Marsh turned away to take his rum.

They held their glasses up and clinked them together.

"Your success, Mr. Dousman," said Marsh.

"Thank you, gentlemen," answered Hercules.

They drank, their manner betraying them. Rolette took his liquor without pause. "Burning his insides," laughed Marsh, who preferred to drink more slowly, though he grew steadily more eager to finish his glass as he proceeded. Hercules kept his eyes on Marsh, a steady gaze, which Marsh returned in his fashion; his fashion was an elaborate pretense—a mummery of gazing from Brunet to Rolette to Dousman, swinging his eyes casually to the door and back again, flickering over Hercules, in the course of which he measured him as completely as Hercules permitted himself to be measured. This was not all; his guard was up; he now believed everything Rolette had said, with only a few reservations, and he thought that Marsh was the more dangerous in proportion to the degree in which his appearance deceived. Yet Marsh had the air of a gentleman, and the manner in which he carried himself, if it appeared indolent and complacent, was nevertheless one of readiness for any contingency. He disliked the thought that Marsh might oppose the Indian policies he hoped to establish.

"I almost landed at Mackinac once," offered Marsh, setting down his glass.

Hercules could not remember that any one had given any clue to the identity of his home place, nor was it likely that Rolette had done much talking beforehand to a man for whom he had so little use. The inference was plain as a pikestaff: Marsh had had previous information of his arrival, and had taken the trouble to acquaint himself as well as he might with Hercules' circumstances. This could not have availed him much. Hercules smiled; his self-satisfaction brought a faint frown of puzzlement to Marsh's brow.

"You'll find these Indians pretty troublesome," offered Marsh.

"I'm used to Indians," he answered, determined that Marsh would get nothing from him. But on second thought, he reflected that if Marsh were to oppose his policies, he had better know from the beginning that he could not count on him for support. "If the Indians are treated justly and handled right, they'll give no trouble."

"You can't trust some of them," said Marsh, exposing his hand with rash eagerness, as if he meant to convert Hercules to his point of view.

Rolette spat with ill-disguised contempt. "I suppose you mean the Chippewas," said he dryly.

Marsh laughed. "Rolette reads a man's mind."

"Pah! Only his heart," replied Rolette, with one eyebrow ranged sardonically upward in a gesture that Hercules unconsciously imitated. "And sometimes," he added, "the interests of his pocketbook."

Marsh shrugged. "Indians are Indians," he said. "You can't trust a damned one of 'em. Have another drink, gentlemen."

"Thank you, no," said Rolette. "We've got to be getting back to the office. Work piles up for me when I'm gone."

"The moral of that is, don't go," said Marsh, wagging a pudgy finger.

Once safely away from the tavern, Rolette began to grumble, flinging his arms around in his anger. "Hah! A fine one to be spouting about morals. What do you think of him, eh? You got a good look at him; I thought you'd put a hole through him."

"I thought at first you were wrong about him," said Hercules, "but I changed my mind. He's a sly one, all right. But he seems to have his good points."

"Damn' right he is. He's a God damned scoundrel, and by God, sir, if I had my way I'd have him horsewhipped as a regular be-

fore-breakfast exercise every morning. Damn me if I wouldn't! Trying to prejudice you against the Chippewas without delay! Damned fool if he thought he could do that, not alone the underrating you, but me,—me,—Rolette! I tell you, my boy, every time I think about him I get so damned hot I could write a letter to Cass that would burn up the paper before it got to him."

"Why don't you?" asked Hercules.

"Don't tempt me," answered Rolette shortly. *"Dame!* it's the Marshes and their ilk that make the going harder for everybody else, but they get rich, they have official approval, they flourish, and the poor devils who try to be honest get nowhere, and if they struggle too much they incur only official disapproval. That," he concluded with a sardonic grin, "is the present state of civilization in Prairie du Chien, Territory of Michigan, Year of Our Lord 1826."

"We'll see what can be done about that," said Hercules quietly.

Rolette looked at him steadily. "Damn me, if I don't think you mean it!" he exclaimed.

A month passed. By this time Hercules was well settled, as fixed in the routine of his new position as if he had known it for years. He had taken infinite pains to familiarize himself thoroughly with the details of the vast trade passing through Prairie du Chien and bound ultimately for Mackinac; he had acquainted himself with all the inhabitants of the village, white, half-breed, or Indian; he had established himself. He took time one evening in late May to write to his father, a long rambling letter designed to supplement the short message he had dispatched at once upon his arrival.

He wrote briefly, precisely about the matters of Prairie du Chien.

There are in the village very few white men: Mr. Lockwood, M. Brisbois, whom you know, M. Brunet, Mr. McNair, and Captain John Marsh. Of this man Marsh, who serves as justice and sub-Indian agent, and has the reputation of knowing more than any one will say directly about the constant Indian trouble here, I shall no doubt have occasion to write at greater length directly. I have taken his measure, and he will not be much longer in

taking mine. As for the remainder of the settlement: it is made up of a great many Indians—Chippewas, Sioux, Menominees, Sacs (or Saukies), Fox, Winnebagos, Pottowatomis—as well as an army of half and quarter breeds and their women. But the village is surely growing.

He looked up from time to time, away from the flickering light of the candle in the Company's office where he sat. He wrote leisurely, occasionally rereading what he had written. The sounds of life in the village at the meeting place of the rivers drifted in to him, and the wind blew fragrance of wild crabapple blossoms into the room, haunting the shadows.

I am permitted to do pretty much as I please. M. Rolette is constantly off somewhere; at the moment he is at Fort Snelling, and I am left to manage.

He put down his pen and read his entire letter over. He had the feeling that he had not written everything. A burst of riotous, diabolic yelling rose in the deep night outside, coming from the direction of Brunet's tavern, where Indians roistered drunkenly. With Captain Marsh's blessing, he thought dispassionately. He went over to the window and looked out. Something still remained unsaid, but he approached his memory diffidently searching. He sat down again, moving the candle a little, and sighed.

A little wryly, he took up his quill again and added a few last lines.

I have had for some time the pleasure of Madame Rolette's acquaintance. She is a woman of inestimable charm, of unquestionable refinement, and a great presence, which is not alone because she has no equal in the settlement.

He read this over twice, before he signed his name and began to fold the letter, reaching for the sealing wax.

3.

We Have Seen These Things

1826-7

SUMMER came and wore gradually away into September, a summer of sweltering heat. No day was free of rumors; always the savages impended, the massacre of the garrison at Fort Crawford might come at any time, the sacking of Prairie du Chien might take place nightly. The village grew used to living in the shadow of horrible death.

Hercules was not unduly alarmed. "In the first place," he said, bidding Rolette godspeed into the Chippewa country late in August, "the Prairie du Chien has for centuries been the historic meeting place of Indians under truce to settle their difficulties; if they were to attack it, such an attack would seem to most of them a bad omen. In the second, they're divided." Firm in this belief, he set about making himself secure, as if he were a general consolidating his position against an enemy advance, precise and certain of himself, not to be deviated from the tasks he had set himself.

He learned more about Marsh, the sub-Indian agent, not alone about his good eastern background, but about his method of informing himself. This was more important to Hercules. It appeared that Marsh was in the habit of entering upon agreements with certain Indians to furnish him with information in advance of general knowledge. Hercules thought this expedient. He lost no time in establishing similar relationships—with Sahcoloquoit, the Rising Cloud of the Sacs, with Kapolequa, the White Nosed Fox of the Fox tribe, with Manitonobe, the Male Devil of the Chippewas; he engaged even a Sioux, The Crazy Bull, Tatonkaweteco, and a Menominee, Waupesuiu, The Wild Potato. But his most informative source was a Winnebago, Wakandjamaniga,

Thunder Walker, who was the most intelligent of them all, and who had an uncanny habit of bringing in reliable information as against wild rumors and inept guesses too often brought by some of the others. Hercules went farther; he arranged that runners be sent to him from Galena, from Fort Dearborn, from Green Bay and even from Detroit and Vincennes to carry news of importance to him in advance of its arrival by the ordinary routes.

Determined to establish himself firmly as a fur trader in Prairie du Chien, he was irritated to discover the lack of adequate maps of the terrain over which roamed the brigades of the American Fur Company. In the summer lull, he made countless trips in ever-widening circles around Prairie du Chien, into the heart of the Michigan Territory along the Wisconsin, into the Galena country and along the Upper Mississippi, and slowly put together a map of steadily increasing importance to the trade passing through the post. His constant travels earned him comparison to Rolette, both among the half-breeds, who called Rolette *King* with great admiration, and among the Indians, who had always respected Rolette's shrewdness, not concealed by his roughness among them. Each night he worked far into the dark adding the substance of small maps, made en route, to the general map he was making. It was no light task: not alone for the difficult travelling into the wilderness all around, but also the juxtaposition of rivers and landmarks to be made on his great map of the Territory's western regions.

He was engaged upon this one night when he was startled by the abrupt silent entrance of an Indian, whose shadow fell athwart the table at which he sat poring over his map. He thought at first it was a hostile Indian, but, coming to his feet, he recognized him for one of the guides Rolette had taken with him, a Chippewa. He was alarmed, but crushed this within him, peering across the candles on the table to the Indian, whose eyes reflected the candle-light.

"What are you doing here, Yellow Head?" he asked in the Chippewa language. "Where's Rolette? Is he all right?"

Yellow Head put a folded paper down before him, his red-brown skin warm in the candles' glow. "Five More send to you," he said.

Hercules took the paper, unfolded it hurriedly, and read it.

"Dousman: As soon as you receive this, please do me the favor of going at once to Jane and preparing her to take the children east for the winter. I charge *you* with this because I fear she might not go if I sent her such word at this time. Rolette."

There was nothing more, no explanation, nothing. Jane Rolette had wanted to go east for some time, Hercules knew. Rolette had not seemed to take her seriously before. He was well aware that something had happened to change Rolette's mind; he suspected what it might be. He turned to the Indian again.

"Where's Rolette now?" he asked.

Yellow Head placed a long finger midway down the line of the Chippewa River on Hercules' crude map. "There," he said. "Go northwest from there. He travel like Zica, the pheasant. I came with the birds. I will go back to meet him here." He intersected an imaginary circle. "He will come back in one moon, the moon of falling leaves."

"All right," he said. "Wait here until I return."

He went out of the office and hurried down the street.

Jane Rolette was still up; so was the half-breed woman who worked for her. It was she who admitted him and went into the children's room to tell her mistress he had come. Hercules paced the floor, taking in the little figurines and colored shells on the whatnot, the handsome grandfather clock in the corner.

"Mistaire Dousman!"

He turned. She stood on the threshold, almost as if she were making an entrance, he thought, her slight figure perfectly framed in the doorway. She held her full skirt daintily in one hand, lifting it just sufficiently to facilitate her approach.

"You are a strangaire, Mistaire Dousman. How is it you do not come to see me? I would expec' it of my husban's partner."

He made a little bow, conscious of wishing that he might indeed come to visit Madame Rolette. "Madame, the charm of your company would distract me so much, I fear I would never accomplish anything; so I forbid myself that pleasure."

She clapped her hands once sharply together. "Mistaire Dousman, you make such pretty speeches! I am delight' with them."

Indeed, he thought, she shone. What a pity Rolette found so

little time to please her with his compliments! "I've just had a message from Mr. Rolette," he said easily, giving it to her. "As you see, I'm discharging my duty immediately."

She read it wonderingly, the fingers of one hand lying lightly against her cheek. He could not help fixing his eyes upon her, marking anew the finely shaped head, the slight body, the small hands. She wore a single earring, he saw; she had removed its companion. Evidently she had been getting ready for bed. She looked up, her blue eyes seeking some key in his.

"But I do not understan'," she cried. "All year I wish' to go east, and M'sieu' Rolette he have always say no, I cannot go, it is too long journey for *les enfants*. Now here it is almost wintaire, and he say go, go now, take *les enfants,* go now at once. I do not think I will go."

He took the message from her and read it aloud, gazing at her helplessly at its conclusion. "You see, I have my duty. Mr. Rolette gives these instructions. I must follow them. I'll have a boat ready for you and the children in the morning. I'll send a letter along to my father at Mackinac, and he'll see to it that you're put on board a packet for the east."

She sat down, drawing herself primly up in indignation. "Mistaire Dousman, you cannot ordaire my life for me!"

"It would give me great pleasure to have that privilege," he answered disconcertingly, smiling at her. "But this is only the discharge of my duty. Mr. Rolette is my superior; I must obey his orders."

"No," she said complacently, "I will not have it. I have always do what I think best. I do not think best of going now. It is almost Octobaire. This is not time to go north. What can M'sieu' Rolette think! Octobaire!"

"By October you'll be at Mackinac," he countered.

"Mistaire Dousman, I will not go."

He could not help liking her fire. She sat before him adamant, unbending only enough to bid him sit down; she did not have the appearance of yielding in the slightest to Rolette's command. He continued to stand before her, looking silently down into her face, thinking dispassionately of her beauty, with his eyes for the line and curve of her cheek, for her lips pressed close in determination,

for her flashing eyes and the light on her hair. So he stood for a moment in silence, annoyingly conscious of not wanting to say anything to break the spell of her beauty upon him, of not wanting her away from Prairie du Chien at all. But the sudden thought of Rolette's motive spurred him.

"Madame Rolette, forgive me, but what is your pleasure as to the time you will want to start?"

She looked at him for a moment with her lips parted, her eyebrows raised. Then she burst into speech. "Mistaire Dousman, I have make up my min'. I will not go. I have do nothing to be ship' away like this. It is true I have always want' to go east, but now I do not want to go."

"Madame must realize that Mr. Rolette must have had good reason for writing this and sending an Indian all the way down from the Chippewa country to give it to me," he said patiently, teetering a little on his toes with his hands clasped behind him. "I think he has. Therefore, I'm going to execute his orders as quickly and, I hope, as efficiently as possible. I trust you will coöperate." He shrugged. "But if not—why, then I shall have the pleasure of personally embarking you."

"Mistaire Dousman—you would not dare!"

"Madame Rolette, I will do it."

She could not outface him, and got up, her eyes snapping angrily. "I am put in this awkward position by my husban' who is more often away from his home than in it, and you tell me I mus' go east, I mus' go at once, tomorrow morning . . . "

"Tomorrow morning, then. That will be wisest!"

"I have not say I will go," she cried.

He bowed once more with almost a mockery of formality. "But Madame will go."

"I am not accustom' to be ordaire' about!"

He smiled. "But you see, it doesn't hurt."

The flush of anger drew away from her cheeks, receding downward, and she began to laugh. "You are vair' masterful, Mistaire Dousman. Almost like M'sieu' Rolette; he, too—when he is at home. And even," she touched the paper, "when he is away. You are two of a kin'. Vair' well, then, I will go. I will go at dawn with *les enfants*. I will expec' you to help me with our things."

"You may count on me," he said.

He hurried back to the Company's office, faintly resentful that Rolette had thrust this task at him, not so much at the task itself as at the necessity of having aroused again all his dormant interest in Jane Rolette. She haunted his thoughts now: the flashing blue eyes, the slight spirited body, the determined mouth. He looked up and saw her face against red Antares, sullen in the southwest. A cooling northeast wind blew, but he hardly felt it in his haste, knowing only that being outside was more comfortable than it had been.

Yellow Head still waited, standing stolidly just as Hercules had left him, as if he were a statue. He did not even turn his head to see whether it was Hercules who entered, or not, but knew just the same that it was he. He knows my step, thought Hercules. He went back around the table and sat down, all in one movement taking up paper and pen. He wrote a short note to Rolette to tell him that his wife and children would begin their journey in the morning. "I will personally see them off," he assured him. He folded it, waxed it shut, and gave it to the Chippewa.

"Take this to Rolette, Yellow Head."

The Indian accepted the message gravely, made a curious nodding gesture with his head and shoulders, and vanished into the darkness outside. Hercules sat looking after him into the place where he had gone. He was disturbed now; Jane Rolette's fire had destroyed something of his self-assurance, and he began to think about the impending Indian attack. He could not understand why Rolette had written no word of explanation, and puzzled over this for some time. He thought that of course it was something about the Indian trouble that motivated Rolette, but in a little while he began to doubt. If it were only that, there would be no reason to exclude it from the message, for it came through a country of Indians who themselves boasted of the coming attack upon Prairie du Chien. He gave it up presently, and returned to his map; but he could not free himself from a growing uneasiness.

In the morning he presented himself at the Rolette house before dawn, and helped load the things Jane Rolette wished to take along. The small craft was crowded with Jane, the two children,

the voyageurs, and Jane's half-breed maid, whom she insisted on taking along. Hercules protested. Some one ought to be there to greet Rolette on his return, to keep the house for him.

"What of me!" she cried. "What of *les enfants?* Men have do such fonny things, and they do not have reason. I have need of her to help care for *les enfants,* at leas' until we get to Mackinac. Then I will sen' her back by the nex' boat. You'll see, Mistaire Dousman. I am a woman of my word." She nodded gravely as if to emphasize this. "Besides, M'sieu' Rolette will hardly be back in a month." She cocked her head a little to one side and looked at him penetratingly. "Or do you think so, Mistaire Dousman?"

"One can seldom say," he said.

"I thought Mistaire Dousman could say for sairtain."

She was laughing at him again behind her grave face. He said nothing, only looked at her from time to time. She stood in the boat and talked to him.

"If he do come back, there will be trouble soon. I know him. You will know him, too. M'sieu' Rolette is a remarkable man; you will see. But he is not like' to risk his scalp for the fur trade, non!" She nodded decisively. "If he come back, tell him I come in the spring. Tell him Eugenie come by the nex' boat from Mackinac. Tell him . . ." She turned suddenly to one of the *engages* and stormed at him in French for splashing water. He grinned at her and spat. She made an elaborate gesture of helplessness, as much as to say, You see how I am being put upon! "You mus' understan' now how I need Eugenie at leas' as far as Mackinac," she said. "She is invaluable to me. She can swim, if one of *les enfants* fall in."

He could not help saying, "Ah, Madame, but what a tragedy if both should go into the water at the same time! Or does Eugenie swim in two directions at once?"

She drew herself up for a puff of anger, but burst into laughter instead.

They swung out into the Mississippi, Jane waving good-bye with a small square of cambric she carried to be sure the boat was not dusty, and slowly they went down toward the meeting place of the rivers. Hercules stood watching them out of sight, partly with relief that they would be out of any danger that threatened,

partly with regret that Madame Rolette would not be in the village for the winter. The morning was clear and beautiful; the early sun lay like wine upon the bluffs across the Mississippi, and the tang of frost mingled with the pungence of smoke in the crisp air. The cloudless sky was given back by the river, a deep intense blue. He was reluctant to return to his work, but he did not linger long.

On the evening of the second day, one of his own Indians came in; this was Thunder Walker, the Winnebago. He was a lithe, dark-skinned Indian who wore little more than necessary, so that his progress in the wilderness might not be impeded. His face was long, with the high cheek-bones so typical of his race; his eyes were alternately bland and alert; he knew something of the ways of white men and considered himself equal to most of them, if not superior. He came into the office just as Hercules was about to go for something to eat, and sat cross-legged on the floor before Hercules.

Hercules went back to sit down at the table and wait.

Presently Thunder Walker began to talk. He had come a long way, he said, and he was very tired. He had important information for him. It was bad. Some of the Indians knew it and they said that the white men were cowards and ready to run away. It was this: the soldiers were to be evacuated from Fort Crawford to Fort Snelling.

"That's nonsense!" exclaimed Hercules. "At a time like this, the thing doesn't make sense."

Thunder Walker said blandly that in his opinion a great many things done by white men never made sense.

"Where did this come from?"

From white men among the Chippewas, answered Thunder Walker. They had heard it from some one at Fort Snelling.

Hercules wondered whether it could have been Rolette. But no, it could not; Rolette and Snelling never agreed; and every moment the two were together it was an armed truce or open war.

"Do many of the Indians know this?" asked Hercules.

Thunder Walker reflected and presently made an elaborate count on his fingers. Actually only two of the chiefs knew of it;

they were friendly chiefs; there was no danger in their knowledge. The white men in question, repeated Thunder Walker, had come from Fort Snelling and not from the meeting place of the rivers. There was no immediate danger, but if the tribe saw the soldiers going into the north, away from the fort, they would consider it a sign of weakness. Besides, there were the prisoners, Wamangoos-garaha and the other Winnebago who had killed the Methodes; they would certainly be taken along, if indeed they were not already dead; some of the Indians said so; it made them all want to take meat in the customary code of the Winnebagos, to kill two white people for every Indian slain; this was traditional; it could not be helped; it was the Winnebago law.

Hercules assured him that the Winnebago prisoners were still alive. "They haven't had their trial as yet," he said. "There's no need to worry. Don't listen to stories that circulate among the Indians."

Thunder Walker reserved his counsel, watching Hercules stride back and forth in the small room. Hercules had no doubt that it was this knowledge which had reached Rolette and had spurred him to send Jane and the children east for the winter. Rolette expected trouble, then, following the evacuation of the soldiers from Fort Crawford. Still Hercules was not convinced.

"Will the chiefs talk in conference?" he asked. "Has any one tried to talk about their difficulties? Why haven't they come to the traditional meeting place?"

Thunder Walker managed to convey an attitude of grave patience. No one had tried recently to talk about the difficulties between the Winnebagos and the whites, and for that reason the chiefs had not come to the Prairie du Chien. It was unfortunate, but white men were not like Indians. If the Indian talked, he said things, he made promises; these things were true; these promises were kept. But if the white man talked, he said much more, he talked about friendship and justice and harmonious living, and he made many promises, he signed his name to papers. What he said was very beautiful, it had the sound of brotherhood, but the white man made it lies; he broke his promises, he disowned his signature; his promises were like scraps of paper and as easily broken as paper was destroyed in fire. Thunder Walker did not appear to be speaking with animosity; he said these things as if

they were common knowledge, regrettable but true. Moreover, Hercules knew very well that the complaints of the Indians were well-founded.

He questioned Thunder Walker a little more. Did he have word of Rolette?

Yes, said the Winnebago, they had seen Five More go up the Mississippi. He was in the north now, in the Chippewa country.

It occurred to Hercules suddenly that if the War Department had issued an order for the evacuation of troops, Colonel Morgan must have had that order at the same time as Colonel Snelling. But no word had come from Fort Crawford. It was possible that Morgan was making an attempt to get the order rescinded; but there would hardly be time enough. He asked Thunder Walker when the order was to go into effect.

Thunder Walker said he did not know.

"All right," said Hercules. "You get some sleep. I may need you later tonight."

He went out and began to walk rapidly over to where the fort loomed into the night sky. He was making not for the fort, however, but for the Indian agency, which stood just outside the walls of the fort, and which housed both Marsh and his wife, and the Indian agent, Colonel Boilvin. He had just remembered that Boilvin meant to spend his winter in St. Louis, leaving Marsh in charge; the colonel might already have gone.

But, no, he had not. He himself opened the door to Hercules: a bluff, hearty old French-Canadian, a little pot-bellied. His black eyes twinkled, his fierce moustache and half beard were constantly divided by the grin so symbolic of his geniality. His little office was crowded with all the trading articles, so that it looked like a general store; there were, besides, many gifts the Indians had brought to him.

"M'sieu' Dousman," he rumbled, "I am not expec'. *Sacré nom!* but I have ev'ryt'ing to do before I go to St. Louis, or I would mysel' have call'. But we are busy, *n'est-ce pas?* Sit down, M'sieu' Dousman, take with me a little *quelque-chose.*"

He drew brandy and water toward him. Hercules sat down.

"You look excite'," continued Boilvin, turning to gaze over his shoulder. "You are excite'?"

"I'm sorry, Colonel, but I've come with bad news. I hope it may cause you to change your plans. We need you here this winter."

"Me? I am flattaire', M'sieu' Dousman, that anybody should need old Boilvin. If it were his *quelque-chose,* now, eh? that would be different matter."

"I'm serious, Colonel," persisted Hercules. "I have information that the troops are to be removed from the fort and transferred to St. Peters, to Fort Snelling." He went on to amplify his statement.

Not a muscle moved in Boilvin's face. His eyes kept their expression of jollity, his mouth held his smile until he brought the glass of *quelque-chose* to his lips and drank it off with great appreciation.

"If that were trut'," he said presently, slapping his rotund abdomen, "I—me, Nicolas Boilvin—I would know it. I do not know it. Where do you hear it?"

Hercules said that he had private sources of information.

"Lak Marsh, hein?"

"Like Marsh, yes," answered Hercules. He went on. "The point is, I think some attempt had better be made to talk to the Indians. You or Marsh . . . "

At that moment Marsh came from an inner room.

"Good evening, Mr. Dousman. I heard my name being taken," he said, smiling frostily. "What brings you here?"

Boilvin explained, volubly, in the process pouring a glass of *quelque-chose* and offering it to Marsh as a fitting conclusion to his little speech, made with great gusto in his quaint polyglot of French and English. The candle glow flickered and gleamed on the liquor and the glasses; it lay like uncertain points of light in Boilvin's eyes, in Marsh's eyes, glinting and vanishing there. Boilvin made expansive gestures to emphasize what he said; Marsh stood quite still, one hand in his side pocket, the other holding his glass. He listened without making any expression of his reaction, save that on occasion his face twitched at that place where his wens grew. His eyes seemed to look through Hercules with an aloof stare.

"In the first place," said Marsh, when Boilvin had finished, "such an act would be madness. I don't believe the War Department

means to move the soldiers away from Prairie du Chien. In the second, even if they did, it would do no good to seek a council with the Indians."

Boilvin nodded.

"It would do no harm to try," protested Hercules.

"I don't agree with you, Mr. Dousman, with all respect to you."

"You mean that you wouldn't make the trial, sir?"

Marsh looked at him with an almost hostile stare. "Well, yes, Mr. Dousman, I suppose I do mean that. You see," he continued easily, "I've had a good many years of experience with Indians, and I must suggest that you defer to my judgment in these matters. My experience . . . "

Hercules interrupted him. "Less than a year at St. Peters, sir, and now this time here. I was born at Mackinac."

Boilvin interjected himself with his eternal *quelque-chose*. "M'sieu' Dousman comes from a place of many Indians," he said, laughing. "You may learn somet'ing, Marsh. Do not be too hasty." He turned to Dousman. "What is it we can do, M'sieu' Dousman? Not'ing. We can do not'ing. *Mon Dieu!* what would it be if we take to run' after the Indians? We're not old women. Besides," he added with grave honesty, "as they are now excite' about that Wamangoosgaraha, it would be dangerous."

Hercules refused another glass of brandy and water; he did not care for it, and he was already like a warming-oven inside from the effects of his first two glasses. "I'm not afraid," he said.

Boilvin answered, *"Sacré bleu!* I am not afraid, do not make mistake. Tomorrow I go to St. Louis. If Marsh want to go, he may; he may talk to the Indians; but do not expec' me to set out now, not when I am read' to go for the wintaire." He shook his head violently, as if by his action to shut out all sound, and at the same time patted his abdomen complacently.

Hercules looked to Marsh. "And you?"

Marsh smiled casually. "Granting that our knowledge of the Indians may be equal, it is still my opinion that any such action as you suggest would be futile. I am in agreement with Colonel Boilvin."

"You won't try?"

"No, sir, I will not."

Hercules got up. "Very well, gentlemen. At least I have tried."

Marsh said, "You've discharged your duty, sir." His voice was unctuous.

Hercules crushed the quick impulse to answer him sharply. He bowed, bade Colonel Boilvin bon voyage, and went out. He knew precisely what he would do. He went over to where Lapiage slept, roused him, and told him the Company's office would be in his charge for a few days. Then he went back to the office, where Thunder Walker slept in his sitting position, just as Hercules had left him. The Indian was awake before Hercules had reached the table, his eyes slitted against the light, still in a simulation of sleep to any careless observer. He opened his eyes gradually and regarded Hercules, watching his preparations for a journey, observing the provisions and presents for Indians which he packed; he understood.

"I'm going to see Red Bird," said Hercules.

Thunder Walker grunted with admirable clarity. "Tonight?" he asked.

"Now." He went into an inner room for his boots, and began to put them on. "How far is he?"

"Eight hours away," replied Thunder Walker.

That would make it morning by the time they got there, Hercules observed. He could not tell from the immobility of Thunder Walker's face whether the Indian was reluctant to go. He said that, of course, if Thunder Walker was tired, they would not go, not now, they would wait until morning.

The Winnebago's vanity was touched; he shifted and shrugged; he snorted in contempt. He was not tired. He could walk or paddle four days and four nights without resting. No white man lived who could equal him.

"Good," said Hercules. "Come on."

He preceded Thunder Walker, who was content to follow him, like a dog at his heels. This was no attitude of subservience, however. Not far out of Prairie du Chien, he called to Hercules and bade him follow, since Hercules' way into the north was not direct enough. "Ten hours that way," Thunder Walker said with a kind of eloquent patience. Hercules acquiesced, quietly amused, despite his respect for the Winnebago's manifest abilities. They began to make their way along devious paths among the sloughs edging the

Mississippi above Prairie du Chien. In one of them the Indian had concealed a canoe.

They went up the Mississippi, keeping close to the shore, deftly avoiding fallen trees, the overhanging vines of wild grapes, sunken limbs. The night was dark, with no moon; stars shone from time to time, clouds rising and passing across the sky from southwest to east; already in the east the stars of winter were rising, the Pleiades, Taurus, Orion striding into the sky. A west wind blew, presaging rain in the fragrance that rode it. Occasionally ducks flew wildly up from the quiet water along the riverbank, migratory flocks resting for the night, and the weird cries of loons rang out. The night pressed close with a thousand secret voices and sounds, a muted symphony against the river's ceaseless murmuring.

At dawn they left the Mississippi and entered the Black River. Thunder Walker pulled into quiet water and left the canoe, jumping lithely to shore. He turned and motioned Hercules to stay where he was.

"How far?" asked Hercules.

Thunder Walker explained that the Winnebago village was but a short distance along the river's shore. He went on to say that because of the agitation about Wamangoosgaraha and the other Winnebago prisoner, the Indians were not too friendly; it might be that they would try to take meat if Hercules came among them without warning. He would go ahead and warn Red Bird of his coming.

"Very well," Hercules agreed. "I'll wait."

He settled himself to wait in the quiet of the pool at the river's edge. The day was breaking strongly in the east now, and soon the first sunlight would be visible. Meanwhile, the woods all around had come to renewed life, the sweet, pungent morning air was filled with the fragrance of fallen leaves, and the voices of thousands of migrant birds, paused for the night in passage. As he sat waiting he could not help feeling some apprehension; but this was soon eclipsed by the necessity upon him. If the trade were ever to be perfected in the Territory, it was necessary to preserve peace; since Marsh was obviously too reluctant to take the initiative, the traders themselves must do it. However, the irony of this lay in the inability of traders to make any binding treaty with the chiefs. He

was conscious of an undercurrent of irritation at the official bungling which made intervention necessary, but he had already realized that the greatest danger to the trade, apart from the promiscuous handling out of liquor to the Indians, was the ineptitude of officials coupled with the careless attitude of the settlers, as well as the occasional brutal disregard for the rights Indians still had.

The time seemed long, and apprehension rose again. He sat quite still, wondering what might have happened to Thunder Walker. A deer appeared in a little glade not far away and began to graze among the tall trees yellow and rose with turning leaves, but presently, his keen nostrils discovering Hercules' presence, he vanished without haste into the deep woods again. The birds flew down all around him, migrants diligently searching leaves and limbs for insects, keeping up an incessant murmuring among them. It occurred to Hercules that Thunder Walker might have been taken and held; indeed, he himself might at this moment be under observation. The thought of active danger stirred him; he stood up, with a kind of sullen, determined anger and without fear, took his gun, and set off in the direction of the Winnebago village. If they had taken Thunder Walker, they would have to reckon with him.

But at this moment Thunder Walker came. He was grave, as always. He said that everything was all right, it would be safe to proceed. Red Bird was waiting for him. He, Thunder Walker, had told Wekau, and Wekau had told Red Bird, and now Red Bird would listen to what Dousman had to say.

They went on up the Black River, and presently came to the village, coming upon it quite suddenly around a bend in the river. The early sunlight lay yellow and warm upon the lodge, and the dwellings clustered around it. Hercules flashed a glance at the lodge pole; no scalp hung there. He was nevertheless conscious of danger. A horde of dogs came clamoring vociferously to the water's edge to meet them, yapping and snarling, as if at meat. A few squaws manifested their curiosity and the children formed an uncertain line to walk cautiously along behind them. Braves stood sullenly by, eyeing them with ill-concealed hatred, some of them with their hands on weapons, and an air among them as if they awaited only the signal to charge Hercules and his guide. The atmosphere was thick with menace, like a tangible thing.

Thunder Walker, however, betrayed himself by no sign; he seemed oblivious of danger. He led the way confidently to the lodge near the center of the village; once there, he stepped aside for Hercules to enter, he himself having apparently not been invited to attend Hercules, who went unhesitatingly into the semi-dusk of the lodge.

Red Bird stood there, a proud, erect figure, well-proportioned, six feet in height, with features hard and fine as a piece of statuary; Hercules thought he had never seen so handsome an Indian. Red Bird wore a dark deerskin suit, and still had on his shoulders the dead cardinals Hercules had seen at the Portage. Behind the chieftain stood the chosen among his braves: a few lesser chiefs, caciques who made no secret of their hostility for Hercules. The lodge was alive with hatred which might explode at any moment. Red Bird made no move. Hercules came to stand before him and waited. He understood that any decision which Red Bird might indicate would decide his fate on the instant, and certainly, if Red Bird heeded the wish of the braves behind him, there could be no question of what would happen. Nevertheless, he was not alarmed; he held to his weapon, and knew he would sell his life as dearly as possible. Then he noticed that Red Bird was holding two pipes, one of peace, one of war, and at the moment that his eyes fell to the pipes, Red Bird extended one of them to him.

It was the pipe of peace. Hercules took it ceremoniously, went through the ritual satisfactorily and with dispatch, and handed the pipe back to Red Bird. The chieftain appeared to be appeased; he sat down and invited Hercules to sit also.

Now that he was here, Hercules did not know how to begin. Red Bird's presence alone had a singular power; he felt the hauteur at the core of the chieftain's mind, he felt himself being keenly observed by the hostile braves around Red Bird. He began at last, making casual small talk about the long friendship between the Indians and the whites.

Red Bird observed that he was a great friend of John Marsh.

The tension increased at this, like a tangible cloud settling down once more within the lodge. The air of Red Bird and his comment might have been meant to convey to Hercules that Marsh, who had married a half-breed of the Winnebagos' Sioux allies, could be

accepted, saying nothing about other white people. Hercules tried again. This time he mentioned Wamangoosgaraha. The result was instantaneous. For a moment all was still; the barking of dogs outside rose like sudden summer thunder. Red Bird slitted his eyes and opened them gravely, slowly, his head held stiffly without a flicker of movement save for his lids drawing upward. Among the braves a broken murmur passed like the sound of wind in the grain.

"What of Wamangoosgaraha?" asked Red Bird.

Hercules assured him that Wamangoosgaraha and his fellow-prisoner were safe, and would be given a fair trial in accordance with the white man's law. Red Bird made it evident that he had no high regard either for the white man or for his laws.

From Wamangoosgaraha, Hercules led into his main subject. "The people at the Prairie du Chien are waiting for battle with the Winnebagos. But the white men will not attack; they would prefer that the Indians also do not attack until a council can be held, either at Prairie du Chien or Green Bay."

"Set Wamangoosgaraha free," said Red Bird shortly.

At this there was again the hush of waiting; every Winnebago in the lodge anticipated Hercules' answer; it was as if they expected him and him alone to decide the fate of the Methodes' murderers. But there was no hesitation about Hercules; he was firm. He explained that such a thing could not be done. In the first place, Wamangoosgaraha was in charge of the military; the civil government of Prairie du Chien had no jurisdiction. Furthermore, it was manifest that Wamangoosgaraha must stand trial for murder. He had committed a crime; he must be punished according to the laws of the country in which he lived; he would get his trial as soon as possible, and would be given his punishment.

"I have heard that Wamangoosgaraha is dead," said Red Bird.

This time the expectation of his answer was ominous. Hercules flashed a glance at the braves, who were regarding him fixedly from narrowed lids; he looked back to Red Bird. He could not help reading in Red Bird's bland countenance that he did not actually believe this rumor, that he hoped Hercules would refute it. He did so, vehemently, permitting a little anger to be manifest in his voice so that the braves might be impressed with his sincerity and his lack of fear of them. He assured Red Bird that this rumor was

untrue, that some one was trying to stir up trouble, to excite the Indians to war. "If you take the tomahawk," he went on, "a great army of white men will march against you, will destroy your homes, slay your women and children. The Great White Father does not like to do this, but he must punish those who do not obey his law, and he has said there must be no war. Let the Indians meet in council with the representatives of the Great White Father, and all things will be made equal."

Red Bird burst into a passionate tirade, his dark eyes flashing, his mouth twisted cruelly. He heaped scorn on the suggestion of a council. What had an Indian ever gained at such a gathering? Nothing but honeyed words and empty promises; nothing but the white man's spreading lies like a plague running over the earth; nothing but betrayal, deceit, outrageous robbery. It was not in his heart to forget his pride, he said. "I am Red Bird of the Winnebagos. I am a chieftain of the Winnebagos. When Red Bird places his mark to an agreement, he keeps it. But the white men do not. I shall not deal with such except in the voice of the tomahawk." He added that he had always been a faithful friend of the white man, but that this indignity wrought upon Wamangoosgaraha was the last of many. Not the least of these was the wanton occupation of the Winnebagos' lead mines in disregard of many treaties made with the whites.

Hercules explained patiently that many white men were the friends of the Indians. Indeed, had he not come all this way from the post by night so that he might warn Red Bird not to make war?

"Red Bird has no desire for war."

"But his braves mutter many threats against the white people of Prairie du Chien."

"Their pride is answering with promises the imprisonment of Wamangoosgaraha. Any one who knows Indians knows that a brave would rather die than be kept in a cell." It was against nature, he explained.

Again a passionate murmur broke the hot, sullen waiting of the braves behind Red Bird. But Hercules remained unruffled; he was confident now that a truce existed and that, however much they hated all white men at this moment, they would not violate the safety Red Bird had promised him. He was patient and began

again, trying to make Red Bird understand the futility of war against an enemy so mighty.

"A Winnebago is proud to die," answered Red Bird stiffly.

Hercules disregarded this, and Red Bird listened without again interrupting. He was not convinced, but repeated that he had no desire for war, even though certain of his braves were eager and ready to take up the tomahawk so that Wamangoosgaraha might be avenged. He shrugged, and went on to say that the Winnebagos and the Sioux were friendly toward the whites; he expressed the hope that this friendship might not be permitted to lapse. His attitude, however, clearly made plain that he considered that friendship long ago dead.

Hercules said that there were men now in Prairie du Chien who were men of honor, who would keep their promises.

A subtle change had by now become manifest in Red Bird. He seemed strangely less skeptical; he betrayed a disposition to consider more carefully whatever Hercules might say; his inclination was in marked contrast to the air of hostility with which he had first greeted Hercules. The braves behind him now were more uncertain, a little puzzled; the attitude of their chieftain undermined their own confidence. It grew clear to Hercules presently that everything which had gone before had its meaning for the disgruntled braves around Red Bird, a sop to their demands upon him. Red Bird was speaking the truth when he declared that he did not want war. Hercules pressed his advantage now, talking long and fully about the desirability of lasting peace in the Michigan Territory, promising a council when he could get word to Governor Cass. These words were not welcome to the braves around Red Bird; they grew restive and muttered. But now Red Bird felt himself strong enough to ignore them, and the volume of their protest was not as great as it had been. Hercules refused even to direct a glance at them, keeping his eyes on Red Bird.

In a little while the atmosphere grew less tense, almost friendly. Hercules felt more at his ease. He believed he had made a friend of Red Bird in seeking him out to urge caution upon him. But he was profoundly pessimistic, nevertheless; this was because it was only too obvious that the Winnebago braves were itching for war, they meant to have it even if they must goad Red Bird into it.

After two hours, he was ready to go again. He made Red Bird a present of a great piece of scarlet cloth. The air of the village was less hostile now, and his going drew only the dogs, as usual.

In the canoe again, he asked about Wabashaw.

Thunder Walker said that Wabashaw was far to the north most of the year, but that just now he was not far away up the Mississippi, at the Winnebago village of old Chief Caramaunee. He understood that the two chieftains were holding a council of war. He would not say; it might not be. Yet his attitude spoke plainly enough that this was what it was.

Hercules was dismayed and a little angered. Nothing was being done to stop these mounting grievances, nothing at all. Boilvin off to St. Louis, Taliaferro and Snelling snug at St. Peters, Marsh worse than nothing with his unholy alliances with the Sioux. And Cass quite unaware of it all, no doubt. The traders and the settlers to suffer, and some among them sharing the blame. Where was the official who would take energetic hold of the problems facing the Michigan Territory and solve them? He thought now not only in terms of his own desire to see the trade and his income therefrom increase and multiply, but also in terms of the future, the years that lay ahead for settlers coming into the Territory in ever increasing numbers.

They went back down the Black River and out again upon the Mississippi, turning north. All afternoon they paddled, under a hot sun until three o'clock, when clouds came up to shut away the heat. At the same time an east wind brought cooling air over the river. Before evening closed down, they took to an island and slept, both exhausted.

In mid-morning they came to Caramaunee's village.

Hercules had asked about him. He was a great chief, Thunder Walker said, much respected by the tribes, though many of the younger braves chose to follow Red Bird. He was friendly toward the whites, and so was Wabashaw.

Once more Thunder Walker went ahead and Hercules was kept waiting.

He saw Caramaunee first. Caramaunee was an old man whose white hair made him look older than he was. He made many protestations of his pride at being visited by Hercules Dousman, the

partner of King Rolette. He was delighted that Hercules spoke the Winnebago tongue, and talked volubly to him. He manifested a tendency to secretiveness, however, as soon as the Winnebago prisoners at Fort Crawford were mentioned.

"It has gone around among the tribes that Wamangoosgaraha must die," said Caramaunee, his eyes wrinkled as if in disbelief. "It is said that they have already been put to death without trial."

Once more Hercules took the trouble to deny this. He argued and cajoled.

Caramaunee protested that he shuddered at the thought of war. "I am an old man now. I do not want war. My people do not want war. We have no quarrel with the whites, except of course, the occupation of our lead mines, and no doubt the whites will presently make this up to us." If he were sincere, he had a touching faith in promises broken countless times within his memory.

Hercules said nothing of the lead mines. He talked about a council. Caramaunee was quite willing, almost eager to come to a council. He made it clear, however, that he would not come because he believed in the white men and their strange, dishonest treaties, but because a council was a time of celebration and he enjoyed these occasions.

Hercules asked presently about Wabashaw.

Yes, said Caramaunee, Wabashaw was in the village. He would leave soon, however, to return into the north where his village was. Did Hercules wish to speak to him? Hercules said he did. Caramaunee sent a runner for Wabashaw.

Wabashaw was tall, like most of the Sioux. He was dressed not like most of his braves, but in a knee-length military overcoat of American design: a relic of the British campaign of 1814 against Prairie du Chien. Around his neck he wore a colorful but rather dirty piece of calico. He was not an attractive Indian; he had an unusually large nose, and a single wide eye, the empty socket of the other being covered by a triangle of black silk which depended from above, the corner of an old handkerchief tied about his head. His mouth was small, and his lower chin receded. Yet he was among the most powerful of the Sioux chiefs. He carried himself with dignity, and sat down next to Caramaunee, with his party of braves ranged to stand beside the Winnebagos.

Hercules made a show of small talk in friendship, and Waba-shaw mentioned his affection for John Marsh. Always Marsh, thought Hercules; always they come back to him. Only Cara-maunee had not mentioned him, but he sat nodding in approval at Wabashaw's words. He went on to talk about his object in com-ing: the impending threat of savagery at Prairie du Chien.

Wabashaw immediately disclaimed any part in this. Why should the Dacotahs fight the white men? Their quarrel was not with the whites but with the Chippewas, who disputed their right to their ancient fishing and hunting grounds, and with the Fox and Sauk Indians, who were the ancestral enemies of the Dacotahs. "It is not the Dacotahs who make trouble. No." He shook his head vigor-ously, so that his black silk triangle flapped against his cheek. "It is the Fox and Saukenauk who make trouble. They do this in the hope of warring against the Dacotahs and the Winnebagos, who are the friends of the Dacotahs. We know this. We are surprised that the white men do not know this. Captain Marsh knows it; he is our friend; he understands how it is between the Dacotahs and their allies, and their enemies. He knows it; it is not good that other white men do not know." There was a slightly ominous note in his voice, and he paused as if for effect before he went on. His single eye flashed and glared. "The Dacotahs have always lived in peace, save with their hereditary enemies. We have not attacked the whites."

This was true, insofar as Hercules knew.

Wabashaw went on to say that it was difficult for Indians to understand the white man's laws, and his way of administering his laws. It would seem, he said, as if the white man had one set of laws to govern himself and another for the Indians. Was this brotherhood? No, it was not. Yet the Indians had endured it with-out protest, other than that which was seemly. They had gone time and again to the councils of their white brothers. And what had they gone for? Why, each time the whites wanted a little more of their land, and before these councils were over, the Dacotahs would be pushed west of the Mississippi like their enemies. He added darkly that there was no assurance that the white men would stop even if the Dacotahs were sent across the Mississippi.

This went on for some time. Wabashaw said that he spoke for

all the Dacotahs in the Michigan Territory, and no doubt he did. His list of grievances was long; he had them well down, as if he kept them constantly in mind. Moreover, he spoke with great earnestness and with a very convincing manner, so that Hercules forgot his unattractive appearance and began to understand why his following was so strong. He stormed about the Dacotahs' enemies, he begged for closer co-operation between the whites and the Indians, he alternately threatened and cajoled, and he put forth his complaints with a properly reluctant air.

But it came to nothing more than Hercules had known before. He made them both presents and took his leave with many protestations of friendship. Thunder Walker had gone before him to the canoe, where Hercules found him waiting with stony indifference.

Did Hercules have enough now? he wanted to know with a faint air of triumph, as if to say, You see how well I have endured this forced trip. Was he ready to return now to the Prairie du Chien?

Hercules examined their provisions and said he was not. "We're more than half way to St. Peters. I'll go on and see Colonel Snelling. Besides, I want to see the fort. Is it so much stronger than Fort Crawford, or so much weaker?"

"Stronger," said Thunder Walker, subdued.

"I'll talk to Snelling."

Thunder Walker estimated that they were at least twelve hours away from St. Peters, possibly more. They went on up the Mississippi, now slowly narrowing save for the magnificent widening at Lake Pepin, beyond which it grew once more steadily narrower. They passed along heavily wooded shores on both sides, and were already sufficiently far north of Prairie du Chien so that they were aware of the advancing autumn in the crimson and yellow leaves here and there, the flaming torches of sugar maples, the scarlet of ivy winding into trees and hanging out over the water. Birds flocked among the wild grapes, feeding. Thunder Walker said he knew a good place to rest, and they made for it, hoping to reach the island before nightfall.

In the next afternoon, they came around a bend in the river and saw Fort Snelling before them: an imposing structure high on a

bluff rising almost perpendicular to the Mississippi. Its white walls shone in the sun, and the flag made color upon the blue, cloudless sky. It was indeed a fort far stronger than that at Prairie du Chien; moreover, it could house five times as many soldiers in complete comfort. A long sloping road mounted to the plateau upon which the fort stood; at the foot of the road were clustered encampments of Sioux. The white-walled fort and its stockade commanded the entire country for many miles around; it would be difficult to take, thought Hercules.

Hercules went up to the fort and asked to see Colonel Snelling. An orderly told him that unfortunately the colonel had gone up river at dawn, and was not expected to return until sundown. That was four hours away, perhaps less. Hercules said he would see the Indian agent, Major Taliaferro.

He walked across to where the agency house stood, looking all around him. This should be an excellent trading post, he thought, commanding lake and river country as it did.

Major Taliaferro was in, a tall lean-jawed man, with sharp eyes and a prim mouth. He wore a fringe of dark beard along his chin from ear to ear. He looked Hercules up and down, scarcely listening to his introduction. Learning that Hercules was a partner of Rolette in the American Fur Company, he softened a little, perceptibly. But his stiffness was not entirely thawed out.

"Do you know John Marsh?" he asked abruptly.

"Yes, in the course of business."

"Damned scoundrel," snapped Taliaferro. "I'd have him cashiered." He had the air of a martinet; Hercules had no doubt he lacked popularity among his men. There had been rumors of some violent disagreement between Taliaferro and Marsh when Marsh substituted for Taliaferro during the major's absence in Washington. He made no comment, but waited patiently for an opening. This came presently, when Taliaferro had exhausted himself upon the subject of Captain Marsh.

He asked whether Taliaferro had had any trouble with the Indians of late.

"Trouble? Young man, they're constantly making trouble. I'm hard put to it to keep civil with them."

"But any trouble, any especial trouble recently, sir?" pressed Hercules.

"Can't say that. Why do you ask?"

Hercules explained that the Winnebagos were planning to go on the warpath, accompanied by some Sioux.

Major Taliaferro was not impressed. "We've heard those rumors from time to time," he said. "They never amount to anything. In the first place, the Winnebagos aren't united sufficiently to do much. Furthermore, they would much rather fight their old enemies among the Indians. As for the Sioux, they do that whenever they get the chance—raid a Fox or Sauk settlement, or a hunting party, and the Fox retaliate. I don't think there's any likelihood of their attacking Prairie du Chien. In any case, Marsh could probably talk the Sioux out of it," he concluded sardonically.

Hercules explained their grievances.

"Why the devil doesn't the military do something then about the occupation of the lead mines? Drive off the settlers for the time being, at least. And why not give the murderers a quick trial and get it over with? There's nothing the Indians think worse than imprisonment. Morgan ought to know that. As long as Wamangoosgaraha and his fellow prisoner are kept locked up, the Winnebagos will be angry. Let them have their trial, shoot them, and put an end to the matter."

A party of Sioux crowded into the room, demanding the agent's attention. Major Taliaferro excused himself and asked them what they wished. They explained ceremoniously, the oldest of them speaking gravely for all of them. It appeared that they wished the major to settle some tribal quarrel. The agent was brusque, almost rude. Hercules had heard that the Sioux had preferred Marsh during his brief agency here; he could understand, seeing Taliaferro's almost insolent manner with his charges, why this was so. The Sioux, however, were very patient, almost as if they understood they had to deal with some one who was to them little different from a child in his reactions; they overlooked his petulance, and he, too, presently modified his manner, made a few suggestions, and sent the Sioux away satisfied.

"This keeps on day in, day out," he said to Hercules. "And it will, as long as the government continues to play Father to them, and lets them feel that the agents are their guides. Why, I believe that the chiefs purposely relieve their own shoulders by sending their troubles to me."

Hercules grinned and expressed the opinion that this would not be consistent with Indian character. The major took immediate issue, and they were soon deep in a discussion which did not end until Hercules rose to return to the fort.

Colonel Snelling was not yet back. Hercules was shown into his quarters, however, and told to wait. The sun was setting, the colonel would be back at any time now. The room to which Hercules was shown was a combination office and dwelling; it was part of the Snelling home. The orderly explained that Mrs. Snelling was not at the post; she had gone to put her daughter Mary into a finishing school in Washington, and expected to be gone a large part of the autumn, if indeed she could get back to St. Peters before ice closed the Mississippi.

Colonel Josiah Snelling was even at this moment entering the stockade from the west. In a few minutes he came into the room, drawing off his gloves. He was in uniform, and cut a good figure; he was ten years older than Hercules, and was growing bald, though there was enough of his red hair remaining to fringe his head and make it colorful against the bright blue of his uniform and the last sunglow in the room. Hercules got up and introduced himself.

Snelling was gracious, though he could not conceal the hostility in his voice when he spoke of Rolette. He sat down, motioning Hercules to do likewise. He listened, opening his uniform a little to ease himself.

"The fact is, we've heard rumors that the garrison at Fort Crawford is to be removed next month," said Hercules. "We're told they're to be sent here, though there's no shadow of trouble up here. I hope to hear from you that it isn't true that the soldiers are being removed."

"Unfortunately, I couldn't tell you it isn't, because it is. Orders from the War Department are explicit."

Hercules protested. He was irritated by Snelling's answer as he was amused by his manner, and could not help wondering whether the colonel's hostility for Rolette had anything to do with the matter. "The sole responsibility for the obeying of that order rests in your hands, Colonel; it lies in your power to hold it temporarily in abeyance."

"I couldn't do that."

"Are the soldiers meant to come for any particular task?"

"No, except to augment my garrison."

"You have a strongly fortified position here; we haven't. You're impregnable to Indian attack; we're not. If there's no particular need for the Fort Crawford men, you have the power to keep them where they are."

Colonel Snelling assumed an harassed air. "I couldn't do it, sir," he said. "An order from the War Department is certainly not subject to my authority."

"Certainly not. Only to your discretion."

"Where do you come from?" Snelling asked abruptly.

Hercules told him.

"Oh, yes, yes," answered Snelling, as if he had known but momentarily forgotten. "Well, in this country we're used to Indian scares. They seldom amount to anything, you'll see. I've lived through them before."

"In this case, the Indians will consider the removal of the garrison as a sign of weakness, and will be emboldened."

Snelling shrugged. "Perhaps. But they know the garrison hasn't gone far, and they're not likely to attack."

Hercules held forth succinctly upon the situation in regard to the occupation of the lead mines and the Winnebago murderers. But it was to no avail. The colonel remained adamant; he would not be moved, continuing to reply that there had been many Indian scares and few, very few had ever produced anything but a solitary scalp, or perhaps, at most, two. No, he could not hold up the War Department's order; even if he could, he would not.

"Think of the people left there, without any one to defend them!"

"Keep your brigades from going out then," answered Snelling, ruffled.

"We can't do that," protested Hercules. "Besides, it's the business of the garrison to protect us."

Snelling sniffed a little and fell back upon his previous excuses, emphasizing once more that danger was remote, that alarms were constant and seldom produced anything promised, that he was bound by the strictures of military law. He went on until Hercules grew slowly, sullenly angry.

"Colonel, if those troops leave the fort, you'll be responsible for whatever happens. If they do go, I'll warrant they'll be back sooner than you think. What's the occasion for moving them up here like this?"

"My dear sir, the War Department's orders are like acts of God. Nobody knows just why such orders are given."

"You know, some of the traders think you're at the bottom of this order—at least, it seems clear that the order didn't displease you."

Snelling's face reddened, and his mouth parted in dismayed anger. "What the devil do you mean, sir?"

"I mean to say that the men don't think you feel kindly toward them, and this withdrawal of troops from Fort Crawford will hamper the trade. I speak for myself as well as for them. Besides, the feud you've had with Rolette is well known, and it is suspected that you have no great use for the American Fur Company."

"Mr. Dousman, that implication is an affront." Colonel Snelling's reactions left Hercules no doubt about this. "I know what you fur traders may think—that I recommended this order simply to interfere with the trade. It's true, I can't get along with Rolette, but that's neither here nor there. I would certainly never endanger a settlement to gratify my personal vanity or prejudices. No, sir, put that down, together with my resentment at your imputation. As for any attempt on my part to hamper the business of the American Fur Company—that would be suicide. I think we understand each other."

Hercules understood very well that Colonel Snelling was informing him that if he or any one else hampered Astor's business, he would not live long to tell about it. He said nothing save to express his gratification that his suspicions were unfounded.

"Believe me, sir," continued Snelling, mollified, "if I have any definite information about the situation at Fort Crawford, I'll order the troops to return there at once; moreover, I'll send part of my own garrison along to back them up." He stood up. "Now, sir, enough of this. Will you join me at supper?"

The impulse to anger had passed; the colonel was amiable, and Hercules was thoughtful. They went together to take the evening meal by candlelight: Hercules, the colonel, and the colonel's oldest

son, Joseph, who, said Snelling, with a tolerant smile, had an ambition to be a writer, to put down Indian tales and narratives of
the Northwest Territory and publish them in a book. They made
no further mention of the garrison at Fort Crawford.

In four days, Hercules reached Prairie du Chien. He went directly
to the Fur Company's building to relieve Lapiage, and found, instead of the voyageur, Rolette. Rolette was at the moment bent
quizzically over Hercules' map.

"Damn' good map, Hercules," he said. "Indians help?"

"I did most of it myself, riding and paddling around. My horse
Major will carry me anywhere."

"You got Jane off, I see," continued Rolette.

"No trouble," said Hercules with a smile. Rolette cocked an eye
at him. "But what brings you back so early. She said you'd not be
back for perhaps a month."

Rolette brushed at his dark beard and coughed. "Jane knows
nothing whatever about my movements," he said dryly. "But
you've been gone, too. Where?"

Hercules told him, briefly, pointedly. He could not conceal his
dismay and disappointment. "Why, it's easier to talk to even the
hostile Indians than to people like Taliaferro and Snelling!" he
cried. "They see nothing!"

"The military are by nature pig-headed," observed Rolette. In a
moment he added casually, "But you're unduly concerned about
these things, Hercules."

"Not at all. If we're ever to make something of this or any other
venture, we must have peace, consistent peace. If the military and
the agents don't bestir themselves, then let the traders be about
it."

"The traders can't do it alone. In this case, I don't know that
we'll have a war. You went to Marsh?"

"I did." Hercules sketched his interview with Boilvin and Marsh.

"Damned scoundrel!" exclaimed Rolette, almost with relish, as
if he were desirous of having a whipping boy, and Marsh the like-
liest candidate. "He's in charge now that Boilvin's gone, too. The
only people who expect co-operation from him are the Sioux. Yes,
and they'll get it," he ended.

"As to that War Department order—it's going through, all right."

"Depend on Colonel Snelling to see to that," Rolette said vehemently. He assailed the order in violent language, without so much as contorting a muscle of his face. That order, he felt, came directly from Snelling's intervention; Snelling wished to show that he was the commander in chief of this portion of the United States; this was one way he could do it. Hercules expostulated mildly, but Rolette would have his say. He went on. Snelling was a good enough man in his way, honest and quite above taking bribes; in this he was like Major Taliaferro. But both of them shared one fault; they were unimaginative. At that, Taliaferro was a far better man than Marsh. "The Indians call him Five Hearts because he treats the five tribes with absolute impartiality. They could call Marsh One Heart." He chuckled.

"I'm glad you're back, just the same," said Hercules. "There are more Indians who will trust you than Marsh."

"But nothing's going to happen; watch and see—not yet."

Rolette was right.

The garrison was evacuated late in October, on a cold, windy day, with leaves showering down after a heavy frost in the night. Wamangoosgaraha and his companion in irons were taken along. The villagers were upset and in terror of their lives—all except old Madame Cardinal, well past a hundred years of age, who created a nine-hour wonder by kicking her third husband, half her age, from her bed and board three days after their marriage. The attack was expected nightly, but nothing happened.

Within the month, the brigades went out; the solitary trappers left for the north country; the *engages* moved toward Mackinac. Prairie du Chien was left to women and children, a handful of decrepit voyageurs too old for work, a few traders and six Americans—Lockwood, McNair, Dousman, Rolette, and Marsh; and there were signs that Rolette would not long be there, the old restlessness to be up and away somewhere taking possession of him. The first alarm was tempered, but the six Americans presently met with Marsh, and Marsh wrote to Governor Cass to warn him that in all probability Prairie du Chien would be abandoned if the garrison were not soon returned.

Just before the ice and snow closed in, a message came from Cass, putting the settlement in charge of Marsh; the governor sent word that a grand council of Indians would be held in Green Bay the following summer, and that Marsh must serve as a delegate to accompany the Winnebagos and Menominees of his agency to that place.

Rolette was furious. *"Sacré tonnerre de Dieu!"* he exclaimed. "What in God's name ails Cass to put a man like Marsh in charge of this place? Might as well invite his Sioux friends in, too—the Winnebagos would follow soon enough. And a council next July— six months away! That council should have been held now."

Hercules pointed out that it was now too late.

"In spring at least, then," countered Rolette. "I'm damned if I'm going to serve under Marsh. I won't do it, no sir, I'll join one of the brigades."

"Thank God Mrs. Rolette and the children are gone," said Hercules.

Rolette nodded. "Had a letter from her. Says she means to come back in spring, as soon as the ice is out. I told her to stay where she was until I sent for her."

Rolette was as good as his word. Within the week he set out with his man, Barrette, for the north country.

Marsh heard of his going and came to the office just too late to intercept him. He stormed at Hercules. What did the man court by going up through Winnebago country at a time like this? What did he mean by going off without his permission?

Hercules observed that Rolette was a free agent, that he was besides a supervisor of Crawford County, that he was in addition a warden of the borough, and not subject to the command of Captain Marsh or any one else.

"But I'm in charge, sir," said Marsh. "I have the direction of this post in my hands by order of Governor Cass."

"Ah, but Governor Cass is a long way off," observed Hercules dryly. "I shouldn't advise you to try directing Mr. Rolette."

"I understand Governor Cass's orders to give me complete authority to do what I think best," said Marsh stiffly, taking a turn about the room. He caught sight of Hercules' map of the Territory suddenly, pinned up against the wall, and stopped short before it,

eyeing it at first in simple curiosity, and then in amazement. "Where did you get this, Dousman?"

"I made it."

"You made it!" He looked at Hercules as if in doubt. "Look here, have you got a copy of it? We can use this in our campaigns against the Indians, if the worst comes."

"I'm sorry; I have no copy."

"Then I'm afraid I'll have to borrow this one."

"No sir. I need that. You don't. There are no campaigns impending, and no men to fight them—unless you mean to foster a movement against the Sacs and Foxes with the aid of your friends among the Sioux."

Marsh spun around, his face dark with anger. "I'm getting damned tired of hearing that canard repeated, sir," he said. "I'll remember that."

He did his best to make his voice sound threatening, but Hercules was unmoved. At his most suave, he said, "Your friendship for the Sioux is well known, Mr. Marsh. Of course, we understand it is all in the family, so to speak."

At this moment Kapolequa came in. The Fox knew Marsh and, seeing him there, went quietly into a corner and stood with his back to him, eloquently illustrating his feeling for Marsh; he would not look at him. Hercules' gaze did not leave Marsh's face, and presently the agent walked stiffly from the room, his eyes smouldering, his mouth working in anger. Hercules did not doubt that he had courted Marsh's vengeance; he was not alarmed; he turned casually to the Fox in the corner.

Kapolequa glanced at him sideways and looked away, to express his disapproval of Marsh's presence. What was that man doing here? he wanted to know. The Fox wanted nothing to do with friends of Captain Marsh, who was their enemy, allied against them with the Sioux.

"My door is always open," explained Hercules, "to white men and red alike. I make no distinction. The Great Spirit said to me not to sit in judgment, and I shall not do so. What brings you?"

Kapolequa was reluctant to talk. The sight of Marsh had stolen the words from his lips, he said; there was a bad odor in the room, the air was contaminated. The Fox said he would open the door

so that everything belonging to Marsh might be blown out by the wind.

"Go ahead," said Hercules. "I don't like it, either."

Kapolequa opened the door and stood behind it making brushing movements with his hands. Only after this ceremony was completed did he talk. The Winnebagos, he said, were gathering. Six or seven hundred of them. They were not going to raid the settlement, not yet; that would come later, perhaps. Caramaunee and Red Bird did not want war, though Wekau wished to take meat. But they meant mischief, even if the older heads among them did not want to make trouble. All they really wanted was to have their lead mines restored. If the squatters would be removed from the lead country, the Winnebago anger would subside. This was certain. They were incensed about the imprisonment of Wamangoosgaraha, but if it were not for the occupation of the lead mines, they would not think about this.

Hercules explained that now with the military gone, there was no way of putting the squatters off the lead lands.

Kapolequa said that the Winnebagos understood the soldiers to have fled out of cowardice. The whites were afraid of the Winnebagos and their allies.

"Are the Sioux in this, too?" demanded Hercules.

No, the Sioux had no quarrel with the whites. But Hercules knew the Sioux, suggested Kapolequa. They would spread false stories, incite the Winnebagos to war; they would do everything in their power against the whites without actually going to war themselves. Let somebody else do their fighting for them.

Hercules discounted some of this as the personal prejudice of any Fox against the Sioux. Nevertheless, the fact that the Winnebagos were gathering was of importance. The fate of Prairie du Chien obviously rested upon the decisions made at the Winnebago council. If the old chiefs prevailed, there would be no war. It was the young braves, who thought fighting against the Americans was a simple matter of descending upon isolated dwellings and slaughtering the inhabitants, who would be for war. The old chiefs knew well enough what would happen if Prairie du Chien were sacked. The weak link was Red Bird; he was young enough to heed the counsels of his younger braves; but he had enough responsibility

to lend an ear also to the old chiefs like Caramaunee. But he was proud, he tended to be vain, his pride and his vanity could be played upon. On the other hand, he had always been friendly to the whites, and particularly to Marsh.

Kapolequa went on, repeating himself. He had a tendency to do this, and Hercules was accustomed to it. After an hour, Kapolequa got up and left, not without presents to reward him. Hercules was irritated that this interruption to the trade should impend after all his efforts; but there was little more he could do. He was pleased that Jane Rolette and her children were not here, and his satisfaction in this assuaged to some degree the feeling of helplessness which was his. He sent word to Marsh that the Winnebagos were gathering, and sat back, like the rest of them in Prairie du Chien, to wait for whatever might come.

They waited in vain.

Winter closed down with heavy snows and ice upon the rivers; this white frozen world held Prairie du Chien until April, when the sun warmed and the thawing began. The birds came back before the snow was entirely gone: bluebirds and robins and vesper sparrows singing with the mourning doves along the river now; and the swallows came to mount the dome of April's blue on the currents constantly in motion above the valley where the settlement stood. The rivers opened, and the waters rose. One by one the brigades returned. So did Rolette, coming in without warning and encountering Marsh just off the landing, whereupon the two of them fell upon each other in a torrent of angry words. Rolette had much the best of this, but fumed for a week thereafter.

At the Fur Company building, they were kept busy sorting and grading the pelts, which were of varying quality, and not as numerous as in the previous seasons. This was already evidence of trouble and discontent among the Indians, and Hercules' dismay was all the more trying because there was now nothing that might be done to alleviate those conditions which made for the trade's detriment.

In May Hercules had word once more from Kapolequa, who paid a night visit to him in great secrecy and said that the Winnebagos were all around the settlement, and that Red Bird meant to

attack Prairie du Chien, kill Marsh, burn the fort, and steal all the cattle. He would kill all the Americans in the village; before that, he would attack St. Peter's and kill Major Taliaferro. Kapolequa said that he would perhaps not come again, while the Winnebagos and the Sioux were congregating so closely; the risk was too great.

Hercules went at once to see Marsh. He found him writing a letter; he seemed disturbed and a little angry. Seeing who it was, he did not get up, only pointed at a chair near the desk at which he sat, and went on writing.

Hercules repeated Kapolequa's warning.

Marsh looked sharply at him, his wens' twitching betraying irritation. "You find these things out almost as soon as I do, Dousman," he said. "But not quite. I had word of this four days ago. I paid no attention to it. This evening I had word from L'Arc. L'Arc is an old and trusted friend of mine, even if he is a Dacotah. He says that we are certainly to be attacked at the full of the moon. That gives us a month, since the full moon is just past. Late in June."

"Do you believe it?"

"I can't believe it of Red Bird. We've never had a disagreement. I think L'Arc has been misinformed. Nevertheless, I'm not taking any chances. I'm writing a letter to Major Taliaferro and warning him to be prepared for an attack. The trouble is, the Dacotahs are apparently in this, too. Some of them, that is. But most of them are Winnebagos. I've also written to Colonel Snelling. We must have a garrison here."

"It's incredible that they should wait so long to attack. Now the brigades are back; we've more men for defense. Last winter they could have overrun the settlement without much trouble. What's stirred them now?"

"It appears they're under the impression that Wamangoosgaraha and his fellow murderer were given to the Chippewas and slain. I don't know who started this story."

Hercules tried to conceal his disbelief. "The Winnebagos see only the Sioux, don't they?" he asked. "So it must have been some of the Sioux."

Marsh said nothing. He sprinkled a little sand over what he had written, glancing away briefly, and presently looked back to Her-

cules, his eyes gleaming in the candlelight. "We've waited for so long, I don't think this will materialize either," he said. "But it's true, L'Arc doesn't repeat rumors unless there is some foundation of fact to them. So I'm preparing, and I hope the garrison can be returned, though I know how Snelling disagrees with the traders, and makes things as difficult as he can for them without being too open about it. There's something to be said for Snelling's attitude; many of the traders have been anything but honest with him, and some of them have committed crimes virtually under his nose."

"I believe that's quite true," said Hercules with equanimity.

Marsh shrugged, as if he had made a great point. "In any case, there's nothing we can do but wait."

May wore into June. The renewed fear of a Winnebago attack was short-lived; the repeated alarms had come to have the effect of a boy calling Wolf! Spring came into its fullest glory, with the fragrance of countless prairie and woodland blossoms lying like heady perfume over the village, blown on every wind. Violets made blue the grass, anemones whitened woodland slopes; the wild crabapples grew overnight from gaunt wintered trees into sweet clouds of blossoms. The migrant warblers went through Prairie du Chien, pausing to fill the air with their songs, and already the fugitive aspects of summer were beginning to make their appearance.

Looking from the window of his office one day in late June, Hercules saw four Indians advancing upon the agency house. One of them, he was certain, was Red Bird. A second he recognized for Wekau. The Indians had been some time in the agency when Hercules realized that they were in war regalia and paint. He seized his gun and made for the door. He was halted on the threshold at sight of the Indians coming peaceably enough out of the agency house, Marsh behind them. They were making the traditional signs of friendly farewell. Hercules stood his gun up against the door-jamb and watched. The Indians went into Brunet's, and presently came out with a keg of whiskey. Hercules felt a warmth of anger against Brunet rising within him. To give the Winnebagos liquor at a time like this! The Indians drank solemnly and went on up the street, carrying the keg. Red Bird

went into Lockwood's house. But Lockwood was gone, thought Hercules; he would come out soon enough. In a little while Red Bird came hurrying out; he seemed agitated. A trader appeared in the doorway from which he had come, and behind him stood Mrs. Lockwood. Slowly the Indians went on down the street and out of town in the direction of McNair's Coulee. They passed McNair's house, however, with not even a glance.

Hercules crossed to the agency. Marsh was still standing there, gazing after the Winnebagos.

"So Brunet gave him whiskey, eh?" he said to Dousman. "They wanted some from me; I wouldn't give it to them."

"They were friendly?"

Marsh shrugged. "As always. Why?"

"Didn't you notice? They were in war paint?"

"Oh, yes—I saw that. I put no significance in that; they do that sometimes without going to war."

Hercules looked up at the sun. In less than an hour it would be noon. He said that the Indians had a good day before them, with an eight-gallon keg of whiskey, thanks to Brunet. The combination of war paint and whiskey was a bad one. Marsh agreed. They stood talking for a little while. The Indians were now out of sight, and presently they separated. Marsh went inside the agency, and Hercules returned to the Company's office.

Hercules had little conception of time. He was standing before his map at noon when he was conscious of some one calling: a distant sound. He thought he had only just now come back from the agency. The sound came closer. It was a woman screaming. He leaped across the room and out of the door. At the same time Marsh came out of the agency, and down the street Brunet peered from his tavern.

A woman with a child on her back running, stumbling, getting up to run again down the street. Her voice was audible now; behind her some of the traders were coming at a run.

"Indians. Red Bird! *Mon Dieu!* They kill' Registre. They kill' Lipcap!"

Hercules came out into her path from one side; Marsh came from the other; they caught her arms. It was Madame Gagnier from McNair's Coulee, just south of the village. Her face was

white, her eyes wide; she was short of breath and could not struggle against them, though she seemed afraid of them, as if they too were enemies. She carried her child like an Indian: the half-breed in her, thought Hercules dispassionately. Her hair straggled down over her face. The traders began to gather around; Brunet came up from below.

"Madame Gagnier, you're among friends. What happened?" asked Marsh. His voice was tense, apprehensive.

"Red Bird kill' Registre! My baby! Old Lipcap! They're on the warpath. I don' know how I got away. *Grace à Dieu!*"

Mrs. Lockwood pushed her way through to where they were. She motioned with her small hands at both Hercules and Marsh, who fell back. "Mrs. Gagnier, if you please. Come with me." She took her firmly by one arm and walked away. Madame Gagnier went passively, bent by the weight of the crying child on her back.

Marsh stood for a moment looking after her.

"Well, it's happened," said Hercules.

"Yes, yes," said Marsh, raising his voice. "You men get your weapons. We'll take out after them." He lowered his voice and stood looking at the ground. "Red Bird," he murmured, as if he could not believe it. "It was the whiskey." He looked up again, but Brunet had sidled away and was now well on his way back to the tavern.

The men scattered and returned, mounted. Marsh got his own mount, and Hercules came with Major, the spirited horse which had carried him safely through the country all around Prairie du Chien. Marsh was still pale; it was not the paleness of fear, but of shock. Marsh was not afraid, but he was amazed and angry; his wens twitched from time to time, his eyes shifted. His wife came out of the agency carrying their child and called to him to be careful; it might be an ambush for them. Before they started, Rolette joined them unobtrusively, but at once it was patent that the men looked to him and not to Marsh as their leader. No one said anything.

Twenty of them set out, and several more rode hard and caught up with them. No one spoke. Dust rose with the smell of horses under the hot June sun; behind them was the hum of an activity

stirred by panic. By common consent, Rolette took the lead; Hercules rode just behind him, and the others crowded around. Brunet was not among them.

They came to the Gagnier farm. A cow was cropping grass just beyond the house; another grazed peacefully on a slope not far distant. A thin coil of smoke came lazily from the chimney of the house. This air of tranquillity was momentary, shattered at sight of Registre Gagnier. He lay spreadeagled in the yard, a great hole in his chest, his head almost severed and scalped. Not far away lay old Solomon Lipcap, red with his own blood, scalped and mutilated. Both were dead.

Hercules had got off his horse to make sure, and some of the others crowded around. Marsh had not moved, save to turn his head a little.

"Snelling will have to send us help," he said excitedly. "He will. Lipcap saved his son's life, he saved Henry from drowning when he was at St. Peter's. Snelling will remember that."

Rolette's voice transcended their shock at sight of the dead men; there was something of urgency in it. "Didn't Madame Gagnier say something about the baby? I think so. We'd better look." His calm was in sharp contrast to Marsh's uneasy nervousness.

Hercules turned and ran toward the house. Inside, it was a shambles. McNair, who came in at his heels, found the baby where it lay under the bed. She, too, had been scalped; moreover, her neck had been gashed and she was bleeding. McNair took her up tenderly, his face twisted with pain, his fine clear eyes clouded.

"Mon, she's breathin'!" he exclaimed suddenly. "She ain't dead yit. Look for yersel', Dousman."

The child was indeed breathing still, a little irregularly.

"I'll take her in to town," McNair said.

He burst from the house and ran to his horse, shouting his discovery. At this, Rolette came to life. He instructed McNair to proceed at once to the Lockwood home, so that Madame Gagnier might know her baby still lived. He detailed four men to stand guard at the Gagnier home, to arrange the remains of Gagnier and Lipcap as presentably as possible, and set off with the rest of them down the road after the Indians. Their trail was

clear; they had broken from the road and gone over fields toward the Mississippi. They were no longer on foot. For they had taken Gagnier's horses; moreover, they had the additional advantage of an hour's start, since it had taken Madame Gagnier almost that time to get into the village, burdened as she was with her three-year-old child. There were fifteen of the men, including some seasoned voyageurs, *hivernans,* who had fought Indians before; some of these went ahead, to make sure that the trail would not be lost.

They came back presently to say that they would not be able to catch up with the Indians. In the first place, there were no longer only four of the enemy, they had met up with a small force of Winnebagos, to judge by certain indications in the wet sand along the Mississippi's edge; they had gone into the water, and all trail was lost; they might have doubled back to the sloughs; the entire party may have gone secretly to Prairie du Chien. It would be best to turn back now and get to the defense of the village as soon as possible.

To this Rolette assented without hesitation.

They reached the village in mid-afternoon. Quiet brooded over everything, save at the fort, whither all the inhabitants had precipitantly fled; there they were now, in abject fear, all of them, save only the Scotchman, McNair, and Mrs. Lockwood. Rolette left them, and Marsh took immediate charge. The first thing, he said, was to repair the walls and the blockhouse of the fort, and to raise an earthwork over that portion at the bottom of the logs which might easily ignite because of dryness and rot. Next, the old brass swivel and the wall pieces would have to be remounted in the blockhouses, and the best-trained men would be stationed there to operate them. Barrels of water must be set in readiness against the walls should the Indians attempt to fire the fort. And every one who had any knowledge whatever of muskets was set to work at once repairing all that could be gathered and brought to the fort. After he had made his speech to rally them, Marsh took count; there were ninety people in the fort, including his wife and their child.

"Now," he said, "I need a man to do something far more dangerous. I need some one to go to our friends, the Menominees.

We must have help; they can go for it. None of us can go in the face of war."

Hercules would have disputed this, but thought better of it. He stepped forward and said that he would go for the Menominees.

Marsh accepted immediately, and made a speech commending him, though it was plain he had no great faith in him.

Hercules was amused. He set off at once on Major and made for a place where he knew he could find Wild Potato, the Menominee who served him. When he stayed there, Wild Potato lived apart from his tribe near the Bad Axe River. Hercules was not afraid for himself; however, there was a disconcerting sound of firing coming from the direction of the rivers, and he went more warily, keeping to the thick underbrush and avoiding open places where he might be attacked from ambush. In this way he reached Wild Potato's dwelling, and found Wild Potato himself just in from the meeting place of the Bad Axe and the Mississippi.

The Menominee was excited and made much talk. He had seen war, he said, while he was concealed along the river. Red Bird and Wekau and some Winnebagos under a leader—he thought Chichonsic—had attacked two keel-boats. They had killed two of the men in the boats, and wounded four before they withdrew. It was war. He knew this. The Winnebagos said that Wamangoos-garaha and another had been slain by the Chippewas on orders of the white men; so Red Bird had gone to take meat. It was the Winnebago law: two for one. But it was not this alone, for they had every action of a war party, and they would probably raid the settlements. Wild Potato was sad; he was lugubrious; he foresaw a long struggle.

Hercules assured him that no long struggle impended. He said that Marsh wished as many Menominee braves as possible to come to him at the fort; at least a hundred, if Wild Potato could find that many.

Wild Potato thought he could.

During the night the Menominees reached the fort, and by morning most of them had been dispatched up and down the river with warnings to all the garrisons; two of them to Galena; two on horseback through the Trans-Mississippi country to Fort Snelling; a lone messenger in pursuit of Lockwood, urging him

to return; two to General Clark at St. Louis; two to Governor Cass, now en route to Green Bay for the council, which would now have to be abandoned, since the first of July was less than a week away, and time and circumstance as well did not permit travel up the river route to the Butte des Morts where the council was to be held.

The first panic of fear had given way now to a more stolid air of waiting, and the foresighted were already looking ahead. Provisions were low; they could not hold out long if reinforcements did not arrive; ammunition, too, was low; they could not conduct much of a defense at present. Nevertheless, they were more assured by morning; they were additionally shamed into greater courage by Mrs. Lockwood's quiet statement that Red Bird had come to her house the previous morning to murder her, but that she had escaped him by running to where a trader was at work in his shop adjoining the house, and so frightened Red Bird away. She said that a man so easily deflected from his purpose could not for long be a great danger to white men of courage.

The waiting began again. Hercules fretted about the business; he was not conscious of any personal fear. When he thought of the danger at all, he was filled anew with a peculiarly warm glow of satisfaction that Jane Rolette was not here to face it. When nothing happened for two days, he left the fort and returned to the Company's office, resuming his life there as much as possible.

On the fourth day Rolette came back from a sudden trip he had undertaken into the west. He was filled with plans for expansion of the Fur Company's business further west, and did not seem greatly concerned over the occurrences at Prairie du Chien, though he had not forgotten it. Poor Gagnier! Poor Lipcap! They were good men, both of them. Before Gagnier retired to farming, he was one of the best *hivernans* on the river. But of course this was before Hercules' time. As for Marsh being in command—who was more afraid, Marsh or the men he commanded?

To do him justice, said Hercules, Marsh was not at all afraid. He was acquitting himself very well indeed. It seemed he could do this in an emergency, and in an emergency only; otherwise he had a tendency to grow pompous.

Rolette was in a hurry to get the Indian trouble out of the way,

thinking only of his business. "And my investments in real estate!" he said. *"Sacré bleu!* what were they trying to do—ruin the value of the land? If this kind of thing keeps up, we won't have a white man wanting to come to this country. If those God-damned white scum could have kept their swinish greed from getting the best of them and kept off the Winnebagos' lead mines, this wouldn't have happened. And if the military had any guts, the squatters would have been absquatulated in a hurry." He went on like this for some time, growing more violent with that peculiarly expressionless face, only his eyes glinting and his lips turned to show his contempt. He spat from time to time, as if for emphasis, looking over toward the fort. Finally he went for the mail which had accumulated for the past month, and which he had disdained to open on his previous visit.

During his absence, Captain Marsh appeared. He was agitated, his wens twitched almost constantly, his eyes were hard and determined, his mouth worked. Hercules put down his pen and went to stand at his side.

"Take it easy, Marsh," he said. "What's the matter?"

"I've relinquished my command to McNair," he replied.

"Trouble?" hazarded Hercules.

No, there had been no trouble. It was only this: Marsh had received intelligence that there were among the Winnebagos many Indians who did not wish to wage war upon the whites, knowing their power. He was sensible of his duty in their regard; he must personally remove them from the battle zone; he must take them up the river route to the Butte des Morts, where undoubtedly Governor Cass was waiting to hold his council. They were late already; today had been set; they could not reach the meeting place for several days, though they were starting at nightfall.

"You can't go at this time, Marsh!" protested Hercules. "There's no need to push yourself into danger."

But Marsh was determined. There was no danger, he said. Besides, it was his duty. He could be well concealed by a body of Winnebagos. Red Bird's braves would not attack Caramaunee's. In addition, some of the Dacotahs would cover their passage for them. He walked back and forth in the small room, looking from time to time toward the fort, as if awaiting some signal which

presently he must have had, for he left the office after exhorting Hercules hurriedly to do all in his power to prevent a slaughter. It was of his wife and son that he thought; he was devoted to them; whatever his faults, thought Hercules, he loves them, and they love him.

Marsh had hardly gone when Rolette returned. The "King" was in a temper; this was apparent in a certain precision manifest in his speech. Rolette had a habit of lashing out with his tongue; though he was almost always blunt and colorful in his speech, and though he spoke with many a blustering oath, he could on occasion be as fine and precise as a rapier's point; he was so now.

"Hercules, a woman is ten thousand troubles!" he began, standing at the window with his hands clasped behind his back. In one of them, Hercules saw a crumpled letter. He deduced that it must have come from Jane.

"You can hardly be troubled by them," observed Hercules dryly.

"I am, sir. I am. Was ever a man so plagued!" He delivered an extemporaneous address upon the unreasonableness, the fickleness, the determination and the aggravating aspects of feminine nature. "I'm cursed with them all in Jane," he concluded. "She was a delicate child, reared by her uncle and aunt, the Brisbois. She has no power to reason, she has no fear; she has too much spirit, she's headstrong as a horse." He shook his head and clasped his hands anew. "I told her she must not leave the East until I sent for her. I haven't sent. She's coming anyway."

"Now!" exclaimed Hercules. He was instantly alarmed, but in a moment thought how absurd it was for him to experience at this information an alarm greater than any he had known since the Winnebago war had begun.

"If on schedule, she'll arrive in Green Bay early in August. A month hence."

"Red Bird may be taken by that time," mused Hercules. "But in any case, you'd better send a message to keep her at Mackinac for the time being."

Rolette looked at him pityingly. "You fortunate bachelor! Do you think Jane would heed that message? She means to come back here despite hell and the Winnebago war. But some one will have to get her. I had thought of sending a message to Lockwood, who

might have been returning from the East then—but he just came in with a load of ammunition. He turned around as soon as he got Marsh's note."

The alarm that Hercules felt was not to be put down. He could envision Jane and the children coming down the river route through all that hostile country. They would be comparatively safe, if the council took place, until the Portage was reached; after that, they might at any moment be attacked. The thought of Jane in the hands of the Winnebagos was suffocating, intolerable.

"Don't concern yourself, Joe," he said quietly. "I'll go myself. I'm fond of Jane and the children; I wouldn't want anything to happen to them, either."

Instantly Rolette's anger vanished. He was delighted; he beamed. He swore once or twice about Hercules' great unwavering friendship and said that now he would be able to go about with an untroubled mind; he was not afraid of Indians, but he was afraid for Jane. Now he need no longer trouble himself about her safety. He did not seem to think that anything at all might happen to prevent his plans from being carried out. He was particularly not convinced even now that an attack on Prairie du Chien would take place. "The time to strike is past; every day makes an attack less likely. *Sacré nom!* do you think the Winnebagos are all fools? Even now, be sure of it, Snelling's on his way with a company or two; every day volunteers are being raised in the country around us. You mark my words, it won't be long and we'll have a formidable force here."

Hercules was impressed by the cogency of Rolette's reasoning, even though he was not entirely convinced. As it turned out, however, Rolette was right once again.

Within four days, Marsh had returned to Prairie du Chien with Governor Cass; they had met en route. Cass had had Marsh's communication at Butte des Morts; he had set out at once for Prairie du Chien, knowing his council could not be held now— though it would be, he said, on August 6—and he had met Marsh near Portage.

Cass was a big man, tall and heavy, with ponderous jowls; he had small, foxy eyes, which twinkled constantly save at moments when he was unusually grave; he was so now. Everything he did

and said was ponderous, in keeping with his appearance. He had an impressive air, from his heavy, fleshy face to his large, thick-fingered hands. He proceeded to the fort and immediately ordered McNair and his company into the service of the United States. Then he made a short address, saying that he would go on to Galena and send back a company of volunteers from there. In the meantime, he had already dispatched an order to Colonel Snelling, who would shortly arrive with aid. From Galena, he would go on to St. Louis and confer with General Atkinson. Meanwhile, Major Whistler was moving down from Fort Howard with a detachment of soldiers and a company of Oneida and Stockbridge Indians from Little Butte des Morts.

When, in a few days, reinforcements began to arrive, the village resumed its normal life once more. Then in quick succession came Captain Fields and a company from Galena, Colonel Henry Dodge and fifty men from the lead country; fifty more, said Dodge, had been left at English Prairie to protect that settlement on the Wisconsin; two companies under command of Colonel Snelling, and finally troops under General Atkinson, commander of Jefferson Barracks and of the Western Military Department. Prairie du Chien took on the aspect of a military post. Daily expeditions went out after the Winnebagos, and after a few days returned, empty-handed. In this way July passed, and Red Bird was not taken.

The end of July brought word that the river routes were open, apparently without any danger from Indians. Dispatches arrived in the sweltering heat from Fort Snelling, from Fort Howard, from St. Louis, from which place came word that Mr. Boilvin had died suddenly, causing rumors to circulate that Marsh would be appointed Indian Agent in his place. But no appointment came from Governor Cass. Word came, however, that the council of Indians would be held, as scheduled, at Butte des Morts on the river route early in August.

On the morning of the day Hercules was to start for Green Bay to meet Jane Rolette, he found a voyageur dozing in the company's office. It was not Lapiage. He walked carefully so that he would not wake him, glancing at him to seek his identity; but he could not see his face well, for the large head, with its shock of

grizzled, graying hair, was bent, his chin rested on his chest, a thick growth of beard concealed the lower half of his face. Quietly as he moved about, he was not noiseless enough. The voyageur raised his head, blinked a little, and grinned at Hercules.

"Drew!" exclaimed Hercules. "I thought I knew that head. Where d'you come from?"

"Ay, and where else but Michilimackinac?" asked Drew in his rough hearty voice. "Ye'll not be sayin' I'm unwelcome?"

"On the contrary. How's Father?"

"Ah, he's well. Ye're mother's not so well, but she's about. They put this hint in my ear to look in on you; ye've not been writin'."

"I know," agreed Hercules. "So much work, and then the war."

"I brought a letter for ye," said Drew, taking it from his pocket and giving it to Hercules. "Ye're father made me wait for it."

Hercules opened the letter hurriedly and read it, his eyes glancing rapidly down the page of his father's familiar script. "Your mother is failing lately. I do not know what it may be, but doubtless she misses the absent ones—and now George has gone off with his friend Solomon Juneau to the settlement of Milwaukee, where they dream of a big city. As you know, John is away at Medical College, determined to be a Doctor, and your brothers Talbot and Presley will soon be leaving for Eastern schools, too; so then there will be no one of all our big brood at home, but the girls. Nancy regrets her Solomon Juneau, of course, and Kate is eagerly looking forward to young Henry Sibley's visit soon. The girls have just received one of his amusing letters from Detroit whither he went from Cleaveland on the steamboat, *Uncle Sam.* 'In compliance with your mother's request,' he writes, 'I send you, Kate, a half barrel of what Mr. Davis says is the very best. I hope it may prove so, inasmuch as I intend to take a hearty draught to your very good health, when I reach Mackinac. . . . I send also by Captain McK. a bottle of walnut, and one of mushroom catsup.' Your mother will be glad of these remembrances. Sibley is always considerate and a fine young man; he is eager to hear more of your wonderful Mississippi Valley, and could easily be persuaded to accompany you. We hope to hear from you, and hope you may get back here soon to help us enjoy the 'half barrel.' "

He lowered the letter, saying nothing.

"Ye might know they'd be worrit about ye now the Indians 've come up again," said Drew gently.

Hercules nodded absently, but he was thinking not of his neglect, which he admitted, not even so much of beautiful Mackinac in its blue waters with the sound of the straits making music summerlong; he was thinking of the trip up to Green Bay. At this moment Kapolequa, for whom he had sent to accompany him north, came in and sat silently on the floor to await his readiness, his eyes narrowed and fixed on Drew; the Fox knew that he had never seen the voyageur before. He sat gazing fixedly at Drew, his fine nostrils flaring a little. Hercules introduced them.

"Look here, Drew," he said then, "I can use you. I'm just off for Green Bay. I don't know of any one I'd rather have along with me. Kapolequa's going. I've got the task of bringing Madame Rolette and her two children safely home. That may not be difficult; on the other hand, with Red Bird and his Winnebagos loose, there's no certainty that we'll get through unscathed. Will you come?"

"Ye'll not need to ask me twice, lad."

Hercules was well satisfied. They set out that day and made rapid progress, so that on the fifth day they reached Green Bay without mishap; save for the country around Butte des Morts, they had seen no Indians, though Kapolequa several times en route said that Indians were watching them from the underbrush along the river. In only one case had these been Winnebagos, he said; they were not hostile. This was obvious, for if hostile Indians had been watching them, it would have been a simple matter for them to slaughter all three. The Indians gathering at Butte des Morts had come for the peace council: Chippewas, Menominees, Winnebagos, Foxes, Sacs, and even a few Dacotahs; they made a great encampment along the river there. It was possible that the Indians who had watched them along the way were also en route to the council grounds.

Jane waited with some impatience at the home of her younger half-sister, Mrs. Therese Baird, to whom she introduced Hercules. Mrs. Baird might at one time have had more of the beauty that marked Jane, but she was clearly growing plump now, so that the fine lines of her features were rounded. A voluble woman, she said at once

that Jane had been eating her heart out in impatience. While he bent an ear to her, it occurred to Hercules that it was she who with her husband had been taken to Mackinac by Rolette on the occasion of the battle of eggs about which Benoit had rambled on at such length during the trip down to Prairie du Chien.

Jane's impatience presently frothed over; she took the first opportunity afforded her in her half-sister's monologue and asked, with flashing eyes, about her husband.

"Where is M'sieu' Rolette, Mistaire Dousman? Why is he not come?" she demanded imperiously.

Hercules explained that Rolette was busy.

"Busy!" she repeated. "Do he think so little of me and *les enfants* that he cannot come to meet us himself?"

Hercules pointed out that Rolette had not sent for her.

"Who am I that I mus' be sen' for?" she asked coldly. "I am Madame Rolette, not M'sieu' Rolette's sairvant." She stamped her foot like a child in a pet; but there lurked in her eyes such a glint that Hercules could not determine whether, as several times before in their acquaintance, she were laughing at him or not. He said nothing. Abruptly she was gentle. "And *les enfants!* Even now they may not have rest' enough from their long journey ovaire the lake. The wataire was vair' rough, too, vair' difficul'. But it seem' I am always subject' to M'sieu' Rolette's plaisir," she went on. "I am a pairson, too. Or pairhaps Mistaire Dousman do not think so eithaire?"

She dared him to say he did not. Hercules was patient in direct proportion to her impatience and wounded pride. He pointed out that Prairie du Chien had for the past months been engaged in a constant waiting game with the Winnebagos, that finally the Winnebagos had struck, that there were things now that needed Rolette's attention, and only Rolette's; he, Hercules, could not settle these matters. Mr. Rolette was Astor's agent, even if Hercules virtually managed the post. He spoke with some asperity.

Mrs. Baird, meanwhile, kept up her monologue. Jane had been this way for some time. Certainly the children had rested enough. God knew they were lively enough, that was something to be sure about. As for Jane, she went on with that magnificent complacence so often second nature to fat people, Mr. Dousman un-

doubtedly knew that for all her seeming petulance and her tendency to be refractory, she was not an unreasonable woman, she thought very highly of her children, only a little less highly of her husband, and held all people in a certain respect even while she railed at them. As a matter of fact, she had some reason to complain of her husband's neglect. She, Mrs. Baird, could vouch for it. On one occasion her husband, who had come up from Prairie du Chien and gone to Mackinac, had met Rolette on the lake. Rolette had been absent from home for a long time. He hailed Baird with joy and inquired about the trade. Then it was the house. It went this way.

" '*Et la cheminée, fume-t-elle?*'

" 'Non, Monsieur,' replied my husband.

" 'And the harvest—how is that?'

" 'Very fine, indeed.'

" 'Is the mill at work?'

" 'Yes, plenty of water.'

" 'How is Whip, my good horse?'

"Everything he asked about—the store, the farm, the business; these matters were discussed. The boats were ready to draw apart. They bade each other good-bye. Only after they had drawn well apart did Rolette think to call, '*Arretez! Arretez! Comment se portent Madame Rolette et les enfants?*' Not until then did he think to ask about Jane. So you see why she is sensitive on this point, Mr. Dousman."

Jane smiled, but she was daunted neither by Hercules' cogent reasoning nor her half-sister's explanation of her. "Now I suppose Mistaire Dousman expec' me to come right with him, right this moment, right now. It is always go, go, go: now; it is nevaire *Is Madame ready?*"

Hercules made an elaborate bow. "Is Madame ready?" he asked.

Her lips trembled; her eyes betrayed her amusement. But she said, "No, Madame is not ready. Please to go until she sen' for you."

He stood unmoving, looking at her laughing eyes, her beautifully drawn mouth, her lovely skin and the sheen of her hair. She wore at this moment a light summer dress with a modified drapery which did not conceal to any great degree the exquisite pro-

portions of her figure; she had dressed her hair a little higher on her head than usual, with side-curls, and her full, flowing skirts lent to her a greater dignity than that she already naturally had. Her manner was imperious, but it was not offensive; it was as if she were playing a game in which she expected every one else to take part; it was the natural outgrowth of her background, the years she had spent with Michael and Domitelle Brisbois, the intermingling of de Viervilles, de Langlades, and Fisher in her person. He thought he had never seen such rare beauty as Madame Rolette's, and could hardly take his eyes from her; it was incredible that this woman, hardly more than a girl still, could have borne two children.

"Mistaire Dousman, will you go?"

"No," he said casually. "I came to get Madame Rolette. I mean to take her back with me. We have no time to spend foolishly arguing. But if Madame enjoys to argue, she may argue to her heart's content once we are on the way."

At this moment the children came in: young Joseph grown chubby, almost fat; Virginia a girl of three now, a frail child with features so fragile that they might have belonged to a wax doll; she was carrying a small bouquet of wild flowers and held them from time to time beneath her nostrils, so that she might drink in their perfume, and she held these up to her mother, as she ran to her arms, meeting Jane's fond murmurs with little incoherent cries which were nevertheless full of meaning to Jane, who seemed to open outward as a flower in the presence of her children.

"Are we going home?" demanded Joseph.

"Hush!" commanded Jane gently, fondling Virginia, who had climbed to her lap. "I am talk' to Mistaire Dousman. Or pairhaps bettaire it would be to say he is talk' to me."

Hercules smiled. "It is Madame who does me the honor of talking to me."

She could not help smiling in return. "Mistaire Dousman, your speeches they are too moch for me. Say to me, *s'il vous plait,* why it is necessaire I go at once with you to Prairie du Chien when my husban' he is too busy to come for me himself?"

"Madame, I'll be honest with you. I want to reach the Butte des

Morts in time to hear what Governor Cass has to say," said Hercules. "The tribes are gathering there now; in a few days they will hear Cass—two days, to be exact. In two days we can reach the Butte des Morts. What he has to say is likely to be important to all of us, yourself included. Perhaps Madame will do me this favor, though I am frank to say that the gratification of Madame Rolette's wishes would give me greater pleasure than listening to any speech by Governor Cass."

"Why go, then?"

"Because the treaty is important to the Territory, and it is my duty."

"Do Mistaire Dousman always do his duty?"

"As he sees it, yes, thank you, Madame. If you will tell me when you can be ready, I will be happy to send some one for your baggage."

She stood looking at him with a peculiarly fixed expression in her eyes, as if she were contemplating something in the future. She did not seem to see him, rather to look through him. She stood this way for fully a minute, during which time Hercules returned her gaze as steadily.

Then she nodded just perceptibly and acquiesced. "Vair' well, Mistaire Dousman, I will make ready now. In half hour, I think. If you have say this at once, it would have save us both time. I am not beyond reason, Mistaire Dousman."

Mrs. Baird smiled knowingly. "You see, Mr. Dousman—it's all in knowing what to say in the firs' place."

Hercules thanked Jane, thanked Mrs. Baird with a broad smile of appreciation, and withdrew.

In an hour they were on their way up the Fox in a *canot du maître,* which was large enough to accommodate them all, and the baggage as well. It would be difficult to handle in the narrows, said Drew, but it could be portaged. The day was warm, with occasional clouds crossing from west to east and shutting away the sun for long periods at a time, the beautiful molded clouds of midsummer, dark and ominous on the turn of their banks, billowing white at the edges. Sullen in the northwest sky lay a haze of nimbus clouds. From these, said Kapolequa, would come rain. The Rain Spirit was lying in wait behind those clouds, and

soon he would come over and it would rain; he must wait for West Wind to grow stronger.

While the children were delighted to be on the river again, Jane was as if oblivious to all the wild beauty along the stream; she was still enraptured by the months she had spent in the East, in Boston and New York, but chiefly in Philadelphia. She talked incessantly. Did Mistaire Dousman know of Emil Edouardt, the famous Belgian artist who was at that time staying in Philadelphia? No, Hercules had never heard of him.

"He has make silhouette of Virginie and Joseph and me," she said. "Joseph, he is hold' a book; Virginie, she has in han' a basket of flowers, and me—I have flowers, too. M'sieu' Rolette will be surpris'. I can show them to you."

"Not now," said Hercules, observing her preparations. "If you please, Madame may upset the boat."

She was indignant. "If Mistaire Dousman do not wish to see," she said coldly, "he should be so kin' as to say so direc'ly, say he do not wish to see, say he have no interes' in these pictaire. I do not upset the boat."

Hercules grinned. Though he was not looking at her, he could see in his mind's eye her flashing eyes and indignant mouth. "Madame makes too much of my words," he said. "I'm interested in seeing the silhouettes. Perhaps when we rest for the night, it will be possible. But not in passage, since there's danger in it, and I would much sooner have the pleasure of beholding Madame in the flesh than Madame in a silhouette."

She was mollified and went on to talk about her visit east. Since she had no immediate family there, she had visited among her cousins and their families. Her social life had evidently been quite constant, and she had enjoyed it. She talked about every one she had met. In New York she had met many fameuse people, among them M'sieu' Rolette's managaire—Le President, Mistaire John Jacob Astor. "He do not say moch. He look' at me long time and ask, 'Madame, are all the ladies of the trading posts as beautiful as you?'"

"And what did Madame answer?" asked Hercules.

"I told Mistaire Astor the truth. I say of course they are not."

Hercules began to laugh; for all its being the truth, he could

not help being amused. He had imagination enough to see Jane standing up to Astor and telling him. No doubt she had told him other things, perhaps less pleasant.

"Mistaire Dousman, are you laughing at me?"

"By no means, Madame—only with you. What else did you say to Mr. Astor?"

She was reluctant to continue immediately, but presently proceeded. "I told him fur business vair' dangereuse. I told him of the Indians and the wintaire, how cold it is, and I say to him that he mus' come out some time and see us and know how we live so that he may understan' it and know why not many women are in the posts." She had said nothing about Astor's methods of business, for which Hercules thanked Rolette's perspicacity in neglecting to inform her. He knew she would have lost no time in assailing Astor, had she known.

Kapolequa grunted from time to time and finally said in his guttural language that Dousman and the woman talked a great deal but said nothing. They make sounds, he said, which go on the wind. They made too much sound, he said. If they were in any danger all that laughing and talk would let the Indians for miles around know they were passing by.

Abruptly, Jane sensed that Kapolequa was talking about her. "What do he say?" she asked Hercules.

"He says we talk too much."

She gave a short explosive puff of anger. "I am insult' by this Indian. Make him stop to talk so."

"He has a right to his opinion," said Hercules with equanimity. "Besides it may be he's right."

"Do you think he is right, Mistaire Dousman?" she asked with icy directness.

"Madame, I enjoy your conversation and would cheerfully do without food and drink so that I might continue to enjoy it . . ."

"Another of your pretty speeches, Mistaire Dousman," she interrupted, her voice betraying pleasure.

" . . . but it's quite possible that Kapolequa is right about our talking," he continued without appearing to notice that she had said anything.

Her silence spoke loudly enough. He was amused. The water

sound of the river, of paddles dipping and rising came again on the air, broken only by the shrill warning calls of birds and chipmunks along the shore of the Fox, and by the small cries of pleasure that the children gave from time to time. Jane had turned impulsively to them, away from Hercules, and presently her voice joined their own, alternately of protest or of affection. He looked back from time to time, moved by her tender concern for the children; whenever she turned to them, she apparently forgot everything else, she became oblivious of the world around her save for the activity of Virginia and Joseph, who trailed hands in the water and asked incessant questions which Jane strove to answer while they forgot their questions in the joyous pointing at birds of brilliant plumage flashing along the river: scarlet tanagers and cardinals passing redly by, goldfinches making their high conversation without ceasing, prothonotary warblers and redstarts darting above the water after midges and gnats humming in air mellow and sweet with the fragrance and pungence of herbs growing somewhere in the lowlands through which they passed. The thick leaf-smell of forests came with the breath of cedar. All the great wild beauty of the country pressed in upon them; all the secret strength of forest and prairie made itself manifest; and they were silent before the wonder and majesty of the wilderness with its lone trail, the blue water of the river up which they went, the river which foamed and churned around rocks and fallen trees and led them deep into the heart of that land.

In mid-afternoon of the second day, they reached the Butte des Morts.

They were in time. One of the chiefs had just risen: old Caramaunee, Hercules saw; he was making a speech declaring the continuing loyalty of his tribe to the Great White Father. He was dressed in all the trappings befitting his rank, and made an imposing figure. But he was not nearly as imposing as Cass, who was in the uniform of a general, with a scarlet, blue and white sash, and many decorations. Caramaunee was the last of the Indians to speak before Cass.

Fully a thousand Indians had gathered to declare for peace. The braves stood or sat in a semicircle around the mound where Cass took his stand to address them, making a colorful showing in the

variety of their dress. On the edge of the semicircle sat the squaws and some children; beyond them tents and makeshift lodges had been erected. Some of the Indians had even brought their dogs, which made a bedlam of barking off to one side.

The Governor gave his address slowly, so that all the Indians might understand from their interpreters what was being said. He warned the Winnebagos to surrender Red Bird, Wekau and Chichonsic, the Gagnier murderers; he pointed to the might of the white armies, and foretold terrible war against the Winnebagos if Red Bird did not surrender. "We will cut a path through your territory," he said, "not with the axe, but with guns." Solemnly all the officers behind Cass nodded; these included, Hercules now saw, Captain Marsh and Major Whistler, whose soldiers, camped across the Fox from the Indian encampment, were ostensibly on the march up the Fox to the Portage. Cass made a fervent plea for peace, but returned again and again to his warning.

During the interval following Cass's address, while the chiefs were moving forward to sit in council with Cass, Thunder Walker found Hercules. He had come up with his tribe. Hercules drew him aside and asked how matters appeared to him.

Thunder Walker said that everything was all right; they, the Indians, would all sign the peace. They were much afraid of the whites, for their scouts had reported great armies on the march toward the river valleys to crush the Winnebagos. They were impressed both by the might of those armies and by the strength of the White Chief's words.

Hercules asked about Red Bird.

Thunder Walker said that no one seemed to know anything about Red Bird, but that Caramaunee had been in touch with him.

Assured that a peace treaty would be signed, Hercules turned to go. At the river's edge, an orderly caught up with him. Would he return, please, compliments of Governor Cass? The Governor would like to see him.

He made his way back through the curious Indians, noticing the predominance of Chippewas, Winnebagos, and Menominees, and faced Governor Cass where the Governor sat before the Indian chiefs, who were smoking a long peace pipe with great cere-

mony. At the moment of Hercules' approach, Marsh swung away
from Cass; he had been bent over him, talking to him in an
urgent whisper. He flashed a glance at Hercules; it was neither
friendly nor unfriendly, but betraying interest.

"Mr. Dousman," said Cass.

"At your service, Governor."

"I didn't know you were to be here, and now I understand
you're leaving, sir."

"I was en route from Green Bay to Prairie du Chien; I stopped
only long enough to hear your address because my interest lies in
peace, as does every one's."

Governor Cass smiled, his grave dignity breaking in the curve
of his lips, the pleasure of his eyes. "My interest lies in your immediate trip to Prairie du Chien. Will you take dispatches to General Atkinson?"

"I shall be delighted to be of any assistance."

"Good." He motioned to an orderly for the dispatches, which
were ready, and handed them to Hercules. "Should you lose them,
give my order orally: for Atkinson and Dodge to proceed with
their companies and the Galena Rangers to the Portage, beating
the country well to put the fear of the white man into those Indians there. Major Whistler will proceed from here immediately
after the conclusion of the council. That should be tomorrow.
Whoever arrives first at the Portage is to wait for the other."

"Very well, sir." He took the dispatches, bade Governor Cass
farewell, and returned to where the canoe waited.

They reached Prairie du Chien without mishap.

Hercules delivered the dispatches to General Atkinson without
delay; the hardbitten General read them and announced plans
to proceed at once to the Portage. Drew said he meant to go along,
and from there go on down the Fox and back to Mackinac, where
he could assure the Dousmans that their son was in good health.
Hercules bade him farewell after several hours together that night,
since Atkinson meant to start on his march in the morning.

But in the morning he himself was ready to accompany Atkinson on his march. During the night it had occurred to him that
the trip offered him an ideal opportunity to know the country

between the two trading posts better than he did; so he armed himself with materials for the making of more maps, and presented himself to Atkinson, mounted on Major. Atkinson said he would be pleased to have Hercules' company; he understood that Hercules had made a good map of the Territory; one could not always depend upon the Indian guides. They must be at the Portage at least by September, and they could not march fast, since not all the men were mounted. It was already past mid-August.

Hercules set out with the regulars, but presently moved ahead with the Galena Rangers, and soon went before even them, taking with him one of the Menominees to scout for hostile Indians who might endanger his work. He marked Indian trails, he marked streams, sloughs, ponds, wherever furs might be taken. He made notes about such flora and fauna as he knew; he indicated the character of the ground, foresighted with the knowledge that the fur trade was slowly but steadily declining, and thinking now that the Territory might soon become even more heavily agricultural. It would be well, he knew, if he were to invest in land, to invest in good land. The Menominee informed him that he need not expect to take any furs in the region of the Prairie of the Sacs, since that country belonged to the Baron Pierneau, who had bought it from the Indians. Hercules was tempted to mount the hill at the lower extremity of the prairie, drawn by the yellow stone house with its curious turret among the trees at the hilltop; but he had his duties to discharge, and he could not be outdistanced by the troops. The Menominee came back from time to time to report Winnebagos in wild flight before them; impressed at the size of Atkinson's force, and doubtless with some intelligence of the force moving up the Fox to join them, the Winnebagos were evidently not making any resistance whatever.

In this manner they moved ahead steadily, day after day, Hercules inevitably returning to camp each night to work long on his maps by the uncertain glow of the camp fires. On the last day of August, they reached the Portage, and found Major Whistler, together with Marsh and over a hundred regulars, in addition to volunteers and friendly Indians, Menominees, Oneidas, and Stockbridge. They made a formidable encampment on the lowland

facing a high bluff, the last in a long ridge reaching into the west. Among them presently appeared to greet General Atkinson the United States Commissioner for Indian Affairs, McKenney: a tall, spare man whose grave mien was accentuated by his gauntness. His tent stood a little apart from the others, and before it sat always two Stockbridge like stone sentinels, one on each side of the flap.

All day and night Indian scouts came in. The Winnebagos were near by, they said. They were preparing to lay down their arms. They did not want to battle an enemy who could so quickly raise so many men. They could not win against such an enemy. But they did not want to go against their tribal code and surrender their hero, Red Bird. It was upon this point that they were divided. Major Whistler proposed to go out after them, to fall upon them and slaughter them. McKenney shook his head. "We'll sit tight," he said.

In mid-afternoon of the first day of September, a Winnebago appeared before McKenney's tent. The Stockbridge gave the alarm, and McKenney came out. Hercules, who had been talking with Atkinson, turned and saw; both of them hurried over.

"What is it?" asked McKenney in the Winnebago tongue.

"Do not strike," said the Indian. He raised his arm slowly and pointed to a place in the sky. "When the sun is there tomorrow, Red Bird and Wekau will come in."

Then he wrapped his blanket around him and turned without a further word, walking into the west.

In the course of the afternoon, three more Indians came, one by one, to convey the same message in the same way: a ceremony attesting their sorrow at this act of submission.

"We may expect them at about three o'clock," said McKenney. They waited dubiously.

Half an hour before the appointed time on the afternoon of the second day, one of the Oneida scouts came in to say that the Winnebagos were on the way. Indeed, they were in plain sight; why had not the white man seen them? He pointed them out.

High on the last bluff in the ridge reaching to westward wound a long file of Indians. McKenney raised glasses; so did Atkinson,

Whistler, and Dousman. There were approximately thirty of the Winnebagos. Leading them was a chieftain carrying an American flag; after him came a second bearing a simple white flag; beyond him in turn came still another chief carrying another American flag. After him came a second Indian carrying a white flag, and the remainder of the company, some mounted, some on foot; all were careful not to pass the flag-bearers. Slowly, steadily, the procession came on, descending the face of the bluff, and on the air sounded a weird keening, the sad singing of a death chant. A hush came upon the encampment and all eyes were turned toward the hills as the chant grew louder.

Major Whistler signalled to his military band; they began to play softly. Pleyel's hymn, thought Hercules; it was appropriate. McKenney made a sign to Whistler, who in turn signalled again, whereupon a detachment of soldiers to serve as an escort went out to meet the Winnebagos. The encampment moved away from before McKenney, leaving the way open for the Indians to come on; the Menominees, Oneidas, and Stockbridge squatted upon their haunches at one side, distant from McKenney's tent. The troops fanned out in dress parade on both sides of the commissioner's tent. Atkinson, Whistler, Marsh, and Hercules ranged themselves beside McKenney. Flanked by their military escort, the Indians came on. Now the chief who led them, old Caramaunee, stepped to one side, revealing Red Bird, who carried the white flag. All eyes instantly turned to Red Bird, who advanced slowly and stood before McKenney.

The Indian was magnificent, thought Hercules. He was dressed in white elk-skin, fringed at the bottom; his sleeves were slit, and similarly fringed; through them his bronze arms showed. His leggings were likewise of dressed elk-skin, fringed at the seams, and decorated with river-shells stained blue. About his neck and across his upper breast and back he wore a wide scarlet cloth, over which lay a collar of blue and white wampum, from which dangled polished lynx claws. On his shoulders he wore still the preserved cardinals which symbolized his name. He wore nothing on his head; his short, black hair had no adornment, and his cheeks only two crescent-like markings painted in green. In one hand he carried a peace pipe; in the other the flag, trembling in

the west wind. His appearance was all the more remarkable since
he did not, save for his color, look like an Indian; his six feet
were perfectly proportioned, his dark burning eyes never faltered
in their gaze, his fine, almost feminine features were unlike those
of most Indians, and his long, slim fingers made his hands singularly beautiful. He stood in stony silence, saying nothing.

It was left for old Caramaunee to advance and take his place
before McKenney, revealing the presence of Wekau, who was in
every respect in contrast to Red Bird—a bent-backed, dirty, gaunt
Indian, whose hostility was not concealed.

"Red Bird and Wekau are here. They have come in like braves,"
said Caramaunee. "We know of no wrong they have done; they
have but fulfilled the tribal law; to us they are heroes. We ask only
this: treat them as braves; do not put them in irons."

The scene had about it the quality of unreality akin to dream,
with a hushed air over all the assembly, waiting for McKenney's
answer. This came presently, accompanied by a restless stirring
among the Indians who grasped its import.

McKenney said that he could promise nothing; it was the military who must decide this.

Caramaunee did not like this; his attitude spoke it plainly. He
asked now that the prisoners might be turned over to one of the
Indian agents: Captain Marsh. Major Whistler said that the prisoners must accompany him, but they need not go to Prairie du
Chien in irons. Moreover, interposed McKenney, Marsh could accompany the prisoners.

During all this, Red Bird had seated himself, his companions
respectfully sitting behind him. When these terms had been agreed
upon, Caramaunee stepped back, and Red Bird stood before Mc-
Kenney, his lofty demeanor indicating that he had no fear of
death, nor had he any sense of wrong-doing. He looked slowly
around him, a little proudly; he gazed at his people, at the soldiers, at Caramaunee with a steadiness that bespoke affection, and
finally once more at McKenney and the company surrounding
him. Then he spoke, his fine, smooth voice grave and proud.

"I am ready. I do not wish to be put in irons. Let me be free.
I have given away my life—" He bent, took up dust between his
finger and thumb and blew it away. "I have given up my life like

that. I would not take it back. It is gone." Here he threw his hands behind him to signify that he was leaving all things of life and going forward into death.

McKenney sighed and began to speak patiently. Why had Red Bird done this thing? Red Bird had always been held in high esteem by the white people who knew him. They could not understand it. Every one knew Wekau for a sly, dishonest Indian, but no one thought this possible of Red Bird.

Red Bird waited for a full minute after McKenney had ceased to talk. Then he raised his eyes to the hills and spoke again. "I took meat," he said. "It is the Winnebago law, and only the women-men among us do not obey this law. I took meat to avenge Wamangoosgaraha because I was told by a party of Sioux that he had been murdered at the order of his white captors. I know now that this was false. I did not know it then. I did not know that the Sioux wished only to involve us in war so that they could fight against the Fox and the Saukenauk and the Chippewa. I do not know that I have done wrong. I come now to sacrifice myself to the white man because it is my duty to save my people from the scourge of war. If I have done wrong, I will pay for it either with horses or with my life. I do not understand the white man's law, which has one set of words for the white man and another for the red. The white men promised us that the lead mines would be ours, but they did nothing to put the men who came to take possession away from them. If an Indian took possession of something belonging to a white man, the soldiers would come quickly enough. We have been patient. We have seen all this. We have seen the ancient burial grounds plowed over. We have seen our braves shot down like dogs for stealing corn. We have seen our women mocked and raped. We have seen the white men steal our lands, our quarries, our forests, our waterways, by lying to us and cheating us and making us drunk enough to put marks on papers without knowing what we were doing. When first the Long Knives came, the prophets told us they would never be honest with us. We did not believe them. We do now. When word came to us that Wamangoosgaraha was slain, I went forth and took meat. I did not know it was false; so I did no wrong. I fulfilled the law of the Winnebago. I am not ashamed. I would not

be ashamed. I have come because the white men are too strong, and I do not wish my people to suffer. Now I am ready. Take me."

At once he went up to Major Whistler, standing against him breast to breast. McKenney said nothing. A platoon of soldiers was wheeled backwards from the center of the line to close in behind Red Bird and Wekau. The Winnebagos fell backward, beginning again to chant the song of death.

But Hercules had seen enough. He could not look longer on this scene. Suddenly all his interest in the events of the past months washed away. He was sickened; the dignity and gravity of Red Bird's speech had taken hold of him; he turned away and walked quickly to his tent, filled with a fierce desire to be back in Prairie du Chien, back at his desk, back at his work, so that he might forget this tragedy grown from the treachery and deceit practised by the whites upon the Indians, who had never yet broken a treaty but that the whites had broken it first. What, he thought, will even wealth do against all this greed, this organized, legal greed? He felt the first upsurging of doubt about the wisdom of his dream; he began to think that perhaps after all he strove for something unattainable, and his intensity of feeling for the trade began to fade a little. He felt stifled, but he was conscious of a faint hope which was bound inextricably with the memory of Jane Rolette, and from this he could not shake himself free. He went into his tent and sat there with the flap drawn a little aside, so that he might see only the blue sky and the trees waving gently in the wind against a white cloud rolling over, the sky under which Red Bird had lived and might have died.

Before nightfall, he set out for Prairie du Chien alone.

4.

Half to Rise

1827-1828

IN August Hercules went north with the boats carrying the season's furs to Mackinac, making the long arduous trip in the summer's height of heat in a plague of mosquitoes and gnats which accompanied them from Prairie du Chien to Green Bay. On the lake, they were free alike of heat and insects.

Mackinac had undergone little change; when the rocky green island emerged from the blue waters of the straits, Hercules had the momentary feeling that he had been away only a little while; but this passed into the conviction that his home lay no longer before him, but behind. He was too restive to stay long; he was haunted still by the image of Red Bird in his cell at Prairie du Chien, refusing food, ready for death; and he could not rid himself of the suspicion that the Territory was not yet freed from the menace of the Winnebagos. His first quick belief that the taking of Red Bird and his accomplices would assure continued peace as well as improve the trade had faded; he understood more clearly than ever that events must take a slower course, and he could not help remembering those years under the British here in Mackinac, when procrastination and delay were constant. He recognized, too, that some great fundamental change would be necessary in the Michigan Territory, to better relations between the Indians and the white men, and this change could not be brought about alone by the traders. Nevertheless, he had reached that stage in his dubiety regarding his fellow men that he was reluctant to remain away from Prairie du Chien any longer than need be; he felt that the wrong impulse heedlessly followed might increase the difficult relations between savages and settlers; and he was all the more uneasy at

thought of Marsh. There was, too, an element of apprehension regarding Jane Rolette; he could not crush it within him; so he no longer sought to do so.

Dousman noticed his son's preoccupation, but was himself burdened with information he must impart to Hercules, whom he did not find alone until the night before Hercules' departure for the meeting place of the rivers once more. They came together that night to the old Astor office near the wharf.

Dousman carefully closed doors and windows. He was grave.

"Hercules, we've heard that Astor and the Columbia Company have come to terms," he said. "That means you'll have no opposition at all at Prairie du Chien, except for individual traders, who don't, after all, have our organization and can do little to take trade from our men."

Though his father had said nothing to indicate it, Hercules understood some inherent warning in his words. "No opposition," he repeated slowly. "What will he do then about liquor for the Indians? He's always said it was necessary in order to carry on against his competitors."

"He'll keep right on shipping it out for sale," said the older Dousman dryly. "In addition, we'll have a little more trouble with him ourselves. You know his sharp practices; you may expect to find them increased to our disadvantage. I have it from MacKenzie, who with Laidlaw will establish a post at the mouth of the Yellowstone. Astor will pay twenty thousand for the Company. The fact is, Astor's just back from London. The scarcity of beavers now makes it too expensive to buy beaver hats, and the enterprising tailors have begun to make a silk hat, which is preferred to the old. Now the fashion is all for buffalo robes: so Astor must have the western territory."

Hercules nodded thoughtfully, appreciating Astor's motive. Nevertheless, he had for so long heard rumors that Astor was preparing to withdraw from the trade in favor of commercial shipping, that he could not at once fully credit this information. "I understood Ramsay Crooks was trying to buy Astor out," he said.

"He is. Astor won't sell yet, not until the demand for pelts subsides even more. But heed me, Hercules: in no circumstances let Astor follow his usual practice with you—taking a mortgage on any

property you may own to guarantee unpaid bills. He won't hesitate to foreclose at once."

"But that's shamefully unscrupulous!" protested Hercules.

The older Dousman smiled. "Astor would call it only good business. I've often found that men change their conceptions of honesty after acquiring wealth."

Hercules shook his head. "Father, I'll disprove that. I promise you I'll be the Northwest Territory's first millionaire—if Astor can do it, I can do it, too."

"But not by his methods, my boy. Let us hope that. But it seems to me such an ambition can have no good end. Money in itself is nothing, and the possession of it is often like wormwood. Money is only a means to an end."

"I'll make it so."

"My boy, you're young," said the older Dousman quietly, dispassionately.

They argued late into that night, with the soft candlelight lying yellow upon the floor and walls of the familiar old room, and the memory of Prairie du Chien looming large in Hercules' mind. He was anxious to be away, to be back at the meeting place of the rivers, at that place he had chosen to spend the rest of his life. And, ceaselessly gnawing at his consciousness like mice were thoughts of Marsh and treachery among the Indians, of Red Bird dying in his cell, of Rolette and their partnership, of Jane.

Two days after his return to Prairie du Chien, Thunder Walker came to see him. The Winnebago was wearing paint which showed him to be in mourning. Hercules was solicitous. Had Thunder Walker lost some one? Why was he daubed? The Indian disdained to answer; he sat cross-legged just out of the circle of light shaded for the papers on the table at which Hercules worked. His eyes gleamed like coals in the darkness beyond; his shadow was a dim outline. Hercules grew uneasy, not for himself, but for what urgence had brought Thunder Walker to him at a time when the Fox and Sauk were approaching the village to trade.

What troubled Thunder Walker? he asked.

The Winnebago said that many things troubled him and all the Winnebagos. They were things which had troubled them only after

the white men came. It was a singular fact, he said, that Indians had had no such troubles before the white men came. It was slowly being felt by all of them that the old time, the old days, were gone; they would never return. The Great Spirit was angry with his people and had sent them this scourge to punish them.

"What scourge?" asked Hercules unthinking, stabbed by the fear of an epidemic among the Indians.

The white men, of course, answered Thunder Walker.

"Ah, well, you didn't come to tell me this," said Hercules.

Thunder Walker shook his head. It was about Red Bird he had come. He did not care about Wekau or Chichonsic; they had always in the first place wanted to take meat; but Red Bird had held back; he was more temperate. Now word had gone among the tribes that Red Bird was starving, that he would not eat. Moreover, the medicine men said that Red Bird would die before his trial. Why did they not try him?

Hercules explained that Red Bird's trial depended upon the arrival of Judge Doty, and the arrival of Judge Doty depended upon God.

Truly, observed Thunder Walker, the Great Spirit was angry with them, or he would not keep Doty so long away.

Besides, continued Hercules, Red Bird saw that he had done grave wrong in taking the word of the Sioux and going forth to take meat without knowing beyond doubt that Wamangoosgaraha lived or had died, and this was his way of seeking passage into the country of the Great Spirit. The Judge would come before Red Bird died, and Red Bird would be sentenced to hang.

"But he will never hang," said Thunder Walker.

"Ah, and why not?" asked Hercules, thinking immediately that the Winnebagos planned to raid the settlement despite the strong company of soldiers now at the fort.

Because the medicine men had said he would die in his cell, answered Thunder Walker. He waited for a long minute before going on to say that the Winnebagos did not like this, the Winnebagos were muttering against the white men, they were angry against the treaty they had signed at Butte des Morts, they did not wish Red Bird to die, for to them he was a hero and he had long been a favorite of the braves. There was much anger, and the old

chiefs were too old to take up the tomahawk. They were likewise too old to hold back the young braves, who wished to do the war dance and save Red Bird.

Hercules listened to Thunder Walker's complaints and, after the Indian had gone, sought out Rolette, who was at work in another part of the building, and repeated this information to him. Rolette was not alarmed.

"Mind you, I don't expect another outbreak," he said calmly, "but with a damn' scoundrel like Marsh in our midst, there's no telling about it. *Mille tonnerre!* if that man should now be named Indian agent in place of old Boilvin! It was thoughtless of Boilvin to die just now."

Hercules came to Marsh's defense. "I don't understand him; sometimes he acquits himself like a brave man, and sometimes he does sly things almost like some of the Indians. But he played a good part in the war just past."

Rolette snorted. "He's been contaminated by his Dacotahs."

Hercules paced restlessly back and forth, his hands clasped behind his back. "We can't have more trouble now," he said. "How can we build up the trade to a point where we can really make money if there are to be always these disturbances and outbreaks?"

Rolette smiled sardonically. "When you work for Astor, it's Astor who makes the money. I told you to invest in real estate; I say so again. I cannot say so too strongly. The fact is, people are coming into the Territory steadily, Indian outbreaks or no, and they're going to want land near the settlements. So buy now. And the trade won't last forever. Even the custom of using buffalo robes won't last long—partly because the public is as changeable as the wind, partly because the buffalo will be hunted as shamelessly and rapaciously as the other creatures, and his numbers will be far too depleted to maintain a reasonable price on the robes." He came around to where Hercules was and took him by the arm. "Look here, Dousman, you're too much alone. Did any one ever tell you that? A man who's too much alone tends to turn in upon himself."

"Perhaps," agreed Hercules.

"Now then, listen to me—this isn't good for you, even if it's good for the Company—and on this point, I can't deny you already know

more than I do about the affairs of the Company; indeed, it's you who are the agent, and I your partner. So why not come and take your meals with us for a while? Jane will be only too glad to have you. We all will. The children, too, have taken quite a fancy to you, as you know."

Hercules hesitated.

"Well, what do you say?"

"Why, yes, I'd like that," said Hercules. "Only . . ."

"Only what?"

Hercules shook his head. "It's nothing, nothing at all."

He would have forgotten this by the following day if Rolette had not promptly reminded him and carried him away to dinner. They found Jane dressed as if for a party, and she herself opened the door to them.

Rolette grinned. Hercules was amazed at sight of her decked out in frills.

"My wife gets too few opportunities to wear her fineries," observed Rolette.

"Mistaire Dousman!" cried Jane in evident delight. "I do not understan' why you avoid us so, that M'sieu' Rolette mus' bring you to our table."

"I'm sorry," said Hercules. "But I'm so busy."

"Even busy men mus' eat," said Jane.

The children clamored at him, and he took the place Rolette indicated for him. Jane too sat down, and the half-breed woman who served her came in to put the dinner on the table. The table was well lit by two candelabra, and conflicting shadows fell upon it and those around it. There was a pleasant warmth in the room, and Hercules was conscious of having missed this in his too often lonely meals. The fragile Virginia gazed at him with the intent interest so often manifested by children; young Joseph tried not to make his own interest obvious; Rolette had apparently forgotten that he was there. Not so Jane; she continued to talk. He was reminded of their trip down from Green Bay, and smiled. Instantly she bridled.

"Have I say fonny thing?" she demanded. "Mistaire Dousman, are you laughing at me?"

"Madame, I laugh only with you," he answered.

"But I have say nothing fonny," she protested, her eyebrows raised in perplexity.

"Jane loves to talk," said Rolette absently.

Jane observed innocently that there was little else to do. She turned to Hercules. "Do you know, Mistaire Dousman, it is the firs' time you have sit at my table since our trip. And there," she pointed with dramatic suddenness to the wall, her eyes aglow, her smile triumphant, "there are M'sieu' Edouardt's silhouettes."

Hercules looked at them: three in a row, with Jane between her children. They were attractively arranged upon the wall. Indeed, the entire room gave evidence of Jane's good taste, her touch was everywhere, in the complementary colors, in the decorations, even in the pieces of furniture, and in that portion of the parlor which was visible from there, revealing the massive piano Rolette had brought down the Fox-Wisconsin waterway for Jane, a piece of furniture which might ordinarily have completely dominated the room but whose effect was mitigated by the skilful arrangement of lesser pieces about it. He smiled and said that Madame could now appreciate, seeing her silhouette constantly upon the wall, what pleasure she must give to the eye.

Jane was delighted and clapped her hands like a child. "You hear that, M'sieu' Rolette? I am not so unattractive, then?"

Rolette grinned and said, "Come, let's eat. *Sacré nom!* it's nothing to do—talk while the food grows cold."

Eugenie, on the threshold to the kitchen, nodded to herself in approval.

Jane suggested that Rolette say grace, which he did hastily.

Hercules could not help grinning mischievously. "Does Rolette still pray?" he asked. "I'm astonished by it."

Jane flashed a quick, amazed glance at him. "Why should he not pray?" she demanded.

"Hasn't he told you? Why, he still owes the Virgin a chapel."

"He do?"

Rolette grimaced and sighed. "I've heard nothing else since," he cried. "Dousman plagues me to death."

"Let me hear of it, Mistaire Dousman."

"Why, it occurred when you were east, Madame. Rolette and I were one day on the river and were caught in a violent storm

which threatened to capsize our boat where the current was strongest. We were laden with furs, besides, and the orders he shouted—well, Madame, the less said of them the better. So he promised a chapel dedicated to the Blessed Virgin if we came through without harm. But your ungrateful husband, upon landing, snapped his fingers and cried out to the heavens, 'Collect my note if you can!' I have waited for the chapel since."

"M'sieu' Rolette, is this true?"

He admitted that it was. "I've been too busy to build chapels," he continued. "Besides, the circumstances . . ."

Hercules laughed. "Then and now are different times, eh, Joe?" He turned to Jane. "You see, I've been at him unmercifully ever since then. And little good it's done."

"M'sieu' Rolette, I am surprise' at you."

He threw up his hands and sighed resignedly. *"Sacré tonnerre de Dieu!* If it is so important, I promise it will be built. Only, let me hear no more of it."

A faint smile touched Jane's lips, and she bent to her food; Hercules' eyes lingered for a moment on her before he, too, resumed his meal.

After dinner, Rolette pushed back his chair and got up. The children sat gazing expectantly at him. "I believe I promised Joseph and Virginie a ride in the canoe," he said. "Shall we take it, eh?"

"Yes, yes," cried Joseph excitedly. "You promised."

Virginia clapped her hands, smiling joyously.

"Very well, we'll go then." He held out his hands. "Come on."

They came to him. Jane rose hastily, going for Virginia's bonnet and Joseph's cap, which she put on them.

"Now be careful," she warned. "M'sieu' Rolette, remembaire they are our children. Mistaire Dousman and I will sit on the verandah and watch you."

She kissed them both and followed them to the verandah, where Hercules presently joined her. She stood at the rail, waving her handkerchief to them where they walked, one on each side of Rolette, down to the Mississippi's edge, where the canoe was. When they reached the canoe, she turned.

"Shall we sit down, Mistaire Dousman?"

"By all means," he said.

Her eyes were held still by the children, but his gaze swung out beyond the three at the canoe. The Mississippi was in constant movement with the activity of men upon it: Indians colorful in their finery of feathers and cloth driving swiftly toward the landing place, voyageurs setting out, a keel-boat coming slowly upriver, lone anglers passing among the islands. From the voyageurs rose a strongly voiced song, sung in unison; it was almost like the old days at Mackinac, Hercules thought, save only that it was on a smaller scale. Rolette's great voice joined the voyageurs' suddenly:

> *A la claire fontaine*
> *M'en allant promener,*
> *J'ai trouvé l'eau si belle*
> *Que je m'y suis baigné.*
> *Lui ya longtemps que je t'aime,*
> *Jamais je ne t'oublierai . . .*

The sunlight lay mellow upon the river and the western hills. All earth was covered still by dense dark green, the last short while now before the colors of autumn began to change the pattern. The pungence of sycamore leaves was strong in air, coming together with the freshness of water riding the wind from the west. Swallows rode the air currents high above the hills, and higher still a great bald-headed eagle soared proudly in the blue; Hercules watched the bird, marking its sureness, its effortlessness, its magnificent grace. In the western sky now a few platelike clouds rose up toward the sun.

Hercules turned to Jane, whose gaze was fixed still upon the trio in the canoe, now skirting one of the islands in the Mississippi beyond the village, smiling when occasionally their joyous cries reached her ears. He thought she looked tired, a little drawn.

"I trust Madame is not unwell," he said gently.

She looked at him, a little startled. "But no, I am all right. Do Mistaire Dousman think pairhaps I look so?"

"Forgive me, but I thought under your brightness there was just a little strain."

"Ah, there is," she admitted. "There are so many things that consairn me—pairhaps it is needless."

"What have you been doing lately, Madame?"

"It is only mon cher Oncle Brisbois; he is so quick' growing blind," she answered. "You know how active he once was. I read to him evair' day, and I mus' help ma cher Tante Domitelle. My poor Oncle Brisbois talk' all time about how he wish to be bury on that hill he own' eas' of the village; he say he will be out of reach of flood watairs, and at same time he can res' even above M'sieu' Rolette. Pairhaps he make his little joke once too often. So I am worry. And I think also about my fathaire; my oncle is so like him. My fathaire he has go off to the Red Rivaire Country so that he can be with his brothaire, my Oncle Alexandaire, who is with the Hudson Bay Company; he has go already when my mothaire have die, and I was so small I was put with my Oncle Michal and ma Tante Domitelle. I think maybe my fathaire will return soon. As Mistaire Dousman know, I have been all time with my Oncle and Tante Brisbois. When I was a little girl, I was sit' on their fence one day when I saw M'sieu' Rolette firs' time; he was han'some; he have on red coat, like British offisaire; he was with the British when they took Fort Shelby in las' war."

Surely, he said gently, these things alone could not disturb her; these were just the outward, tangible signatures of time passing. Certainly Madame had no fear of time.

She shook her head. "No, I have no fear. I am not afraid. You are right, it is not all, Mistaire Dousman. I do not look forward to time when Virginie and Joseph mus' go eas' to be educate'; M'sieu' Rolette, he insis' upon this. I do not wish to part with them. M'sieu' Rolette, he has long ago sen' his daughtaire, Elizabeth, by his firs' wife, eas', and she is now in St. Louis, all this time without see' us. And it will soon, some day, be the same with Virginie and Joseph —for so long time, and so far away. Mr. Crooks, he has promise' that they will be take' good care of, since he is in eas' also." She shrugged her shoulders with resignation on her features. "And then, there are so many sick in the village, especially *les enfants*—and I cannot bear to see children suffaire, I will not, I mus' do what I can, and they count on me to help them, to nurse them and care for them."

"Madame need not do that," he protested.

"I need not, but I do, I will, I know they need some one, and who will help them if I do not?"

"The doctor at the fort . . ."

"Oh, he cannot be there all time; he come only when they call him. No, no," she shook her head, "they look to me. I will not disappoint them." She exclaimed suddenly. "There, they are coming back!"

She sprang up and ran down to meet her children, Hercules following more slowly after, reflecting that beneath all her fire there were deeper currents, primitive almost; the image of her in his mind's eye was strengthened immeasurably, and he felt a sensation almost of pain possessing him at the thought that Rolette had had the advantage of knowing her before him.

In a little while Hercules was established in this routine. He came regularly for his meals, and for a time he enjoyed coming. The summer turned to autumn, and still he came. But presently it was with steadily growing reluctance; he found himself once more strongly attracted to Jane; he could not keep his eyes from her, and her singular beauty haunted him in both his waking and his sleeping hours. Yet he came to his meals at the Rolette home. As long as Rolette was in Prairie du Chien, he could not easily escape coming; Rolette would take no excuse. He had settled this matter for Hercules, and he would not take Hercules' refusal. What can I say to him? wondered Hercules from time to time. "I'm sorry, Rolette, but I can't come to your home any longer on these terms; I've fallen in love with your wife!" He could hear himself saying any such thing! And he could imagine also Rolette's untroubled laughter. But he was beginning to feel that if he were to speak the truth to Rolette, he must say this or its equivalent, for so dominant had Jane grown in his daily thoughts that he could not any longer deny it even to himself. Despite her quick temper in regard to him, despite his unqualified firmness with her whenever necessary, there was between them a silent bond which needed no word to make it known. But she, certainly, did not recognize what had happened to him, thought Hercules; and she need never know.

Nevertheless, his preoccupation with Jane hindered his work. Rolette noticed this but withheld comment. Meanwhile, there was no further intimation of trouble with the Winnebagos until late autumn, when Red Bird was growing steadily weaker. At this time,

Rolette illogically decided to go up to Fort Snelling. Now that Astor had bought out the Columbia Company, he wanted to talk the matter over with the traders in the region of St. Peters. His absence gave Hercules the opportunity to discontinue going to Rolette's home for his meals; he made his apologies to Jane; he said a little stiffly and stuffily that it would not be in accordance with convention and propriety if he were to come to the house so often during Mr. Rolette's absence, as Madame Rolette would understand. Jane thought he was being unnecessarily ridiculous and said so at length.

"I have nevaire care what people say," she cried. "I have always do my duty, and I have not need to do more. Whatevair people talk, Mistaire Dousman mus' eat, and he look bettaire since he began to eat at our house."

But Hercules would not be moved. He was sorry, he said, but he could not come again; besides, he was very busy, and now with Red Bird's plight, no one knew what might happen. He wished to be at the office without feeling that he should be gone at certain hours for his meals. But he knew, with a hollow feeling inside him, that he would miss seeing Jane across the table from him; he would miss her more than he cared to say.

The season's first snowstorm fell in December, a thick heavy fall drifted rapidly by the northwest wind. In a short time the world was obliterated; white snow covered everything; chickadees, sparrows, and brilliantly feathered cardinals huddled close to buildings. The air, however, stayed only moderately cold, and the Mississippi did not freeze over.

Hercules stayed in his office. He worked still, from time to time, on his map of the Michigan Territory and that portion of the trans-Mississippi whose traders came to the post at Prairie du Chien. The wind tore at the old building, the snow sifted pleasantly against the window, on the hearth burned a bright fire which made shadows dance upon the walls and spilled a ruddy glow like old burgundy upon the floor and table and chairs.

In the midst of the storm, Kapolequa arrived. He was caked with snow and walked over to the fireplace so that he might warm himself. Hercules looked at him in some surprise, watched him sit

down, and waited a few moments. But the Fox was apparently not yet ready to speak; so Hercules resumed his work. In twenty minutes, Kapolequa shifted his position a little so that he could look at Hercules; he grunted.

Hercules looked up. "Will it be a long snow?" he asked.

Kapolequa said that it would be comparatively long. After the snow would come quick, sharp cold; the river might freeze; he thought it would. After that would come more snow and cold with a little warm weather. It would be a long winter. He said that he had come a long way from the north and the fire warmed his bones, frightening away the frost spirit.

"It must have been important to bring you to me," said Hercules in the Fox tongue, "in weather like this."

It was not snowing when he started, explained Kapolequa. He had come from the Prairie La Crosse where the Winnebagos were making mischief.

Hercules sighed. What the devil was it now? Did the Indians intend to take a lesson from their white brothers and break treaties? He assumed that they were sullen because of Red Bird's dying. But Red Bird had chosen his own manner of death, and it was no fault of the white men. He would be executed in any event.

Nevertheless, the Winnebagos were making trouble, continued Kapolequa imperturbably. He had seen it. And the Sioux and the British traders were urging them on. The Sioux had learned from the British the art of persuading others to fight for them.

Always the British, thought Hercules dispassionately. He felt a sharp twinge of memory; his mind retreated swiftly into the past, far and yet near in moments like this, back to the siege and occupation of Mackinac, and he heard as if yesterday his father's sharp comments about the British and their use of Indian allies.

"What kind of trouble?" demanded Hercules. "Have they said anything?"

No, they had not. It was what they were doing. The braves killed by the men in the keel boats during the past summer were lying unburied on a scaffold at the settlement of Indians below Prairie La Crosse; above the platform on a pole, the Winnebagos had affixed the scalp of the Frenchman, Gagnier. The White Brother understood what this meant.

Hercules understood that Gagnier's scalp was a symbol of the Winnebagos' ill feeling, boldly expressed. He nodded.

Kapolequa had also heard talk. The Winnebagos muttered among themselves and wished to take meat. He did not know whether the threat was made against Prairie du Chien, but he thought Dousman should know.

Did the Indian agent know? asked Hercules.

Kapolequa shook his head. He would not tell him because Marsh might hear. He did not know whether it was possible to trust Marsh. Many of the Winnebagos trusted him, and all the Dacotahs did, but he, Kapolequa, would have nothing to do with him. Marsh hated the Fox and the Saukies, and he would not believe them.

"Very well," said Hercules. "You can sleep tonight by the fire here, Kapolequa. The agent must know this."

"Do not say a Fox has said it to you," cautioned Kapolequa.

Hercules went out into the storm and made his way blindly to the agency house. The new agent had arrived only a short time before: a Virginian, General Joseph Street. He had been a newspaper editor, and if he had any qualifications for the agency, he had not as yet shown them. But he was a gentleman; he seemed to know his mind; he could not be put upon by Marsh. It was no secret that he could not get along with Marsh, nor Marsh with him. Their disagreement had begun at once. Marsh had expected Cass to appoint him, but some one had apparently pressed Cass to make a different appointment; as a result, Marsh resented Street, all the more so since it was true that Street had had virtually no contact with Indians, and lacked all the experience Marsh had. Hercules, pleased that Marsh had not been given the agency, was nevertheless dubious about Street's abilities.

Street was in his office: a model of cleanliness and order now, in contrast to Boilvin's time. He was a tall man, florid-faced, with a clipped moustache and a military bearing, for all that he had never had any military training. He had a habit of fixing his gaze immovably upon any one who spoke to him, as if in a conscious effort to disconcert people. He accordingly fixed Hercules immediately upon his entrance, greeted him politely and sat to listen to what he might have to say.

Hercules explained wearily that it was the Winnebagos again.

"Is there no one here who knows how to handle these Indians?" asked Street absently. "I thought they just signed a treaty six months ago."

"They have. But it's entirely possible they've learned to adopt the tactics we've taught them: to break treaties. Besides, Dodge and his volunteers have camped on their lead mines and are helping themselves like all the other greedy settlers in that region. They have grievances."

"Well, what is it this time?"

Hercules told him.

"Is that a bad sign?" asked Street.

"Beyond doubt. It means that the Winnebagos are harboring a grudge, and the scalp's hanging there is an indication that the Indians mean eventual war."

Street turned and called Marsh from an inner room. Marsh came in: a little saturnine, eying Hercules with faint, aloof and slightly patient scorn. "I suppose we're having trouble again?" he said as if he did not believe it possible, and much less so coming from such a source as the Astor agent.

"Looks like it," said Street. He told him.

"Gagnier's scalp, eh?"

"Mr. Dousman feels that something must be done."

"Ah, what precisely?" asked Marsh, turning to look at Hercules.

"The scalp must be taken down," replied Hercules promptly. "You know as well as I do that if we can succeed in taking down the scalp, they'll understand that we defy them. So it must come down."

"I suppose we can just write them an order to that effect," countered Marsh lightly. "They will no doubt be glad to obey, while the memory of Atkinson's force is still green among them."

"I think the effect of that has been overrated," said Hercules, ignoring Marsh's sarcasm. "It wouldn't in any case be as simple as that. Some one must take that scalp down; obviously, we can't expect the Winnebagos to do it."

Marsh raised his eyebrows and his mouth made a quick grimace of alarm; he shot a glance at Street. Street was grinning, and there was an almost furtive look about his eyes. He turned his head slowly and gazed at the subagent.

"Don't you think well of Mr. Dousman's suggestion, Mr. Marsh?"

"I hardly know what to say."

"Don't you think he may be right?"

"Oh, he's right, of course. The only thing is, how to accomplish such a feat without setting the Winnebagos about our ears."

Street continued to gaze at him with a sly guilelessness in his eyes. "A resourceful man could do it, don't you think, Mr. Marsh?"

"Anything is possible," agreed Marsh.

Marsh had forgotten all about Hercules now; he was engaged in a rapid duel with his superior, and he was well aware that beneath Street's casual, deliberate manner lay a well-formed plan involving him. He was careful not to put himself into a position from which he might not easily retreat if the necessity were forced upon him. He watched Street with an almost feline intensity, but it was Street who was catlike in his soft gentle probings, his apparently indolent manner, his mask of slow thought.

"It would mean invading the encampment at Prairie La Crosse and talking down the scalp by night, alone, I should think," Street went on. "It could be done in the course of one night, I believe. Couldn't it, Mr. Marsh?"

"Yes, I believe it could." He looked away; he had steeled himself sufficiently now so that he could remember Hercules. "But perhaps Mr. Dousman has a better suggestion to make. Mr. Dousman is well liked by most of the Indians who know him; indeed, many of them have fallen into the habit of calling him *Father* in the same manner as they address their agents, if not with more genuine warmth." His lip curled upward slightly, and his eyes grew sly. "Mr. Dousman is an intrepid explorer; we all know that his map of the Territory knows no equal, and is the best map obtainable."

"Ah, is that so?" asked Street. "Is it true you know the region very well, Mr. Dousman?"

"I have some familiarity with it, Mr. Street."

"Well, sir, I'm glad to hear that. We couldn't have anything happen to a man who is so well acquainted with this region, could we, Mr. Marsh?" He did not wait for Marsh to answer. "So I think you had better go, Marsh, as soon as the river freezes over. I think

you can take care of this matter with your customary dispatch and success."

Hercules expected Marsh to argue, but Marsh did not. "Very well, sir," he said. "I'll inform my wife."

After he had gone, Hercules protested mildly. Surely it was a dangerous mission on which to send a lone white man? The Winnebagos were in an ugly mood, and it might not go well with Marsh.

"A man must do his duty," said Street, a little sententiously. But he was evidently very well pleased with himself; he had got rid of Marsh for the time being, and could in any case take the glory of Marsh's success. Presumably, if Marsh failed, the attempt would be to the credit of his memory at least.

Hercules took his departure not without a feeling of having unwittingly been Street's accomplice in putting Marsh to this dangerous task. He was not pleased. He did not like the agent's tactics any more than he liked Marsh's, but doubtless Marsh had provoked Street's decision; certainly Marsh had wasted no time seeking to influence Street to suggest that Hercules go, as soon as he himself had sensed which way the wind blew. He went back to the office and sat in the candlelight mulling over Marsh's predicament. Marsh had a wife and child; it would have been a task more fitting to Hercules. It was characteristic that Hercules did not think of his plans for his future at the moment.

He woke Kapolequa, who lay asleep before the fire, his copper skin aglow with the flames' reflection. Kapolequa blinked at him slowly, turning his head a little from the brightness of the fire, so that he might see Hercules better. He grunted and sat up.

Hercules asked about the way to Prairie La Crosse. Were there many encampments of hostile Indians between?

None, said Kapolequa. But deep woods. Take snowshoes. Clearly he assumed that Hercules had made up his mind to go.

Hercules did not disabuse him. It would be possible, then, to come upon the camp of the hostile Winnebagos without necessarily being seen and risking being reported to the camp?

Kapolequa agreed that it would. Unless, of course, he travelled making noise and so letting them know of his approach.

"All right. Go back to sleep."

Kapolequa grunted, lay down, and turned toward the fire once more, rolling a little. Hercules went over to the window and stood looking out through the now thinly falling snow to where light burned in the agent's window.

In the morning he saw Marsh on the street. Marsh was restrained in his greeting; but this was no new thing. He was bundled up against the cold and carried snowshoes, as if he were preparing to make his trip.

"Look here, Marsh," said Hercules. "It doesn't seem right that a man with your family responsibilities should take this risk. Why not let me go?"

"Thanks," said Marsh dryly. "Street wants me to go. You could see that. Besides, I'm no coward. There might be as much risk in not going, you know."

His faults, thought Hercules, stem not from cowardice, but from a different kind of weakness. "When do you plan to go?" he asked.

"Late this afternoon."

At sundown Hercules was ready. He saw Marsh set out, gave him a little time to get started, and set out after him, pausing only for a few words with the boy he had put in charge of the office until his return. The cold had not abated, but the wind had gone down entirely, so that rapid movement served to keep the blood circulating and held warmth to the body. The evening was clear; low in the southeast Sirius gleamed frostily, and in the west the last daylight drew slowly down beyond the rim of snowbound earth. Snow lay everywhere in treacherous drifts, and Marsh was making every effort to avoid them, Hercules saw.

He had no difficulty keeping to Marsh's trail. It led directly to the shore of the Mississippi and followed the stream along the ice at its edge. The river was not quite frozen over, since a dark stream, choked with ice-floes, coursed openly between two shelves of ice grown from the shore on both sides. Coming presently to a place where Marsh had paused and put on his snowshoes, Hercules did likewise. He pressed on, anxious to find Marsh within sight before the absolute darkness of the winter night closed down. The cold air made his skin tingle, his breath was a cloud of vapor, some of which became white rime along his fur cap and coat collar. Above, stars were coming into the dark blue of late evening sky, twinkling

and gleaming, distant and cold, with naked branches of trees gaunt against the dome of heaven, and the night's stillness was broken only by distant yawping of foxes and the eerie hooting of great owls invisible in the dark woodlands. Before him he heard occasional sounds which gave evidence of Marsh's passage.

Abruptly, rounding a bend in the river at an island, he came upon Marsh. Marsh had been waiting for him.

"I heard some one behind me," he said. "What do you want?"

"I'm going along with you, Marsh."

Marsh gazed at him incredulously. "There's twice as much danger that two of us may get caught, as there is that one may be found out."

"It was partly my fault that you got into this," continued Hercules. "At least, I can make getting caught a little more difficult."

"Look here, Dousman—what are you after?"

"Nothing. Unless you might put it that I'm after some kind of permanent peace so that a man can pursue his living without interruption. As far as my going along is concerned, it can be a secret between us."

Marsh looked at him for a moment in patent doubt, suspicion of him manifest in his hard eyes and grim mouth; he was undecided. Plainly, he wanted company, and yet he had the impulse to go on without Hercules. But he did not yield to that impulse; he hunched his shoulders, turned abruptly, and went on, saying no word.

Night had grown deep now, but still the line of earth and sky stayed clear by virtue of the white emanation from the snow, a dim, spectral illumination marking off earth from sky, save where the woods pushed upward into the night. The cold was still, penetrating. Their passage was soundless, save for the whispering of snow underfoot, and the occasional crunching and cracking of ice on the river. They kept to the shelf of ice along the Mississippi, but from time to time found it necessary to invade the woodland where the ice had broken away, and made their way with difficulty among the deep drifts there. A lynx screamed at them, a sudden ululant scream that brought Marsh to a stop. Behind him Hercules stopped, too. The tension around them was suddenly electric; it was such a cry

as might have come from a human throat. For a full minute they stood waiting, alert for any further sound; there was none.

"Was it a cat, do you think? Or a signal?"

"A cat," said Hercules, certain.

They pressed on.

At midnight they came within sight of the Winnebago encampment, compact in a broad open space in the woodland at the river shore. Woods were dark all around, but not so close that attackers might utilize them with impunity. Marsh paused cautiously and waited for Hercules.

"They'll expect people to come along the river," he whispered. "We'd better make for the woods here where we can do it without making too much noise."

Hercules agreed. It would be better in any event to come upon the village from behind, he said.

They stood tense, almost painfully alert lest their whispering be heard and answered suddenly by the sentry's warning cry, or perhaps even by the discharge of a weapon to bring the entire village upon them. They skirted the encampment through the close-pressing woods, keeping themselves well concealed among the dark-shrouded trunks, made denser here and there by cedar groves. They came to a stop finally within a half circle of cedars from which they could see clearly into the Winnebago village. There was some activity still among the wigwams, though for the most part quiet held the encampment. A large fire burned in the center of the place, and the snow around it gave evidence that a council and a dance had been held there. It was not comforting to reflect that the Winnebagos might have done the war dance, because it was easy to imagine what would happen to them if they were caught by Winnebagos in whose veins flowed war-fevered blood. Hercules grew coldly alive to every sound; fear left him before the necessity for the utmost alertness; he studied the village until he felt assured that the Winnebagos had had not only a war dance, but also a celebration of some kind; there was still a vague aroma of liquor in the quiet air.

Not far from the fire stood a scaffolding, upon which lay dark mounds: the frozen bodies of those Indians slain near the Bad Axe during the summer uprising. Above this rose a pole, from which dangled a solitary scalp, its long hair swinging a little in the wind

and, in turning, catching a subdued gleam from the firelight's glow. This was the object of their dangerous mission, and if it could be obtained, their cold, dark-bound trek would not have been in vain. But between the scaffolding and the clump of cedars stood an unbroken expanse of snow—and the wigwams of Winnebagos, each one of whom might rouse from his sleep to the attack upon them.

They waited, crouched close together, so that they might not feel the cold too much. All around them the dark woods stood over, and the night was soundless. In his mind's eye Hercules walked back into the months and years just gone, back to that time when the British had taken Michilimackinac with their Indian allies, and he thought that now once again the British traders were doing their best to stir the Indians to trouble against the white men. What was it Kapolequa had said? The Sioux had learned from the British the art of persuading others to do battle for them. He smiled in the darkness. He thought of his determination to know the power of wealth, but at the same time he was overcome with the venality of his fellow men, and the evidence of it he had seen even in his short time: their greed, their selfishness, their cruelty, so often hiding the vein of goodness when it was within them at all. Inevitably, his thoughts drove back to Jane. He contemplated her almost with guilt, as if he had no right to think of her in any but the most superficial manner.

Marsh turned suddenly and touched his arm. "All right. I'm going," he said. He took off his snowshoes and stood them against one of the cedars.

Hercules removed his own. He shifted his gun and followed Marsh's dark shadow slipping from the cedar grove.

The Winnebago settlement was still; the fire was dying down; the wind was growing, pulling at wigwams, making Gagnier's solitary scalp to dance above the bodies of the dead. Hercules was alert for the sentries; he saw one of them presently, sitting in the snow with his back to the fire. Abruptly they stood motionless, but in a moment the breath hissed from between Marsh's teeth in relief; the sentry was asleep. There was still at least one other sentry to be accounted for, but they could not find him. Nevertheless, there was no irresolution about them; they passed soundlessly among the

wigwams, keeping as much as possible to the shadows away from the fire, and came at last to the foot of the platform with its gruesome burden. Marsh paused and looked cautiously around. There was no evidence of the second sentry; perhaps he too lay asleep somewhere, perhaps none had been sent out. Hercules was not confident; he fingered a large stone he had picked up from beside one of the wigwams. There was no sound, but he reflected that a hostile eye looking from a wigwam made no sound. Marsh hesitated no longer; he mounted shakily to the platform, and Hercules came soundlessly after.

On that instant the second sentry appeared, coming catlike from among the wigwams, his gun held in readiness in the crook of his arm. He came looking all around him, his eyes gleaming like coals in the reflected glow of the fire. Marsh caught his breath, and began to raise his gun unsteadily. Hercules pushed the gun gently away, shaking his head. The sentry came on; almost at the fire, he turned and looked suspiciously behind him. If he reached the fire, he would almost certainly kick his fellow sentry awake. Without hesitation, Hercules acted; he took the stone from his pocket, aimed at the Winnebago's head, and hurled it with all his force. His aim was true; the stone struck with a muted thud; the Indian crumpled forward and lay still.

"God!" hissed Marsh.

"Get to it," urged Hercules.

In the dim spectral luminosity of the snow, the dead Indians lay as if asleep. But they were not asleep, wrapped in their blankets; even in that dim light the evidence of decay before the bodies had frozen was visible in their gaunt faces. Snow still lay upon some of the bodies; from some it had blown away on the wind which was even now swirling it from the platform. Above them Gagnier's scalp flapped in the wind, slapping the air with short barking sounds. Rickety as the platform was, the pole Marsh now had to climb was even more shaky. But after another quick glance toward the wigwams, he began to climb, the pole swaying dangerously, and the platform creaking and groaning with its movement. Hercules stood tense, watching for any sign of wakefulness among the wigwams. The moment was endless, held in a shell of apprehension, with danger all around, waiting upon any accident to spring to

activity. Marsh reached the scalp and tore it away, stuffing it into his pocket. He came cautiously down again.

"Got it?" asked Hercules in a whisper.

Marsh nodded. "Come on. Let's get out of here."

They stood for an instant more, wary of any possible ambush; but the Winnebagos trusted to their sentries; they had evidently all celebrated well, for there was no sign of wakefulness among the wigwams. The fallen sentry still lay quiet. They descended to the ground and loped rapidly out of the settlement to the grove of cedars, where they paused only long enough to put on their snow-shoes, and then circled to the river once more, turning with the wind into the south, where they went without sound as swiftly as the snow and ice would permit.

Shortly after dawn they reached Prairie du Chien, coming into the village from opposite directions, so that no one might know they had been together.

Now for a time there was release from the fear of Winnebago ill will. Word of Marsh's exploit went from mouth to mouth and he was praised. Street shared in his praise; the villagers spoke of the courage and determination of the Indian agents. Hercules alone was not certain that the taking of Gagnier's scalp removed the menace of dissatisfied and angry Winnebagos, and in this belief he was presently joined by Lockwood and McNair. Even when Thunder Walker came in to say that the Winnebagos at Prairie La Crosse had been impressed with the resourcefulness of the white men, Hercules was not inclined to put down his skulking convic-tion that the Indians had not yet finished with their anger against the whites.

Early in February Rolette came back from Pauquette's post with information that the Winnebagos were gathering again. They were ostensibly in a fury about Red Bird's wasting away; their medicine men had foretold Red Bird's death soon, and they were determined to take meat. However, said Rolette, they had given up Red Bird and were not really concerned about him, though they were telling the English that the Americans were poisoning him; it was Dodge's occupation of the lead mines that angered them. Rolette was sardonic.

"You see how little our efforts amount to," he complained, walking up and down in the Company office, his hands in his pockets. "If it isn't the agents, it's the delinquency of the military. No one has done a thing about the occupation of the lead country, and the past treaties have all guaranteed this land for the Indians. *Sacré bleu!* how many more Indians and white men will die before this matter is settled."

Hercules sighed and pointed out that settlement would be made only one way; it would not be a closed matter until the whites frankly owned the lead-mining region. Surely Rolette knew that?

Rolette did. He said he would go over and talk to Major Fowle and learn if possible what action would be taken.

"I'll go along," said Hercules. "I'm going to talk to Red Bird if he's still able to talk."

They walked over to the barracks, Rolette commenting absently upon the broken-down appearance of the fort. They would certainly need to build a new one soon. Not of wood, however, since it was clear that with water four feet deep inside the barracks every time the river came up after the thaws in spring, no wood would long withstand decay. He gazed casually around him and said that, with all his holdings, it was a pity he would have little to sell to the government, since it was obvious that the best place for the fort was that high knoll, where the Indian mounds were, the place where Doty had wanted a courthouse built, and Lockwood owned that. They entered the barracks and separated.

Lieutenant McKenzie conducted Hercules to the blockhouse. Red Bird had a room of his own, a bleak room, barren of all ornament. It was high-ceilinged and beamed in rough oak. Only one oblong window permitted light to enter the room, and this was crossed with bars and high, so that Red Bird could see little but the sky. A fire burned with desperate cheeriness in the dark room. Red Bird himself lay on his pallet against one wall, his head turned toward the window, his eyes fixed upon the blue sky, with a longing so strong that it was as of physical pain, his whole being seeming to be given to the outer air while his flesh languished here within these walls. He was clad still in the white suit in which he had surrendered at the Portage, but he was now pitifully wasted and gaunt, a man certainly with the mark of death upon him.

Hercules walked into the room and stood where Red Bird could see him. Slowly the chieftain turned his head.

"Do you know me, Red Bird?" asked Hercules.

Red Bird said that he did and named him.

Hercules sat down, in the cross-legged manner of an Indian, and told him why he had come. He spoke of the unrest among the Winnebagos, and said that some word from Red Bird would be good to carry to them now, lest they rise up again and suffer worse massacre.

Red Bird agreed with this, but he would not send word. "I will not betray them. I am no white man. What could I say to them? If I told them to trust the white man, they would say, 'Red Bird is out of his mind; the Great Spirit has taken Red Bird's mind already.' I would not give them this hope. When the white man first came into our country, we trusted him, we welcomed him as a brother. He came among us as a friend, but we did not know him. We saw him as a creature like ourselves, a creature who walked on two legs and had arms and could speak and make himself understood in a manner similar to ours. It is now years since then, and we have come to know this white man who calls himself our brother. Their traders made us drunk and robbed us of our justly earned goods and our women; their settlers stole our lands; their soldiers shot us and hunted us and the Great White Father made us presents with one hand and broke his treaties with us with the other." He spoke slowly, with an effort, and it was painful to listen.

Presently Hercules said that in so far as the Winnebagos were concerned, they believed that Red Bird was starved, and they should at least be told that this was not true, for it was apparent that Red Bird took food.

"But I starve," answered Red Bird in a voice terrible for its sudden strength and the imprisoned violence of it. All his fierce longing came tearing out of him now, and his voice made tangible the poignance of his imprisonment, the shutting away of this primitive child of the wilderness, whose kinship had always been to tree and bird, to flower and cloud, who knew the pungence of the massasauga and the voice of the wind in the trees, who read the message of turned blade and leaf, who knew the portents of the

seasons in their majestic passage and responded to them, spoke to them in his spirit without word or sign beyond the intangible oneness of himself with nature. "It is not of the body. It is my spirit that starves. The red man was never meant to be put into a narrow room. If the soldiers mean to kill me, why do they not do so? Since it has been decided that a rope is to be put around my neck, why is it not done? If I have earned the punishment, let it be inflicted upon me. But I have done nothing to earn this slow death. They have put me away where I cannot see even the Big River, the Father of Waters. They have put me into this dark room where I know when the corn is in the tassel only by its sweetness on the air, and I know the green has come upon the earth only by the warming rains, and the winter by its snow. If I have committed a crime, let me be punished honorably. But they will not; they will wait until my spirit leaves my body pale and feeble for its journey."

As he spoke, the aspects of earth that came from his lips became tangible in the room; so great was the terrible nostalgia in his voice that Hercules could smell the stirring fecund fragrance of corn in bloom, the wonderful fresh sweetness of rains on the spring soil and foliage, the frosty coldness of the snow. When Red Bird finished, he turned his head to the wall and would say nothing more, lying motionless, already walking in his spirit into the world beyond, passing into that place where no one would shackle him and wall him away from the beautiful land, away from the familiar spirits with whom he had communion, from West Wind, and Water Spirit, and Thunder Eagle, and all those other intimate old friends, those servants of the Great Spirit, Gitchee Manitou.

There was nothing for Hercules to say. He left the room silently, and McKenzie, who had waited outside, locked the door again. He was taken again with the same violent depression which had come upon him at the time of Red Bird's surrender, for everything the dying chieftain had said was true; the traders had enslaved many of the braves to liquor, causing them to plunder and murder; the settlers had stolen their land and slain all their game with a wantonness which betrayed their complete and devastating ignorance of the laws of nature; and finally the soldiers aided the government in its shameful abrogation of those treaties signed in all good faith by the Indians. It had been so from the beginning; not

alone in the Michigan Territory, but as far away in place and time as early New York State. Even more moving was the mnemonic image of Red Bird imprisoned: the slow dying of this proud spirit removed from the nurture of his familiar earth. This image tore at him, ate at his mental peace insidiously, gnawing away throughout his waking and his sleeping hours, all the more tenaciously because of his inability to aid Red Bird in any way, since he knew the refusal of officials to act, the passing of authority from one hand to another and so achieving endless delay, the binding tape of laws designed almost as if alone to hamper kindness and temper mercy.

In mid-February Red Bird died, and soon intelligence of the Winnebago mutterings against the white settlement at Prairie du Chien reached the village. When the snow was going out, Thunder Walker came by night to where Hercules worked in his office and informed him that one of the Winnebago chiefs, Corumna the Lame, was coming in to lay his grievances before the agent, Street.

"What grievances now?" asked Hercules.

Thunder Walker expressed his displeasure at Hercules' short memory. It was the lead mines, of course. Hercules had knowledge of this for some time, for many moons. And the Winnebagos were growing steadily more angry about this illegal occupation of their lands. "This man Dodge beats his chest and says he will protect the settlers, and always more come; they take the lead away from us and they use our land."

"When will Corumna come?"

"In the morning. When the sun is so high." He made an angle to indicate the sun's height at ten o'clock. He went on to say that Dodge had armed fifty of his men and they were determined to keep the lead mines. Dodge had even brought in two black men to help him, and they had raised as much as two thousand pounds a day. The Winnebagos were helpless, unless they wished to shed blood; they did not wish to do this now. He went on to speak at great length of all the wrongs inflicted upon the Winnebagos, and he said that it would not be long now until the white men would try to remove them to the trans-Mississippi; their medicine men had foretold it because it had happened so with all the others.

Then he went out, having worked himself into anger at the white men.

Hercules was troubled, though he anticipated no danger. He knew, if indeed he had not known before, that it was not the Indians the trade had to fear, but the rapacity and greed of the white settlers who stirred the Indians to anger and bloodshed.

In the morning he went to the agency a little before ten o'clock. Street and Marsh were both there; Street was busy writing a report to Governor Cass. He had already learned of the occupation of the lead mines and of Dodge's success in holding them; he was accordingly writing to the governor to inquire as to what action might be taken.

"What will be the effect of these high-handed measures, I'm at a loss to say," he said to Hercules. "What can I tell the Winnebagos?"

"Tell them you are their friend," said Marsh dryly.

Street glared at him, his patrician face pale with sudden anger. He turned to Hercules again, waving his pen and saying, "I don't understand Dodge or men like him. They know they're causing trouble and needlessly exposing innocent people to slaughter."

"I think Dodge is not a gentleman," observed Marsh with the same dry humor.

At this moment Corumna came, walking with upright dignity despite the lameness of his right leg. He was accompanied by ten braves, eight of whom stayed outside. Two of them came in with him and sat down cross-legged on the floor, one on each side of Corumna, who stood before Street, his lined old face leather-brown and free of paint now. He shrugged out of his blanket, though he held it to his sides and abdomen with partly folded arms, and he made a little speech to say that he had found it necessary to see the agent.

Street assured him that he was there for the purpose of listening to the Indians and of speaking to them about their differences among themselves and with the white men. If there were anything he could remedy, he need but to know it.

Thereupon Corumna launched at once into his grievances. He told about Dodge and his occupation of the lead mines. It was true that white men had occupied the mines before this time, but

they had left them again during the search for Red Bird. After this Dodge had come with armed men to take the mines and he had driven all the Indians away, threatening to murder them if they returned. "We did not expect this, and we want to know when this will stop. The hills are covered, more white men come each week, and shove us off our lands to make the lead. We want our Father to stop this before blood may be shed."

The implied threat was so mild that it was some moments before Street was aware of what Corumna had said. When it came to him, he betrayed his alarm by the sudden narrowing of his eyes and the paling of his cheeks. He controlled himself quickly, brushing at his narrow moustache. Did the Winnebagos mean to fight? he demanded.

Corumna nodded slowly. If the white men were not put off their lands, they would fight. How was it, he demanded, that each time an Indian went on a white man's land, he was driven off, but when a white man took an Indian's land, nothing was done to him? "Is the law different for the red man? Is there one law for a red man and another for a white man? Why is this? Why has it always been so?"

Street said that the law was precisely the same for both white men and red. "We are brothers," he repeated several times.

"We would not call such men our brothers," said Corumna. "We would put them out of the tribe for doing these things to us. But you have done nothing to them, and if you do not we must."

Street turned and took up the letter he had been writing. "Even now I am writing to our Father, the Governor, to ask him what to do."

Corumna looked askance at the paper waved before him. "The Winnebago does not trust the white man's words or his papers," he said with great dignity, drawing his blanket around him in preparation for his leave-taking. Besides, he added, did the agent write letters each time the Indians did anything wrong? No, he did not; he sent the soldiers. Why was there again this difference?

There was no answer to this but action of some kind. On the moment, Street made his decision; he turned away from the letter and glanced at Marsh, who read his superior's mind and pressed his lips firmly together, lest he make some outburst.

"I will show you," said Street, "that we are brothers. I will send Captain Marsh to the hunting ground of the Winnebagos. He will speak to Dodge and send him away in peace."

Marsh grinned with patent mockery.

Corumna was delighted, as Street doubtless foresaw. He knew the Winnebagos believed in Marsh, and he could assure Street that the Winnebagos would withhold their action against the settlers until after Marsh had been there. He did so volubly, his protestations almost embarrassing Street.

Street said he would write a letter ordering Dodge to move at once, and give this into Marsh's hands for delivery. He would send Marsh without delay. He sat down, suiting his actions to his words, and took up his pen, making such a show of this trivial business that Corumna was persuaded to believe his mission accomplished; accordingly, he ceremoniously bade Street farewell, accepted presents from Marsh, who gave him far more than customary with the sole desire to pique Street, who goggled at Corumna leaving the agency with an armful of things Marsh had handed to him. He could hardly wait until the Winnebago chieftain had left the building before he turned angrily to Marsh.

The subagent was ready for him. "This playing at brother to the Indian is expensive, eh?" He smiled disarmingly. "Of course, if you can do so with some one else's property and life at stake, it's easier."

Hercules got up and slipped unnoticed from the building. Far down the street Corumna went on his horse, his braves riding slightly behind him. Always tomorrows, thought Hercules; always promises to mature on some tomorrow, a tomorrow that never comes, and is never meant to come.

Marsh came back from his mission within the month. He had gone along the river to English Prairie, and had then travelled overland to the place the miners called Dodgeville, in honor of their bold leader. He had given Dodge Street's message, had read to the assembled miners the agent's order and the treaty guaranteeing the Winnebagos their lead lands. But Dodge had spoken as soon as Marsh had finished, to say that in his opinion there were no definite lines of demarcation between the lands ceded by the

Chippewas and Ottawas and other Indians of the Territory, and those of the Winnebagos; until such lines were put down, he intended to stay where he was. So did his men. Marsh reported that Dodge had already put up a small stockade and that twenty or twenty-five log houses were in evidence, together with much lead, being mined by over two hundred armed men. Dodge had said he might leave the country when it was convenient for him, but he had also said that, if the Indians wanted their lands, they might try to take them from him.

Street was incensed. He ordered Major Fowle to evict the miners. Major Fowle replied that he had but a little over a hundred men fit for duty, and simply could not do so. The trouble about the Winnebago lead-mining country became a little drama of wills. Clocking its pulse from the office of the American Fur Company, Rolette was stirred to frequent hilarity. Hercules, however, was downcast.

"What will it come to?" he asked. "Do these men have no shred of honor?"

"Oh, give Street his due. He's trying to do what the law tells him he may do. But of course it's easy to make the law and then forget to send up enough men to enforce it, and so veto it anyway. *Sacré bleu!* do not be so young, Dousman. As to what it will all come to—why, that," he said slowly, with relish, "that is the most obvious thing of all: it will come to another treaty. The Indians will be asked down to parley, they will load them up with presents and liquor, they will sign papers, and all will be well— until the glow wears off, and then the Winnebagos will begin all over again. You'll see."

Hercules had no doubt that Rolette was right. He was. The mutterings, the grumblings, the sudden panics of unreasonable fear: these manifestations continued throughout the spring and summer. In August Governor Cass met with the principal chiefs of the Winnebago nation at Green Bay for the purpose of purchasing the mineral lands of that nation. There was little else he could do, since by that time ten thousand settlers had forced their way into the lead country. There was even less the Indians might do, and they surrendered eight million acres of their most beautiful land.

"Now perhaps we'll have something like a lasting peace!" cried Hercules.

Rolette was sardonic, as always. "Not as long as Marsh serves the Sioux," he said unequivocally. But he would not predict what might happen, save to say that the Winnebagos would presently regret their loss of the lead country, and the dissension would start all over again. "God help them," he said, "because it's certain the white men won't."

Hercules felt a queer, angry tightening at his heart. Memory of all his resolves and intentions rushed upon him, overwhelming him, leaving in its wake a cloying bitterness at the futility of trying to teach men justice. God help me, he thought; I am becoming wealthy by virtue of the things I hate! It was true, for despite the disruption of the trade from time to time by the dissensions among the Indians, despite the partiality of the military, the greed of the incoming settlers, the invasion of the lead mines and the destruction of the wilderness with its inevitable pushing westward of game, his income from the trade did not appreciably diminish, and his circumstances steadily improved. But if his desire for financial security was being satisfied, the far greater desire for social service was not. His father's caution came to him: *a man must compromise between what he wants and what he can have.* He looked at Rolette's back and thought dispassionately of how much Rolette enjoyed life; and he thought, too, that he was no stranger to compromise, for he had compromised about Rolette's wife, though the image of Jane still held tenaciously to his mind's eye from day to day.

He sighed, depressed, and turned to the maze of figures on the table before him.

5.

And Half to Fall

1828-1830

THE year wore on.

That summer Rolette went to Mackinac with the furs, not because he wished especially to make the trip, but because he had certain business matters to settle in Cincinnati, and because he was to go from there to St. Louis and meet Elizabeth, his daughter by the wife who had died before he had known Jane Fisher save as the child in the Brisbois home. Elizabeth, now fourteen, had completed her education in the private school of Madame de Lechene, and Rolette wished to make full settlement for her edution before she left for Prairie du Chien.

When the older man came up from St. Louis, he found Hercules restive and depressed. It was a hot day in late summer, with the dusty air dry and unpleasant. Hercules scarcely noticed the quiet girl who stood behind her father, her shy brown eyes held to Rolette. He was introduced, and seemed absent, a certain preoccupation apparently dividing his interest. Rolette took his daughter home and came back to the office.

"What's wrong, Hercules?"

"Nothing."

Rolette fixed him with his keen eyes and presently decided that Hercules might in his own belief be speaking the truth. Nevertheless, something was there to make him restive. He was shrewd enough to divine the cause of Hercules' unrest, though he could not know how largely Jane loomed in his partner's thoughts, how disturbing the constant thought of her might be to Hercules. He sat down.

"D'you know Scott Campbell, Hercules?"

"Yes."

"He's the son of John Campbell, an Indian agent sometimes known as Archibald Campbell. His mother was a Sioux, and his wife is half French and half Menominee. D'you know his daughter, Margaret?"

Hercules was mystified. What is he getting at? he wondered. "Why, I may have seen her. I don't remember. I don't have much time to look at women, Rolette."

Rolette slapped the table with the palm of his hand. "What burns you, Hercules? A man needs a woman. You're twenty-eight now. A man your age isn't cut out to be a bachelor." He snorted.

Hercules chuckled. "I've managed to get along without a woman," he said. But he thought of Jane, and he could not help thinking, too, of the futility of his love for her. And he was conscious that he had not heeded his own belief in compromise insofar as Jane was concerned. It was true; his restlessness now stemmed from his growing dissatisfaction with his lonely existence, the knowledge that Jane was bound inextricably away from him.

"There are many attractive women in or near the settlement," pursued Rolette.

"I don't think I can persuade myself to take an Indian or half-breed mistress," said Hercules bluntly. "In any case, it would be on my initiative."

Rolette stood up casually. "Certainly, certainly. *Mille tonnerre!* I'm too busy to order any one's life for him. And by the same sign, you're too busy to burn needlessly." He shrugged and went out.

Hercules looked thoughtfully after him.

In two days Rolette came in with Scott Campbell and his daughter Margaret. Campbell was a broad-shouldered man of an indeterminate age; he hardly noticed Hercules. Neither, for that matter, did Rolette, save to indicate Margaret casually and say to Hercules, "I've a little business to attend to with Campbell here; I'll leave his daughter in your care."

Hercules got up and bowed. "Will you be seated, Miss Campbell?"

"Yes, thank you." She sat down and looked demurely at her hands clasped in her lap.

He went on with his figures, but in a few minutes looked up. If she were marked by her breeding, it was only in her high cheekbones, betraying her Indian ancestry. She was not only not an unattractive woman; she was physically good to look upon, a dark-eyed, dark-haired woman, whose growing maturity was manifest in the curve of her breasts and the slight thickness of her thighs. He thought of her as comely, marking the full, broad mouth, the straight, well-formed nose. She had long, pointed ears. He returned to his work but presently looked up again, conscious that he ought to say something and not leave her sitting there as if she were no one.

He observed that it had not been his good fortune to see Miss Campbell before.

She smiled uncertainly, exposing two rows of perfect, if somewhat large, white teeth. "I saw Mr. Dousman at a maple-syrup party at the brook last spring," she said. "He was with Monsieur and Madame Rolette."

He cast his mind quickly back to the party. "Indeed," he said, "I'm afraid I was much occupied that day. I believe they gave me some work to do."

She nodded. "Yes, they did. They put you to watching the boiling."

"So you see, I had little time to look around." He smiled.

"Yes, I know," she said. Her pleasant smile faded, and her eyes fell once more to her hands.

He saw that she had long, thin fingers, and stared at them a moment, still gripping his pen.

"I don't believe I've seen you at any of the dances," she said casually, without looking up. "Don't you dance?"

He laughed. "Why, I do, but it's true, I haven't danced much here. I've been very busy, you see. The fur trade——"

"I know about the fur trade," she said.

He put down his pen and regarded her frankly. He did not have a doubt that Rolette had deliberately arranged for her to be here alone with him so that Hercules could see how attractive she was. Hercules was disconcerted. In the first place, the woman *was*

attractive; she did not have the look of a half-breed; she had, moreover, an air of passionate intensity which held him, a tangible presence which escaped her determination to be demure before him. He could not help wondering whether Rolette had said anything to her.

At this moment Rolette came back, talking busily to Campbell, and, again without seeming to notice Hercules, went on through and out of the office. Margaret got up, excused herself, and followed them.

Hercules gazed after the three of them with amused tolerance for Rolette's subterfuge and a faint interest in Margaret Campbell, who stood so still waiting in the late summer sunlight for her father to finish his business with Rolette.

Within a fortnight he saw her again. He had gone to the ball at the fort, intending to stay only long enough to have the pleasure of a dance with Jane. The officers and ladies of the fort were few in number, and the ladies were augmented by some of the younger half-breed women from the village. Among these was Margaret Campbell. Hercules did not see her until he was dancing with Jane. Seeing her then in her more formal clothes, he could not help looking at her longer than he might ordinarily have looked.

"Ah, Mistaire Dousman has see some girl," said Jane softly. "He stare so, his eyes they show. Is she pretty, Mistaire Dousman?"

"Why, yes, I guess she is. But Madame well knows that all beauty fades before her own."

Jane smiled. "How wondairful it would be if my huban' would say such nice things to me. But he do not. He is too busy to think of them. Or pairhaps he do think of them and do not have time to speak them. Where is this woman?"

As decorously as possible, he indicated Margaret.

Jane looked at her openly, critically. "Well, yes, she is pretty, Mistaire Dousman. Of course, she is half-breed. I do not know what to say to you. Do you like her then?"

He laughed. "I have but a speaking acquaintance with her."

"Could you love a half-breed woman, then?"

"I don't know," he answered, laughing again. "I've never tried."

"Nevaire?"

He shook his head. "Surely Madame must know that my heart is hers, that I am doomed to a hopeless passion?" He said this in so bantering a manner that she was deceived and accepted it again as a jesting tribute to her.

She smiled and half-closed her eyes. "Will you dance with this woman?" she asked presently.

"I think I may," he said. "But Madame will understand that it's only because it's impossible for me to take all the dances with her."

"My Oncle Brisbois he have tell me long ago to pay no attention to men who flattaire. Mistaire Dousman, you are flattaire' me."

"Ah, Madame, the truth can never be flattery."

She sighed and held tightly to him, so that he was loath to release her when the fiddlers stopped playing. Rolette came over to take her from him, and Colonel McNeil made his way toward them. Hercules excused himself and sought out Margaret Campbell, who was momentarily alone. He introduced himself anew.

"I remember Mr. Dousman very well," she said quietly.

He asked her whether he might have the pleasure of a dance in the course of the evening, the next one, perhaps?

She nodded quickly, and in a few moments they were on the floor together. She danced well, she stood well in his arms, complementing his height, she did not make any unnecessary conversation, answering his questions when he asked them, and otherwise dancing with an easy effortlessness. He found himself liking her very much. She was not in any way undignified and yet managed to be gay; she could show that she enjoyed herself only by the glowing of her eyes and her shy smile. Presently, he asked whether he might dance with her a second time.

During his second dance with her, he found himself asking whether he might call on her some evening.

Yes, of course, he might, she said.

But he did not go. He thought of Jane and could not go, haunted by the tenacity of her in his memory.

He grew steadily more restive. Seeing Jane from time to time, he became always more conscious of the futility of his affection for her, she who was content to be the wife of King Rolette, twenty-three years older than she, to live in the most imposing house in

Prairie du Chien as the wife of a man slowly but surely growing rich, a man who gratified her every wish without the necessity of himself thinking overmuch of her save as his possession. His restiveness mounted finally to become almost unbearable. He paced the floor, unable to work. He found new things to do, all to no avail. He could not always live a celibate life; Rolette was right. He could not live alone all his life. This restlessness impaired his work. He thought more often of his dream of wealth. How could he achieve any end at all so long as he was scourged by his flesh and the normal need of his flesh?

Rolette came in one night while Hercules was in the midst of his fleshly agony.

"I was just passing," he said, sitting on the edge of the table Hercules used for his desk. "Saw your light. I just saw Campbell off. The man thinks himself rich ever since McNeil took over his coulee for a military garden. He's gone to the Portage to help build the new fort there—so he says. But he's a trader; not a builder." He looked around him. "Are you at work?"

"In a fashion," answered Hercules wryly.

"I may send Jane east for the winter," Rolette continued casually. "She might enjoy it again. I'll be gone most of the winter anyway, since you can handle the Company's affairs better than I can. I never had much head for figures."

Hercules spoke only in monosyllables.

Rolette looked at him with his keen eyes from time to time. Presently he said that it was clear Hercules meant to be alone. "A man burns better alone," he said. "If he insists upon burning," he added pointedly. He came to his feet and added casually that the weather was turning colder slowly; the autumn was coming in. The brigades would soon be going out again. He added from the threshold that wonders would never cease, Judge Doty was going to try Wamangoosgaraha and his companions at last during this month of September. "Unless he changes his mind again," he added. He vanished into the night.

Hercules scarcely heard him. He thought of Jane's going east again. If she went, he would be more alone than ever, denied even the sight of her. But in a moment he thought that this futile love would only be kept alive by the occasional sight of Jane, and the

futility of it might never be lessened if she were always within reach. He put out his candles and stood for some time in the darkness, peering out into the night-bound village. A south wind blew gently into the room carrying the fragrance of the rivers and the sloughs, the pungence of dying leaves and herbs.

Slowly, the image of Margaret Campbell rose before his mind's eye. He began to contemplate her, at first with hesitation, at last with growing interest. His thought of her was coupled with a certain bitterness at the fullness of his realization that his love for Jane was hopeless, destined only to failure. His pulse quickened, and he thought with shame that his flesh stifled his heart. But he understood that he could not forever endure this agony of loneliness, this fierce desire for something unattainable, the pounding demands of his healthy young body.

He went hesitantly to the door, opened it, and stepped outside. He went through the business of locking it, tried it, and finally turned to look into the night. A light still shone at the agency house; in Brunet's tavern a few Indians sat, revealed in the open door; at the fort a dozen windows showed yellow. He looked up; the sky was cloudless, swept with stars in their cold distance, with the Pleiades and Aldebaran mounting the east, and the stars of the summer night sloping westward, Arcturus winking its amber eye low in the northwest. Dogs barked across the Marais de St. Feriole, a staccato sound breaking sharply into the night's quiet.

He sighed and looked briefly at the dark shadow of Rolette's house, reared upward with no light to mark its windows.

Then he turned and began to walk slowly, inexorably toward Scott Campbell's house.

Margaret opened the door to him. She stood for a second on the threshold, not knowing what to say; then she moved back, so that he might come in, saying nothing.

"Are you alone, Margaret?" he asked.

"Yes," she said quietly, closing the door and standing momentarily with her back against it, her eyes burning toward him in the semi-dark of the little hall.

He took her hand and led her toward the parlor. "I'm alone too," he said. "I think sometimes I've been alone too long."

She followed him without protest, even to allowing herself to be

drawn down beside him on the sofa. He sat looking at her quietly, marking her intense dark eyes all over again, as if he had not seen them before. He thought that if she were pliable, there was still within her a core of pride.

"I don't see you out very much," he said. "Surely a girl as attractive as you are, Margaret, has beaux?"

She gazed at him fixedly. "I don't go out," she said presently. "If I have beaux, I haven't encouraged them."

"But surely there's some one you like?"

She nodded shyly, a smile lurking at her lips.

"Perhaps I can help," he said, smiling.

"I'm afraid not. You see, it's Mr. Dousman."

His pulse quickened. For a moment longer he was still; then he drew her into his arms and met her lips, warm and eager for his own.

In December the Indians were stirred into activity once more. This time it was not against the whites. But any activity was dangerous, since no one could predict with any degree of certainty what an Indian might do next. Chief Morgan of the Fox had raided the territory of the Sioux and fallen upon a hunting party of Dacotahs, killing a squaw, and abducting the wife and child of a chieftain. The Crazy Bull reported it to Hercules, with heated anger; he went also, at Hercules' behest, to the agency house and alarmed Street by his graphic account of the outrage and his dire threats of reprisals. Street was beset by visions of massacres in which the victims were predominantly white. He had a fine feeling for panic, in any case, and dispatched Marsh at once to find Morgan's camp and take from him the squaw and her child. "Make any threats you care to make!" he ordered. "Tell Morgan the army will wipe out his camp if he does not return the captives."

Crazy Bull came back and reported this to Hercules, repeating his threats.

Hercules calmed him. What good could be achieved by making war now? The Dacotahs could not fight a war against the might of the white men. They knew this very well. He was cogent and resourceful.

Crazy Bull was subdued to mutterings and grumblings.

Marsh set out on the edge of winter and came back in February.

Within a week, Street appeared at the Company's office. He was in a towering rage. He could hardly speak, but walked up and down muttering angrily against Marsh. Hercules could not quiet him. What had Marsh done? Surely nothing worse than some of the things he had done previously.

Street replied directly enough. Marsh had done much more. "He carried a war challenge to the Sioux from a band of Chippewas he met on the Black River. Think of it—my subagent serving as an ambassador for the Indians! I had it just now from one of the traders. The Sioux are sending runners to all their warriors and ordering them to return to their villages. What do you expect that to do to your business?"

Hercules agreed that it would do no good.

"I should think not. I don't know what to believe of that man," he went on. "Sometimes I think he's brave and resourceful; but now I think he's just a plain damned fool! Conceive of it, if you can!"

Hercules replied quietly that he could imagine it very well indeed. Marsh had always been partial to the Sioux. His wife was a Wahpeton half-breed. Still, it must be admitted that the Sioux would have received the Chippewa warning whether or not Marsh had brought it.

"Nevertheless, I'm writing General Clark at once," pursued Street. "This isn't the only thing. You know very well how assiduously he's done everything he can for his Dacotahs. I'm going to file charges against him."

Hercules gave it as his opinion that Marsh might be better in the agency than out of it.

Street made no effort to understand this. He was in too great a fury against Marsh to heed any defense of his subagent. He went back to his agency and wrote a letter filled with charges against Marsh, and presently, with the slowness so characteristic of government, the War Office notified Marsh that he had lost his office.

Within two days Marsh had bought a house from Brunet, a house fronting on the Mississippi. Within a week Prairie du Chien knew that Marsh had opened a store to sell merchandise. What Kapolequa informed Hercules at once was not generally known: that Marsh

was also selling guns, rifles and ammunition to the Indians in direct defiance of the law.

This was to be expected. Rolette, who was in the office at the time Kapolequa came in, said shortly that there was nothing Hercules or any one else could do just at present. "As long as he's still a justice of the peace, he can fine himself. And he would, too. Besides, the military are too concerned now about the new fort rising across the Marais de St. Feriole, and one trader more or less selling guns to the Indians can't make much difference to them."

Hercules protested. Surely it was madness to permit this sale, especially when Marsh's partiality for the Sioux was so well known.

"Are you motivated by the business or by humanitarian considerations?" asked Rolette.

"Both," answered Hercules. 'You know very well that every time trouble stirs among the Indians, the volume of furs goes down. And if the trouble increases, it won't be long before the Indians are packed up and moved west."

"It won't be long in any case," said Rolette dryly. "Have you thought of buying land, Dousman?"

Hercules smiled. "I've already bought some," he said. "I've arranged to take over the land occupied by the old fort as soon as the new quarters are ready. I think some day of building a house there on the mound where the fort stood."

"Buy more. After the trade is done, the land will remain. People are coming in, every year more of them."

But this talk did not settle the matter of Marsh and his business. Rolette gave it as his opinion that if Marsh were left alone, he would settle himself in the course of a short time. Besides, he would be certain to do very little illegal business for the next few weeks because already Indians and commissioners were converging toward Prairie du Chien for the grand council which every one hoped would settle all the Indian differences. He reminded Hercules that he was to sit in at the council.

Hercules assured him that he had not forgotten.

"By the way," said Rolette, coming back from the threshold, "the new surgeon has just arrived at the fort. Comes from Mackinac. Says he knows you."

"What's his name?"

"Beaumont. William Beaumont. They say he's a great one for experimenting."

"Why, of course I know him. He's the man who saved Alexis St. Martin's life when he was shot in the abdomen at Mackinac. One of the Company's men. No one expected him to do it." He got up. "I'll go over right away."

Rolette sat down on the threshold, facing outward. He complained of the heat, his voice rumbling after Hercules on his way to the fort.

Beaumont had not changed. He was a slight, spry man in his early thirties, with a head of thick, curly hair; he was very energetic and emphatically voluble. His eyes gleamed with pleasure at sight of Hercules, whom he recognized while he was yet some distance away from where Beaumont stood. He came hurrying forward, clasped one of Hercules' hands in both his own, and shook it violently, his smile broad.

"Dousman. How good to see you! You look well, too. We're here now, all of us. And what do you think? St. Martin is back with me! I've got him to come back, and now I shall learn all about the digestion."

He was enthusiastic, though Hercules did not immediately understand his reference. His last intelligence of St. Martin was that the voyageur was back in the trade. He interrupted Beaumont's reference to his wife to make further inquiry about St. Martin. What did the doctor mean by saying he had got him to come back?

Why, it was very simple, Beaumont explained with that slightly vexed air so common to people who are perpetually in a hurry and expect others always to apprehend their full meaning no matter how slight their reference. St. Martin's gunshot wound had never entirely healed; there was an opening, a hole directly into his stomach so that Beaumont could see what went on there. He had hoped to make several experiments in digestion and record his findings, but St. Martin had gone off before he could do so. Now at last he had persuaded him to come back into his service. He was here now, at the fort. He paused to look around him, seeking among the officers and privates moving constantly about the compound making ready for the visitors scheduled to arrive for the Indian council, and, seeing the voyageur presently, hailed him.

St. Martin came over. Him, too, Hercules recognized; he had seen him often coming in with the brigades at Mackinac; he had heard his voice raised in the carefree songs of the voyageurs. St. Martin had long ago won his feather of merit. But for all that he was still a young man, though he was bearded and moustached, and his busy eyebrows jutted forth above his blue eyes. He was not, apparently, in a pleasant mood, though he was courteous enough to Hercules in his careless way.

"You'll miss Michilimackinac, St. Martin," said Hercules.

"*Oui,*" agreed the voyageur shortly. He indicated Beaumont with one thumb and added. "He pull me aroun' all over to see into ma insides." He was evidently very tired of Beaumont's direction.

Beaumont waved him away, warning him to take care of himself, to remember the opening, not to jeopardize in any way the success of the experiments he hoped to perform. He turned back to Hercules and said that he must meet Mrs. Beaumont; she had gone to their quarters, but would doubtless be pleased to see him.

At that moment one of the officers confronted them: a man of medium height, whose full face was distinguished chiefly by his firm, uncompromising mouth and his striking eyes, now fixed upon Hercules. But he addressed the surgeon. Was his companion by any chance the Astor agent, Hercules Dousman?

Assured that he was, the officer made a curt bow. "Colonel Zachary Taylor, the new commandant, at your service, sir. Mr. Caleb Atwater, the United States Commissioner, has just arrived and is anxious to see you before the Indian chieftains begin to come in tonight or tomorrow. Would it be possible for you to see him now?"

"Certainly," replied Hercules.

Taylor turned and motioned to a fellow officer. "Lieutenant Jefferson Davis will conduct you to Mr. Atwater. You'll excuse Mr. Dousman, Doctor Beaumont?"

But Beaumont was already hurrying in another direction. Lieutenant Davis came up: a slight, soft-eyed young man with fine, almost feminine features. He acknowledged his introduction to Dousman with a faint air of condescension, but this was defensive, for he was soon talking companionably. He had never before been

this far north, he said. He was a southerner by birth and inclination. Did it grow extremely cold here? Hercules assured him that it did. The lieutenant spoke of Colonel Taylor, he mentioned his daughter, Knoxie, with a singular animation, so that Hercules guessed that at least some part of his inclination was held to the north.

The Commissioner sat on the sagging verandah up against the fort wall, well out of the hot summer sun. He was a big man, broad-shouldered, large-boned, with a long, rectangular face, full and broad, and made even broader by heavy side-burns. His flinty blue eyes examined Hercules as he approached, his square, prognathous jaw moved a little from side to side, as if he were chewing at something. His big, hairy hands held firmly to the arms of his chair until he got up.

"Mr. Dousman, my pleasure." He shook hands and offered Hercules his seat.

"Thank you, no," said Hercules.

"Walk with me, then." Atwater stuck his thumbs into his waistcoat pockets, holding his long light coat back, and began to walk slowly down along the verandah, keeping well out of the sun. "I have good fortune to see you so quickly," he said. "The military have sent to Washington all manner of accounts of your good offices on behalf of peace, and of your influence among Indians of all kinds. For that reason, we anticipate your influence on the council a few days hence."

Hercules deprecated the military reports.

Atwater would hear nothing of his modesty. They were all well aware of what a burden it was to strive for peace in such wild country as this, and especially when there was always the constant danger of war among the tribes themselves. He understood the situation between the Chippewas and the Sioux, as well as between the Fox nation and the Sioux and Menominees. The Indians were coming in now, all under the flag of peace, of course. Almost four hundred Winnebago men and many more women were already encamped just outside Prairie du Chien. The leaders of other tribes were coming in. It was possible they might have trouble, since there would be Chippewas, Sioux, Ottawas, Fox, Sauk, Menominees, and Pottawatomis present in addition to the Winnebagos.

Hercules pointed out that some effort would have to be made to rectify the stupid errors which had been permitted to occur.

Atwater stopped in his stride, his hands clasped together across his abdomen, his thumbs still holding to his waistcoat pockets. "I agree with you most emphatically," he said. "We've bought forty tons of goods for the Indians—just to make good all those earlier promises which were never fulfilled!"

Hercules said that this would certainly be of great help.

"Now then," continued Atwater, raising his voice a little. "We've set the opening of council for day after tomorrow in the morning, at about ten o'clock. I'll expect you then." He shook hands again and returned to his seat to wait, he said, for the Indian agent, Street, for whom he had sent an orderly.

Hercules went around to Beaumont's quarters, paid his respects to Mrs. Beaumont, and returned to the Company's office, where he reported to Rolette his conversation with the Commissioner.

Rolette guffawed, his hearty laughter ringing loudly into the quiet afternoon. "So now they wish to appease the Indians!" he shouted. "God damn it, why didn't they treat them like human beings in the first place, eh? They always say an Indian is ignorant, but he's not half as shortsighted as most of the white men he must deal with. Forty tons of goods! *Mon Dieu!* how wonderful that will be for all the traders! They will feel like leaping up and saluting the Commissioner on both cheeks—I don't say! I'll tell you one thing—if they don't push the Indians west of the Mississippi, they won't have peace."

Hercules asked whether Rolette wanted the Indians pushed westward.

"*Sacré nom!* Me, want? No, certainly not. But it's either that or stop the greedy settlers from coming in and taking the Indian lands. And you can be sure they won't do the latter. You must take the practical view of this thing, Hercules."

"I'll try," said Hercules.

The council began as scheduled, but slowly. A shade had been erected near the fort by order of General McNeil; under it stood a raised bench for the commission to sit so that they could face the Indian chiefs. On each side of the commission stood the officers of the army, all in full dress; beyond the shade stood the soldiers,

bright in the sunlight. Behind the commission sat the ladies of the garrison and some of the citizens. Among them Hercules saw Jane Rolette, with her daughter Virginia, whose bright hair she was fluffing absently. She saw him and nodded. The Indian chiefs sat in a semicircle before the shade, chiefs of all nations, even more colorful in their dress than the military and the women behind the commission. The Indians who had come in to the post for the council now numbered well over two thousand; these sat behind their chiefs.

Hercules took his place under the shade, spoke briefly with Pierre Pauquette, who had come down from the Portage and, seeing him, came over to talk, and turned to look among the chiefs. Presently catching Atwater's eye, he said that most of the chiefs were present; only Black Sparrow Hawk of the Sacs was not there.

"Oh, their part of this so far is all right," said Atwater. "I can't say as much for our side of the question. They tell me I must not expose myself between sessions, as if these Indians meant to attack us. This fine feeling of mistrust is not a good note upon which to begin. I'll stay with these people until the treaty is signed. McNeil can do as he likes, and Menard can be in 'ill health' as long as he pleases."

Hercules silently approved.

It was not until almost noon that the council opened. Atwater made a brief, pointed speech in which he said that the council had been called to settle as far as it was possible to do so all the differences that existed between the white men and their red brothers, and especially to ratify the agreement of 1828 in regard to the Winnebago lands, since that agreement had been repudiated by certain of the chieftains. He spoke moderately, making no threats, asking only the co-operation of the chiefs. But it was apparent in his address that he recognized that separate treaties would have to be made with the Winnebagos on the one hand and the Ottawas, Pottawatomis and Chippewas on the other. After he had finished, Menard spoke, bristling a little, and after him, General McNeil, bristling still more; this was calculated to put fear into the chieftains, but there was no sign that they had been impressed. They grunted approval of Atwater's speech, made small sounds after Menard's, were silent after McNeil's.

One by one the chieftains rose and made lengthy protestations

of friendship for their white brothers. As yet, they made no complaints, but it was certain that before the terms of the treaty could be discussed a list of grievances would be presented. This, however, did not come until the third day, when Keokuk rose to speak for the Sacs.

Keokuk was a dignified, middle-aged Indian; he spoke slowly. He began, as customary, with a recital of his long friendship for the whites. He had never been involved in any action against them. He would never be. He trusted the white men, though they had time and again betrayed his trust. But he cogently assumed that, even as there were bad Indians, there were also bad white men. It was true that whereas the Indians would never put bad Indians in positions of power, the white men seemed to follow another practice in this regard. His address rambled presently into a listing of grievances. The white men had squatted on Indian lands and had not been driven off. They had cut down the Indians' wood and had sold it to the steamboats. They had taken the lead mines, they had plundered the hunting grounds, killing game needlessly, they had fired woodlands to make more clear land for themselves. It did not matter to the white man how many animals died to make his clear land; it did not seem to the white man that he, too, was an animal, and that he had no more right to live than lesser animals. It would be well if the white man could look upon the living of animals. They did not fight among themselves. They did not arm themselves and hunt their brothers. They lived upon each other as the Great Spirit ordained, but surely Gitchee Manitou had not meant that His pale-faced, two-legged animal, man, should slay with his guns all the animals around him and leave them to rot? There were years when the buffalo roamed over the Michigan Territory. Where were they now? They were in the West—those which had escaped the white man's rapacity. Already the white man was beginning to slay the beautiful colored pigeon, the passenger bird, not for his food, but for his hogs, which had more food than they could eat in the earth itself. Soon they too would be no more. This was the way of the white man; it was his custom thus to foul his future generations on the earth; it was his custom to make worthless the land by cutting away the beautiful trees; it was his custom to permit rain to wash away the loam. So be it. The red man could

not live in that manner, but he had hoped to live in peace with the white brother. But the white brothers had come and taken the land and lived upon it and desecrated the Indian burial grounds and the corn-hills and made a mockery of the Indians themselves. Was this brotherhood?

He went on like this for some time. The Indians were silent behind him; they were in agreement. The commissioners were sympathetic, the military attentive. Keokuk spoke well, without bitterness, but as with a great weight of sorrow. When he sat down there was no sound, but soon another chieftain rose. This time it was Little Elk of the Winnebagos, a tawny Indian of middle age, gaudily bedecked.

"Many years ago the first white man came among us. He was a Frenchman. He came often, and he brought his brothers. When he came among us, we spoke to him in this fashion: 'How beautiful is the sun, O Frenchman, when you come to visit us. All our village awaits you, and you shall enter all our cabins in peace. It is good, my brother, that you should visit us.' He lived among us as we did. He painted himself, he smoked his pipe with us, sang and danced with us, and married one of our squaws, but he wanted to buy no land of us. Then the redcoat came, and he made us many presents and asked us to fight against the Long Knives from south of the Shawnee country, and the bluecoats from beyond that to the east. And then at last came the bluecoats who wanted to buy our lands and stole them. We thought we knew the white brother when the Frenchman was among us, but the Indians understand the white brother much better now!"

A grunting of approval interrupted him briefly, and he waited, unmoved, his eyes fixed on the commission. After a few moments, he went on, more impassioned now, making many gestures to illustrate his points.

He recapitulated the history of the Winnebagos in their dealings with the whites. Did ever a Winnebago entice a white chief into his wigwam, put into him the evil spirit in the bottle, and then make him sign away his land when he did not know what he was doing? No. No Indian would do that. But the white man would. He had done so, not once, but many times. Did the Winnebagos sign treaties with lesser chieftains and ignore the chieftains whom

the Indians followed? No, they did not. But the white man did. "Even now there is not among us today Chief Black Sparrow Hawk of the Saukenauk. He is bitter across the Father of Waters because the white man enticed the old and feeble chieftains to sign the treaty of 1804 at St. Louis. Who were Pashepaho, Quashquame, Outchequa, Hashequarhiqua? That is his cry. That is our cry, for each nation among us has this same grievance."

He had finished and made his way back to his place, settling himself again with great dignity. One by one, the other chieftains rose to speak, but they said much the same thing; their grievances were all the same, save that there were different dates and chieftains and nations involved. This statement of grievances continued until all the chieftains were heard, so that it was well over a week before the commission had its turn to answer the Indians. All this time Atwater stayed among the Winnebagos, and was convinced that the treaty with that nation was of the utmost importance. He strove accordingly to have the agreement of the commission on this point. Hercules pressed his arguments home to them, and Menard finally conceded that it would be best to deal first with the Ottawas, Pottawatomis and Chippewas. Therefore, Atwater addressed himself first to them.

He listed the concessions the United States asked. He said that payment by the Great White Father would be generous. Sixteen thousand dollars annually forever; twelve thousand dollars in goods as a present now; fifty barrels of salt to be delivered to them annually forever at Fort Dearborn; and the assignment of money and lands to certain Indians and half-breeds would be made. After some further explanation of the terms, the council sat to discuss the area of the lands to be conceded and the payments made. The rights and lands were not as great as those of the Winnebagos, but there was great dissatisfaction and several days were required to come to an agreement.

Finally the chieftains signed, two weeks after the council had opened.

Immediately negotiations were opened with the Winnebagos. Atwater asked Hercules to state to the Indians in their own language what land was required by the Great White Father. Hercules got up and spoke slowly and distinctly, so that every one could

hear. He expressed his friendship for them all; they were well aware of this. He tried to explain why the Great White Father needed this land, but he could not feel that he had been very successful because he was not sympathetic to this movement to gratify the greed of the settlers in the lead regions. He set forth at last the boundaries of the land.

Eight million acres.

This terrain encompassed the entire lead region of Wisconsin and Illinois, without even the exception of the Galena mines about which the Winnebagos had been disgruntled for years. He sat down in silence. There would be no word from the Winnebago chieftains until they knew what they were being offered. They were, in any event, cautious, since some of them had put their marks to a treaty made in the previous year and disposing of this land. They waited for Caleb Atwater to speak, since they knew it was he who headed the commission and could speak directly for the Great White Father. They paid no attention to Menard, who made a conciliatory speech.

Atwater got up finally and stated the terms the United States was prepared to offer. These were, he thought, substantial. Eighteen thousand dollars annually for thirty years would be paid to the Winnebagos, part of it at Prairie du Chien and part of it at Fort Winnebago in proportion to the population centered about each place. At this time, before the council was over, if the Winnebagos signed the treaty, thirty thousand dollars' worth of goods would be presented to them. For the same time, that is, thirty years, the Winnebagos would receive annually three thousand pounds of tobacco and fifty barrels of salt, divided as the annuity had been divided. Certain money, more than twenty thousand dollars, would be paid at once to cancel Indian debts and obligations at present outstanding; land would be assigned, as in the case of the earlier treaty, to Indians and half-breeds; and to Therese Gagnier, widow of the late murdered Registre Gagnier, the Great White Father would pay for fifteen years an annuity of fifty dollars.

The chieftains answered him. Snake Skin wished to know whether the Winnebagos would retain their right to hunt on that land, to which Menard replied that if this activity did not interfere with the white settlers, they might hunt. Whirling Thunder rose and

made a long talk about the evils of war; he listed again all the grievances held against the whites by all Indians, but particularly by the Winnebago, citing at the last the treaty made during the present council with the Ottawas, the Chippewas and the Pottawatomis who had disposed of land which only the Winnebagos owned. To this Atwater replied that the Great White Father had bought the land from both of them, but particularly from the Winnebagos. Four Legs also made a brief speech, entirely conciliatory. After much bristling talk on both sides, it appeared that the chieftains were amenable to the suggestion of the Great White Father that they part with their valuable land for these pieces of gold.

On the first of August they were ready to conclude the council by signing the treaty. The Indians signed first; after them the members of the commission and their staff, Atwater calling out their names: "Charles Hempstead, Joseph Montfort Street, John Kinzie, subagent for Indian affairs; Lieutenant-Colonel Zachary Taylor, Henry Gratiot, William Beaumont, Charles Chouteau, James Estis, Jesse Benton . . ."; and after them, the interpreters placed their signatures.

The council was over.

For this last meeting, Rolette had come over. He now leaned toward Hercules, who had risen from his seat near the commissioners, and said, "How does it feel to take part in such a swindle, Hercules?"

Hercules smiled wearily. He saw it as his partner did, but said nothing.

Menard, however, bridled. His eyes flashed, his lips trembled. "Have a care, sir," he said. "We've conducted this council without coercion of any kind . . ."

Rolette interrupted him suavely. "Ah, Commissioner Menard! I trust the ill health which came upon you every evening and caused your retirement into the safety of the fort will no longer trouble you."

Menard flushed and turned abruptly to Atwater.

From among the officers' ladies, Mrs. Taylor pressed forward. She touched Rolette's arm lightly, smiling mischievously. "Oh, Mr. Rolette, I would not be engaged in the Indian trade," she said. "It seems to me a system of cheating the poor Indians."

Rolette was momentarily taken aback. "Let me tell you, Madame, it's not so easy to cheat the Indians as you imagine. I've tried it these twenty years and never succeeded. Believe me."

Hercules turned and made his way from the shade. He walked among the Indians, absently greeting those he knew. The sun was hot, and a shimmering of heat held to the air. From the concourse of Indians rose a variety of odors, some of them unpleasant, some stimulating, the crushed herbs and spices, the pungent medicine roots carried or worn by Indians and their squaws among the Winnebagos. He looked around for signs of discontent, but there were none; the Winnebagos were making preparation for a celebration that night. He thought with deep relief that now at last peace would come, but presently he was conscious of a lurking fear about the Sioux and their hereditary enemies; neither of them had signed treaties during the council, not enough of their chieftains had come. His fear was rooted in the association between them and Marsh, the former subagent, and he wished heartily that Marsh were gone from Prairie du Chien. Nevertheless, he was convinced that a time of peace lay ahead, and he hurried back to the Company's office as if to work with dispatch before that time might be over. He lost no time in sending runners for all the traders working for the American Fur Company, so that he might acquaint them with the terms of the treaty. He wrote a long and detailed letter to Ramsay Crooks, setting forth these developments. "I am looking forward," he wrote, "to some prosperous years."

The first of the traders came in, and he sat back to wait for the others.

That evening he went over to see Margaret. He met Campbell on the way out, and had the momentary suspicion that the trader had seen him coming and was absenting himself by design; but this could not have been, because it was already dark when Hercules came. After talking briefly with Campbell, who said he was going to one of the islands to meet one of the Indian chiefs, he went into the house. The night was warm, and the house was not comfortable. Off to one side, it had a small vine-covered porch, where, this evening, moonlight filtered whitely among the leaves, making a magic pattern on the floor and walls. It was to this that Margaret led him, complaining of the closeness inside.

He kissed her now with an easy familiarity. Since that initial visit he had come often to see her, and he had grown fond of her. There was no comparing Margaret with Jane, but she offered him a quiet, often shy companionship, betraying time and again her affection for him, and he found himself at ease in her company, rested by the small conversation she made, and growing alive to her ways, the inflections of her voice. She lacked Jane's fire, she did not have Jane's beauty, but she was not unattractive, and her retiring manner was pleasant enough; moreover, she was not bound to a husband, she was free.

On this evening she was dressed becomingly in white, and she was especially quiet. Hercules could not help inquiring about her tiredness. Had she been working too hard?

She shook her head. "No. But papa is very trying sometimes. I think maybe he wants to be rid of me. He would like a different life, I think."

He laughed. "Campbell does as he pleases, it seems to me."

"Unless I do not want him to."

"Oho! But you can't run Campbell. Your father's been his own boss too long for that, Margaret. You ought to know that."

"He tells me often enough. I guess I ought to." She laughed gently and turned from him to look out toward the moon. "Isn't the moon beautiful tonight, Hercules? Look how bright it is outside—and in here, where it's the only light in the darkness."

"There's the light of it in your eyes, too," he said softly, drawing her to him.

The moonlight slanted across her face, pooled in her eyes like black light, its gleam shot through the darkness. An irregular leaf-shadowed patch of it lay across her bosom, all the brighter for the strong, unrelieved white of her dress. He kissed her, his lips holding to hers, releasing her only when she drew away a little. She lay in his arms now, her eyes closed, her lips parted.

"Hercules," she whispered. "I've been in love with you for a long time. I know it isn't something a woman should say, but you, too—I know you're fond of me, even if——"

"I am," he said quietly.

Her eyes flashed open, and she held him closer. She kissed him, and again, her arms tense around him, her body trembling faintly,

holding to him so long that presently her fire was communicated
to him, and his pulse became a wild, frantic drumming in his ears,
and the desire that rose in him could not be put down, the fierce,
exultant primitive power until now strange to his flesh. The moonlight's magic became witchery, a bright glowing, like the night's
eyes upon them.

He picked her up and carried her, stumblingly, into the house
and its darkness.

The year wore on through a wet flaming autumn. The brigades
went out, lone traders made their way into Indian country to the
north and west, and the Territory was at peace. Every sign pointed
to a good year for the trade. Every night found Hercules in his
office. Rolette chided him from time to time. "A man needs so
much sleep, and if he fails to get it, he suffers," he said. But Hercules demurred; he had this or that to get done. He had bought
the land in a certain coulee and meant to put up a mill there if
he could find some one competent enough to run it. He was thinking of putting some money into steamboating. He said that since
his brother George was now in Milwaukee with Solomon Juneau,
he wished to look into the advisability of buying land there; he
thought he would do so. Meanwhile, there were countless details
of the trade which needed attending to, and there were several
quarrels among certain Indian villages which he intended to settle.
Rolette shook his head and left him; the old restlessness was upon
him again; he had not yielded to it for so long that he had begun
to drink more than was his custom, to assuage the hunger for
travel which he did not satisfy. But he would go soon again; the
hunger was too strong in him.

One night some one entered the office while Hercules was in the
back room. Thinking it one of his Indians, Hercules made no
haste to come back; an Indian needed a few moments to meditate
before he spoke, in any case. When he entered the office, he was
surprised to find Scott Campbell there, looking dourly at the fire
on the hearth. Flakes of snow still clung to his heavy beard, and
his fur cap bore a crown of white, melting slowly now in the
room's warmth.

"Evenin'," he said.

"How are you, Campbell?" He sat down, expecting no answer, mildly curious as to the reason for Campbell's visit.

"Mon, I'm fine, e'er since I heerd the news," said Campbell.

Hercules looked up and faced the older man's grave eyes. "What news?" he asked.

Campbell looked incredulous. "Ye don't know?"

"I pride myself on knowing most things as they take place. That's a necessary part of my business, Campbell," said Hercules. "But your actions seem to indicate that you know something that's escaped me."

Campbell expanded his great chest and let forth a long blowing breath. "Mon! I'm to be a grandfather! And I'm thinkin' ye ought to know, Mr. Dousman." His tone changed suddenly, became sly.

Hercules was only momentarily startled. He was then instantly overcome with mingled emotions. Of doubt he felt the least. In the space of a minute he made a rapid revision of his plans for the future, but no sign of it was betrayed in his features. It was indeed possible that Margaret might have his child. He did not feel shame at all, save only that it should come like this.

"Are you sure, Campbell?" he asked.

"Mon, she would na' tell me, till I made a show of beatin' her. My Margaret's no common woman, Dousman. There's been no other mon but you a-callin' on her. But don't alarm yersel'. I think maybe something can be done. If ye'll make me a small payment, we'll say nothing about it."

Hercules got up abruptly, so suddenly that Campbell was startled and half rose in turn. "Don't think to come here begging for money, Campbell," he said coldly. "What's happened is between Margaret and me, and you'll have no part in it. You'll oblige me by staying here until I come back. I want to see Margaret alone."

Campbell nodded, open-mouthed. It had not occurred to him that Hercules would do anything but give him money, as he had suggested. He was disgruntled, but was wary of showing it.

Hercules put on his fur cap and greatcoat and left the office. Snow fell quietly; no wind blew; the night was not cold, for December was not yet far advanced. He thought dispassionately that he had not seen Margaret for some time now; so she could not have told him herself even had she wished. His child! It required

a certain readjustment in his mind to accustom himself to the idea of fatherhood, but with characteristic steadiness, he made it. The Campbell house loomed before him sooner than he thought it would.

When Margaret opened the door to him, he saw that she had been weeping. She strove to conceal the redness of her eyes by keeping her face turned a little from the candlelight when she sat down. He said nothing, took off his coat and cap, and went over to her. Seeing an angry bruise on her forearm, he touched it gently.

"Was it your father, Margaret?" he asked quietly.

She nodded.

He sat down beside her. "You've been crying, Margaret. Did he beat you?"

"Not much."

"I didn't want him to go," she cried. "I tried to keep him from

"Your father came to see me. Is it true, then?"

going. I wanted to tell you myself—if you were to know it at all. But he said . . ." She stopped and would not say more.

"Go on, Margaret," he urged gently.

"He said men like you were not responsible."

"He's wrong," he said without anger. It was difficult for him to go on; he hesitated for a moment in order to gather his words clearly before he spoke. "I don't know that I love you, Margaret. I don't know that I'm sure what love is. But I'm fond of you, and I couldn't let you have this child alone any more than I could have a child of mine born away from its father, without its father's name. If you say the word, we'll be married as soon as possible—tomorrow. I can go to Father Badin tonight, still; it isn't too late; he'll be up. He can marry us in the morning."

She took his hand in her own strong fingers. "Hercules, I couldn't ask a man who didn't love me to marry me."

"Margaret, I've always been honest with you. You understood; you knew. I'm still honest with you. Whatever either one of us may feel, we must now consider the child—our child. I would not want a child of ours to run these streets fatherless, even if no one but you knew its father. Would you?"

"No." Her voice was almost inaudible.

"Very well then. We'll be married tomorrow or any day you say."

"Tomorrow, then."

"Do you need clothes, anything?"

She raised her head proudly. "I have everything I need, Hercules."

He caught her chin in his hand, bent, and kissed her. Then he took up his greatcoat and cap, settling it on his head. "I'll go to see the priest then," he said. "I'll leave you to tell your father. He may be disappointed."

He went out into the falling snow again, the flakes cool and wet upon his face, and turned to walk in the direction of the priest's house.

They were married in the morning, quietly, and moved into a small house near the Company's office, bought by Hercules a month before.

Rolette came back in the spring. He was enthusiastic about his trip, but Hercules saw that he had not foresworn his liquor. He took long drinks from a bottle he carried with him, striding up and down as if irked by the confining walls of the Company's office. He had heard that Hercules was married. An Indian runner had said he had taken a squaw. He did not know whether it meant marriage until a travelling missionary among the Indians said that Father Badin had performed the ceremony. No doubt now the caliber of Hercules' work would improve still more. It was evident that ever since he had begun to call on Margaret Campbell he had been less disturbed by restiveness. This was true enough, and Hercules took no trouble denying it. Nevertheless, Rolette was somewhat surprised at the suddenness of it. How had it come about?

Hercules told him of Campbell's visit and his own prompt action.

"Well, she's a good girl. She'll make you a good wife," said Rolette. "But you wouldn't have had to marry her. God knows, most of the men have Indian or half-breed mistresses; it's nothing, nothing at all. There are so few women in these settlements, you know it's only what one might expect. *Sacré bleu!* if all the traders followed your example, they'd have a dozen wives and plenty of children who run the streets would turn up with some well-known names."

"Including Rolette, eh?"

Rolette sniffed and coughed; but he did not deny it. "However, you've married her, even if that disappointed Campbell, to whom money meant more, no doubt. And as I've said, she'll no doubt make you a good wife."

"Yes," admitted Hercules. "She does. I don't know that I ever loved her, but she does everything she can to make me comfortable."

Rolette waved his hands about. "A great deal of importance has wrongly been attached to love."

"Besides," continued Hercules, "I wouldn't want a child of mine running the streets fatherless. It may be that the other traders have a different code in such matters; unfortunately, I don't find it so easy to adopt that code. The child is mine; there's no doubt of it in my mind, and I would like to think that I have a little more consideration for a woman I have taken than these other traders."

Rolette shrugged eloquently. He went on to talk about other matters. It would be Hercules' turn to go to Mackinac with the furs in the summer, he said. Perhaps now that he was married, he might not want to go?

Hercules said that he meant to go on. "I want to see Ramsay Crooks. Besides, Margaret's expecting soon—about April, I believe."

Rolette assented. Hercules would go then, in late July or August, if not earlier. He spoke briefly about the Indians. They appeared to be settled now, but it was well known that the trader Marsh was thick as syrup with the Sioux, selling them guns and ammunition. "Make no mistake about it—Marsh will have yet to be dealt with," said Rolette.

Hercules nodded gloomily. "Kapolequa has set himself the task of watching him as well as he's able. We'll see."

"God damn it, I'm a patient man," said Rolette, "but this thing has gone just about far enough. I wouldn't be sorry if some one disposed of Marsh."

"I think it can be handled without violence," said Hercules, smiling. "After all, the only difference between him and the traders in our Company is that we have the license and he does not. The end, it seems to me, amounts to the same thing. If he's reported, something will have to be done. But if he's left alone, he'll be sure to do

something which might enable us to get rid of him altogether."

Rolette objected to waiting but he had no definite plan of action to offer. He filled the room with anger against Marsh and what he called Marsh's innate sense for treachery. He damned the ex-agent for a scoundrel and a knave at such length that presently Hercules found himself in Marsh's defense. From time to time Rolette took long pulls at his bottle until it was evident that he was no longer in full control of his faculties. Observing this, Hercules thought of Jane and contrived to persuade Rolette that it was necessary for him to superintend the pelt sorters at work in the yard outside the building, so that he might be more sober when he went home. Lapiage's brigade had come in, he said, and Lapiage himself was under the weather. Marsh was forgotten.

Hercules woke one night in mid-April to Margaret's voice. She was in labor. Since they were alone, it was he who had to go to the fort for Doctor Beaumont. He ran swiftly through the fragrant April darkness, the sound of the rising river making a constant rushing in his ears.

Fortunately, Doctor Beaumont was still up, busy writing reports of his experiments, which he hoped, he said, to put together for a book. He hardly heeded Hercules' admonition to hurry in his eagerness to talk about his patient. He said he had never enjoyed so much seeing a man eat, even if he himself never ate again; it was enough just seeing what went on in St. Martin's stomach. He could tell now just what happened to different meats, to bread, to green vegetables, to potatoes. . . . In this manner he rambled cheerfully on until they reached Hercules' house, where now all was still.

Hercules was apprehensive, but his fear was groundless. Margaret controlled her agony as well as she could, withholding the soft moaning which had awakened Hercules.

"Get LaBuche," ordered Beaumont, forgetting St. Martin now.

Hercules went for the midwife, waking her and telling her where to come. He went back without waiting for her.

Margaret lay still, her eyelids pressed shut, her lips firmed together. Beads of perspiration lay across her forehead and on her upper lip; the color was gone from her cheeks; her hands were

clenched at her sides. Hercules glanced in Beaumont's direction; the doctor seemed not at all alarmed. He observed casually that it would take a little while yet, but that he did not believe it would be anything but an easy delivery. He talked as volubly about Margaret's pelvic structure as he had about St. Martin's digestion. He said she should have no difficulty whatever bearing children, but of course there were always unknown factors. No one could ever tell for certain. Some day it might be possible.

The midwife came in: Menard's wife, though she was still called by her familiar maiden name. She was a large, capable-looking woman who did everything with an air of authority and confidence, as if she knew that she was the best nurse and midwife available in the settlement and for miles around. She glanced casually at Beaumont as if she were the doctor and he the nurse. She went directly to the bed and looked at Margaret, after which she went to the door and held it open so that Hercules might leave the room.

"If you please, M'sieu' Dousman. In here until we need you."

Hercules went obediently into the adjoining room and sat there. Presently LaBuche came in to say that somehow she had forgotten her herb medicines and would he go back to her house after them, her husband would give them to him. He did not understand that this was a ruse to take him from the house.

Menard found the herb medicines only after an extended search, gave them to Hercules, and grumbled his way back to bed. Hercules hurried back to his house. During his absence the baby had been born; its thin wailing filled the house. As he entered by the front door, LaBuche came from the bedroom carrying the child.

"It's a girl, M'sieu' Dousman," she said.

He looked at the child, realizing that he had not much cared whether it was a boy or girl, and now feeling briefly that he would have preferred a son. LaBuche was smiling tenderly at the child in the uncertain candlelight.

"How's my wife?" he asked.

"Go in."

Margaret lay looking toward the door by which he must enter. At one side stood Doctor Beaumont, humming a little, and watching her with a keenly professional air. Hercules went over and

came down beside the bed. Doctor Beaumont went into the adjoining room, from where his humming drifted back, broken by comments to LaBuche.

"Margaret, do you feel all right?"

"Just a little weak, Hercules."

He nodded confidently. "That will pass." He felt awkward suddenly. "I've seen her. What shall we name her?"

"I thought—Emily," she said with an effort.

Doctor Beaumont came in, bustling a little. "She should rest now, Dousman."

Hercules kissed her and went out. LaBuche carried the child back to Margaret. In a few moments Beaumont came out. He stood at the window looking into the night, apparently in no hurry to get back. Hercules asked about the delivery. Beaumont admitted that it had had some complications. Hercules remembered with sudden shock that LaBuche had not answered his query about Margaret.

"How did she come through it?" he asked Beaumont.

"She came through all right," answered the doctor. "But she's not out of danger."

Hercules came to his feet, went over and gripped the doctor's shoulders. "Beaumont—what's the matter? I demand that you tell me!"

"There's some hemorrhage, Dousman. I've tried to stop it as best I know how. I may have succeeded." He paused and looked away. "I may not." He shrugged. "In any case, I'll stay until I find out."

He stayed for an hour before LaBuche came to the threshold and called Hercules. She held the child again, murmuring to her. Beaumont stood at the head of the bed, looking at Margaret with troubled eyes. Hercules went over, dropped to his knees beside the bed, and took hold of Margaret's hand. She turned her head slowly and smiled. Her respiration was regular but very slow and shallow.

"Emily," she whispered.

LaBuche came immediately to the bedside with the baby, holding it so that Margaret could see. Hercules looked at Beaumont, who closed his eyes and shook his head a little. There were suddenly a hundred things he wished to say to Margaret, but even as he

opened his lips to speak her fingers relaxed, her head sank a little into the pillow. She was dead.

He got up slowly, relinquishing her hand, hot tears forcing their way from his lids.

"I'm sorry, Dousman," said Beaumont gently.

Hercules did not seem to hear him. He took Emily for a moment from LaBuche, glanced at the still figure beside him, and smiled through his tears at the child. My child, he thought. My daughter. He gave her gently back to LaBuche and went outside into the close-pressing aromatic April air, where he walked alone and fought to control a grief he did not know he could feel.

When he wrote to his father three days later, his grief was tempered. "Since last writing to you, I won and lost a good wife. I have left to me now a daughter of but a few days in age, named Emily——"

6.

Each Believes His Own

1830-1832

*T*HE spring deepened.

Pussy willows blossomed, catkins changing from gray to yellow, and their fragrance spread on the wind from the Mississippi bottoms through Prairie du Chien: a sweet heady perfume mingling with the odor of the river's thaw water, and the rich fragrance of turned earth on land occupied by American families filtering into the town in the westward migration. Days lengthened steadily, and of an evening the robins carolled, turtle doves mourned dulcetly in the village, and killdeers flew overhead wailing and crying among woodcocks twittering high above in mating flights. The hyla choir sang nightlong, and at last whippoorwills called from the dark hill hollows. Slowly and steadily the Mississippi rose for the late spring inundation of the island town, the water darkening a little here and there with silt brought down from slopes denuded of trees and undergrowth. The stars of spring rode high, led by amber Arcturus, and already bright Vega wheeled summer into the sky.

Alone once more, Hercules bent again to his work, keeping long hours. By day he worked often among the sorters, he interviewed traders, he sought new avenues of incoming pelts, he gleaned from the traders all manner of information about the land over which they had travelled, and he added from time to time to his map of the Michigan Territory and the trans-Mississippi to westward; by night he worked on his records, he wrote long, detailed reports for Ramsay Crooks, he wrote letters of inquiry about the season in pelts to Chouteau's outposts, to Astor's Yellowstone River Post, so that he might better acquaint himself with

the potentialities of the country beyond Prairie du Chien. It was once again usual to see his light burning in the office window, the pale yellow glow dancing sometimes in the wind, the same wind that bore the ineffable sweetness of wild crabapple blooming all around the village now, of wild plum along the deep woods, of cedar disseminating its fragrant pollen into the May night.

There were nights when he found himself unable to work, stirred by the pulse of spring, by the mysterious odors of growth, the miasma of the earth itself aroused by the mounting sun; and he sat for hours thinking of the years ahead, thinking of all the things he meant to do, dreaming with a certain practical common sense of the slow accumulation of wealth which must certainly give him soon the power to rectify the evil that flourished all around him among the white men as well as between them and the Indians. He did not think of power as his end, but only as his means; even as he thought of wealth as means to power. I will be strong, he thought often, and a strong man is twice strong if he can defeat the unscrupulous who may try to destroy him. His dreams were not idle. He sat at the table with his head in his hands; he walked a little outside; he stood at the window gazing out into the May night, where the wild plum and crabapple trees stood spectrally bending and swaying, showering their petals into the south wind.

While he sat at work one night, he heard a light tapping at the door. He looked up, hesitating. He knew it was not one of his Indians, for they walked in always, unfailingly; at the same time, he was aware that it could not be one of the voyageurs or traders, for none of them would have made that gentle knocking. He called out, and the door opened. Jane Rolette came into the room.

He got up immediately. "Madame Rolette! I'm sorry." He came around the table and placed a chair for her. "If I had known Madame stood at my door, I would have gone without delay to answer her knock."

She smiled faintly and thanked him, taking the chair he had set forward for her and disposing her full skirt about her. He looked at her keenly, noticing an air of distress about her: in the uncertainty of her eyes, in the faintly puzzled lines of her forehead, in the lower lip caught by her teeth now. He went gravely back to his place and sat down again, "with Madame's permission."

"If you please, Mistaire Dousman," said Jane, nodding. "No doubt you think it vair' fonny of me to call on you at this hour. But I have good reason."

Hercules smiled. "I'm sure that Madame does what is right and best. But tonight you're troubled? I hope it's possible for me to help."

"Oh, Mistaire Dousman, I do hope you can. My Oncle Brisbois is just now gone, and besides, he is not well, he is going blind, as you know. I do not know to whom I can turn. I would nevaire think of go' to a strangaire, but you are no longaire a strangaire, Mistaire Dousman."

"I sincerely hope not," agreed Hercules.

She nodded, her brow cleared, her eyes rested on him, and a little smile touched her lips; but her trouble was not gone, for all that. Her hands played nervously with a small reticule she carried, pulling at it this way and that.

"I do not know how to say," she cried. "It is about M'sieu' Rolette. Do you know what he do?"

"Madame Rolette knows very well that he does a great many things, so many it would be impossible for me or any one other person to be acquainted with them. He does all of them well, too," he added.

Her eyes entreated him, seeming to say: Do not make it difficult for me! He waited, his hands quite still on the table before him, his blue eyes fixed upon her with disarming guilelessness.

"You know how he drink," she said. "I have ask' him again and again not to drink, and he do so anyway. I do not know what I will do. I cannot have him come into the house like that when the children are there. I am sure I do not know what it is that trouble him, but he do not act like M'sieu' Rolette when he is dronk."

"Does he come home drunk?" asked Hercules.

She nodded emphatically. "He do. He is not nice to me. And when I talk to him, he say to hold my tongue, I am spoil', he cannot have talk. *He* cannot have it. He do not think of me. It is all right, if I want a new dress; always he use' to ordaire it for me and pay for it; but if I say something he do not like, he become vair' angry."

"I was not aware that Mr. Rolette went home intoxicated," said Hercules.

"But he do," continued Jane. "And you know he drink so."

Hercules nodded. "Yes—for almost a year now I've known it. But perhaps he has troubles about which you know nothing?"

"If so, then, do I not have the right to know them? Sairtainly I do. But M'sieu' Rolette, he tell me nothing. He say this is none of my business, and how am I to know or how can I help him? Not that way."

She stirred restlessly, leaning forward a little, so that her face came more clearly into the light, and its fragile fine beauty, softened by the light's glow, flowered in the room. Seeing her there, he was moved, as always, by the singular beauty of her features, and he was struck by the observation that she had been crying.

"Does he strike you?" he asked suddenly.

"He would not dare!" she exclaimed, drawing herself up. "If he strike me once, I will go from him, I will go back to ma Tante Domitelle; he know this vair' well; he will not strike me."

Hercules nodded absently. "Of course, Madame Rolette appreciates the difficulty of my position. I can talk to Rolette; I can promise nothing. It would be better if he stopped the drinking."

She drew back again, so that her face was shadowed. "Mistaire Dousman, how do a man like M'sieu' Rolette begin drink'?"

"Madame knows very well that it is impossible to say why men do things. I have said, possibly he has troubles. He hasn't said."

She got up abruptly and began to walk to and fro. "I cannot endure this," she cried. "I will not. M'sieu' Rolette is not to come into our house in such condition. What can he think! What can Virginie and Joseph think to see him as they have do? He do not think of me. He have nevaire think of me. If it is something I want, that is different; he can buy it; he do not think of money. Until now. Now he do not want even for me to have new clothes. He has say he will not pay for them. He distrac' me when he is like this."

"I'm sure he'll pay for the things you need," said Hercules in a quiet voice. "Do you storm at him when he's drunk?"

Her eyes flashed at him. "I say only what is necessaire. I do not storm. Mistaire Dousman know vair' well I nevaire storm."

He stood up to conceal the twitching of his lips. "Does Madame Rolette wish me to speak to him?"

"I wish some one to do so. I have do so, but he do not listen. My oncle is not here. My fathaire is dead. My brothaire George seldom come. My Oncle Alexander is all time up there, in Canada; he nevaire come, I do not think he will evaire come away from the Hudson Bay Company. I do not know to whom to say this; so I come to you. After all, Mistaire Dousman is my husban's partnaire."

He sat looking at her without saying anything for a few moments. She was patently upset, though she held herself well under control apart from the superficial fire she made manifest. He had before this already understood that her spirit, while genuine enough, was never permitted to befog a certain innate core of good sense and judgment. But he could not help playing to her fire.

"Madame is upset," he said casually.

She clapped her hands sharply together. "Madame is not upset," she answered tartly. "Madame know vair' well what she do."

"Then doubtless you have thought what you must do if Mr. Rolette cannot be persuaded to do his drinking elsewhere, or to cease drinking altogether?"

She shook her head. "I have not think of this much. But I will not endure it. That much I say now. I will not endure it. He say to me that if the children mus' not see him, then I should sen' them away. He know they mus' go eas' to school after a while. But Virginie is so young, so small; I could not bear to part with her yet. She is so lovely, so good a child—how can he ask that!" She stopped suddenly and gazed at Hercules, who met her proud eyes without lowering his own. "Do not Mistaire Dousman go eas' this summaire?"

He nodded. "If all goes well, I will go."

She was suddenly conscious of something more. Dismay touched her mouth. "Oh, I am selfish! I do not think. I come so soon aftaire—aftaire your wife die, and you have trouble, too, your own child."

"Please don't distress yourself," he said quickly. "Emily is well taken care of. I've placed her with LaBuche, and I see her almost every day. I did not want to do this, but I'm unfortunately not able to give her the care she needs."

"Oh, why do you not bring her to me?" she cried.

"Surely Madame Rolette has enough to do for children of her own without troubling herself for me."

"Mistaire Dousman, it would have been no trouble," she said earnestly. "But I may go to see her?"

"I wish you would. Especially if I go east."

"Yes, yes," she said quickly. "If after all the children mus' go eas', they should go with you. Then it is only right that I look to your Emily since you will look to my Virginie and Joseph."

His thoughts returned to his partner. It was true that Rolette's drinking was increasing, but he had not known until now that Rolette had exposed Jane to its effects upon him. He did not know what to do, but he could not betray his uncertainty to Jane. He got up and came around the table to where Jane stood.

"If Madame Rolette will leave her problem with me, I will think about it," he said. "Now if she will permit me to see her home . . .?"

"Oh, do not take this time from your work, Mistaire Dousman."

"It's late, too late for Madame to walk alone. If you please?" He held open the door.

She looked at him with that quick indignation so much a part of her spirit, but her face broke into smiles. "Mistaire Dousman is vair' masterful," she said with light mockery.

She went out. He left the light burning, since he meant to return. They walked in silence, she with her thoughts retreating to her husband's drinking, to her children, he thinking dispassionately of her distance from him. The night was wonderfully aromatic; the fragrance of late crabapple blossoms still haunted the darkness, and all around them moved the sentient spring air, filled with the sounds and odors of life at the height of spring, the mysterious furtive sounds of nocturnal creatures, the primitive stimulation of unknown perfumes riding the light south wind, and over all, the powerful headiness of the river's smell, heavy with the thaw water from the north. From the Mississippi's shore came the yawping of foxes, the wild screaming of lynxes, the clamor of night birds and hylidæ.

They were nearing her home before she spoke. "You see, Mistaire Dousman, we have meet no one. There is no dangaire."

"Danger doesn't give warning," he said. "Besides, I couldn't ex-

pose myself to the danger of losing Madame's occasional good company."

A horseman came riding out of the darkness from the direction of the coulee to the east. He swerved to avoid them and rode on, but pulled up his horse suddenly and turned to call back.

"Is that you, Dousman?"

"Yes. What is it?"

"Street. I need to see you."

"Go on to the office, then. It's open; I'll be right there."

The horseman swung away, and Hercules turned once more to Jane, who had stood waiting for him to finish with Street.

"M'sieu' Rolette is not now at home," she said quietly. "He has go out somewhere, but he was worse for drink. He do not know I have gone to you. Pairhaps it would be bettaire if he do not fin' out."

Hercules laughed. "He needn't," he assured her. "But let Madame feel no compunction about calling upon me whenever I can be of service to her."

He left her at the door with mingled feelings. All the old delight in her company, all the old impulse toward her which he had thought put down within him, had come back, and he could not rid himself of the image of her that held to his mind's eye. He stood for a moment looking back at the Rolette house, that house so imposing in the village, the house King Rolette had built especially for his lovely young bride, and he thought that serious trouble must threaten Rolette that he should now oppose Jane's wishes, to say nothing of his having taken to drink. He turned and hurried back to the office, striving to put her from his mind.

Street stood on the threshold waiting for him. He turned into the room before Hercules and leaned over the table.

"Sit down," invited Hercules.

The Indian agent shook his head. "It just occurred to me," he began. "I need your help. You know as much about the Indians as any one around here, and I need a careful hand to deal with them."

Hercules held up a deterring hand. "I'm too busy now to go into the woods," he said.

"No, no, it isn't that. It's here. I'll tell you." He sat down then, straddling a chair, and began to talk rapidly. There had been trouble among the Indians for a long time; of this Hercules was well aware. The Fox and Sacs on the one hand, the Sioux and the Menominees on the other. It had come to Street's ears that they were carrying challenges from one tribe to another. If it now came to an Indian war, it was certain that some whites would be massacred. Hercules well knew that an Indian brave drunk with the thought of war is not careful whom he kills.

Just what information did he have? asked Hercules.

Street told him. There was no doubt in his mind that the bad feeling between the tribes had grown steadily, and would soon burst forth. "I need hardly tell you that a good deal of it comes from the Sioux, who feel so much stronger now that Captain Marsh has been selling them guns."

"In regard to that," began Hercules.

Street barked a short laugh. "I haven't been able to catch him at it, though I know he does it." He went on with his talk. He had in mind calling a council in the following week and wished Hercules to serve on it. All the Indian chiefs knew Dousman, they called him *Father,* they trusted and believed in him. This was more than could be said of almost any one else in the settlement. Would Hercules serve?

Hercules sighed. The thought of Indian trouble had not occurred to him. There had been treaty after treaty, and he had felt that the settlement of last year would bring lasting peace to Michigan Territory. "We've robbed them of everything," he said bitterly.

Street agreed. "Of everything but their enemies. They can still fight," he observed. "And of course, they must not."

"Very well. I'll be there."

Street impressed him with the necessity of secrecy. He wished the council to begin without its occurrence being noised about. He had already sent messages to the chiefs, and Kettle with a band of his Foxes and Sacs was on the way. He had some hope of settling the differences among the tribes in a friendly council, not without warning that a tribal war would bring the military back. If Hercules talked to them forcibly, this, together with what Street could say to them, might possibly prevent bloodshed which showed every

sign of ultimately involving the settlers at some point along the line of battle.

The Indian agent got up, reassured by Hercules, made a little small talk about the rapid growth of the settlement now that the Americans were coming in in such numbers and occupying the land south of the new fort, and took his departure. Hercules stood looking after him, thoughtful now. He felt a sullen annoyance with himself that he continued to believe in the possibility of justice for the Indians, and permitted himself to become once again a party to these negotiations in the hope that again justice might be done. It was no longer appeasing to himself to reflect that perhaps there might be even grosser injustice if he were not present. What can one man do against the conniving greed of scores of men, the all pervasive selfishness that infects high and low alike, he thought.

But presently he forgot the Indians, he forgot his sore dissatisfaction, and his thoughts turned to Jane.

In the morning he sent one of the men from the post out to summon Kapolequa, so that he might inform himself about the nature of the quarrel between the tribes. The Fox had not come to the office for months, and Hercules had missed him. For that matter, none of his other informants had appeared either; this, if anything, was a sign of peace in the Territory.

That morning, too, he saw Rolette.

Rolette was still showing in his bloodshot eyes the effects of his drinking the night before. He was evidently also in a bad temper, for he came scowling into the office, barely looking at Hercules. His black beard was fierce, his eyes stormy. Hercules, however, was not to be put off. He stopped him when Rolette would have gone on through the office toward the warehouse.

"Look here, Rolette, there's something I want to say to you."

Rolette turned and came slowly back. "So? What now? You can run this business without my help, Hercules."

"Perhaps so," agreed Hercules. "But it seems to me you're needing help of a different kind. You're drinking far too much."

Rolette snorted contemptuously. "*Sacré nom de Dieu!* That's my affair, and only mine," he said angrily. Who was Hercules to inter-

fere in anything Rolette did? He had the tongue of a woman when he spoke like that, said Rolette.

Hercules was unmoved. "No, sir, I disagree with you. That's not just your affair alone. You're forgetting your wife and children. They have every right to expect you to remain sober at all times."

Rolette swore indelicately. He tipped a chair and turned it, sitting so that his great arms were folded across its back. He began to talk rapidly. What did Hercules know of his affairs apart from the trade?

Hercules admitted that he knew nothing and had no wish to know anything. But if he meant to say that his affairs were in a bad way, Hercules would be bound to point out that he, Rolette, was solely responsible. "I've told you time and again not to loan money to people who come begging for it without any kind of security," he said. "They know you're soft-hearted, they rely on your reputation for kindness, they know you won't prosecute them if they don't pay. Some of them have left the village, they've gone, God knows where, and so has your money. You'll never get it back."

"It's not only that," said Rolette savagely. "God damn it, my wife uses too much. She dresses like a queen."

Hercules observed not without truth that she bore herself as a queen might. It was well known that all the French and French-Canadian women in the settlement looked upon Jane Rolette as a woman set apart; they worshipped her, and she had as great a reputation for kindness and generosity among them as any one could have.

"That might all be true," Rolette admitted. "But it can't go on. I won't stand for another cent on her clothes! It's a damned shame."

"When I came here you were the richest man in the settlement," said Hercules. "What's happened?"

"I put a lot of it into land, and right now I'm not realizing enough on that land. I make a small profit, true, but not enough. Then, as you said, I've lost a great deal on loans and on bad investments. And it costs something to keep up the house, to send Jane east, to send the children. They should go to school pretty soon. *Mille tonnerre!* it's one damned thing after another."

Hercules observed dryly that it was always a matter of one

damned thing after another, no matter what a man did. This was an age-old problem.

"I lose money wherever I turn," cried Rolette.

Hercules replied that it could not be so bad as that. He was losing money only because of bad judgment. Drinking certainly did not help to remedy that fault—or did it? He pressed Rolette to say.

Rolette swore proficiently for two or three minutes, during which Hercules waited impassively, his mind seeking some avenue by which to help Rolette from whatever plight in which he might now have found himself. Drinking did not help, perhaps, but it took Rolette's mind from his troubles. He could no longer even enjoy his trips into the north. It was pathetic; he loved to roam into the woods. If it were only a matter of losing money, that would not be so bad. But he could not go away with the thought that perhaps Jane would not have enough to live on until he came back. And when he did come back, there was no telling what new situation might have to be faced before income mounted sufficiently again.

"You own a good deal of land, better than fifty percent of the available land within the village, don't you, Joe?" asked Hercules presently, interrupting Rolette's voluble recitation of his troubles.

Rolette looked at him, grinning. "God damn it, man, I'm land poor! I've got the money in it, and I can get it out, only I don't get it out fast enough."

"All right," said Hercules. "Suppose we go into partnership in real estate. I'll buy half your holdings."

Rolette looked at him in amazement. *"Sacré bleu!* D'you think you've got enough money for that?"

Hercules assured him that he had more than enough. "I go nowhere, I spend little, I invest carefully, I don't make inadequately secured loans," he said. "In that way I've managed to save a little something."

"A little something," repeated Rolette, his great laugh ringing through the building. It would take more than a little something to buy half his holdings in Prairie du Chien, much more.

Hercules said that "a little something" was only a comparative term, as Rolette would in the course of time understand. "The point is not whether I can pay, but whether I can buy. Will you sell?"

"If you can put money down to cover, I'll sell."

"I can put it down."

Rolette trumpeted a figure he computed rapidly in his mind, looking with a faint air of triumph at his partner. Hercules smiled casually and said that the money would be waiting for Rolette in forty-eight hours, if Rolette would be so good as to make out the necessary papers.

Rolette stared at him for a moment as if he did not credit what he had heard. He sat as if waiting for Hercules to smile and so proclaim his offer but a jest. But Hercules did not smile.

"That would help you for the time being, I presume," he said gravely.

"You know it would," assented Rolette. "But, Hercules . . . God damn it, man, can you afford to do this?"

"Much more easily than you can afford to drink the way you do."

Rolette made an irritated gesture, grimacing. "As to that, I'll do as I like," he anwered shortly. He got up. "I'll have the papers ready in two days, then."

"I think you can tolerate me as a partner," said Hercules, smiling.

"My boy, if you're only half as good in real estate as you are in the trade, we'll both make money."

Hercules nodded. "*I* intend to," he said. "But you'll still need to stop drinking."

Rolette turned on his heel and went out, without a further word. In the afternoon, Kapolequa came in. He sat down cross-legged against the wall and waited while Hercules finished with two traders who had come in to complain about the decline in numbers of otter in the sloughs, as if Hercules could remedy this condition. After they had gone, he asked Hercules why he had sent for him.

Hercules told him what he had heard from Street.

All that was quite true, admitted Kapolequa with equanimity. It had been true for some time, for years. Hercules knew this very well. There was no war between the tribes, though the challenge had been brought to the Foxes by a friendly Winnebago. The Sioux and Menominees were equally hated by the Foxes and the Sauke-nauk, and they in turn hated them. Kapolequa did not think war impended.

Nevertheless, Street did, interposed Hercules.

Did the agent think that the Indians meant mischief? asked Kapolequa.

Apparently he did, explained Hercules. It was true that Street was inclined to be more than usually nervous, but he had had plenty of time to accustom himself to the ways of the red men. Moreover, he was no longer likely to believe every rumor he heard. So if Street believed there might be trouble, it was possible.

Kapolequa did not understand what he could do about Street's suspicions and fears.

Hercules was uneasy and showed it. Did Kapolequa know that old Chief Kettle was on the way to council?

Kapolequa did.

"I have information that a war party of Sioux and Menominees joined forces near here," continued Hercules, now relaying information given him by one of the traders. "Kettle does not know this. They've gone down the Mississippi, and Kettle's coming up. Some one ought to tell Kettle that they're on the way."

Kapolequa understood that Hercules expected him to find Kettle, and agreed to do so. It was well known where Kettle and his braves would camp for the night if they approached Prairie du Chien. It would be at the Prairie du Pierreaux, something like fourteen miles south of the settlement. He would have the lesser chiefs, Broken Face and Piermosky, with him, thought Kapolequa. However, he did not much like the suggestion that he run crying warning, since it would not be dignified of him to approach Kettle, who was one of the fiercest warriors among the Fox, and one of the bravest, notwithstanding his age. He shook his head to indicate his unwillingness, despite his agreement.

After half an hour of cajoling and pleading, Hercules prevailed upon him to go, and Kapolequa set out immediately for the Prairie du Pierreaux.

Just before dawn, Hercules was awakened by the sound of scratching at his window. A light sleeper, he rose at once, went barefooted to the door, and opened it. It would be Kapolequa, he thought.

It was Kapolequa. But it was not the same Kapolequa as he who had left the Company's office the previous afternoon. On the threshold stood an Indian daubed with war paint, and with the smell of blood about him.

Hercules stared at him for a moment as if he could not believe

his eyes. Then he stepped back hurriedly, beckoning Kapolequa inside. Behind the Fox the eastern sky flowered with a pale amethyst and shell pink fanning upward before the sun.

"I will say only a little," said Kapolequa.

It was evident that the Fox was enraged; this was betrayed in his clipped speech, his hard, set eyes, his war paint. Hercules began to dress; it was in any event time for him to be up and about. From time to time he looked at Kapolequa, who stood there like a statue, watching him. Kapolequa was on the warpath. He had not been drinking. He was cold sober. Nevertheless, with the courtesy so common among the Indians, he waited while Hercules dressed, despite the urgency of his message.

"Now, then," said Hercules, dressed at last. "What is it? Why are you wearing the paint? Have you taken up the tomahawk, then?"

Thereupon Kapolequa unburdened himself. He talked stolidly, unemotionally; it was Hercules who could not control his emotion, his mounting shock and anger. Kapolequa had come to Prairie du Pierreaux just too late. Kettle, Broken Face, Piermosky and all of their party save one boy had been massacred at the camping place by Sioux and Menominees, who had broken the boy's arms and sent him to Dubuque so that the Fox village there might know of the defeat and death of Kettle. It was a challenge to war, and the Fox and Saukenauk were already sending runners to the villages. Hercules might tell the Indian agent, Street, that the council could not now be held.

"But I can't understand," cried Hercules. "Street worked in the greatest secrecy."

Kapolequa looked at him and made an obscene gesture together with a word picture.

"Marsh!" exclaimed Hercules.

"Marsh sold the guns. Marsh told them Kettle was coming. We know. Tell Marsh we have not forgotten his wife and son carry the blood of Sioux in their veins. He is evil, and we have always said it."

"But he can't have done this!" protested Hercules.

Even as he cried out, he knew with that conviction which permits no disbelief that Marsh had indeed betrayed Kettle's party.

He had all along expected something like this of Marsh; now it had come; it was useless to fight against it. He had the same conviction as Kapolequa, but he was filled, too, with a kind of sick horror, which was responsible for his attempt to discredit Kapolequa's message.

"Tell Marsh," said Kapolequa again.

If Marsh had done this thing, he would be put out of Prairie du Chien. Hercules promised Kapolequa this.

The Fox shook his head. The white men would never do it. They lived to protect the weak and the evil ones among them. They were stupid people. It would take the Fox and Saukenauk to avenge the massacre of Kettle.

He padded softly to the door and turned on the threshold. "Good-bye, Dousman. You will not see me again," he said. Then he was gone.

Hercules stood where the Indian left him, his impulse to go at once to Street, but some sense of caution holding him back. So reluctant was he to believe this intelligence from Kapolequa, that he wished further confirmation of the slaughter at Prairie du Pierreaux before he sought out either Street or Marsh.

It was not long in coming.

The early morning activity of Prairie du Chien had hardly begun before the victorious Sioux and Menominees began their triumphal march through the village. Braves, squaws, children—all marched. They were painted for war, their faces were smeared with the blood of their victims, and they were fully equipped for battle, wearing feathers, carrying tomahawks, war clubs, scalping knives. They had been cunning enough not to bring the guns Marsh had sold them. Moreover, they announced their coming by sounding drums and rattles, so that all the settlers could view their victory parade. A few of them carried scalps waved on high poles; but most of the Indians, braves and squaws alike, bore aloft more grue-some trophies of the slaughter: arms, hands, legs—some with long strips of skin flapping bloodily against their faces—heads, torn flesh. All were dancing the scalp dance, all yelled monotonously, with shuddersome shrieks and ululations. They went up and down the streets, going several times past Marsh's house, and past Rolette's.

Hercules watched the scalp dance with mounting rage. He could

understand Kapolequa's feeling very well. This was Marsh's handiwork. Rolette had always called him a damned scoundrel; at this moment Hercules thought his partner had been too lenient with Marsh in his thoughts. The dance went on for over two hours, until it seemed that the savages would never tire of it. At the end of this time the Indians retired to a small mound just outside the village, to roast and devour the heart of Chief Kettle, which would inspire them with courage and gladden their hearts. No one interfered with them, but by this time word of the battle at Prairie du Pierreaux had reached Street, he knew his plans for a council would have to be given over for the present, and he sat down in an effort to fix upon the source of the Sioux' information about the approach of Kettle.

By the time that the Indians retired to devour the Fox chieftain's heart, Hercules could contain himself no longer. He walked rapidly down the street to the house where Marsh lived, and from part of which he conducted his trading post.

Marsh was in his store, a little pale at what he had just seen. He was preoccupied, but waved Hercules to a chair.

"I didn't come to sit, Marsh," said Hercules bluntly.

Marsh gazed at him, slowly flattening his hands upon the counter before him.

"You saw the scalp dance?"

Marsh nodded, his eyes warily narrowed, his mouth defiant.

"How did you like your handiwork?" Hercules did not wait for him to answer. "It's generally known that credit goes to you for betraying old Kettle and his braves coming to the council. The Fox especially knew it. And they've not forgotten, as you seem to have done, that your wife and son have Sioux blood in them."

The defiance washed out of Marsh's handsome face. He grew pale. "You don't think they mean . . ."

Hercules interrupted him. "I was asked by one of the Fox this morning to carry the challenge to you."

"Then they mean to strike at me through them," said Marsh.

He was ashen now, and his eyes betrayed his fear. The scene held timelessly for a minute: Marsh isolated in his apprehension, Hercules aloof in his angry judgment. The room seemed to close in about them with dark foreboding, and the parallelogram of sunlight on the floor grew spectral.

"Didn't you think of that when you betrayed the Fox and Sacs to the Sioux?" asked Hercules. "Couldn't you look ahead? You've done one of the most despicably cowardly things possible for a white man to do. The Indians may retaliate against the entire settlement in the course of taking vengeance on you. I tell you now I knew there was something of the scoundrel in you when I first laid eyes on you in Brunet's tavern years ago. I've had every evidence of it since then. This, however, is the greatest piece of knavery you've done; it's plain murder, and there's no other name to call it. To have done such a thing at a time when the Fox and Sacs were on the way to a peace council here makes your crime all the worse. I'm going to be frank with you, Marsh—you're not the kind of man, white or half-breed, we want to see in Prairie du Chien."

"Are you telling me to get out?" demanded Marsh with harsh bravado.

"I could say it more plainly: get out."

Marsh got up and kicked his chair back, anger bringing color to his face. "I'll thrash you, Dousman."

"Don't force me to soil my hands. I have no objection to handling ordinary curs and scoundrels, but I have some sensibilities left. I care nothing for cowards. I'm telling you now, in time—get out—before something happens to you. We've had enough trouble with the Indians without the meddling of a man of your obvious tastes. We've tried again and again to stabilize the trade in the Territory, but if it isn't the Indians themselves who cause trouble, we can always depend upon people like yourself, it seems. The Indians at least live by a strict and, to their own conception, honorable code; you know nothing of honor. You sold them guns; you told them where to use them; you probably saw with some satisfaction that they revealed none of them. All of this without thinking of anything save your Sioux friends. Now you have something more to consider—the danger in which you've placed your wife and son, to whom we all know you're devoted—if that, too, is not just a mask. And you have to consider, too, that no decent person in Prairie du Chien will so much as pass the time of day with you after this."

Marsh sat down slowly, covering his face with his hands. "There's nowhere I can go," he said.

"You might go among the Sioux to whom you seem so attached."

Marsh looked at him. "Not as a trader!"

"In whatever capacity you like—because after this fear passes, doubtless you'll be up to your old habits. And when that time comes, I know we don't want you here. I can't speak more plainly than that. You're not to be trusted. I've seen evidence of your bravery from time to time, but I know that the same tenacity which characterizes the brave man in you also works the scoundrel."

He went out, his anger tempered by contempt. From beyond the village came still the voices of the Indians, making a noisy cater-wauling; on the wind also came the smell of roasting flesh, unpleasant in the fragrance of May all around. As he went along, he saw the signs of excitement; people stood in groups around doorways, in the road, heads together. Some of the military were moving here and there, their blue uniforms bright in the morning sunlight. When he crossed the road toward the office, General Street came upon him. The agent rode past before he identified Dousman, turned his horse around and dismounted in the middle of the dusty village street. He was white-faced, and his mouth trembled with fury.

"It was Marsh!" he almost shouted.

Hercules nodded quietly. "I know all about it. I just came from there," he said, adding, lest some of the villagers standing not far away might overhear, "Come into the building, Street, where we can talk without being heard."

He led the way, Street following and talking volubly, somewhat incoherently.

"My hands are tied, I can do nothing. I wish I had the right to do something about this cowardly outrage. I'd have him shot now, at once. I told the War Department a long time ago that he was a menace to the settlement, to the Territory, but Cass managed to uphold him until just recently. Even now he'd prevent my doing anything about this. But I'm in such a mood I tell you, sir, if a convenient accident happened to Marsh, I would applaud, I would indeed." He sat down in response to Hercules' gesture.

"What about the council?" asked Hercules.

"Council!" shouted Street. "Do you think we can have it now?"

Hercules shook his head.

"Of course not. I've had runners in since dawn to say that the

Sioux challenge has been accepted; it's war, that's what it is. All because that damned murderer Marsh couldn't remember he was a white man, and not a Dacotah."

Hercules interposed smoothly. "Forget Marsh for the moment. The council is more important. While it's obvious that it can't be held right now, we must however absolutely insist upon a council of peace within the next few months."

"August or September then."

"You forget that I'm planning to leave in mid-July for Mackinac. I may not return until late in autumn; I don't know what plans Crooks may have for me, but I believe he means me to go back east with him. I think if they can be persuaded to come together here in August, they can be cajoled into doing so early in July."

"We'll make it that date, then." He got up. "Now I'll get on to Marsh."

Rapidly, Hercules told him what he had said to Marsh. Street nodded approval, adding that his feelings against the ex-agent were so strong that he could tolerate seeing him publicly horsewhipped.

"I know what he'll say. *Lex talionis*—he gave his Sioux friends a chance to avenge themselves upon the Fox and Sacs for previous raids into Sioux country. But no white man has any business meddling in Indian affairs. And he must learn that."

Hercules shook his head slowly. "He'll never learn that, Street."

He watched the agent ride on down the road to where Marsh lived, a bitter smile on his lips. In his thoughts the very name Marsh sounded like anathema; and yet he could not entirely understand the impulses to which Marsh gave heed from time to time, the impulses which could arise in a man with so good a background and education, unless it were the impact of the great wilderness and its people whose codes he could not assimilate upon a nature unprepared for that contact. He could not help thinking of a passage from Pascal, with Marsh and his misdeeds in mind. *All wicked men are ignorant of what they ought to do, and what they ought to avoid; and it is this very ignorance which makes them wicked and vicious. Accordingly, a man cannot be said to act involuntarily merely because he is ignorant of what it is proper for him to do in order to fulfil his duty.* But he had no doubt that fear would now

drive Marsh from Prairie du Chien, and he hoped he would go from the Territory, far from the Mississippi country, so that even the echo of his deeds might not reach the settlement at the meeting place of the rivers.

Captain Marsh was not a coward.

He had been vain and venal in his time, and he had been foolish. There came always, however, an aftermath, and this came upon him now when he had listened to Hercules and to Street, when he had seen how people avoided him on the road, turning their heads and refusing to speak in reply to his greetings. He understood now that he had transcended a code stronger than the Sioux code he had temporarily adopted. There came to him that hindsight which revealed with remarkable clarity what his fate might be, and he had an uncomfortable premonition that he had unconsciously altered the entire course of his life. As with so many men, he looked too late upon his action not alone with eyes for himself, but for others, and the effect of his action upon others. The simple retaliation he had wished out of friendship to afford the Sioux had grown into a complicated web of horror, fury, and hatred, and he found not only himself now firmly enmeshed in that web, but also Marguerite, his son, and perhaps also his daughter. In addition to having incurred the undying hatred of the Fox and the Sacs and their allies, he had also stirred the Indian agent to such a pitch of contempt and anger that there was no telling what he might do in his efforts to bring Marsh to some kind of retribution; more than this, he had put the Astor Company directly against him, and the voyageurs and their followers could ruin his trade, to say nothing of what the Company itself might do to him. Marsh well knew that Astor himself was the Company; he knew that fraud and force were its chief weapons; the Company was a law in itself, ignoring all laws made by Congress; there was a time when it would not stop at murder to achieve its ends, to quell the complaints of defrauded Indians, to prevent the encroaching of other traders upon its territory.

Marsh was not a coward, but he now recognized that he had, by this single friendly act to the Sioux, raised against himself such a wall of opposition that he could not fight it, especially now that

his family was involved. He might have dared it alone. It took him only until mid-afternoon to make up his mind to give up temporarily his trading business and to seek an appointment of some kind among the Sioux a hundred miles to the north, in the village of his old friend, Wabashaw.

He sat down at once and wrote to Governor Cass, setting forth his wishes.

With great difficulty, the Indians were prevailed upon to come in to a council for peace in July, and on the seventh of that month the sessions began with the usual speeches. Hercules chafed at each day the council was drawn out, though it was apparent that it would not be a matter of many days. He was anxious to be away, knowing that Crooks would be waiting for him, though he had sent a message on to Mackinac to inform Crooks of the reason for his delay. In addition to all this, Rolette had abruptly decided, spurred no doubt by Jane's indecision, that Virginia and Joseph could go east to begin their schooling, and the children were to be entrusted to Hercules, who had made arrangements also to take with him his daughter Emily, to be cared for by LaBuche until the child reached his mother's home in Mackinac. The furs were ready, the voyageurs were impatient, a steamboat was held in readiness to take Hercules and the children as far as Fort Winnebago.

But the council dragged on. The attending chiefs made many protestations of friendship for their enemies, signified their desire for lasting peace again and again, but there were ominous signs. In the first place, the Indians were entirely willing to sign whatever the white men proposed. In the second, they were evidently not expecting gifts. In the third, they bore over all an attitude as if they were at play. These factors made it clear that the Indians had no intention of abiding by any treaty they might sign at the council, that they had considered the present war a matter which was theirs alone to settle, and not within the province of white men to order. As if these signs were not enough, there was an even graver indication: the most important of the Sac chiefs was not present; Black Sparrow Hawk had not seen fit to attend the council, and it was he who had the most grievances against the whites, who had invaded the old Sac burial grounds at the mouth of the Rock, and

destroyed the Sac village there, and it was he, too, who was most bitter against the Sioux.

In eight days the council drew to a close. Governor Cass made a great address which was apparently approved by all the Indians present, and the Sioux on the north, the Sacs and Foxes on the south ceded a strip of territory twenty miles in width on each side of the boundary line established in 1825. This separation of their territory was repaid with annuities, and the promise to furnish the various tribal villages with blacksmith shops, agricultural implements, and the things necessary for a higher standard of communal living. It did not come as a surprise to Hercules when the Governor announced the awarding of a contract for the erection of a blacksmith shop near the Sioux village of Wabashaw to John Marsh.

Cass went back to the territorial capital well satisfied with his accomplishment, but Street was not sanguine, and neither was Hercules. Nevertheless, each of them believed there might now be at least a breathing space, and each was certain that no white man would be involved in the Indian struggle—unless it were Marsh. Marsh had undergone the kind of punishment which made itself felt; he had been snubbed by the white inhabitants of Prairie du Chien, he had been jeered at by the half-breeds, and among the Indians, all but the Sioux turned their backs on him, refusing to look upon him and defile their eyes. Hercules was confident that for a while at least Marsh would cause no further trouble, since it was known that Marsh would remove his entire family from Prairie du Chien to take up residence among Wabashaw's band of Dacotah Sioux.

Two days after the council was concluded, Hercules was ready to start for Mackinac. The voyageurs in their large canoes set out with the furs ahead of the steamboat; Lapiage and Benoit had gone several days before with the boat which was to carry Hercules, LaBuche and the children down the Fox to Green Bay.

Rolette came early to the river's edge at the landing place. He was in a temper. Seeing Hercules already on board the steamboat, he called up to him that he would undoubtedly have to wait. Jane insisted upon making a great ritual of the children's departure; she could be depended upon to hold up the sailing. There was no

way to hurry a woman in her moods. Hercules was needlessly annoyed, for presently Jane came.

LaBuche and Emily were already aboard, and now Rolette turned to where Jane was making her way down the road, the children held by the hand. *"Sacré nom!* Hurry up, Jane. Dousman has been waiting long enough already."

She did not answer him; she did not even appear to notice him; her attention was all for the children. As she drew closer, Hercules saw that she held tightly to a handkerchief; she had been weeping. Her intense love for her children made this parting difficult, and Rolette's growing daughter Elizabeth was no substitute for the bright liveliness of Virginia. Rolette continued to hurry her, though Hercules saw no need for it.

The morning sun was bright and warm. Virginia was dressed in a pale-blue frock, Jane in deeper blue, with an odd little dark hat, which framed her face and strengthened her dark beauty. Hercules came down off the boat to take charge of the children.

"A few moments more or less mean nothing," he said shortly to Rolette.

Jane flashed him a look of gratitude, but Rolette only laughed and said that the more a man made concessions to a woman, the more concessions she would want. He brushed at his beard in his irritation, brusquely ordering Joseph aboard.

"But a few moments more, M'sieu' Rolette," begged Jane.

"Woman, you've had all the time of the council," he answered. "We can't keep these furs waiting forever. And more important, we can't keep Crooks waiting."

"I'll answer to Crooks," said Hercules quietly.

Rolette snorted. "No matter. Come now."

Joseph kissed his mother and father and went sturdily aboard the steamboat. Impulsively Jane ran after him, kissed him again, and hugged him close to her. In this interval Rolette took Virginia's hand and began to lead her aboard. Jane came running back, her eyes flashing angrily, her mouth set in a stubborn line.

"M'sieu' Rolette, I will take her aboard."

Rolette released the child's hand and stepped back. Hercules returned to the boat, apprehending that some quarrel must again have taken place between them to account for Rolette's unnecessary

stubbornness. He thought Rolette, who was not by nature or habit so, was being needlessly firm. But he saw too that Rolette also felt deeply about this parting from his children, and concealed his own feelings behind his gruffness, as if ashamed to reveal his emotions; so that all his actions were designed simply to hasten the parting and its effect upon them both.

Jane had now come aboard with Virginia. It was obvious that she was making every effort to remain with the child as long as possible: straightening her dress, murmuring words of endearment to her in French. Rolette shouted at her from the landing, but she did not seem to hear him; she gazed at Virginia with such a depth of longing in her eyes that for a moment Hercules had to look away. When he glanced back, he saw that she had resigned herself to the parting; she was biting at her lower lip to keep back her tears, and yet she was trying to smile. She was stepping backward, feeling her way from the boat; he went forward and took her arm. The children came to the rail and waved at her, calling in their thin voices. She waved back, her damp handkerchief fluttering limply. Rolette stood a little beyond her, his hands clasped behind his back, his expression tolerant. There she stood still, waving and calling to them when the boat began to drift down the Mississippi toward the mouth of the Wisconsin, her voice rising even above the shouting of the steersmen and the noise of the boat. Hercules stood behind the children and thought how little, how forlorn she looked there, and he had misgivings at the thought of leaving her with no one but Rolette and Elizabeth. But she would survive, he thought confidently.

LaBuche came hesitantly to take the children, but he motioned her to leave them where they were as long as he himself stood there; so she retired again to where Emily's shrill crying rose. In a little while Jane vanished, the village fell away, they entered the mouth of the Wisconsin and began to pull slowly upstream, making a snail's progress at first while the steersmen sought the channel of the lesser river, crowded on both banks by the deep green of mature foliage, and, in open places, by thousands upon thousands of orange hawk flowers and white daisies, by yellow St. John's wort and bright blue spiderwort. Only a short distance from Prairie du Chien, they were in the heart of the wilderness, with birds crying

out against their intrusion, and animals vanishing from the water's edge whither they had come to satisfy their thirst.

The children were entranced, crying out at each kind of bird, demanding that Hercules tell them the names of warblers, of grosbeaks, of indigo buntings, whose bright feathers caught their alert eyes. So, amused, he sat down at the railing with them, answering the questions they threw excitedly at him, sharing in their ecstatic appreciation of the wild earth's great beauty. They were untiring in their curiosity, and he did not permit himself to tire, so that none of them marked their slow pace up the River of the Thousand Isles.

At noon of the second day they reached the Portage, where Lapiage and Benoit were impatiently waiting in the bateau. In consequence of the number of passengers the boat would have to carry, the amount of furs packed beneath the tarpaulin fastened down and over the sides for the protection of the pelts had been lessened, some of them having been transferred to the other boats which had gone on. Lapiage, who served as bourgeois, had six rowers in their places; the messbasket had been packed with roast prairie chickens, bread, butter, biscuits, tongue, chocolate, wine and brandy, all prepared in advance by the wife of the Indian agent, Kinzie, at Fort Winnebago. The boat carried, in addition to all this, two tents and bedding for overnight camping.

Lapiage was anxious to be off. He said that the air smelled of rain, that they might outdistance it if they started at once; but he was not sanguine. There were clouds low in the northwest, and an east wind blew. Hercules did not know whether to go on without permitting the children some time on shore. He asked the children.

They were ready to start, despite the temptation of taking luncheon at the Indian agent's house, Mrs. Kinzie having come down to the steamboat among those of the military who had been drawn from the fort at sight of the craft, for some of them still novel, and asked them up. The agent, Kinzie, stood for a while talking to Hercules, who had asked about the Winnebagos in the region of the post, telling him how peaceful they were.

They were at the Portage less than an hour, only long enough to transfer from the steamboat the baggage belonging to the Rolette children. Then they set out once more to follow the meandering

path of the Fox River into the northeast. For a little while there were continuing signs of habitations by trappers and Indians. Before they found themselves in the wilderness again, they passed a canoe moving toward the Portage. The Indians paddling were from the Green Bay post; Lapiage hailed them. Benoit saluted the young man and woman in the small craft; Hercules looked at them fleetingly, seeing the young man's soft hair and proud eyes, the woman's apparent apprehension showing through despite her attempt at interest in the wilderness.

After they had passed, Benoit shouted to Lapiage. "You know heem, Lapiage?" And at the bourgeois' negative added proudly, "Me, I met heem wan tam when he go to school, to place call' Harvard. I paddle heem, me, Benoit. Hees fathaire vair' seeck; he die, maybe. Then *he* ees Baron Pierneau."

Hercules looked after the retreating canoe with interest. So it was he who lived in the house of yellow stone high on the hill south of the great prairie of the Sacs! But the canoe was already too far up the river for Hercules to distinguish any more than the woman's lavender dress and Pierneau's white shirt.

At evening of the tenth day, Mackinac rose out of the blue water of the straits, lying like a great emerald and white jewel under a mound of cumulus clouds magenta and old rose on the turn of their banks, and the sky above amethyst and aquamarine. They landed before dark in the cool winds that broke the heat of their passage.

Hercules was met at the wharf by a dark-haired young man with intense dark eyes and an incipient black moustache; these features stood out; he had, on second glance, a good mouth, finely lined eyebrows, a strong but not prominent nose.

"Dousman," he said. "I'm Sibley, Henry Sibley. Crooks and your father sent me. They're waiting for you at the office if you can come."

"I'll be right with you." He turned and directed Lapiage to see to it that LaBuche and the children reached the Dousman home; then he took Sibley's arm and propelled him quickly forward. "We were delayed a little," he explained. "I hope I haven't kept them waiting too long."

Sibley said he thought not; in fact, Crooks himself had been gone for some days, and now he planned to go east, as Hercules knew. A packet was being held in readiness for Crooks now.

Hercules looked Sibley over with frank curiosity. He had read enough about him in his father's letters; for the moment he forgot whether it was Nancy or Kate who was fond of him. He asked presently whether Sibley was now with the Company.

"Yes, this year," said Sibley, a little uncertainly. "I don't know that I'll stay, though. I wasn't cut out for this work, you know. Educated in law, but got tired of that. Always liked to hunt and fish; so I came west—from Detroit," he added with a boyish grin.

Hercules laughed. "Wait a bit before judging the work. There's always room for young men in it."

"To tell the truth, at the moment I'm too much taken with your sister Kate to be aware of anything else."

"Ah, that will pass," said Hercules casually, not wishing to be drawn into any discussion about her.

They came to the office and Sibley stood aside so that Hercules might precede him. The two men who waited were bent over the table; a lamp in a bracket above shed an uncertain glow upon the map they studied. The older Dousman looked up and, seeing his son, came quickly forward to embrace him. Crooks raised his great body, casting a dark shadow over the table before him. He extended a heavy hand.

"Ah, my boy, late, but still in good time."

They shook hands. Crooks had not changed; he was still the same heavy man with the big face; there was still about his small eyes the look of cunning which had first marked him for Hercules. He had an easy manner, a capable air; at the moment he dismissed Sibley with a wave of his hand; he motioned Dousman back to his place before the map; he told Hercules shortly to sit down, murmuring something about the problem that engaged them at present, that of unifying the area around Lake Pepin in the upper trans-Mississippi a little more efficiently. "Efficiency is after all one of the chief factors in making a living," he opined dryly.

Hercules agreed. He thought that if Crooks had summoned him only to sit here while he and the older Dousman pored over a map,

he might as well have gone on to pay his respects to his mother, and to see to it that the children were adequately disposed.

But it was apparent presently that Crooks was quite capable of doing two things at once. While he traced an outline with one index finger on the map before him to guide Michael Dousman's notes, he talked to Hercules. He spoke casually about the quality of Hercules' work in the Company, interrupting from time to time to clarify the wanderings of his finger.

"I can say that we're well satisfied with it. I've taken occasion more than once to commend you to the old man. I say this conservatively. You seem to have a directing genius, Dousman. You've succeeded in paring the expenses of the post at Prairie du Chien to a minimum, and yet you've been lavish enough with presents to keep the Indians friendly. We have reports as to this from other sources than the Company itself.—No, no, Dousman; not St. Peters, there; bear north.—Your father has already acquainted you with the fact that I'm going back east, and that I wish you to go along. If he hasn't done so, I say it to you now. But he's done so, for we're already informed about the passage of the Rolette children. How is Joe, by the way?"

Hercules said that he was in good health, but the shortness of his manner did not escape Crooks. His eyes narrowed.

Were there difficulties between the Rolettes, by any chance? He did not wait for Hercules to answer, but went on to say that he had always thought it unwise of the old Brisbois to marry off their niece at fifteen to a man twenty-odd years older, even if he had been the best match in the region. And Madame Rolette's father dead now, after so long a time in Canada, with the Company's oldest rival! He forgot Rolette except to say that as far as the Company was concerned now Rolette might not be in existence at all since Hercules had taken over.

The older Dousman interrupted with a question, and in a moment they were bent together over the map once more. Hercules contained himself, though it was difficult for him to do so, since he had begun to concern himself about the faring of Jane's children and his own Emily. But presently Crooks was addressing him once more.

"We'll set out day after tomorrow if you can be ready in that

time," he was saying, with his eyes still fixed on the map. "You appreciate that we must hurry if you're to be back at your post by the time the winter sets in. There's a packet waiting to take us to Detroit, where we'll ship on another boat and go on up through the Erie. As you know, there are rumors every year that the old man means to sell out; if he does, I want to be there when it happens. Astor's a hard man to deal with, but I think I can handle him at least capably enough so that he won't find me too easily put upon." He laughed with perfect assurance and self-confidence. "Can you be ready?"

"I'm always ready, Mr. Crooks."

"Well spoken—and not idly. We have every evidence of that. Word came to me recently about your exploit with that ex-Indian agent after the scalp the Winnebagos had hung on a pole in their village. I've heard, too, much about your work on the council, and one of the military sends us word that your map of the Territory in the vicinity of the meeting place of the rivers is the most accurate known. The Schoolcraft and Carver maps are apparently in error. So you see, we're not ignorant of your accomplishments, not by any means, my boy." His finger had come full circle on the map before him now, and he said to the older Dousman, "Now, you see, the line runs from Lake Pepin to the British Line, thence to the headwaters of the Missouri, and back to St. Peters in this manner. Headquarters, I presume, are best left where they are, at St. Peters. That marks the Northwest division." He turned to Hercules again and stood before him, slapping his abdomen. "Now then, my boy, where were we?"

"On the way to New York, I believe."

"Oh, yes, yes, of course. Day after tomorrow then. We'll take the packet *Aquila* at the wharf."

He shook hands again, shook hands with the older Dousman, put his beaver on and walked from the office in a shambling trot, his footsteps drifting back in the darkness. Hercules turned to his father.

"Well, Father, since I haven't been home, I'd better go. Sibley brought me here at once."

Dousman hummed a little. "What did you think of Sibley?" he asked.

"I had too little time with him to formulate any opinion. I know you think well of him. Perhaps tomorrow I may have a little time to know him better. He leaves a good first impression."

"Wait a little—I'll go with you."

He got up, blew out the lamp, and they went outside to walk together up through the village and out along the road past Fort Holmes and the cemetery to the farm. The stars were remote and clear almost as in winter, with Vega winking down from high near the zenith, and Arcturus already westward. A ceaseless movement of air came with the water's sound, the old familiar voice of waters in the straits, and a fugitive fragrance rode the wind, a pungent minty odor taken partly from leaves of beebalm growing alongside the road, partly from the aromatic pines and cedars growing on the island. It came to Hercules casually that the last time he had walked so with his father was during the habitation of the island by the British, on the evening of the battle before the Dousman farm. He was curiously warmed at this memory, not at the sentiment of it, but purely at its recurrence. Time stood between that moment and now this, he thought—almost twenty years! It did not seem so long ago; it did not seem to him now, walking thus with his father, who had perceptibly aged in these five years, that anything could ever be as long ago as actually it was. The call of the sentry at the dark fort brought him back to that night when he had gone for Lieutenant Hanks at his father's behest, had brought him to the farm to learn the bitterness of knowing he must surrender in the morning to the overwhelming attack of the British. This event, like that other, was held in a curious shell of timelessnss, and he thought that all events great in any life are preserved so in memory, made greater by the balm of time.

Here on the old road little was changed. They went through the red pasture gate into the front yard and so on into the house. Like parts of a puzzle, the familiar aspects of the old place fell into place to obliterate the time between those past events and the present. The door stood open and, hearing his voice, his mother came to the threshold and stood there waiting.

He embraced and kissed her gravely and asked at once about the children.

"They're eating," said his mother. "Your Emily among them. My first granddaughter," she added with pride.

He went into the kitchen and saw them; of one accord the two Rolettes turned to look at him, and for a moment sat thus, their spoons poised, before grinning shyly and turning back to the food before them. The efficient LaBuche had grimly put the baby Emily into a high chair and was determined to teach her to help herself. Hercules laughed and turned back into the front room to fill the house with the warm delight of reminiscence.

On the second morning he found himself oddly reluctant to take his leave of Emily. Emily was sleeping; LaBuche and his mother were united against him; the child needed all the sleep she could get; he could bid her good-bye and hello upon his return, all at the same time; she would not miss him. The Rolette children had been made ready to accompany him. Virginia had cried a little for her mother, but had resigned herself; nevertheless, her great luminous eyes affected Hercules strangely. They were part of Jane; he could not escape knowing this. The boy was more like his father, sturdy, direct in his manner, eager for new adventure, and already marked by a lust for travel.

Ramsay Crooks was on board, but he had not been there long. He welcomed the children heartily, but expressed some doubt in regard to their travelling so great a distance without feminine companionship. Hercules assured him that both were good travellers, reminding him that children of such a roamer as Rolette ought to be.

Crooks wasted no time. As soon as they had followed their baggage aboard, he ordered the boat away, shouting over the rail some parting instructions to Sibley and the older Dousman, who had come down to see them off.

"We'll have a good trip," he said to Hercules then. "Huron is smooth, the air's still, the ship makes good time."

Mackinac fell away, the sound of the straits diminished, and soon the *Aquila* was on its way along the east coast of Michigan on its journey to Detroit, and thence through Lake Erie to Buffalo, where the Erie Canal began.

The trip, as Crooks had foreseen, was uneventful; they escaped storms, and soon reached Buffalo, where they transhipped to a canal boat for the journey up to Troy and thence down the Hudson to New York. The contrast between the country they had left and the land bordering the canal was great; here the aspects

of wilderness had been left behind, the beautiful Mohawk Valley
was a succession of well-kept farms with the appearance of having
been long settled; life along the canal was gay and industrious, but
not hurried; the low canal boats offered a greater intimacy with
the passing scene than the steamboats on the lake, and the almost
somnolent countryside bespoke an advanced civilization free from
frontier dangers in the casualness of its scenes: men driving stock
along the roads, the horsemen along the canal shouting to each
other in passing, the settled air of the villages they passed, the traffic on the canal, the boisterous familiarity of rival boatmen. Some
day the Michigan Territory, too, would be like this, thought Hercules.

The journey was ended at last. They reached New York at night,
but Crooks knew his way around. They went first to deliver the
Rolette children safely into the hands of Jane's cousins who were to
take Virginia to the Academy at Georgetown and Joseph to Philadelphia. Then Crooks ordered the driver of their carriage to take
them to a certain lodging house near Maiden Lane, since, as he
explained, he wished to be near the waterfront for business reasons.

In the morning, Hercules found himself alone. Crooks had left
a note to say that he might be gone all day, he did not know; if
he was not back at the lodging house by evening, he would send
word. Hercules dressed himself, ate breakfast, and went out to
make a tour of the shops. The streets along the waterfront were
crowded even at this early hour. Ships which had docked along
South Street during the night were unloading; kegs, bales, boxes
were piled high along the wharf; across the road, the counting-
houses were open; there was a constant flow of men across the
road, so that traffic was from time to time impeded, and horses
pulling loaded drays had to wind around piles of merchandise.
There were packets from England, from France, and many American ships; a foreign flavor permeated the waterfront. Hercules
dawdled, making sure of his directions, for he found himself reflecting that though he would find no difficulty in making his way
about in the wilderness country with which he was familiar, it
was possible for him to go astray and miss his lodgings in this
maze of streets, alleys, and tall, four-storied buildings.

He left the waterfront after a few hours and found his way to a tailor's shop, where he had himself fitted with a frock coat and trousers to match, these to be marked with his name and delivered at his lodgings by sundown. At another shop he bought himself a handsome white shirt whose texture was less stiff than most, and added to it a high black stock neckpiece with a bow. At still another, he ordered five hundred segars shipped to him at Prairie du Chien. After he had taken his lunch, he hailed a cab and had himself driven to the address where they had left the children on the previous night, to assure himself that all was well with them; but there he found only a servant, who informed him that the children were already on their way. He had himself driven along the waterfront and presently returned to his lodgings.

There he found a message from Crooks ordering him to leave his present lodgings and take rooms for both of them at the Clinton House, where Crooks would join him as soon as it was possible for him to do so.

It took Hercules the remainder of the afternoon to effect this change. Then he went around to the tailor to change his address for shipment of his clothes, but since these had already gone forward, it required still further effort to eliminate delay. As it was, his new clothes preceded him to the Clinton House, so that he found a rather irate tailor's assistant awaiting him with a bill which obviously he thought he would never collect. Hercules paid him, tipped him, and took his clothes upstairs. He shaved himself and dressed; his glass showed him a young man of striking appearance whose long dark hair fell almost to his shoulders, straight except for an upward curl at the ends; his white shirt and tie were ruffed from his tight black frock coat, and almost shone. His trousers were well-fitted, and not too tight. While he was thus surveying himself in the glass, a knock fell on the door of his room.

He opened the door and confronted a middle-aged man who was garbed in the dress of a footman. "Mr. Dousman?"

"Yes."

"Mr. Astor's compliments, sir. Will you join him and Mr. Crooks as soon as you can?"

"Where are they?"

"At Mr. Astor's town house. I'll take you there whenever you're ready."

Leaving the door ajar, Hercules turned back into the room, put on his beaver, and came once more to the threshold. "I'm ready now."

The footman led the way staidly to a handsome brougham at the curb outside the Clinton House. He opened the door for Hercules, saw him seated, and went around to mount to his place. The carriage rolled away over the cobblestones.

He was received by a butler, and conducted at once to a small room not far from the entrance. If he would be so good as to wait there, Mr. Astor would see him as soon as it was convenient for him to do so. The butler withdrew, bowing his tall white-knickered, black-coated person out of the room. Hercules sat alone. Judging by the babble of voices rising mutedly from the depths of the house, some kind of gathering was in progress; there were also sounds of a harpsichord and some one singing.

Hercules had been directed to a seat near an inner door and now, as he sat there, he became conscious of voices in the adjoining room. One of them was recognizably that of Ramsay Crooks. The other was a dry, almost rasping voice, which could on occasion be pleasant enough. Hercules could not help overhearing the conversation, which, on the part of Crooks' interrogator, was casual.

"Now, then, about this man of yours."

"Of ours," corrected Crooks.

"As you like. Of ours, then. I understand he's done very well in unifying the traders in that area, with which we've always had difficulties, not only because of the encroaching of the Hudson Bay Company—damned blackguards!—but because of independent traders and Indian uprisings."

Crooks deprecated this positively.

"Spare me," said the other. "Continue with what you were about to say."

"I've had opportunity to write you time and again about his remarkable executive ability, his fine hand for organization. That position has always required a man of sound and cultivated judgment; the district is so extensive that only a man who has infinite patience and an executive head on him can succeed there.

He's shown his ability to deal equally well with savages and voy-ageurs. In addition, he's never taken sides in any intertribal war, and has friends among all the nations. Though he does not have the title, he's nevertheless in complete charge of the largest area in our Company—all the country north and west of the post to the British boundary except, of course, the land immediately around the Falls of St. Anthony."

There was a brief silence now. Hercules felt a warm glow in-side him, all the stronger because he had never thought of himself in such terms, and did not now; nevertheless, it was he about whom Crooks talked, for the territory described was that in charge of the agent at Prairie du Chien. And it was he who did not have the title, and was yet in charge.

"You've found him trustworthy?"

"Eminently. I've known his father for years, and I've had every experience with him in his position. As you well know, there's been none of Rolette's haphazard method since Dousman came in."

"I believe he must be here by this time. We'll have him in."

The door opened suddenly, and Hercules found himself con-fronting a tall thin-haired old man in his late sixties; he had a long sharp nose, hawk eyes, a thin, cruel mouth in a straight small line. He was elegantly but not flamboyantly dressed, and had evi-dently always been a slim man, though in his present years there was evident a tendency to corpulence.

"Come in, Mr. Dousman," said he.

Hercules crossed before him and greeted Crooks, who had come to his feet in mild surprise. Hercules recognized that his superior did not know Astor had intended to place Hercules in a room where he might overhear everything Crooks said. Crooks intro-duced him to Astor. They shook hands, the old man examining him critically with hard, almost unfriendly eyes.

"I have been hearing about you, Mr. Dousman," said Astor. "Sit down."

Hercules sat down, and Astor resumed the seat he had left to admit him.

"I have just now heard from Mr. Crooks of your abilities, though, to be honest, I should admit that not only Mr. Crooks but other sources have written me about your fine talent for or-

ganization and leadership. These are attributes vitally necessary to the success of the American Fur Company." He spoke with a thick accent, his German ancestry pronounced.

Hercules said modestly that he hoped always to serve the Company to the best of his ability, but that he was unaware of having performed any startling deeds in that service.

"Ah, he is modest, too," observed Astor, smiling wintrily. "I had a curiosity to see you, Mr. Dousman. I had imagined that you might be one of these colorful woodsmen; now I find you quite impeccably dressed."

"I had opportunity this afternoon to visit a tailor," admitted Hercules.

Astor laughed.

Crooks, who had regained his composure and was once again his old self, joined in, remarking that he had not recognized his travelling companion in such clothing. "However," he went on, "Dousman pays a great deal of attention to his clothes. He could hold his own very well here in New York, I have no doubt." He turned to Hercules now. "We've been talking, Mr. Astor and I, about the possible sale of the Company."

Hercules shot a quick glance at Astor, who remained imperturbable, his eyes masked.

"Does the sale impend?" asked Hercules.

"Not yet," said Astor shortly. "I confess, however, I've thought about it. Much of my interest at present lies in shipping, and admittedly, as we all know, there's a marked decline in the trade."

Crooks observed that the trade would always have its ups and downs, and went on like this for a while until Astor held up his hand suddenly and said that they must be getting back to the party, they must not keep the others waiting.

"Of course, Mr. Dousman will join us? Please."

He led the way into a great parlor, from which had come that murmur of voices heard earlier by Hercules. At once a group of gentlemen, who had been watching the door of the library, pressed forward, and in a few moments Hercules' brief attention for the gay party was eclipsed by the introductions Astor was making.

"Mr. Lenox, Mr. Dousman, Mr. Vanderbilt, Mr. Boorman, Mr.

Jones, Mr. Ogden, Mr. Gracie. . . ." Hercules could not begin to remember half of them. At last there was but one left, and Astor beckoned him forward. "Ah, Mr. Van Brugh, you'll be interested in Mr. Dousman. He, too, has Dutch blood in him. His grandfather was a certain Baron Van Dousman who fled persecution in Holland with his sons and their tutor to settle here." He turned to Hercules a little roguishly to say, "You see, I am not entirely ignorant of the men who serve the American Fur Company."

For a week Crooks did everything in his power to persuade Astor to change his mind about the fate of the Company; he met him repeatedly; he entertained him; he brought Hercules to tell in detail the hazards of the trade in that country, as if Astor were not aware of them; he foresaw the ultimate end of the trade because of the rapid influx of settlers who were interested in the pursuit of agriculture and commerce limited to small agricultural centers.

Astor was unmoved; he would not sell. He admitted that he was disappointed in the slow decline of the trade, but he was satisfied that this was not due to any failure on the part of the men who made up his great fur empire, as he himself jokingly called it. Crooks was nettled, but he would not show it.

In the meantime, Hercules was not idle. He found opportunity to meet the heads of various enterprises, either through his own effort, or through the intervention of Astor and Crooks, and in this way he established relationships which might in time be of use to him. He did not meet men in trade alone; he went to the waterfront again to meet shippers and boat men; he sought out the grain buyers, foreseeing the time when the fur trade must of necessity give way to the raising of grain—and its sale. At the same time, he took frequent hours to familiarize himself with the city; he went out and bought presents for those at home, saving Jane's present until last because he did not know what to bring her. He would have liked to bring her a ring, but this, he felt, would not have been quite proper. It was not until the day before his departure that he happened upon a little, out-of-the-way shop in Ludlow Street, and found there a beautiful silver teapot, which he bought without hesitation for Jane Rolette.

At the week's end, Hercules took his departure, leaving Ramsay

Crooks resigned to Astor's refusal to sell. But he was not discouraged. "The old man will sell as soon as he realizes that his margin of profit will go down, you'll see," he said. "Then we'll be in, and of course you understand, Dousman, I've all along wanted you for a partner, and perhaps we can plan something to include Chouteau as well. Only wait."

In this hope, they parted.

Early in September Hercules returned to Prairie du Chien.

He was anxious to be back, partly because he was concerned for the trade during his absence, partly because he worried about the intertribal warfare which almost certainly brewed among the Indians. The effect this might have upon the already declining trade was difficult to gauge, particularly in view of the increasing numbers of settlers coming every month from the east. Coming down the Wisconsin to the meeting place of the rivers, he thought he had never seen so many craft on the stream. Captain Kinzie, who went down to Prairie du Chien from Fort Winnebago, said that houses were going up around the fort at the Portage, and that some of the trappers had erected crude dwellings even along the Barribault River which fed into the Wisconsin midway between the Portage and the northern rim of the prairie of the Sacs. The lead regions, however, were still receiving the greatest numbers of newcomers; but the important fact remained that all these people were bringing their families; they were settling down to live, not just to work the mines and pull up stakes once more.

It was evening when the canoe came to the landing at Prairie du Chien. Kinzie went immediately to see Lockwood, and Hercules hurried to the office, where he found evidence that Rolette had been in charge. He sat down at once, after arranging for his baggage to be taken to his house, and drew the books to him.

In half an hour, drawn by the light in the Company's office, Rolette came over. He blinked at Hercules, who saw that he had been drinking.

"God damn it, I thought we were being robbed," he said. "When'd you get back?"

"Just now. I came right here."

"Glad you're back. I never did like the business of taking care of

affairs like this. I'll take the work outside, away from the books. How's Crooks?"

Hercules said that Crooks was in good health. So was Astor. He described his meeting with Astor at some length. He spoke also about Crooks' plan for the American Fur Company if and when Astor could be persuaded to sell out.

Rolette listened with interest, but he was clearly not sanguine about the outcome of Crooks' plan. Crooks had very definite ideas about running the Company, he knew. Crooks' ideas did not always agree with his own. He did not believe he could get along with Crooks, and would not hesitate to tell him so. "In any event," he finished, "I have enough irons in the fire."

Hercules asked for an explanation of several entries, and Rolette made them easily. He got up finally to go.

"I hope you don't plan on working too long," he said. "There's a ball at the fort tonight, and you'll want to go."

"Are you going?"

Rolette tugged at one ear and said he did not know.

"Jane would enjoy that," said Hercules.

Rolette nodded with a dry smile. "Her brother George's here, George Fisher. Companionable fellow."

He went out.

In a little while Hercules put the books away, went to his house and dressed for the ball; he put on the same clothes he had worn on the occasion of his first visit to Astor. Already in the warm September air, pungent with the fragrance of falling leaves, the music of the fiddlers at the fort across the Marais de St. Feriole sounded distantly. Lest he arrive too early, he set about unpacking his baggage, setting out the teapot he had bought for Jane, the segars he had brought Rolette, and various other gifts.

It was nine o'clock by the time he reached the scene of the ball. While he searched in vain for sight of Jane, he was discovered by Doctor Beaumont, who seized upon him at once and carried him off to inquire about his eastern trip.

"I'm afraid," he began dejectedly, "that they do not think too well of me there, Dousman. You see, I have had to disagree with some of the best authorities on the digestion, and I am much of the belief that they consider me an upstart. If they could but look

into St. Martin's stomach, they would not think so any longer; they could see it as I do."

"How is St. Martin?" asked Hercules.

"You ask it as if you expected him to drop dead at any moment," said Beaumont in an aggrieved voice. "He's very well, only a little impatient with my experiments, which go forward all the time, as much as I can afford with my meager salary; you know how little I have to live on. But the things I have discovered! Dousman, you would not believe it."

"Perhaps more easily than the scientists who have previously conceived notions," countered Hercules, laughing.

"For instance," continued Beaumont in a more animated voice, "I have ascertained that the digestion is aided if food is chewed very well."

Hercules could not help pointing out that the Indians wolfed their food.

Undoubtedly, said Beaumont, the Indians had many a bellyache, but of course, being stoic, made no mention of it; they endured them as they did lice or similar afflictions, as an act of Gitchee Manitou.

At this moment Hercules saw Jane. She had come in not with Rolette, but on the arm of a dark-haired young man whose facial resemblance to her identified him as her brother. He excused himself and went over to where she stood talking to Colonel Taylor, who was squiring his wife. He bowed to them all, turned to Jane, and asked whether Madame Rolette would do him the honor of taking the dance with him.

"Mistaire Dousman flattaire me. But of course; I will be delight'." She turned as the Taylors walked away, and tapped her escort's arm. "Mistaire Dousman, this is my brothaire, George. He has come to live in Prairie du Chien."

They shook hands. In the fleeting glance he gave him, Hercules thought George made of weaker stuff than Jane. This was apparent not only in the laxness about his mouth, but also in his casual manner. But he had little time for Jane's brother in her presence. It was absurd how his pulse bounded forward when she came to his arms for the dance.

She asked at once about the children. How had they taken the trip?

He told her they had borne it very well, adding that he had left his own Emily with his mother.

LaBuche had told her how it went to Mackinac. After that she knew nothing, but of course her cousins had written, and the headmistress of the school at Georgetown had written, too, to say that Virginia was a well-behaved and apt pupil, that she had missed her mother, but would get over this. "I have hear' from the pries' that Joseph have accustom' himsel' to life in Philadelphia."

For over half the duration of the dance she talked about the children with an animation which failed to betray her loneliness, her love for them, the apparent manner in which she clung spiritually to them. He felt his sympathy rising for her, and yet knew that in the event of trouble again among the Indians, the children were better where they were. He said so, and she reluctantly agreed.

Presently he asked after Rolette. Where was he?

At once she seemed to tauten in his arms. "M'sieu' Rolette do not see fit to come," she said stiffly. "M'sieu' Rolette he have bettaire things to do. He sit all night at Brunet's tavern and drink his whiskey."

"He's still drinking then?"

"He has nevaire stop!" she cried indignantly.

He maneuvered her into a more quiet corner, from which fled at their approach pretty Knoxie Taylor and her Lieutenant Davis. They sat down.

"Now then," he said. "If Madame will tell me?"

"But there's nothing to tell," she cried. "It is jus' so—M'sieu' Rolette drink too much, he drink too often, he become drunk, he say bad things to me, he say he will not pay for my clothes, he will not give me any money."

"Did he pay for the clothes you ordered from St. Louis just before I left?" pressed Hercules.

She nodded. "But only with vair' great reluctance. I do not like his drink' like this. But I cannot talk to M'sieu' Rolette; he will not listen to me. He will not listen to any one."

"I'll talk to him again."

She shook her head. "It will do no good, I know. He is worse now. He show his tempaire now, and he take my brothaire with

him some time, and George grow drunk, too. Elizabeth and I, we do not like this. I do not know how long I can endure it. Mistaire Dousman can pairhaps imagine how hard it mus' be for me."

Hercules assured her that he could. He pressed her, however, for more details. Surely there was some reason for Rolette's drinking. He had thought he had at one time helped to solve the older man's difficulties. If he had never stopped drinking, what reason might he have given himself for his failure?

But she knew nothing. "He do not tell me anything. I am a woman, only a woman. I do not understan' business, he say. How can I understan' what he tell me nothing about?" she cried indignantly.

"Has he quarrelled with you recently?"

"He quarrel all the time. Whenevaire I ask him for something— a hat, shoes, a dress—then he become angry, he quarrel. He is not kin'. M'sieu' Rolette is not like the man I have marry. He has grow different; there are now sairtain things about him I cannot endure, I cannot get accustom' to. Today I wish' to send an ordaire to Stambaugh for a new dress, and M'sieu' Rolette has counterman' my ordaire. I do not know what to do, but I say again I will not endure this long. If M'sieu' Rolette pairsists, I shall leave him."

Hercules expressed the opinion mildly that Rolette would be a helpless man left alone. Consider how much he had his man Barrette with him, both at home and in the wilderness. Barrette's companionship was constant, both in the capacity of valet and guide. He did not like to think of Rolette left alone.

"M'sieu' Rolette always have his Elizabeth. She would nevaire leave him," retorted Jane with some asperity.

Hercules laughed. It could not be as serious as Jane made it, he was certain; he said so. She was indignant and stood up. Quite easily he put his arms around her and swung her away into the gayety of the dance again. After a while, he questioned her again about Rolette. Did he not at times seem worried?

"He figure on papaire vair' much," she agreed. "But he have always do this. I do not know what it is he write."

He told her briefly that before he had left for the East, Rolette

had been in some financial difficulties, and that, in order to alleviate his temporary condition, he had taken a partnership in Rolette's real-estate business. He could not help adding that, with
the influx of settlers, Rolette should now be taking in enough
money.

She replied that he seemed never to be without money. At least,
he seemed always to have enough to drink all he wished and to
lend to worthless people. "Oh, I am patient," she cried. "I try to
do as he would wish me to do, but I cannot endure his tempaire
and his drink', and the way he talk and act now."

He made a mental note to see the trader, Hill, and to speak once
more of Rolette. Then he changed the subject to speak to her about
his trip. He said he had brought something west for her, and he
would bring it over to the house, or send it in the morning.

"Could we not, George and I, walk ovaire with Mistaire Dousman and obtain it now, tonight?" she asked eagerly.

He was a little taken aback. "I suppose you might—but it isn't so
important; it isn't anything so big. It's nothing much, just a little
something."

"Whatevaire Mistaire Dousman may bring, I am sure it would be
the bes'."

She was laughing at him behind her eyes in her old manner.
Quickly he responded. Madame well knew that even the best paled
beside her, and therefore he must perforce deprecate anything
which was presumed to stand beside her.

"Then we can go to your house and obtain this little gift now?"
she insisted.

"All right." He gave in, knowing the futility of argument and
the triviality of the issue.

But when they looked for George after several dances, he was
nowhere to be found. Lieutenant Davis reported presently that
Madame Rolette's brother had left the ball shortly after his arrival. No one knew where he might have gone, or whether he would
return.

Hercules hoped that he would have the pleasure of seeing
Madame home, unless she preferred that he not do so.

"I have not forgot' we are to secure what you have bring for
me," she said. "We shall go before you forget."

The night had turned cool, the air was crisp, and leaf-fragrance was strongly pungent. No wind blew, save for the occasional rustle of furtive breezes among the dying leaves. The gay music from the ballroom at the fort rolled after them pleasantly, vying with the barking of dogs and a man's voice somewhere uncertainly singing *En Roulant Ma Boule*. Jane held firmly to his arm.

Well away from the fort, she said gently, "I know where my brothaire have go. He have go to where M'sieu' Rolette is. They will take each othaire's company when they drink."

Hercules laughed. "You make too much of an issue of this."

"No, Mistaire Dousman, I do not. I know M'sieu' Rolette. I know my brothaire. M'sieu' Rolette is strong in many things, my brothaire is strong in none."

He was silent. The moonlight shone down into her face and left him breathless; for all the inner turmoil that she suffered because of the change in Rolette, there was no mark upon her face to show that she had been deeply affected; she wore still that same air of serene and ageless beauty. He turned away presently and would not look at her again until they reached his small house.

She stood outside decorously while he went in and brought out the teapot.

She was delighted. "I have always want' such a teapot," she said. "I have always hope' to have one. I do not know how to thank you, Mistaire Dousman." She held it up so that the moonlight made a soft sheen upon its surface.

"There is no need to thank me," he said. "I am repaid a thousand times by the pleasure Madame has shown."

"What did you bring for M'sieu' Rolette?" she asked, walking with him again toward her own home.

He told her.

She made a moue. "Segars. He will smoke up the whole house. But then, it is his house, so why shall he not do so if he wish?"

They came quickly enough to her door and stood briefly before the house so pretentious for its environment here on the frontier. He was reluctant to part from her; she seemed no more eager to enter the house herself. They made small talk. There was no sign of life about the house; even Eugenie, said Jane, had taken the

evening off, and had gone somewhere, she did not know where, but the life in the growing village was rapidly passing beyond her ken. She could no longer keep up.

But at last she said she must go in. She came close to him and looked earnestly into his eyes. "I know I have a good frien' in Mistaire Dousman," she said. "I know he is frien' to M'sieu' Rolette as well as to me. I hope he will not judge me too harsh' if I mus' leave M'sieu' Rolette."

He looked at her fine precise features in the heady moonlight and closed his eyes. "If Madame Rolette does not go immediately into her house, I am afraid I shall do something I will regret," he said stiffly.

She tightened her hand on his arm. "Mistaire Dousman would not dare," she breathed, half in earnest, half in mockery.

In answer he swept her to him, and kissed her almost savagely. For a brief, incredible moment, she did not resist; then abruptly she pushed him from her.

"Mistaire Dousman forget' himself," she cried.

"I'm sorry," he said. "I warned you."

"You do not soun' sorry," she answered sharply.

Hercules smiled now and looked into her eyes. The words were necessary, he explained, but the feeling could not be artificially created. "I'm sorry," he said again, "and I know I do not sound so. And if Madame continues to stand there and look at me like that, I shall have to be sorry all over again."

Jane pressed her lips firmly together, caught up her skirt a little, said "Good night, Mistaire Dousman. Thank you!" very austerely, and marched into the house, closing the door behind her with a spirited slam.

He stood looking at the dark house thinking only of the loveliness of her mouth and the taste of her lips upon his own. For these fleeting moments he forgot that she was Rolette's wife, and when, in a few seconds this realization came to him, he crushed the sudden shame he felt as resolutely as he put down the surging of longing he had so often known for Jane.

He sent for the trader, Hill, in the morning. Hill was on his way east and was in a hurry: a great, big-boned man, with heavy flesh.

He came a little truculently and wished to know why Hercules had sent for him.

"I understand Madame Rolette has ordered a dress from Stambaugh which you're to bring back to her?" he asked.

Hill nodded. This was true enough. But Rolette had countermanded the order, and of course Madame could not pay for the dress herself.

Hercules wrote a brief note and gave it to Hill at once. "Give this to Stambaugh and bring her the dress. She shall have her clothes. Rolette isn't well, and this note will assure Stambaugh that, failing Rolette's payment, I'll pay for the things she buys myself."

Hill felt it his duty to point out that the King might not like this.

"Rolette and I are partners, Mr. Hill," replied Hercules shortly. "Each of us does business in his own way regardless."

Hill went out, grumbling. But he would bring the dress.

Rolette came in around noon. Hercules had waited all morning for him to appear, and he was at this moment in the store adjoining his office, pulling out a pair of red leggings, for a Winnebago who had come after them. He settled with the Indian and made his way hurriedly among the piles of blankets and cloth into the office, before Rolette could go into the warehouse.

Rolette, however, had sat down at the table where Hercules' books still lay open. He was regarding them thoughtfully when Hercules entered.

"Ah, I'm glad to find you still here, Joe," said Hercules. "I wanted to see you. It seems you've kept right on drinking to excess . . ."

Rolette interrupted him with a profane exclamation. "I didn't promise to stop. *Sacré tonnerre de Dieu!* A man can go to the devil in his own way, surely?"

Hercules pushed this aside. There was no reason to speak so. No one had said Rolette was going to the devil. But it was nevertheless true that by his actions Rolette jeopardized not only his relations with the American Fur Company, but also with Madame Rolette. Rolette listened, his face reddening with anger. Hercules went on, setting forth his arguments with biting scorn.

At last Rolette got up, kicking back his chair. "What the devil

business is it of yours, Hercules?" he demanded. "I can drink as much as I like. In any case, you've got charge of the books. I don't interfere."

"And Madame Rolette?"

Rolette had a ready answer for that. Jane spoke for herself, he said. She spoke very volubly. She spoke day and night; so that it was a mercy to escape the house from time to time.

Hercules said that in his opinion Jane was not a nagging wife. Nor would Rolette countenance any suggestion that he had said this. "Still, she talks too much. I don't get the rest I should."

Hercules shrugged, thinking it useless to point out that if Rolette lacked rest, he might find some if he gave up carousing at night. "I understood this morning from Hill that you had countermanded Madame Rolette's order for a new dress," he said instead.

"Mille tonnerre!" exclaimed Rolette angrily. "That Hill talks too much."

"But it's true?"

"Of course it's true! God damn it, Hercules, I'm a patient man, but I've had to put up with new clothes on every trip a man makes to Stambaugh. I'm getting tired of it. Why, Jane's got almost an entire room filled with all kinds of fancy things which she'll never wear."

Hercules protested gently. He had been through the house more than once, and had seen nothing of this room. Where was it?

Rolette ignored this. "So I stopped Hill and told him he would accept no more orders from my wife without my approval." He flung his big body toward the door, his dark beard bristling, his eyes flashing. "I tell you, Hercules, you're a lucky man to be unmarried!"

Hercules went around and sat down, saying quietly, "I gave Hill orders to bring whatever Madame Rolette ordered with the understanding that if you didn't pay for it I'd do so myself."

Rolette went out, but instantly returned, his mouth open in astonishment. "What was that?" he asked, as if he had not heard aright.

Hercules repeated what he had said. He added that he had set no time limit on his promise; so he would evidently have good

opportunity to know to what extent Madame Rolette ate up Rolette's income.

"What is the point of this, Hercules?" asked Rolette, more amused now than irritated.

"Why, we're partners, Joe," said Hercules dryly. "I believe in sharing the crosses you must bear as well, though you see, I'm not convinced Madame Rolette is a cross."

"Not yet," said Rolette. He shrugged. "Well, it's your own affair, if you want to humor her, but it's poor business, poor business. You'll never succeed that way, Hercules." He went out, shaking his head.

Hercules followed him to the outer door and looked thoughtfully after him. Rolette walked to the center of the road and stood there, torn between his desire to go down toward the river where Brunet's tavern was, and to cross the Marais de St. Feriole to where his home stood. At this moment George Fisher came along, caught hold of his arm, and together they walked down toward Brunet's.

Hercules sighed and re-entered the office. He was disappointed, but he had no time to concern himself further now. He had had no word of the intertribal warfare he had left behind him, and he meant to find out, so that he might know what to expect in the way of influence upon the trade for the coming seasons. He closed his books, put them away, and went out to where Major was stabled. He mounted his spirited horse and rode leisurely eastward to the coulee where the Indian agent had his house.

Street was at home and glad to see him. Hercules asked at once about the Indians. Street shook his head.

"Fighting, raids, massacres—they go on all the time. Many of them we don't even hear about," he said. "But I don't think there's much danger for the whites."

Hercules was pleased to hear this at least. But any fighting among the tribes would impair the trade; if the braves were kept from hunting and trapping, the number of pelts would become less in direct proportion to the time spent at warfare. He asked about Black Sparrow Hawk.

Street shook his head. "He's apparently quiet in the trans-Mississippi region, though I understand he goes to see the British

agent at Malden, and he has a very unreliable advisor, White Cloud, who calls himself the Prophet."

They talked for some time. Reassured, if not entirely relieved, Hercules went back to work with renewed vigor and determination to raise the total of pelts taken above last year's, to justify the faith Crooks and Astor had in him.

Two days later, Hercules met Jane on her way to visit Madame Fernette. She stopped short before him, fixing him with flashing, almost angry eyes. She did not return his greeting, and for an instant said nothing at all, standing as if waiting for him to speak again. When he did not, she spoke.

"Mistaire Dousman owe' me an apology for what happen' the othaire night."

He had gone toward her with the intention of offering her an apology, but in the face of her indignation, he could not; the desire to tease her came over him too strongly to resist it: besides, this light mockery was a weapon she had often used to advantage, and it had been in part at least responsible for his yielding to the sudden impulse which had beset him.

"What happened the other night?" he asked, widening his eyes in amazement.

That he should have kissed her at all was in her estimate enough of an affront; but that he should have forgotten it was incredible. Her natural vanity was piqued. Her lips parted momentarily in astonishment before she could prevent it, and she seemed unable to make any reply to him, who stood with a polite air of inquiry before her. Then a quick angry blush suffused her fine features.

"Mistaire Dousman took the liberty to kiss me," she said.

He saw that he had touched her more than he meant and was instantly sober. "Yes, of course, I remember it very well. I do offer you my apology."

"Well, that is bettaire," she said, mollified.

"But in all honesty, I must tell Madame that I cannot be sorry for its pleasant effect upon me. I believe it is beyond me. If I say that I am sorry for yielding to the impulse, Madame must understand that her presence gave too much strength to the impulse, so that I could not overcome it."

She cocked her head a little to one side, and a glint came into her eyes. She strove very patently to remain firm, but a hint of amusement touched her lips. "You talk vair' much, Mistaire Dousman," she said. "Are you sorry or are you not? Which is it? Say yes or no, and do not make so much excuse."

"Yes and no."

She gave a short sharp exclamation and turned to pass him.

"I could not truly be sorry," he said quickly, "for anything which in my mind would seem to deprecate Madame's beauty."

She paused and eyed him doubtfully.

"For no man could be sorry he had kissed some one as beautiful as Madame," he went on. "But if I have offended Madame, I am sorry for that. I am sorry for the weakness which permitted me to yield to the impulse—but I am not sorry for the kiss itself, and I am afraid nothing on earth can make me sorry for that."

While she was trying to make up her mind what to say to him, he bowed and said, "But I am keeping Madame. Forgive me."

When he looked back from the threshold of the office he saw her going swiftly down the street swinging her parasol with a vehemence that bespoke the strength of her reaction, whatever it might be. He could not help laughing softly to himself, amused that her mockery could have been so well turned against her.

Autumn wore to winter, and winter to spring. The snows were heavy and held to the earth until mid-March, when the south wind began to bring the spring with infinitesimal slowness up the Mississippi, the white-throated sparrows began to sing, the red-winged blackbirds cried cheerily from the reeds along the river. All winter the village had known peace; the trade had flourished despite the deep snows; Indians and independent traders came and went; Rolette vanished northward, toward Lake Traverse, having made it clear that he had no intention of putting an end to his drinking.

Hill came back from the East in May. Stambaugh had sent Jane's dress, and Hercules paid for it, unknown to her.

In the same month Marsh came back from Wabashaw's village to open his trading post again. He brought his family with him and showed every sign of settling for good. Hercules was vexed and especially angered when Rising Cloud came to see him in the night

and reported that Marsh was selling guns secretly again to the Sioux. Hercules sat for a while in deep thought while the Sac waited.

Hercules asked presently about Black Hawk.

Rising Cloud said without emotion that the Black Sparrow Hawk would soon speak to the war birds; he would hold the dance; his braves wished him to do so. He had that spring come back from a visit among the British in Canada and found the ancient burial grounds of the Sacs overrun with settlers. He had not sold the burial grounds nor the village at the mouth of the Rock. This was now the second time such a thing had happened, though anything was possible of a white man. Black Hawk was enraged; he had torn up fences and dug up gardens; he had warned the settlers to go away from the Sac village. They in turn had written lies about Sac atrocities to Governor Reynolds of Illinois, and he had chased the Sacs across the Mississippi, followed them, and forced the Black Sparrow Hawk at the point of a gun to write his name to a promise that he would never cross the Mississippi again. That was the way white men liked to make treaties, said Rising Cloud. And some of them, like Marsh, sold guns to the old enemies of the Sacs, to exterminate them; they all knew white people.

"Look here, Rising Cloud," said Hercules, "I want you to do this thing: after a little while, come with others and buy guns from Marsh, if you can. Then you must be ready to show them and testify against him, and I will have him brought to trial. In that way you can be rid of Marsh, and so can we. We don't like him any better than you do."

Rising Cloud was dubious. He said he would try it. But every one knew that Marsh did not sell to the Sacs and Foxes, whom he hated, and who hated him. But perhaps they could persuade certain of their allies to trap Marsh.

Hercules made him a present of a red-and-brown blanket and sent him away.

He was concerned about Black Hawk's calling for the war bird dance. Are we never to have peace! he thought, thinking angrily about the decline of the trade inevitable enough without such additional factors to stimulate that decline. He was more than ever angered at Marsh, but there was nothing he could do without proof.

He observed that people continued to cut Marsh on the streets of the village, but Marsh appeared to have hardened himself to this now. Nevertheless, Marsh did not have the appearance of a man at his ease. He avoided the military, he avoided Street, he crossed the road when he saw Hercules; he did not, in fact, come much into the public eye, but stayed close to his trading post with his wife and son, who was now in his fifth year.

The spring passed over without alarm, a tranquil time. Settlers came, passengers for Fort Winnebago came up the river, commerce between Mackinac and other points north increased with Prairie du Chien, Dubuque, St. Louis and New Orleans; the movement of people made the Michigan Territory seem less a wilderness than ever before.

But Indian trouble impended always. Large parties still came to the village, camping just outside, and spending a day in trading, a night in roistering before going on again. Sometimes they stayed for a week or more, so that there was still a constant encampment of Indians on the islands and the prairie east of the settlement.

On the last day of July a party of Menominees camped on the island directly opposite the land upon which the old fort had stood, now Hercules' property. Among them were some of the same braves who, with the Sioux, had massacred Chief Kettle and his band in the previous year. They had brought their squaws and a few children, and were bent upon roistering there. For most of the night their yells and calls resounded, keeping Hercules awake until but a few hours before dawn. This was no isolated roistering; those Indians who had been initiated into drink, who had not refused to "put an evil spirit" into their bodies, were accustomed to such debauch. However much it was to be regretted that the Hudson Bay Company and its rivals following the older Company's initiative had brought firewater to the Indians, it was now too late to prevent drinking.

In the morning Hercules rose early to watch as much as possible Marsh's store, to see whether the Menominees went there to buy weapons. The sun rose and the village came to life; no sound came from the encampment on the island. But presently a solitary Sioux appeared on the river, drove swiftly in his canoe to the land-

ing, and went directly to Marsh's store. Hercules waited patiently.

In half an hour the Sioux came out. He carried nothing but what he had taken into the store. But immediately behind him came Marsh, carrying a large bundle to the canoe. His manner was clearly one of great agitation. He hurried from the canoe back into the store and came out with another bundle; this one the Sioux took, and came back. Then, after a lapse of perhaps five minutes, Marsh appeared again, accompanied by his wife and son, dressed for a journey. His wife, Hercules could observe, was protesting bitterly, but Marsh only shook his head, hurried her to the canoe, kissed her, and literally forced her to join the Sioux and their son, who had gone willingly into the canoe. The canoe pushed off, with Mrs. Marsh's protests rising still, and Marsh stood waving after it as long as it was within sight on its way down the Mississippi.

The entire procedure had taken less than an hour.

Hercules was astonished and perplexed. Impulsively he went quickly over to the store and made a soundless entry. Marsh was standing at a counter making small pillars of silver; he was white-faced, his hands were trembling, he was patently in a panic of fear.

"Is it retribution, Marsh?" asked Hercules shortly.

Marsh whirled and fell back a little, reaching for a short-arm. He regained something of his composure when he saw Hercules.

"Dousman! I thought it was . . ."

"The Foxes, eh?"

Marsh stared at him. "Then you know about it? Who told you? A Sioux was just here."

"I saw him. What did he tell you?"

Marsh began suddenly to tremble. "What's the matter? Wasn't he a Sioux? Oh, God! I sent Marguerite and Charley with him. I thought—but it *was* Antoine, I know him; of course it was. What are you trying to do?"

"Nothing at all. You seem to be doing very well by yourself. What did he tell you? I asked you before."

"About the Menominees on the island—all butchered by the Foxes while they slept, every one. Antoine found them in their blood."

"You can thank yourself for that, Marsh," said Hercules, when the shock of this information had passed.

"It means that the Fox are around us. They'll come after Marguerite and Charley. They haven't forgotten."

"Pull yourself together," said Hercules curtly.

Marsh made an effort to control the shaking of his hands, the revealing uncertainty of his glance, moving from door to window and back, as if he feared that at any moment a raiding party of Fox and Sacs might appear somewhere to take their vengeance upon him for his betrayal of old Kettle.

"But I'm still too smart for them," he said after a little. "I've sent Marguerite and our son down to the Concord Settlement on the Sandridge, in Illinois."

"They'll be going through the Fox and Sac country," Hercules pointed out.

But Marsh had thought of this. He had sent them up the Wisconsin to Green Bay, and thence down the lake past Chicago into the Illinois River to the settlement. It was the longest way they could take, but it was also the safest for them. He knew now that the Fox meant to kill his wife and son if they could get at them. Where they had gone, they would be safe; it was not a village to which Indians came with the freedom and latitude that they came to the posts.

"Just in case it might be necessary, where would we reach Mrs. Marsh?" asked Hercules smoothly.

Marsh blinked and swallowed uneasily. "They're at Doctor Pantier's. Everybody down there for miles around knows Uncle Jimmy Pantier." Abruptly he changed the subject. "But I don't know why I'm telling you all this. You don't like me, and I don't like you, and we've made no bones about that."

"I don't dislike you, Marsh—I dislike only that part of you which plays at being Sioux, that part which sells the Sioux and their allies guns and ammunition. For the bravery and resourcefulness of the man behind, I have only admiration. Nevertheless, because of those other parts, you know I'll seize upon every chance to get you out of here. You're a troublemaker; Rolette told me that when first I came, and I've found it out since. But I have no personal feeling whatever; you misjudge me and my motives. I'm thinking only of the good of the trade."

Marsh laughed bitterly. "Like all of us, you think only of your own good. You don't fool me, Dousman. If you want war, you'll have it. I'm not afraid of you, and I'm not afraid to die, as long as nothing happens to my family."

Hercules left Marsh alone and hurried back up the street. By this time the alarm was out; the Menominees had been discovered. He thought with a quickening pulse of irritation that they would have it to do with the Indians all over again, and he went thoughtfully back to his work, earnestly probing for some solution, some end to this constant warfare which harassed the trade without ceasing.

The turmoil among the Indian tribes continued.

It was manifest that preparations were being made for war, and it was certain that isolated whites had every reason to fear attack as soon as the war began. No one could say when that would be. Hercules' Indians failed to come in. Kapolequa, at any rate, would come no more; he had been killed by a party of Sioux, and intelligence of his death reached Hercules through Rising Cloud. Hercules was saddened by the relentlessness with which the Indians pursued their intertribal warfare.

Meanwhile, the trade was disrupted. Not only were the Indians engaged in nothing else but preparations for war, sending runners among the villages both in the Territory and in the trans-Mississippi, but traders found certain areas inaccessible to them. In addition to this, prices paid for pelts declined. The trade, to a man, were furious at Captain Marsh, whose betrayal of Kettle's party over a year ago had set in motion the sequence of events which threatened now to engulf the upper Mississippi region in war which, however ostensibly it must be concerned with the Indians alone, would inevitably involve settlers and ultimately the military.

Information was fragmentary. Traders carried stories. Certain Indians who came to Prairie du Chien told that the Prophet, White Cloud, promised all manner of aid from the British at Malden, but it was not clear whether these British were agents of the Hudson Bay Company or whether they had connections with the government of the dominion to the north. Indian agents writing to Street informed him that the struggle would apparently involve not only

the Sacs and Foxes on the one side, and the Sioux and Menominees on the other, but also Winnebagos, Pottawatomis, and members of other tribes. Hercules was exasperated. He sent runners to the various chiefs to learn their intentions. Most of them would not say. Keokuk came out openly and said that he would not lead his tribe into war, no matter what events took place. The implications in the information which Hercules received in this manner pointed clearly to one man among the tribes; this was Chief Black Sparrow Hawk. It was he who must make the decision, and, whatever it would be, the other chiefs, with the exception of Keokuk, would abide by it.

The trade declined inexorably, and Hercules redoubled his efforts to remove Marsh from Prairie du Chien. But Marsh was cunning; he was aware of enmity and he knew guile. He continued to sell arms and ammunition to the Sioux and Menominees and was not detected at it. Hercules was not alone in his anger and bafflement; Lockwood, Rolette, and Street, together with the French settlers led by the Ducharmes, La Pointes, and Fernettes were bitter that a white man's greed and lack of honor could have brought the settlements along the Wisconsin and the upper Mississippi and their tributaries to the threat of war once again.

Destiny, however, waited upon Captain John Marsh, and with ironic indifference struck at him that autumn. Marguerite, the Wahpeton half-breed to whom he was so devoted, lonely and homesick, escaped from the Pantier household on the Sandridge, in Illinois, and with incredible courage and resourcefulness made her way through hostile country on foot in bitter weather, filled with the fierce desire to be once again in her home country, to be at the side of her lord and master. But the effort was too great; in her last week of pregnancy, she survived only to drag herself across Marsh's threshold and die in his arms, unable even to speak, so great was her exhaustion. Marsh was shaken in his grief. He hurried at once to the Concord Settlement to assure himself that his son was still alive and in good hands, since his wife had not been able to tell him herself.

During his absence Hercules had word of the intentions of Black Hawk. This came not from Rising Cloud or from any other among his Indian agents, but from the young Baron Pierneau, who came down ostensibly to sell a pack of fine otter pelts, and remained to

betray an almost hopeless idealism and a thorough lack of knowledge of the background for the Indian struggle, thinking all the
intertribal warfare had been brought about solely through the
machinations of Astor's Company. Nevertheless, Hercules was
patient with him; he bought his pelts, paying more than he need
have for them. His patience was rewarded, for presently Pierneau
informed him that war was inevitable between the settlers of
Illinois and the adjoining part of Michigan Territory and the Sacs
under Black Hawk.

Hercules apprehended at once that Pierneau had some definite
knowledge. Accordingly, he pretended that his own was less than
it was. "You believe the Sacs may attempt to reoccupy the Rock
River lands again?" he asked.

Pierneau said that he did, nodding his fine head, his mouth a
straight line between his soft moustache and carefully trimmed
beard. His gray eyes, Hercules saw, were firm, commanding; his
supple hands those of an aristocrat born.

Hercules pressed him for further information. What made him
speak so? He could rid himself of the idea that the traders could
prevent hostilities. He knew as well as Hercules himself did that
war was the last thing the traders wished to face.

"I'm convinced that nothing can stop Black Hawk from reoc-
cupying his home territory again," said Pierneau.

Hercules agreed that if the Sac did so, war would be inevitable.
He did not say at once that the Sioux and their allies would be
drawn in, ostensibly on the side of the whites, but in reality only
in retaliatory blows against their old enemies. In any case, Hercules
was certain, the Sacs would not move across the Mississippi to the
mouth of the Rock until after the coming winter had passed.
Pierneau agreed.

After they parted, Hercules looked up Lapiage, whom he knew
to visit Pierneau on his occasional trips along the Wisconsin.
Lapiage was at his lodgings, making ready for the night, saying
that he felt unwell and needed to rest. His fat face, however,
creased into a smile of pleasure at mention of Pierneau, whom he
praised volubly.

"Where does he get his pelts?" asked Hercules. "He brought in
the finest otter furs I've had for some time."

"He has three *engagés* living at his place," said Lapiage.

Hercules shook his head patiently. "I know. He had two of them along when he went over to Lockwood's. But these otter pelts never came from the Sac Prairie country; they're much finer quality than any we've taken from this part of the Territory."

"I understand he has Indians delivering pelts to him—some of the Sacs from Black Hawk's band."

"Ha! I thought so. Then we may depend on it, the Hawk will invade Illinois in the spring!"

That uneventful winter was one of the poorest in the history of the trade. Yet Astor demanded income, and the agents suffered. Marsh came back and began to sell arms and ammunition once more, despite the pointed warning of General Street. Fewer Indians than ever came to Prairie du Chien that winter, and there was about those who came an inexplicable air of waiting. The aging Manitonobe came in to inform Hercules that word had gone around that the spirit of Tecumseh guided the Prophet, whose influence upon Black Hawk was great. All the Indians revered Tecumseh as the generation before had looked upon Pontiac as the supremely great leader. It was now thought that Black Hawk might be the third of them.

This was not a good omen, since it presaged greater support for the Sacs than they might otherwise have got. And the signature of war was everywhere apparent; war was certain to come as soon as the snows passed, unless Keokuk could prevail upon the Black Sparrow Hawk to seek a council.

In April came Manitonobe once more to say that Black Hawk had crossed the Mississippi with a band of some five hundred Indians, braves, old women and men, squaws, children, and all their belongings. They had come not to make war, he said, but to reoccupy their lands; however, they had gone deep into Illinois, the settlers had become alarmed, Governor Reynolds had issued a call for volunteers, and the hue and cry had begun. All up and down the river—at Galena, Apple River, Kellogg's Grove, Armstrong, Winnebago—the forts were arming. At the Blue Mounds, at Union, Defiance, at Hamilton's and all the lead diggings preparations for battle were being made, and General Atkinson was being called.

So it had come at last, thought Hercules. He sent word up to General Street, and would himself have gone to the fort had he not been interrupted by the arrival of a boat from St. Louis carrying as passenger an Hungarian Count, who introduced himself to Hercules as a cousin of Pierneau, and wished to know how best to reach his cousin's place on the Wisconsin. Impulsively, Hercules went himself to accompany Count Brogmar to the prairie of the Sacs, so that he might inform himself of the character of the land there and return to Pierneau the favor of bringing him information about Black Hawk's movements. Already in his mind, however, was the thought of the land and its usefulness in raising grain, for it was apparent that the trade would decline with or without Indian wars to help it along, and he foresaw that in grain lay the next source of income, after the trade was done, and the sale of the lands had been accomplished. He talked about this to Pierneau, preparing him for the change he knew must come.

He returned then immediately to Prairie du Chien to wait for word of the war. This came soon, with many conflicting stories. The first battle had taken place near the Rock River, where Black Hawk had sent two braves to offer his surrender, and, these two having been murdered by the whites, he had then set upon them and routed them, a handful of Indians scattering ten times their number of volunteers. From this point on, it appeared that the Black Hawk War became grotesque. In the first place, none of the promised assistance came to the Sacs; they fought virtually alone. In the second, Black Hawk tried repeatedly to surrender, but the whites chose to believe that he was laying waste the country, killing all the settlers in his path, and generally spreading carnage. This was not wholly imagination, for in reality some of the Sioux had killed several isolated settlers and left the marks of Sacs there to inflame further the whites against their hereditary enemies. The Sioux themselves took up arms against the Sacs, as did their allies among the Menominees. These Indians were led by no less a leader than Captain John Marsh, who sold them their arms before proceeding upon the dangerous mission of tracking Black Hawk.

The Sacs, meanwhile, continued to retreat up the Rock, coming at last to the place of the Four Lakes in the Michigan Territory,

where realization came to them that they would be safest across the Mississippi again. They accordingly made their way as rapidly as possible overland until they were caught by Colonel Dodge and his men at the heights of the Wisconsin River valley directly opposite the high hill upon which Pierneau's house stood at the south end of the great prairie where once the proud Sacs had had their village, where Black Hawk himself had been born. Here they fought, the Sacs holding the Heights until nightfall, when both sides encamped, Black Hawk again tried unsuccessfully to surrender, and, failing, then executed a strategic withdrawal down the Wisconsin.

At the first sign of battle, Marsh's Sioux turned tail and ran. Having for so long depended upon some one else to do their fighting for them, they had grown cowardly in the face of battle, preferring to butcher only parties considerably less in number. They found opportunity to do so when the retreating Sacs reached the Mississippi at the mouth of the Bad Axe River on the first of August. There Captain Marsh, on board the *Warrior,* defied destiny once more by disregarding Black Hawk's final attempt to surrender himself and his band by firing upon the Sacs huddled for surrender, venting his Sioux-like fury and hatred upon them, and encouraging the Sioux to slay without mercy squaws, children, and old men without distinction when these remaining Sacs attempted to swim the Mississippi to the haven ambushed by the Sioux, whose bravery in annihilating the helpless Sacs was outdone only by Marsh's further treachery.

The war had not left Hercules idle. If the trade were temporarily ruined, he could at least redouble his efforts to watch Marsh. Furthermore, excited by the conflict, encouraged by his own passion for letting the blood of the enemies of the Sioux, Marsh grew careless. Hercules waited and watched.

The battle of the Bad Axe ended the war; not long after, Black Hawk surrendered to friendly Winnebagos at the dells of the Wisconsin, and was brought to Prairie du Chien. In mid-September General Winfield Scott called a council at Rock Island to force the Winnebagos to sign a treaty giving up their lands east of the Mississippi, as punishment for aiding the Sacs and Foxes, and to make a settlement also with the still friendly Sac chieftains, led by Keokuk. This was Hercules' time. He took passage at once for Rock

Island, had a private audience with Scott and laid before him his evidence of Marsh's sale of arms and ammunition to the Indians, before and after the opening of hostilities. Without hesitation, Scott signed an order for Marsh's arrest.

Hercules left Scott's quarters and sought out Marsh, who had come to attend the council and had already signed the Winnebago treaty. He found him alone, as he wished to see him: the same slightly arrogant young man, a little despondent now, with his cheek and wens twitching more than ever, and his mouth more cruel.

"Sit down, Dousman," he said. "This war's ruined my trade. How about yours?"

Hercules shook his head. "All trouble does that for the time being. But your trade in weapons must have been good."

Marsh narrowed his eyes. "Dousman, some day you and I will have to settle a score of long standing."

"I came to settle it today, Marsh," said Hercules, grinning without mirth. "I have already settled it, in a manner of speaking. Not for my sake: I'm too busy a man to carry grudges of any kind. But I said long ago that Prairie du Chien was too small a place for your kind of man, Marsh, and I've never had reason to doubt my wisdom. I'm settling this score for a great many Indians—Sacs and Foxes chiefly, old Kettle, yes, even Black Hawk, who sits in prison now after attempting five times to surrender, the last time to see his people butchered by Sioux you had rounded up to carry on that carnage."

"I'm not afraid of you, Dousman."

"I believe you're not. But you won't have to answer to me. I've just laid information about your sale of arms and ammunition before General Scott. Not only information, but proof also."

Marsh got up slowly, his color gone. "You don't know a thing. I've been careful. God damn you, Dousman . . ."

"Take it easy, Marsh. I'm telling you this now, tonight. Scott's just signed an order for your arrest. There's still time for you to get away." He did not add that if Marsh cared to stay and stand trial, he might get off with a light sentence, knowing that once Marsh took to flight, he could never return to the Territory with the order for his arrest still waiting to be executed.

He stepped to the threshold, looking back briefly at Marsh. "You've finished your trouble here, Marsh. I was sorry for you once, when your wife died. I'm not sorry now. Good-bye."

In the morning, as he had expected, Marsh was not to be found; the officer who came to arrest him reported his absence; some one else had been left a message saying that Marsh had gone west, and the order was posted, to be fulfilled as soon as Marsh returned. Hercules was satisfied, and yet he could not rid himself of a feeling of loss now that his enemy and the enemy of the trade and the settlers was gone. He regretted the necessity of striking at Marsh at all; for himself he could have dealt with him; but it was impossible to establish any basis of lasting friendship among the Indians as long as there were white men who so aggressively took sides. But he found himself, after so long an opposition to Marsh, already realizing that he would miss this opposition, he would miss the zest and keenness of Marsh's challenge, and however much a scoundrel Marsh was, he could not help entertaining the fugitive thought that perhaps Marsh might return to face trial.

But Marsh did not return, and now that both the Indian trouble and Marsh's activities had come to an end, Hercules went back to Prairie du Chien filled with a sense of well-being, determined and eager to build up the trade again to a point exceeding even Astor's expectations.

7.

And Goes His Way Alone

1834-1835

*D*ESPITE the decline in numbers of the Indian trappers and hunters, the trade flourished.

Hercules was pleased, regretting only that peace could not have come sooner and more justly, so that the trade could have been so much greater in those earlier years. Yet he could not help knowing that the trade must eventually fall before the settlers; it could move westward for a time, but it would not be for long. There were signs, too, that Astor was tiring of his empire; this meant but one thing—that the trade was no longer paying him returns sufficient to justify his continued interest. Nevertheless, Hercules wrote enthusiastic reports to Crooks, and for the second year since the Black Hawk War, he suggested that Crooks carry his report to Astor. "I do not know what the old man thinks of us out here," he wrote. "I never hear from him, naturally, nor does any one else; I suppose if it were put up to him, he would say that it was for this correspondence that he retains you.—And not, of course, just for the collection of his percentage."

Crooks replied cryptically, saying that he thought it better not to show Hercules' report to Astor. He suggested that perhaps Hercules might write another, less enthusiastic, which would serve as well. Hercules was puzzled. He knew that, while the number of pelts had declined, their quality was generally of a high order. Lapiage, Souligne, Benoit and the others had opened up new territory in the heart of Wisconsin along the tributaries there and in the lake country in the north woods. He began to suspect Crooks' motives, presently, but he was not kept in doubt for long.

Late in summer Crooks appeared without warning in Prairie

du Chien, walking into Hercules' office one afternoon and seating himself before Hercules was aware of his entrance.

"Damn me, sir, it's hot," he said, sighing.

Hercules recognized his voice and looked up, startled. "Crooks! What brings you here?"

"I'm just passing through, so to speak. I'm on my way to see Chouteau. He's in St. Louis, expecting me."

Hercules raised his eyebrows in interrogation. "Is the old man thinking of selling out?"

Crooks nodded. "That's why I didn't feel the time opportune for your good report. You have a happy faculty for making glowing reports, Hercules, but just at this time, when he's on the verge of selling, I don't think Astor should see such a report as this. No," he went on, shaking his head, "it would never do. It might change his mind; he might go up on his price. It would be poor business, you see."

Hercules said that he understood it very well. It was an action which Astor himself would appreciate.

"Are you ready to come in with us?" pressed Crooks. "There will be just yourself, young Sibley, and of course myself for the Northern Department. I think Chouteau will take over the Missouri River region. I don't know how much it will come to, but I'll buy for as little as we can. Sibley's an excellent man. I had all I could do to persuade him to stay with the Company. He was for going east, though he confessed that he liked the country here. I thought of him for the post at St. Peters and the Northwest portion of our holdings then. He's ready to come in."

"You know I've always been," said Hercules.

"All right. I thought I could count on you. I think this time we have Astor. He's been dissatisfied with things out here, the Black Hawk War, the other uprisings—all these things eat into his profits, and he's a man who feels chiefly through his bank account; that's his heart, candidly. Besides, right now he foresees great events in commercial shipping, and he's investing heavily. The steamboat has revolutionized things, as you know." He paused briefly, to add, "Steamboats on the Mississippi might make shipment from St. Louis more practical for you hereafter, Hercules. You'll stay at Prairie du Chien, of course, no matter what happens to the Company, and I'll keep the New York office, as always."

Hercules nodded. "What terms will lie between us?"

"We'll be in simple partnership; that should increase our earnings all around. No more of this buying from Astor at prices too high, and paying sometimes with mortgages on land—which he prefers; no more of his percentages. Even with the decline in trade, we should be earning more. How does it sound to you?"

"Very good. As you know, I have an ambition to be free of the necessity of grubbing. This business of working for some one else has never appealed overmuch to me. You find me ready, Crooks."

"Good. I'll get to it as soon as possible, then."

"But there's one thing we've not touched upon," resumed Hercules. "What happens to Rolette?"

Crooks shrugged uneasily. "Oh, he can have an interest, certainly. But the three of us must be in full control." He hesitated, got up, and stood to look out of the window, his broad back to Hercules. "You know," he went on, "I believe Astor has bills against Rolette's and Aird's holdings. I suppose he'll follow his usual procedure and foreclose. Where will that leave them—Rolette in particular?"

Hercules thought of Jane, whose bills came to him still from time to time for payment. "I don't know. I don't think Joe's too well off. But I can't say what he's done with his money. I'll tell you— if Joe doesn't owe Astor too much, that is, too much more than the land's worth, make a deal with Astor for me. In any case, the land's a good investment. Besides, it will be a means for Joe to pay for his interest in the new Company. I suppose you mean to keep the old name, if Astor sells?"

Crooks nodded. "That would be only good business, yes." He came back to his chair. "Look here, Hercules, I'm going east directly from St. Louis. Astor expects me, and he knows why I'm coming back so quickly. I'll send you word as soon as I know what the old man will do. Now I want to see Rolette before I go. Where will he be?—If he's in Prairie du Chien at all."

Hercules smiled wryly. "You might try Brunet's tavern. He keeps on spending time there."

"Still drinking?"

"As you might expect."

Crooks shook his head. "I feel sorry for Madame Rolette. By the way, I had a good letter from the boy, young Joe, just before I

came west. He asked to be remembered to you." He got up again. "Now I'm off."

"Good luck, Crooks. If you see Rolette, tell him I want to see him when you've finished—if he can take a little time away from his glass."

They shook hands, and Crooks left the Company's office.

So the old man might sell out! thought Hercules. He had not given Crooks any indication of how earnestly he hoped Astor might indeed step from the Company; he had long ago computed the precise income the old man derived from his agents and, while it might not be a large sum for Astor, it represented a considerable addition to the income of even the best of the agents. He would be pleased enough to share it. In addition to this, he would be responsible to no one but himself.

he didn't make quite clear was my own position in the new Company, if there is to be one. I don't think Astor will sell, but I may be wrong. I've been wrong before."

"It's assumed that you'll want an interest."

"Of course, I'll want one," answered Rolette, raising his voice. "God damn it, man, I do want one—but what am I going to pay for it with?"

"Why, I wasn't much concerned about that, Joe," said Hercules smoothly. "The fact is, you've probably got some land you can let me have in payment. How much of your holdings belongs to the old man by mortgage?"

"Practically all of it."

He was still in contemplation of the future when Rolette came in. Rolette's shaggy beard had begun to gray a little, streaked here and there, and his face had grown more lined. At the moment it was obvious that he had been drinking; his voice was edged with thickness, his eyes were inflamed, but there was no unsteadiness about him, and his manner was direct enough. He straddled the chair Crooks had but recently vacated, and fixed Hercules with his commanding eyes.

"So Crooks hopes to talk the old man into selling out, does he?"

"He told you, eh?"

Rolette nodded. "*Sacré nom!* he has no secrets from me." Hercules took this with doubt, but he said nothing. Rolette went on. "What

"That bad?"

Rolette nodded. "Things just went from bad to worse, I guess. The old man was there, willing enough to extend credit for mortgages. I suppose he'll foreclose now, too. I don't know what will become of Jane if she has to leave the house."

Hercules was astonished. "You've mortgaged the house, too?"

"Yes, I did. Not so very long ago."

"Joe, you shouldn't have done that. Why didn't you come to me?"

Rolette shook his head and said nothing.

"Then if the old man forecloses, you won't have anything left, Joe?" pressed Hercules gently.

"I believe not."

"I think perhaps he can be persuaded not to foreclose immediately. I'll see what can be done. We'll save the house, in any event."

Rolette expostulated. He said he would get the money somewhere and pay Astor back. There was no use expecting that Astor would be lenient; the old man was hard as flint, and every one knew that. He himself cared little, but for Jane and the children. As for Jane, she was not spending so much for clothes, it was true, but there was now the cost of keeping the children in school. He wished them above everything to have a good Catholic education, and the Academy of the Visitation at Georgetown was certainly one of the best, though if he had it to do over again, he would not have sent Virginia so far, rather to Florissant at St. Louis. Joseph was all right where he was, near Cincinnati.

Hercules heard him out without comment. When Rolette had finished, he repeated what he had previously said, adding that Crooks would no doubt come to some satisfactory terms with the old man. Certainly Rolette was to count on an interest in the new Company, if it materialized; if it did not, Astor would not foreclose; in either case, Rolette had nothing to trouble himself about. Except one thing.

Rolette's eyes narrowed. "What's that?"

"The bottle," said Hercules quietly. "I've told you time and again, Joe—it's your only fault, but it's a bad one. I don't like to see you drinking like this, and I can tell you Jane won't stand for it much longer."

Rolette laughed. "Jane has stood for it so long, she's used to it."

"Jane will never get used to anything of the kind," said Hercules with asperity. "You should know her better than to suggest that."

Rolette got up. "God damn it, Hercules, oblige me by not talking about my habits," he said, raising his voice. "If I want to drink, I'll do it. I'm drinking because I enjoy it, not to please any one else, not to drown my sorrows, not to celebrate. If Jane finds herself unable to bear it, let her start reforming her brother. He drinks ten times as much as I do."

"Yes, as to that," replied Hercules, "there isn't much evidence that he drank to excess before you took him in tow. You have to answer for that, too, you see. Hold on, don't run off . . ."

But Rolette had gone, closing the door angrily behind him.

Hercules shrugged, thrust his partner and his habits from his mind, and turned back to the work laid out before him.

In mid-September he had a brief message from Crooks to assure him that Chouteau would buy the Missouri River trade from Astor, and that he might go east. They would in any case be on the way when this letter reached Hercules. Crooks directed Hercules to go up to St. Peters and examine into conditions there, to list all such things as might be needed by Sibley when he came, so that Sibley could know this before he left Mackinac, and to visit among the Indians there to be certain what manner of co-operation Sibley could expect. Hercules set out at once, and returned in ten days.

He arrived in the evening, and found Lapiage in charge.

"Where's Rolette?" he asked, taking the place at the table vacated by Lapiage.

The voyageur shrugged. "No one knows. He may have gone to Mackinac; you know how he enjoys the journey. Madame Rolette especially would like to know. They've been looking for him."

"Why? Is anything wrong?"

But yes, said Lapiage, something was wrong. Rolette's brother-in-law had been found drowned three days ago; he had just been buried this morning. He was evidently drunk and fell into the Marais de St. Feriole; before he was discovered, he had drowned. In fact, he was not found until toward noon of the following day.

"Young Fisher?" asked Hercules.

Lapiage nodded.

Small wonder Jane wished to know where Rolette was. Hercules got up again; he was not too tired to go over at once to the Rolette house. "Stay a little longer," he told Lapiage. "If I'm not back directly, lock up."

He hurried through the village whose crisping evening air was sweet with the pungence of dry leaves turned early this year. Outside the Rolette house, Elizabeth raked leaves to a bonfire burning redly at the edge of the lawn. He paused to greet her and asked whether her stepmother was inside.

Yes, she was there, Elizabeth assured him. But she was very much upset. The girl was dubious about his visiting Jane.

Nevertheless, he went to the house and rapped on the door.

Eugenie came presently, to stand formidably on the threshold. "Madame weesh to see no one," she said.

"Nonsense," said Hercules, and made his way past her.

Jane sat in her parlor. She was dressed in black, her face was pale, her mouth betraying in its firmness her withheld anger. Seeing him, she came to her feet.

"But of course I will see Mistaire Dousman," she cried. "It take somebody to die before he come to see me." She came over to him impulsively, lowered her head to his shoulder, and began to weep softly. He put an arm around her tenderly and held her there for a little while before he led her back to the sofa from which she had arisen.

"Now then, pray dry those tears, Madame."

She touched her eyes with her handkerchief. "I cannot help it," she murmured. "I have know all time it is too much. Where is M'sieu' Rolette?"

"Madame knows as well as I do where he is. I do not."

Her voice grew more animated now; the fire of her rising anger came to supplant her grief. "You see what he have do while you are away!" she cried. "This is too much! I have tolerate' it as long as I can. I cannot longaire do so." Impulsively she caught hold of his hands. "Mistaire Dousman, you mus' help me."

"Madame knows I am at her service," replied Hercules. "But what has Rolette done to upset you so?"

"Has no one told you? Surely some one has inform you of this

terrible thing—my brothaire has drown'. M'sieu' Rolette has do this."

He deprecated gently. "Madame does not know what she is saying. Rolette could not be guilty of such a thing."

Her fingers closed more tightly about his own. "Mistaire Dousman know vair' well I know what I speak about. My poor brothaire never drink before M'sieu' Rolette teach him to do so. Since that time, George get dronk vair' often. No one could speak to him but M'sieu' Rolette, and it was too late to say anything. Now he is gone, and it is M'sieu' Rolette's doing. How can you think it is not? Did not M'sieu' Rolette take my brothaire constantly to Brunet's? Did not M'sieu' Rolette encourage George to drink? Mistaire Dousman know vair' well this is so. Then it mus' be clear to him also that George would be alive today if M'sieu' Rolette have not drink so and show my brothaire to drink also. Do Mistaire Dousman wish to argue this?"

Yes, retorted Hercules, he did. He spoke with some heat, himself stirred by what he felt was Jane's unjust accusation. Madame was overwrought; she would not have spoken so, if she were not. George's weakness was his own, no one else's. However much Rolette had sinned, George's death was not on his soul. Besides, Rolette had not even been in Prairie du Chien at the time of George's death. One might as well blame Brunet; after all, he may have sold George the liquor.

"I will not listen to you. You try to distrac' me," she cried. "I know what I have go through. I am done with M'sieu' Rolette. Pairhaps it is true I should nevaire have marry him; I am not sartain. I do know I can no longaire live with him. I have endure his drink' long enough."

She got up and began to pace up and down the room, clasping and unclasping her hands. He watched her for a few moments in silence, thinking with disapproval of her unreasonable charge against Rolette, but understanding its source. He could not help reflecting that in her distress she was more beautiful than ever. Presently he got up and caught hold of her hand.

"Come, sit down." He led her firmly to the sofa, and with one foot turned the seat from the piano so that he might sit on it, facing her. "Now then," he began. "Rolette has many troubles of which he does not speak. He thinks too much of you to bother you with his affairs."

"Or too little to trus' me with them," she retorted, her eyes smoldering, her mouth uncompromising.

"Don't interrupt me," he said. "I'm trying to do this for your own sake."

"Mistaire Dousman will realize I am able to help myself. I am determine' to leave M'sieu' Rolette."

"Do you mean to divorce him?"

"Mistaire Dousman know we are both vair' good Catholics. No, we will live apart from now on."

"Where will you go?"

"As long as the house of my Oncle Brisbois stand, there is room in it for me."

"Then think of Rolette. What will become of him?"

"He will have all this house to live in. And Elizabeth will take care of him. She is vair' fond of him, and she do not min' his drink'."

"And your own children. Think of them."

"I have think often of them. They would not like their fathaire to be like this. I would not want them to see him. But they will not be back yet for four or five years, until they have finish' their education. Oh, how could he do this when he know I am so lonely for our children and have such a hard time to bear their absence from me!"

"What if Rolette now ceases his drinking?"

"I hope he may. Then I will go back to him. But now it is the end; I have endure' this too long. Now he is not even here so I can tell him I am to leave him. I do not know where he is, but he will know where I have go. And it will not do him any good to follow me there; if I say so, my Oncle Brisbois will not let him in the house. And I will say so, I promise it."

He remonstrated with her anew. If difficulties were besetting Rolette, her withdrawal would only serve to make his lot harder to bear.

"Drink has made it easiaire," she said shortly. "I have watch' it five years. If he has trouble, I do not know it; he have nevaire tell me; he will not tell me. I do not read his min'. It is not my place to do so."

She was adamant, and not all his persuasion could change her mind. He reflected that it was possible that the shock of her leaving

him might bring about a change in Rolette's habits; but he was not too sanguine. He faced her angry eyes, her determined mouth; he was depressed, and yet he could not entirely escape a feeling of relief. He had not liked the situation any better than she had, but at least she had a right to rebel; he did not, because he understood that his reaction depended upon his regard for Jane; apart from this, Rolette might do as he pleased so long as his activities did not hamper the progress of the American Fur Company. He sat looking at her in silence now until she got up, turning from him, and began to pace up and down the room again.

"Mistaire Dousman do not know what I have go through," she cried. "It has been so since we were marry'. Not the drink—that came las'. But all time M'sieu' Rolette treat me like a piece of his property. Indeed, in the vair' first year or so that we were marry', I know he had anothaire woman. I endure' it because I promise' to be a good wife, and I was so young, my fathaire had go away, I had been burden to my Oncle and Tante Brisbois long enough, I would not have know what to do. Then it was always his go' away, I did not know where, he jus' went, he did not let me know, I did not know where he was until he come back again. And now it is the drink, and the talk about how he will not pay for my clothing."

"But of course, he does."

"He mus', because the clothing come to me, and Mistaire Stambaugh would not sen' them if they were not paid. But he talk so, he scold, he say he will not pay, I buy too much, I do not know what to think."

"But the clothes come," repeated Hercules. "Perhaps Rolette's bark is worse than his bite."

"Oh, M'sieu' Rolette's bite is not bad, but it is the drink that bite' him I will not endure. So I will do without M'sieu' Rolette, and if I do not have anothaire new dress for five years!"

"Madame Rolette could make that sacrifice easily enough," he said.

"What do you mean?" she demanded quickly.

"Madame Rolette would be kind to the eye even in rags."

She half-smiled, but looked at him with suspicion; she did not know whether he joked or whether he was serious. Presently she

decided that he joked, and said, "It is all vair' well to say so, to flattaire me, but I know the sacrifice I am mak'. I know it bettaire than any one else."

She continued to walk back and forth, up and down, until he went to her again, took her firmly by one arm, and brought her back to the sofa. "If you please, Madame, sit down. You wear out not only this lovely Brussels carpet—you see, there, the flowers you've walked on are all worn in the pattern—but my patience also."

She looked in naïve amazement and bewilderment to the pattern of the carpet and then to him, but sat down obediently enough. She withdrew a little, clasping her hands firmly in her lap, and fixed her eyes stonily on him. "I do not think Mistaire Dousman take me seriously enough. Is it so?"

"Madame Rolette knows I take her far too seriously."

"This is not a mattaire for joke', Mistaire Dousman."

"I assure you, I was never less in the mood for joking," said Hercules. "I think Madame is acting hastily, but as she says, it is her problem alone, and no one else's. She cannot expect me to help her in this."

"Ah, but I do. I want you to tell M'sieu' Rolette why I have leave him. I want him to hear it from you, rather than from my Oncle Brisbois, who do not like him vair' much, or from Elizabeth, who like him too much. This you will do for me, will you not, Mistaire Dousman? Say."

"Yes, I can do that. I wish to serve Madame Rolette whenever possible, but I could wish to serve her in a more happy task."

"Life is not all happy, Mistaire Dousman. You do not need me to tell you that."

"Assuredly not," he agreed. "Still, you have been apparently happy until this most recent trouble came upon him."

"Recent!" she exclaimed, interrupting him anew. "Do you call something five years old recent? I think Mistaire Dousman is playing Devil's Advocate."

"Hardly as bad as that."

"He sound so. Do not hold M'sieu' Rolette up to me. I know him bettaire than you do. I should. He is a man you cannot talk to unless he has a min' to hear what you have to say. I have try and try again."

"Perhaps Madame talked too much."

She drew herself up. "Mistaire Dousman, I am not glad to see you if you come to insult me."

"I have no wish to insult Madame." He went on, speaking rapidly to press any advantage he might have. Rolette deserved another chance; she should give him one. She should tell him without sub-terfuge that she intended to leave him unless he gave up drinking. She should put it to him squarely where she stood.

She could hardly contain herself while he spoke. "He do not de-sairve anothaire chance. I have give him too many already. Besides, he know I will leave him if he do not change, and he do not. So now I will leave him, I will teach him I do not speak idly, I will do as I say, and if he wish now to change, I will forget what is pas'. But do not ask me to give him anothaire chance; I will not."

He got up, spreading his hands in mock helplessness. "I must go. When does Madame intend to leave the house?"

"In the morning."

"When does Madame wish her husband informed?"

"As soon as he come home. Do you know where he is?" She searched his face for any betrayal he might make; she was satisfied that he spoke truthfully when he said he knew nothing of Rolette's whereabouts. "Vair' well, but he will come home, and when he do, I wish you would speak to him. I do not know what Elizabeth may say to him, but she love him vair' much, and even if she is fon' of me, she may tell him something different, I do not know, and for that reason, I wish you to speak to him."

He promised again that he would speak to Rolette.

She walked to the door with him, silent now. He thought she was in a mood; she held to her frown, and bit at her lower lip as if in agitation. But the good night she bade him was cool and self-confident; she had come to a decision and meant to follow it; however much he thought that she might change her mind by morning, he did not actually believe that she would. She gave him her hand gravely, and he held it for a moment, looking into her eyes, before turning from her.

In the face of this break between the Rolettes, the importance of Jane to him came surging back into his consciousness. He was disturbed, because he had thought he had put her from his thoughts

before this. But he had thought this before, and always she had come back, always she had reappeared; it began to crystallize in his realization that he would never be entirely free of her. He wondered what might have happened had Margaret lived; inevitably, sooner or later, he would have betrayed himself; she would have been unhappy. Jane's tenacity in his mind's eye was nothing he could wash away; her superiority over all the other women in the settlement, her singular beauty, her spirited self-confidence—these aspects were unique; any one of them alone would have been enough to account for his love for her. But his love was something more than a mere attachment to her attributes; it was something far more deeply rooted, something which he bound, deep and silent, within him, something which even in the secrecy of his thoughts he dared not contemplate. He forgot the problems of the trade, he forgot for two days even to send Crooks the report he wanted, and he grew apprehensive for Rolette's return and the distasteful task facing him.

Jane went to the Brisbois house and established herself there. Elizabeth kept Eugenie, with Jane's permission, and stayed on at the Rolette house. The two women remained amicable, strangely enough, for a stepmother and stepdaughter.

On the fifth day after her departure for new quarters, Rolette came back to Prairie du Chien. He came into the Company's office before going home, talking animatedly about the improvements being made at Fort Winnebago until he noticed Hercules' fixed stare. Then he stopped and looked at his partner.

"Sit down, Joe," said Hercules.

"I'll stand. What is it? Has the old man taken my house?"

Hercules shook his head. "No, not that. You've lost something more precious. Jane's left you."

"Left me!" He looked incredulous. "You mean, she's gone?"

"Yes, five days ago."

"Where to?"

"She went to the Brisbois, to live with them."

He swore suddenly, violently, and flung himself into a chair. "She can't do that to me. God damn it, she's had it nice enough. Even if I do drink a little from time to time—*mille tonnerre,* I don't bother her. I told you women were nothing but trouble; I say it again. What about Elizabeth?"

"She's at home with Eugenie."

He smiled bitterly. "At least one of them stands up for me."

"She asked me to tell you that as soon as you stopped drinking to excess, she would come back to you. She blames you now for George's death. Did you know of that?"

"Yes. I had word at Winnebago; that's why I came back." He sighed and lowered his great head to his hands. "God damn it, I've tried, but it's no use. I guess I'm a little old for Jane." He shook his head. "The Brisbois—they'll spoil her."

Hercules smiled mirthlessly and observed that Madame Rolette was a woman who encouraged easily the impulse to spoil her.

"Yes, I suppose I've done my share," agreed Rolette. "But then . . ." He shrugged. "Well, I won't go crawling to her. Elizabeth's old enough to run the household, and with Eugenie's help . . ."

"You'll still have to make some provision for Jane, Joe."

"I will, as much as I'm able. I don't know how much that'll be." He got up restlessly. "I can take care of the children all right, and if the new Company emerges without too much loss for me, I can take care of Jane, too, whether she's with me or not." He shrugged.

Hercules was unable to determine whether Rolette was deeply wounded or not. Something of the older man's reaction was concealed by the shaggy moustache and beard which covered half his face, and his eyes betrayed nothing but a certain hardness which had always been there. However much Rolette might be hurt, he was not the man either to show it for long or to let it affect him permanently. Hercules came around his table and stood beside Rolette, who had gone to the window to look out; he put an arm loosely around his partner's shoulders.

"She may come back, Joe," he said. "I haven't given up trying. In fact, I've seen her only once. But it was the drinking, and her brother's death—you can understand how she must feel. Jane is a fine woman, and her sensibilities are easily aroused. She's spirited, yes, of course, but when her good sense is appealed to, she can respond readily enough; I've always found it so, and perhaps if you'd taken a little more time, you would have found this, too. But it seems you've always been too busy for Jane, and she's proud enough to resent that, too. After all, isn't it easy to give a woman a little

money, a few gifts, and to clothe her instead of giving her something of your time or yourself?"

"*Sacré bleu!* I'm a busy man, Hercules," said Rolette. "I can't fawn upon my wife. You can't expect it."

"No one has asked it. Only pay some attention to her—you carry on your business with some laxity, but with far greater perseverance than you attend to Madame Rolette."

Rolette shrugged his arm away and turned, his hands clasped behind his back, his frock coat swinging open so that the gold chain across his waistcoat gleamed dully in the room's light. He walked nervously to the threshold of the inner room, and back again. Hercules went slowly over to his table and sat down, watching his partner. Rolette was concerned, but not deeply upset; his pride and anger had been aroused much more than his affection for Jane.

"Then, too," continued Hercules, "there's the matter of Jane's clothes."

Rolette shook his head impatiently. "Enough of that. We've settled that. I refused to pay for them, and she's resigned to it."

"Is she?"

"Yes." He turned suddenly upon Hercules, his eyes narrowed.

"Do you think a woman like Jane would sit quietly with hands folded and say nothing if she could have no new clothes for years on end?"

Rolette came over to the table and bent above it, his hands flat upon its surface. "Hercules, you haven't been buying clothes for my wife all this time?"

Hercules nodded. "You know that all your household bills come to the office for me to settle while you're away. When Stambaugh's bills for Jane came, I honored them, too, thinking you could pay me back if you wished, since I have the money, and you were apparently hard pressed. In any case, I disliked the thought of Jane being deprived, and I told you I would help you out in that. You and Jane have done much for me, and I can do so little for you in return. As for Jane, I haven't found her too extravagant. True, she does occasionally get a dress which she might do without, but not often. Not often enough to warrant all the distress you caused her by ranting at her about it."

Rolette disregarded this last. "Then I owe you a considerable sum."

"No. I took this upon myself, and there's no reason why you should reimburse me, or, if you insist, why you should be in any hurry about it. I wanted to discover whether Jane bought too many clothes, as you said; I'm satisfied that she doesn't. Of course, Jane knows nothing of this; it is among Stambaugh, yourself, and me, and no one else knows about it unless it was the trader, Hill, who has gone elsewhere now. And I shall expect you to say nothing to Jane if the matter does come up in conversation. Let her think you softened and paid her bills after all. If anything, that's to your advantage."

Rolette looked at him wordlessly for a moment. Then he said, "I don't understand you, Hercules."

"I suppose no one of us ever fully understands any one else," said Hercules casually. "The fact is, I'm fond of Jane, I like to see her little vanities gratified, and, as I said before, I was interested in learning just what the amount of this expense was to which she put you and caused you to rebel against. I found it not large, as I told you, and that leaves me still more in the dark about the reason you took to drink."

Rolette straightened up and sighed. "Hercules, there was no reason. I always liked whiskey, and I drank it before it was known here that I did; but it's true, in the last years it's got beyond control. Perhaps it was because I worried about what the old man might do about those mortgages."

"Stop worrying about them. Crooks will take care of them for us."

Rolette shrugged. "I'm going home," he said, turning toward the door.

"Aren't you going to see Jane?"

"Not now," answered Rolette. "I may later—if the Brisbois will let me in." He laughed dryly. "You know, the Brisbois were always anxious for Jane to marry me—I was the best catch in Prairie du Chien, in this part of the Territory, then; I was wealthy. Old Fisher never seemed to care one way or the other; after his wife's death he went to Canada and never came back. But in the last few years, the Brisbois do not act as if they were especially pleased with the arrangements they made."

He went out. Hercules could not believe that he was not going immediately to see Jane. He followed to the threshold and stood

looking after him. The older man went with no sign of haste to his own house.

In mid-October word came from Crooks. Astor had sold out, as Crooks had predicted, and they themselves were now masters of the American Fur Company. Hercules might expect Sibley as soon as that young man could organize for his journey to St. Peters. Crooks appended a note to say that the matter of Rolette's mortgages had been taken care of, which Hercules assumed to mean that he himself now owned most of Rolette's land in Prairie du Chien. He went at once in search of Rolette.

Rolette was at home, at the moment in his shirtsleeves assisting his daughter to move furniture.

"Elizabeth says we must clean house," he said, wiping perspiration from his forehead. He sat down in a chair which had been moved to the center of the room. "What's up?"

Elizabeth came in and asked gently whether they would not rather go outside, since they made it difficult for her to work.

"*Sacré nom!*" exploded Rolette. "Can't a man even sit down in his own house without being told to go?"

"If you please, Papa?" Elizabeth persisted, her grave eyes fixed on him steadily, and without alarm at his shouting.

Hercules took Rolette firmly by the arm and walked outside with him. "Joe, you're as bad as some of those women you talk about for arguing," he said. "Sit here on the verandah; we'll be more comfortable."

Rolette's irritation washed away in a wave of grumbling.

"Look here, I've had word from Crooks. Astor's sold out."

Rolette inclined his head toward the house behind them. "What about that?" he asked. "Did Crooks say?"

"Yes. The matter's settled. I bought Astor off, and you're to pay me back when you can. That shouldn't be long, because the new arrangement will bring us all a better income than we've had heretofore."

"That's very good of you, Hercules," said Rolette soberly.

Hercules could not determine whether Rolette was pleased or irritated at his action. However, he went on. "I couldn't afford to lose you, and the trade certainly couldn't. So I thought that the best

arrangement all around; you needn't concern yourself about the repayment, and you're free of worry about what Astor might do. But I thought, if you would prefer, I could keep some of the land you had mortgaged to Astor, and so lessen the amount."

Rolette glanced at him quickly. "You cleared everything? Not just the house?"

Hercules nodded. "Everything. I thought it best."

Rolette grinned. "God damn it, Hercules, you're not a good business man. I don't know that the land's worth as much as you're paying for it if I take you up. Besides, you ought to hold me up for a better sum with such a weapon as this house."

Hercules shook his head. "That's not my way of doing business, Joe. I continue to believe that if you do your best for a man, he'll do his best for you."

"And what if he doesn't?"

"He may regret it."

Rolette looked at him steadily. "And what do you expect of me, then?"

"Give up drinking. Try at least. Go back to Jane."

"Why are you so set on this, Hercules?"

"Because I wish to see her happy, to see you both happy. Because I'm not easy in my mind with Jane away from you." He did not say why, distrusting even his own quickened pulse at thought of her.

"You forget that it was Jane who went away; so I can't go back. It's Jane who will have to make that compromise."

"She will, if only you stop drinking."

Rolette shook his head. "Let's have no more talk of this."

"Very well. As you say, it's your affair. Have you seen Jane?"

"Once." He was short, almost gruff; plainly, he did not wish to discuss their meeting.

"As for the land," resumed Hercules where he had left off before, "I think it's worth a good deal more than I paid for it, and if you don't agree with me, we should have no difficulty in coming to a working agreement between us in regard to the amount due on your house and the other mortgages."

"We won't. Let's each work out a schedule of values, eh? We'll settle the matter sooner than I could have settled with the old man, thanks to Crooks."

Hercules agreed and got up to go. "Get back to your house-cleaning, Joe," he said. "That girl can't do it very well by herself. The piano alone is too heavy for half a dozen of her."

"She's a good girl," said Rolette. He stood for a moment gazing at Hercules before he put out his hand. "Thank you, Hercules. You've taken a load off my mind. If it had been any other man, I'd have been enraged by what I considered his meddling. But not you, not you."

Hercules walked down the road and paused to look back. Rolette was just re-entering the house. Hercules gazed at the two-story building which was considered so pretentious and had no rival, save only the Brisbois house, which had only recently been erected. He wondered how much this place had cost Rolette, and whether after all he had had it built only to gratify Jane's wishes. It was imposing enough, with its verandah, its blinds; it might very easily have belonged to a New England village, save for the French architecture most noticeable in the construction of its dormers. He stood for a few moments before he turned, crossed the street, and went impulsively to the Brisbois house.

Jane was at home. Moreover, she was alone. The Brisbois servant showed Hercules into the parlor, where Jane sat in deep concentration over some needlework. She looked up at Hercules' entrance, and he thought again how queenly was her appearance with its touch of hauteur.

"So Mistaire Dousman come to visit me?" she said a little proudly. "How long is it since he see me? An entire month."

"Madame will forgive me, I know," he said. "I came today to tell you about the Company."

"What of the Company?"

He told her, meanwhile looking all around him to see how comfortable Jane had made herself. But his eyes came inevitably back to her; she was attired now in a chenille house dress with wide flowing skirts in a soft shade of blue, a color which complemented very well both her dark hair and blue eyes. Her thin hands worked with great rapidity while she listened.

"You mus' forgive me," she said when he had finished. "I mus' have something to do; so I do this work. Is it not pretty?" She spread it out for him.

He assured her that it was indeed a fine piece of work, and asked her what it was.

"Why, it is a samplaire, Mistaire Dousman," she said, as if he ought to know. She drew it carefully back and looked at him, with a faint air of laughter behind her eyes in that expression he had come to know so well. "Now, about the Company—I know Mistaire Dousman do not come jus' to tell me this. Why do he come, then?"

"Madame Rolette knows very well that it is a pleasure for me only to see her."

"You continue to flattaire me," she said, smiling. "But this time is not time for flattaire' me. Did M'sieu' Rolette sen' you?"

He laughed. "Your husband is quite capable of running his own errands," he said. "Do you think he did?"

"I do not know." She shrugged elaborately. "Men do many fonny things. Me, how should I know what he do?—or what Mistaire Dousman do, for that mattaire."

She was demure with gentle mockery. Hercules bent forward a little, commanding her eyes while his pulse beat faster, uncontrollably, as it had never beat for any woman before. "Did Joe come to see you?"

Her eyes flickered to meet his and lowered again. "M'sieu' Rolette was here. But he do not make any promise." She shook her head. "He say to me what do I mean by running away from him, he say to me to come back and live in his house, and he will go elsewhere to live if I do not wish to live with him, but I say no, I cannot do this, I will not do it, I am away from him and I will not live with him or in his house until he do me the favor of no longaire drink' as he do."

"What did he say?"

"He jus' shake his head and say he make no promise he may not keep."

"Did you explain your departure?"

"I explain everything. But I have explain' before, I have threaten' —all has do no good. I do not know that it will do good now. I do not believe it will. M'sieu' Rolette is a man of strong min', and he think his min' is bettaire than mine or any one else's, and no one can do anything with a man who is like that."

"Or a woman."

"Yes." She caught herself and looked squarely at him. "Do Mistaire Dousman mean to suggest I am like that? Do he?"

"Did it seem so to Madame?"

"Yes." She gave a positive nod. "I think Mistaire Dousman mean me."

"Does Madame then have a bad conscience?"

Her cheeks were tinged with red of sudden fire. "Mistaire Dousman know vair' well my conscience is clear. It is M'sieu' Rolette who should have the bad conscience. You are try' to make me angry, to upset me."

Hercules observed that in so far as his acquaintance with her permitted him to know her, he was convinced that she could be upset only from within, and not by some one on the outside. She smiled.

"Each time you make me angry you say something nice, and I cannot longaire be angry," she said. "But I will tell you this to say to M'sieu' Rolette; I have told you before—I will not go back to him unless he give up his drink'. Say that to him. I have say it to him myself, but he has hear it so often from me he do not believe it."

"He's heard it often enough from me also," interposed Hercules.

"Nevairetheless, he will listen to you. He do not even listen to me. He will stop up his ears; he will not hear." She put her needlework impulsively aside. "I tell you, I do not think I will evaire live with M'sieu' Rolette again. He is stubborn, he is proud, and as long as he has Elizabeth to care for him, he do not need me."

Hercules shook his head and said that Rolette might need her, but he agreed that he would be too proud to admit it. However, he could not so easily accede to her wishes; he did not think it good to speak again to Rolette, or too soon again at least, since he had been at him too constantly, and if this kept up, Rolette would finally become angry and would listen to him in nothing. He asked whether she had given orders that Rolette be kept out of the Brisbois home.

"No, I have not do that. If he wish to see me, he know where I am. He have come once to see me. No more. It was a short visit," she added reflectively and in faint surprise. "But I should expec' that, because M'sieu' Rolette is too busy being occupy' with himself to think of me or any one else."

"I suppose you got at him about George."

"Sairtain' I did, what do you think?"

"Why, then it's easy to understand why he didn't stay longer. He says George's death is no fault of his, and you say it is; you could never agree about it. So why do you keep on about it? After all, George is dead, and neither one of you can bring him back to life again. Or does Madame think she might?"

She got up abruptly, angered. "Mistaire Dousman had bettaire go now before I become angry with him, too."

He bowed. "So, that's better. I am always too likely to become too fond of Madame, who shows her wisdom in treating me like this." He smiled thinly, unable to conceal a gentle mockery of his own, thinking that he would give her back something of her own manner. So thinking, he bade her good-bye and left the house.

When he looked back she was at the window, gazing after him with a puzzled frown over her eyes.

In the morning he set out for Mackinac to complete the details of the new status of the American Fur Company. Crooks was coming in from the East, and would possibly already be on the island in the straits by the time Hercules reached there. If the weather in the East was as conducive to travel as it was in the Michigan Territory, there was little doubt that Crooks would precede him—clear, sunny days, warm with Indian summer warmth, the air sweet with perfumes and pungence of dying leaves, of leaf-fire smoke, of herbs and the fresh odor of waters; crisp, frostbitten nights, which were never too cold.

The waterway was well travelled now, and Hercules made good time; in a small stern-wheeler to the Portage; by canoe to Green Bay; by a lake boat to Mackinac. Crooks was already there. Hercules stopped briefly to see his parents before going on to visit Crooks, whom he found slightly irritated and in some agitation.

He explained that it was about young Sibley. Now at the last moment it began to look as if Sibley might not come in after all. Here were the papers ready to be signed, and Sibley hesitated. He went on at some length to wonder what had got into so promising a man.

"Has he definitely refused?" asked Hercules.

"No, he hasn't."

"Then let's hear what he has to say. Meanwhile, let me look over the papers."

In half an hour Sibley came in. He greeted them both a little uncertainly and sat down. Hercules looked at him sharply; he seemed a man acting against his impulses, against his will. Sibley had grown more mature; he had a firm, strong look about him; he had a capable manner despite his temporary indecision. Hercules remembered what his father had written so often, and concluded that Crooks was right; Sibley must be kept in the Company.

"What is this we hear of your doubt now, Sibley?" he asked gravely.

Sibley was eager to explain. "I owe it to you and to Mr. Crooks to say what lies behind this apparent change of front. In the first place, frankly, my parents are strongly opposed to my staying longer in this country; they've been opposed all along, of course, but now that it seems I am to go even farther west, they are firm. Besides, in the second place, I've been offered the position as cashier in a Detroit bank, and also in another in Huron, down in Ohio, both positions at a handsome salary. I grant that you have taken over my contract with the old Company, but I don't grant you the right to insist upon my remaining to fulfill it. However, out of respect to you and to myself, if you'll release me from my engagement, I'll pay the new corporation a thousand dollars."

Crooks put down his pen and looked at him carefully, his massive frame impressive in the small chair he occupied. "When last I spoke to you, Sibley, you were enthusiastic about the post at St. Peters. I can't believe that you could change so easily in so short a time. Is it your personal feeling that you should not go along with us?"

"No, sir, it's not."

"Do you personally feel that you'll earn more for yourself and made a greater success as a cashier in a bank than with us?"

"No, sir, I don't."

Crooks leaned forward and spoke persuasively. "You know that I hold you in high esteem, Mr. Sibley; I'm fully aware of your abilities, and I feel that we could not get a better man in the Company, nor a better man at the post. I hope you will not insist on leaving; you are just the kind of man we want—no, not just the kind, just the man himself. I ask you not to minimize the place of agent at St. Peters, because you'll have under your control not only a vast area of country and many trading posts, but also a small army of traders, clerks, and voyageurs. For the past five years you've discharged your

duties like a veteran, and I can promise you terms that will be satisfactory. We've been over all this before, and you know as well as I do that your future lies in the West, not in the East."

Sibley agreed, but there were other factors, he countered.

"Isn't it a fact that your parents alone are influencing your decision?"

Sibley hesitated. "Well, sir, I suppose it is."

"If you permit your parents to make your decisions for you at this age, you have my sympathy."

Sibley made no reply.

Hercules began to talk. Knowing how devoted to field sports Sibley was, he described the region around Lake Pepin. There were many buffalo and elk there and to westward, he pointed out; the woods were filled with bear, deer, lynx, raccoons, and game of all kinds; the lakes and waterways abounded with wild ducks and geese, with swans and lesser aquatic birds, and the waters were filled with fish. As for the country itself, it was singularly beautiful, ranging from the land around St. Peters north to the British line, and west to the headwaters of those tributaries flowing into the Missouri River. Surely Sibley could not expect to do any such hunting and fishing in the vicinity of Huron, or even of Detroit. He grew more animated, depicting the territory served by the post at St. Peters in glowing terms, and it was patent presently that Sibley was impressed.

Crooks pressed the advantage Hercules had clearly gained. "You need not give your consent immediately, if you'd rather go west and look over the country, Sibley," he said. "After all, that should be your privilege."

"No, if I go, I'll make up my mind now, today."

"As for capital—as you know, I can furnish all the necessary capital myself. The important factor is to get this new Company of ours into action. I needn't point this out to you."

"No, of course not. I'm fully aware of it. If I went, what time would you want me to start?"

"As soon as possible."

"You could return with me," said Hercules.

"When do you go?"

"Tomorrow afternoon."

"That would be too early. I would need at least a week to prepare.

And then there would be additional preparation to be made at Prairie du Chien. From there north is virtually unmapped wilderness, I understand."

"Not quite. I have a map," said Hercules. "And as for your preparations there, I'll get things ready for you."

Crooks stood up. "Then we can take it you're in, Mr. Sibley?"

"Yes, sir. You may. Dousman has convinced me. He knows I can't resist the hunting. But I've known all along you were right, I needed only to be convinced against my parents' will, so to speak."

"Your hand on it, Mr. Sibley."

They shook hands joyously, and Crooks brought out a bottle of dry wine to drink a toast to the new American Fur Company.

Within a few days of Hercules' return to Prairie du Chien, Sibley arrived. Hercules had prepared for him, assembling provisions, and instructing the trader, Alexis Bailly, who had four stations within Sibley's district and who was en route to St. Peters, to wait for the new agent and serve as his guide. He had, moreover, detailed five voyageurs to accompany Sibley and Bailly north, and had taken upon himself the problem of asking Sibley to permit in his company young Duncan Campbell, Margaret's sixteen-year-old brother, who wished to join relatives in the country northwest of Lake Pepin. In addition to Bailly, who knew the river route best, Hercules had arranged for a Winnebago guide and all the horses the party would need. He had not, he told Sibley, stored too much meat, since it was possible for them to take venison on the way, and he added also that they would not wish to miss eating the wild honey they could find if they sought for it.

Sibley was anxious to proceed, since it was already late in autumn, and snow might be expected to fall. Nevertheless, he stayed in Prairie du Chien four days, discussing the new Company with Hercules and Rolette. On the fifth day he was ready to set out for his permanent post.

"I know I've made the right choice," he told Hercules. "And thanks largely to you. I'll not regret coming in."

"I don't think you will," agreed Hercules. "Any more than we will keeping you. Now keep in touch with me; if anything goes

wrong, send a runner at once. Depend on me to do everything I can to help you establish yourself."

Bailly was already pushing ahead with the Winnebago guide, and the voyageurs followed. Sibley swung into line, holding his spirited horse from making a show of himself, turned to wave farewell, and rode into the north.

Now that the affairs of the trade were for the moment over, Hercules' thoughts went unerringly back to Jane. Rolette had not gone again to see her; she had made no attempt to communicate with Rolette. Apparently he was quite content to have Elizabeth working for him, and Elizabeth was satisfied to have Eugenie come occasionally to help her. Moreover, whatever might be the situation between Jane and Rolette, Elizabeth visited Jane from time to time, and there was no animosity between them. In this manner, doubtless, Rolette learned about Jane's activities, and she about his without the necessity of words between them.

Hercules determined to make another effort presently to eliminate the difficulties between them, though he knew that Rolette still drank substantially, and that doubtless Jane was well aware of this. However, he hesitated. Affairs at the post with the coming of winter kept his attention. The Company's store was filled with goods, colorful red blankets and leggings predominating in consideration for the Indian's preference for red; the warehouse was beginning to receive furs, and the sorting had begun, so that Hercules found little time even to be in the office, save at evening. Daylong there was a constant stream of visitors to the store or warehouse—Indians blanketed against the cold, voyageurs, some of them grumbling because the money for their pay had not yet arrived, and not pleased that Hercules had had to send a runner to St. Louis for funds to come by dogsled. Deep snow fell early, and the trade picked up rapidly. As for Rolette—he spent far too much of his time in his own office near Hercules', with a bottle constantly at his elbow, though he worked among the men in the warehouse, his costume as picturesque as theirs, so that he was often unnoticed among them. Of them all, only Hercules dressed as impeccably as if he held an office in the city.

In January, when still deeper snow kept many of the traders and

Indians from coming to the post, Hercules went over to see Jane, who sat reading to her old aunt. The older woman, thinking that Hercules carried word from Rolette, left them alone. They sat together briefly in silence broken only by the sifting of snow against the windowpanes, neither knowing what to say.

Hercules presently asked what intelligence she had from the children.

"Oh, I am so lonesome for them," she cried. "I cannot tell you how I miss them!"

"More than Rolette, no doubt," he said.

"Much more," she agreed. "I love my children. I do not know whether I have evaire love' M'sieu' Rolette."

He raised his eyebrows. "You find that out rather late, do you not, Madame? Or was it the liquor which enabled you to discover this?"

"Partly," she assented. She seemed not to have her customary fire, and he was a little disappointed. "But I have always know this, I think, only I never say it to myself. Do you understan' that, Mistaire Dousman?"

Yes, he said, he could understand that quite well. There were things which he too knew about himself, but did not, could not say to himself. "We dislike to admit many things to ourselves," he added.

"Mistaire Dousman is apparently in a mood for philosophy," she said, smiling with her eyes.

"Events turn us to philosophy, Madame," he said. "Tell me, does Rolette provide adequately for you?"

"He do what he can."

"Do you find it ample?"

"Yes, I do. But he still do not pay for my dresses, he say."

Hercules laughed. "Don't you think it a little too much to ask of him, that he honor your bills when you no longer live with him? Or do you find that quite consistent? I shouldn't think so."

She covered her mouth with the fingers of one hand, as if to hold back a sharp retort. Color drove to her fair skin and receded. "I suppose it is unreasonable of me to expec' that," she admitted finally. "But I do not know why he make such absurd statements, when he has pay for my clothing until now. Always he say he do not pay, and yet Mistaire Stambaugh nevaire sen' me bills."

"Oh, Rolette has a good heart underneath his gruffness," said Hercules casually.

"I have nevaire doubt' that," said Jane.

"You've thought no more of returning to him?"

She shook her head. "I have made up my min', and M'sieu' Rolette have make up his. We are oppose', and we are sairtain to remain oppose' because neithaire of us will give in. I am right, and he is wrong. Maybe he think it is the othaire way aroun'; I do not care. He say he do not need me, and I know I do not need him. If he miss me then I miss him, too; but no more than jus' a little; it is only because I have got use' to him, as no doubt he got use' to me." She nodded a little, as if to emphasize her decision. "I do not dislike him, and he do not dislike me, but we do not agree, and that is all there is to it."

Hercules got up. "I must go," he said.

"Mus' you? Why? Why do you not come more often to call on me?"

"Surely it would not be proper, Madame," he said with gentle mockery. "After all, you're still a married woman, and we must consider society and its code."

His mockery was momentarily lost on her. "Yes, that is true," she agreed. Seeing how his eyes twinkled, she drew back. "I do not live by that code; I have a bettaire one of my own, thank you. Mistaire Dousman, you make me vair' angry, you make fun of me."

"Only deservedly, Madame," he said, still smiling.

He left her half angry, half amused.

In March he saw her again, at her own direction. Rolette fought his way through a downpour of rain to the Company office and told Hercules that Jane wished to see him at once. He had just come from a brief visit to her, he said, and he had been obliged to tell her certain things she should know, in the course of which he had unwittingly put Hercules in an unfavorable position. Hercules would learn, if he had not known before, how Jane could be when she was angry.

Hercules was amused. He observed that nothing could be urgent enough to take him out into a downpour like that; so he waited.

When finally he came to the Brisbois house, he found Jane await-

ing him. She stood in the center of the Brisbois parlor, and could hardly contain herself until Hercules strode into the room.

"There, Mistaire Dousman, there are the things you have buy for me," she cried, pointing dramatically to a heap of dresses piled on the sofa.

Hercules remarked quietly that Madame had quite a flair for dramatics, and sat down, making himself comfortable.

"Take them, take all of them. I do not dream it was Mistaire Dousman who pay for my clothing!"

"Does Madame then expect me to wear the dresses?" he asked, grinning. "If so, I fear I shall have to disappoint her."

"Take them," she cried passionately. "It is no consairn of mine what you do with them. They are yours. You have pay for them."

"With all reason, Madame should spare me this scene."

"Do you think it not reason when I discovaire that anothaire man has pay for all my clothing? Yes, I should think so, indeed! Here I have all along think that M'sieu' Rolette make a joke with me, and pay for my clothing anyway. Now I fin' that he do not joke after all, and that you pay for them."

"Who said so?"

"He. M'sieu' Rolette say so. He was only jus' now here."

Hercules remained undisturbed. He listened until Jane had talked herself into a breathing space and then said only that if Rolette himself had no objection to Hercules' paying for her clothing, she need not have.

She cried out again. "But what do people think if they knew?"

"They don't."

"But why have you do such a thing?"

"Well, in the first place, as Madame well knows, I am fond of her; I would not like to see her deprived of the things she considers necessary. In the second, Rolette suggested that he might pay me back later, but I myself said that would not be expected. In the third, I was interested myself as a friend of both Rolette and Madame, to see just how much it was that Madame spent on her clothes, whether she could be blamed for extravagance and augmenting Rolette's worries. Besides, I have from time to time had occasion to pay other bills for Rolette; it is a business relationship, and I felt that this could be considered in a similar manner."

She shook her head angrily. "That is almos' like—as if you conduc' a social experiment with me as subjec'! Mistaire Dousman, I have seem vair' patient, but I assure you I cannot tolerate this. Take these dresses; I do not want them."

Hercules looked at her with disarming frankness. "Has it ever occurred to Madame that she's very beautiful when she's angry?"

She turned away, disconcerted. "That is beside the point."

"Beauty is never beside the point," he said, getting up and coming over to her. "Now, look here, Madame—I don't want those dresses; I have no interest in them; even if I had I would not take them; I can't be bothered with them. They're yours, and if you insist upon giving them away, you'll have nothing to wear, because I promise you that Rolette will absolutely not pay for your clothing. Will you try to understand that? I appreciate your objection, but pray believe that my action had no other motives but those I mentioned, and that the matter of a financial transaction is between Rolette and me, and you have no part in it. I did not ask for permission to pay for Madame's dresses; I assumed that right as a friend of both Rolette and yourself, to relieve Rolette at a time when he was hard pressed, just as sometimes I paid for his segars, or his new coat, or his other bills when they came to me during his absence from Prairie du Chien."

She shook her head as if she wished to hear no more. "Mistaire Dousman have put me in a vair' difficult position. I am obligate' to him."

"Not at all," he replied immediately. "Madame owes me nothing. If any one is obligated, it's Rolette; and I absolved him from obligation some time ago. No, Madame, we'd better let the matter rest just where it is."

"I am so upset I could cry," said Jane.

"Well, cry then," he said. "It may help you."

Her eyes flashed, and her mouth grew briefly firm. "Mistaire Dousman's sympathy is not strong. I should be ashame' if I torment' some one so."

"Madame can understand then how I feel," he said. "Now I shall go, so that you will have ample time to arrange your clothing again."

The delicate mockery of his tone stirred her anew. "I will not. I will not keep them. You have pay for them, and you shall have them. I will sen' them to your office. . . ."

He turned casually to the door. "No, Madame—you'll keep them, and please to say no more about them to me. I'm busy, too busy to argue with you about them—much as I enjoy to discuss matters with Madame."

He went out, with her voice calling angrily after him.

He was in a fury with himself, but it was not because of the dresses. It was because he realized more than ever that he was drawn to Jane as he had no right to be, and he thought of himself as belying his own wish each time he urged Jane to return to Rolette, because he could not believe that honestly he wished her to. He was all the more annoyed because it was evident that thought of Jane superseded everything else; now that the trade flourished as well as it could in this time of change, he could not rid his mind of her image, he heard her laughter ring in his ears sometimes when he had not paid her a visit for weeks, her voice echoed in the channels of his memory, and he saw again every gesture, every movement of her features as if he only just turned briefly away from her.

It was incredible that he who had never so much as consciously troubled himself emotionally about a woman before should be in love with Jane. But he was. He was too intelligent to make any attempt whatever to deceive himself. And he knew that there was no comparison between his love for Jane and the affection he had borne Margaret, an affection which had come too late, in any case. As he went along, rain began to fall once more, but he did not mind, he did not even seem to notice; he was intent upon seeking some escape from the emotional problem which pressed ever more persistently upon his mind. What he had to struggle against was not alone his affection for Jane, but also his impulse to be as direct about this problem as he was in his business: to patiently but swiftly remove all obstacles to achieve his end. As long as she remained Rolette's wife, he could do nothing; no one of them could; each must go his way alone, and none could speak even what lay in the innermost places of the heart.

8.

Interlude:

What Thin Partitions

1836-1839

WITH the insistence of Jane in his thoughts, Hercules flung himself furiously into his work in an effort to stifle his feeling for her. His concern now was no longer only the fur trade, but also with his plans for agriculture and the shipping of such grains as might be raised successfully in the Territory. At the same time, his investments in real estate were beginning to pay him many times over his original capital, particularly his Milwaukee holdings where the property advanced rapidly in value as a consequence of the steady flowing in of settlers from the East and from abroad. He grew steadily more wealthy, and found it difficult to reinvest his income. Despite all the minutiæ of his existence, he could not keep Jane from occupying his thoughts.

Early in that year she left the Brisbois home and went to live in a small house on an island directly opposite the lower part of Prairie du Chien. She took Eugenie to stay with her, explaining to Rolette that she needed more privacy than the Brisbois home permitted her. Rolette remonstrated with her and finally carried his grievance to Hercules.

Hercules liked her move no better than Rolette. "But of course, she owns the place," he said. "She can do as she likes."

"But it's so isolated—to have to cross the river each time she wants to come to the village."

Hercules pointed out that she did not come to the village often enough to matter. As for its isolation, she undoubtedly preferred being alone.

"*Sacré bleu!* She could be alone with a dozen people all around her," he said. "What the devil does she need to go to an island for?"

"Well, Joe, perhaps she wants to get still farther away from your drinking. Who knows?" He shrugged. "If you dislike it so much, you might try modifying your taste for liquor and permit her to come back to you without losing face."

"That has nothing to do with it," said Rolette gruffly.

"Oh, it has everything to do with it," countered Hercules casually.

"I won't hear that again," shouted Rolette.

"Very well. We won't talk about it. Here, take a look at this schedule of prices." He handed a letter from Crooks to Rolette, who took it in bad humor. Hercules went on, making conversation. "Only ten years ago we were paying as high as thirty cents for prime muskrat skins, better than that for raccoons and minks, as much as seventy-five for a good fox pelt, and up to five dollars for number one otter skins. See to what an extent those prices have come down since then."

Rolette nodded, shifting his big frame uneasily in his chair.

"The fact is," Hercules continued, "for any one who will see, the handwriting's on the wall for the trade. At the same time, prices generally were down then, whereas now they're up—twenty dollars for a barrel of whiskey, when it was seventeen ten years ago, for instance."

Rolette put Crooks' letter down. "For that matter, the trade's been declining ever since the last war with England," he said absently. "It's good for ten or twenty years yet; it'll have its bad years and its good years, as always."

Hercules folded the letter and put it away.

"Right now," resumed Rolette, "I'm more interested in what to do about Jane."

Hercules laughed. "I should think that by this time you'd have realized that there's nothing whatever to do with Jane; if she's of the mind to live on that island, she'll live there, and you won't stop her."

"Perhaps you might be able to do something," suggested Rolette. "After all, she calmed down quickly enough about those dresses last year."

"I'll call on her some day, when time permits," Hercules said.

But he put off calling on Jane because he knew very well that he was too eager to go. He permitted everything to keep him from

visiting her where she now lived, and when at last he was ready to go he was held to his office by word from Colonel Taylor that a messenger from the President of the United States would shortly present himself to Hercules and wished to take an hour of his time. Hercules was mystified, but he was grateful for this further excuse to put him off from calling on Jane, whose very presence shook him now.

The messenger presently came, a tall, grave man of middle age, who introduced himself as Captain Kenilson. He had a military air, but more commanding was his dignity, broken every little while by an almost boyish grin, so that, while he had an air of gravity, his smile had a puckish way with it. He apologized profusely for taking up Hercules' time, but he was bearing a commission from President Van Buren.

Hercules said that he was surprised to know that President Van Buren was aware of his existence.

"Indeed he is, sir," protested Kenilson immediately. "A good many of us are. We all know your reputation. The War Department commends your map highly; the surveyors find it most exact, only here and there a few miles out of the way. We are all aware of the high esteem in which the various Indian chieftains hold you, and this speaks well for you. Governor Cass speaks highly of you, and, I need hardly add, Mr. John Jacob Astor."

Hercules snapped to attention. "Mr. Astor?" he repeated.

"Yes, indeed, Mr. Astor," went on the captain. He continued to sing Hercules' praise until Hercules became uneasy. He did not know what Kenilson's visit portended, but presently the captain began to drive toward the reason for his visit. As Mr. Dousman perhaps knew, the eastern part of the Territory was this year to become the State of Michigan.

Hercules said he had been aware of that for some time; his father had written him as long as a year ago, he felt sure. He was still not certain of what Captain Kenilson was driving at.

"The remainder of the Territory will be given the name Wisconsin, after the river which runs through it," continued Kenilson. "And of course, it will now have to have a governor in place of Cass."

"Ah, will Cass stay in Michigan. then?"

"For the time being at least," Kenilson went on. The President, of course, would need to appoint a governor of Wisconsin Territory, preferably some one familiar with the country. Unfortunately, there were few persons of promise in the Territory.

Hercules protested. What of Colonel Henry Dodge, for instance?

The President had considered him, but the fact was, the strongest representations had been made for another name, and if at all possible, the President would prefer to appoint him. In short, it was Hercules Dousman.

Hercules stared at him for a moment in amazement. "Some one has mentioned me?" he asked, as if he could not believe Kenilson. "But I've done nothing. As a matter of fact, I would never have considered myself. . . . No, no," he shook his head, "I'm too busy. I can't conceive of it."

"The War Department and Governor Cass have been especially loud in your praise, sir," said Kenilson patiently. "And the President earnestly hopes that you will accept the appointment."

Hercules had never thought of taking any kind of public office. He said so. He pointed out that he had always felt himself best able to serve his country as a private citizen, and he hoped to be permitted to continue as before.

Kenilson protested. After the most careful sifting of names, Dousman's had remained. It had been agreed that any one who so assiduously and quietly managed to convince the Indians with all their intertribal wars of his sincerity and honesty would make an ideal leader in the Territory, which would itself now move toward Statehood, certainly.

Hercules got up and walked slowly to the window, his hands clasped behind his back, his head shaking. "No, I can't do it," he said again. "I wasn't cut out for such a position. Believe me, I'm sensible of the honor the President means to confer upon me, but I consider that I'm more necessary to my various enterprises. In any event, I'll always be available to any governor who may be appointed." As he talked, he wondered about Kenilson's offer, and who had been the instigator of it; it might well have been the military through the War Department; it could not have been Astor, who had little interest in the Territory, apart from such lands as he still held, lands won through foreclosure of mortgages at the

time the American Fur Company had changed hands. These lands, however, were largely in the Green Bay area.

Kenilson stood up. "I hope your decision isn't absolute, Mr. Dousman. Shall we put it this way? I'll be back in the morning for your answer."

"You may if you like," replied Hercules, "but I can give you my answer now; I have given it. It's no. Frankly, the office is one I never contemplated; in fact, I've never contemplated a public office of any kind. I would much prefer to be left alone to attend to my enterprises here."

"You're much too modest, sir."

Hercules shook his head. "No, it's not modesty; it's only good business. I'm responsible for enterprises covering more country than the proposed new Wisconsin Territory right now. And I must be here in Prairie du Chien, where it's unlikely that a capital will be established. So I say no."

Kenilson made a military bow, once more expressed his disappointment at Hercules' decision, and took his leave. Hercules looked after his retreating back, a mixture of emotions assailing him. He was faintly proud that he had been thought of, but he was even more astonished; he had held to his work for so long and steadily, that it did not occur to him that in all this time he had done anything at all to merit attention; he had done only what needed to be done to further the good of his businesses and of his community.

He turned and went philosophically back to his work—the countless infinitesimal details of that business which kept him constantly occupied.

In mid-morning of the next day he went over to see Jane. The house in which she now lived was a small, one-story building, sturdily built, with a narrow porch running its length on the east, facing toward Prairie du Chien. Its setting was ideal; tall cottonwoods towered overhead, lacy birch embowered it; and behind it grew a large patch of bergamot, whose minty fragrance held the sun-warmed air, and along the porch Jane had planted other wild flowers which were now in blossom.

When he approached the house, he saw Eugenie at the pump.

She had seen him before she caught his eye, and watched him come on with a friendly smile. Seeing that he had observed her, she nodded and pointed helpfully toward the house, to indicate that Jane was there. He waved to her and went on.

The door stood ajar. He knocked and looked in, his nostrils informing him that some one had been ironing clothes. From the back of the house came Jane's voice, calling sharply to Eugenie. Eugenie called in reply to say that it was Mistaire Dousman who stood at the door, and presently Jane appeared, momentarily flustered.

"Mistaire Dousman, come in. I am sorry, I do not know who it was come to see me. Sit down."

She sat down before him, clasping her hands laxly in her lap, and looked at him as if she were expecting a lecture, her eyes gazing up at him from beneath lowered brows, her lips just faintly touched by a smile.

He remarked that she had an attractive small house here, he had no idea it was so kind to the eye, he had no doubt Madame's energy and ingenuity were largely responsible for transforming the old shack into the house it had become. "But why," he ended up casually, "did Madame see fit to come here?"

"Because I do not longaire wish to impose upon my aunt," she said promptly. "And I own this, this is mine. I can do with it what I wish."

"But it's inconvenient for you, surely. And it's rather isolated," he protested. "I can understand the wish for privacy, but surely this is a litttle too much?"

"Is Mistaire Dousman then concairne' about me?" she asked, sucking her cheeks in as if to prevent herself from smiling.

Hercules felt an impulse to impatience, but withheld it. Certainly he concerned himself about her, as she had good reason to know long before this. He objected, quite frankly, to having been put to the additional trouble of wondering about her safety here on this island; after all, he pointed out, on a similar island not too long ago almost twoscore Indians had been slain without a sound that reached the village.

She laughed, and assured him that she was quite capable of taking care of herself. "I have nevaire been accustom' to hide behin' any

one," she said simply. "I do not considaire it necessaire' now."

"Rolette is himself very much upset about this," he said reflectively.

Again she laughed. "How strange it is that evair'one make so much bothaire, and M'sieu' Rolette especially. He do not think enough of me to say he will stop his drink'; so why should he now concairne himself about what I do? Men are such strange creatures, I do not understan' them, I think sometime' they do not understan' themselves. What do you think, Mistaire Dousman?"

She was apparently gravely serious, but there was laughter in her eyes.

Hercules answered with a straight face that doubtless women appeared quite as strange to men on many occasions. The difference between them was really quite a simple matter for any one who chose to examine it.

"Indeed?" said Jane in a voice that amounted almost to a purr.

Hercules remained sober. Yes, really quite simple. It amounted to this, he said: men were essentially reasoning creatures, while women were emotional. It was patent that women were rational only up to a certain point, after which they became emotional—usually violently so; this was no doubt the natural escape to conceal the lack of greater reasoning power. He said all this without smiling.

She looked in vain for any sign of his jesting; there was none. "In my opinion," she said with cool precision, "we are all creatures of the emotion on sairtain occasions."

"Doubtless there are occasions," admitted Hercules.

Jane retreated to Rolette. "Do M'sieu' Rolette think I should come back and live once more with my aunt? If he do, is that for his convenience so he can call on me more easily, or do he think of me?"

Hercules supposed that Rolette thought of her.

"He think first always of himself," she said. "I think all men are this way."

Hercules nodded. As reasoning creatures, men doubtless realized that the self is all-important—just as Jane did when she left Rolette. Would Madame call it selfishness?

"No, I think not," said Jane. "I would call it self-protection."

Hercules said bluntly that they were different names for the same thing.

"There is no reason why I should sacrifice myself," cried Jane. But abruptly she stopped, in sudden irritation with herself. She unclasped her hands and made small fists of them. "Why is it we have always this argument?" she demanded. "Why is it evair' time you and I are togethaire, we have this fight with words?"

Hercules smiled, and said that doubtless the reaction was fundamental in their natures and could not be avoided. He thought that surely Jane must be aware that underneath this constant tugging between them there lay his fondness for her, a fondness which found no expression in words; but if she were not aware of it, so much the better; it would not do to have her appreciate the depth of his affection for her; since she remained nominally Rolette's wife, this knowledge would serve only to distress her.

She got up abruptly, excused herself, and went into the kitchen, where her voice rose in conversation with Eugenie. He took these moments to look around him. On the wall were the Edouardt silhouettes of Jane and her two children; they were arranged above the piano, which Jane had apparently had moved from the Rolette house, for it was the same massive piece which had been brought in sections down the Fox-Wisconsin water route. From the look of the music on the piano, as well as of the piano itself, it was apparent that some one played quite often. He thought it would be Jane. On the small round table near her sofa she had placed a bowl of columbines, from which arose a delicate but subtly present fragrance. On another wall hung a sampler in a neat wooden frame; he recognized this for the piece which Jane had worked when he had called on her at the Brisbois house. The chairs and sofa were arranged almost carelessly to make a half circle facing toward the piano; there was a careful artlessness about the room which was attractive to him.

Jane came back in. "Eugenie says it is almost time for dinnaire," she said. "I hope Mistaire Dousman can stay and join us. It is long time since he have dinnaire at my table, and it is time now he do so again."

"I believe I can stay," said Hercules, "but I would not wish Madame to go to any bother on my account."

"Oh, it is no bothaire, believe me, Mistaire Dousman. You are like an old friend of the family," she replied. "Even though there

is at the moment no family." She laughed gayly at her sally.

He laughed with her, though with mixed emotions.

"And now let us not fight any more," she said. "You come so seldom to visit me, it is not right that we should quarrel each time you do. Tell me what news there is, what has happen' in the village since I have move' here, how is your business—jus' talk to me about things we do not argue ovaire."

He grinned and said that disagreements were natural enough between any two people as forthright and sure of themselves as they were. He began then a prosaic recital of events in the existence of the village. Did Madame know that the Pest House had occupants again? Four children and a woman. All had smallpox. Doctor Foote feared that an epidemic was about to begin. So perhaps on that score it was better that Madame had chosen this time to move to the island.

"Do Doctaire Foote take care of them?" she asked. "Who are they?"

He named the sick, whereupon she was filled with dismay. She knew them all, and filled the room with cries of pity. He said their illness was apparently serious, and Doctor Foote had good reason to be worried about an epidemic. The smallpox was feared with just apprehension.

"Doctaire Foote, he mus' have his hands full. Do he stay there with them? How do he do his work if some othaire pairsons take sick?"

He shook his head. "Oh, no, Foote could never take care of them. That's not his job, you know. He looks in now and then, but he can go no farther."

"Is it LaBuche then? Or one of the Indian women?"

It was neither, Hercules assured her. There was no one.

She cried out. "They have no one? Ah, *les pauvres enfants!* What do they do? How can they live then?"

"I believe the woman who is with them does what she can," he said. "It can't be very satisfactory, because she's ill herself."

"But they will die, they will all die! Mistaire Dousman, something mus' be done for them. They can't be allow' to suffaire and die alone—like dogs. What do the people think to do this?"

Unfortunately, Hercules pointed out, sentiment could not be per-

mitted to endanger the entire community. Regrettable as their confinement without some one to wait upon them was, it could not be helped. There was no way of forcing any one to take care of the sick; Madame could understand that, certainly.

"But how cruel!" she replied. "It is not human. It is like the animal who leave his sick one alone to get well or die; he do nothing."

"Madame, at bottom we're all animals; it would be futile to deny it. We're all sorry about the contagious sick who must go into the Pest House, but it can't be helped. If no one wishes to play nurse to them, we can't make them do so."

"Has no one offaire'?"

"Not to my knowledge."

She cried again about the helpless little children locked away from their homes, from all comfort and solace but that of a woman herself sick perhaps to the death. It must not be endured; it could not be permitted; some one must be sent to nurse them. It was barbarous, and she declared that man with all his accomplishments should have arranged for such an emergency as this. The intensity of her sympathy for the imprisoned children was so great that it brought tears to her eyes, and she wiped them unashamedly away.

He strove to change the subject, but she would hear nothing else. She plied him with more questions, wishing to know where the disease had first become apparent, what was being done to prevent an epidemic, whether the gravity of the pox was great enough so that they might expect many of the unfortunate victims to die. She kept up her questioning throughout the entire meal, scarcely eating at all, crying out again and again about the unfortunate children so incarcerated without care.

"But I am glad to know about this before it has got worse," she said at the meal's end. "I think I know some one who can take care of them."

He cautioned her not to send Eugenie; it was bad enough for the two women to be alone on this island, but one alone would be far worse. If it were another of the French-Canadian women among whom she had so much influence, he suggested also that she send some one who was not herself bound to a large family, so that

if anything happened to her in this duty, she would not be so grievously missed.

She seemed now impatient for him to leave; this was apparent in her restlessness, her inattentiveness; so he got up, thanked her for the dinner, and left. Rowing over to Prairie du Chien, he thought with no attempt to control his imagination how pleasant it would be to take his meals always with Jane, contemplating this as he might consider something remote in a distant time never to be attained.

When he reached the office, he found a runner from the nearest Sioux tribe waiting for him: a young man, agitated, and not at his ease. Hercules flashed a curious glance at him; he had never seen him before. He sat down and asked what he wanted.

The Indian introduced himself: Running Deer. He had come at the request of one of the chiefs who was ill to say that the Indians were all very sick, dying many of them. They did not know what to do; they had no food.

Hercules thought fleetly how fortunate it was that Jane knew nothing of this. "What is it?" he asked. "The pox?"

Running Deer nodded, his coal-black eyes smoldering in distaste and fear.

"Go back and tell them I will send them food and whatever else it is they need."

Watching Running Deer go on his way, he reflected that if the Sioux had the pox, other tribes might well also be afflicted. He sighed. He might as well prepare to make provision for them all.

In late afternoon Doctor Foote stopped in. The sun had gone behind a bank of clouds portending storm, and the calm, waiting air had grown sultry and very hot. Doctor Foote, who was tall and muscular, came in wiping perspiration from his temples and his thick moustache. He was young, in his thirties still, and impatient in his eagerness. He flung himself into a chair with a manner presaging his rapid departure again very soon.

"Dousman, thank you. That was a fine thing you did. I would not have believed such a thing possible of Madame Rolette, but I've misjudged her. A wonderful woman! Who would have thought it! She says you were in part responsible; I've thanked her as much as I'm able; now I thank you, too."

Hercules listened in amazement, wondering to what Foote had reference; certainly the doctor could not yet know about the supplies Benoit and his men had taken to the Sioux. "I think you're taking advantage of me, Doctor," he said when Foote had finished. "I don't know what you're talking about."

"Indeed? You didn't know that Madame Rolette entered the Pest House this afternoon to nurse the sick there?"

For a moment Hercules was as if thunderstruck; the shell of his wonder burst into a fountain of needling fear for her. "Jane!" he exclaimed. "Madame Rolette—gone into the Pest House herself?"

"Why, yes—yes, I assumed you knew of it. She said . . ."

"I knew nothing of this," he said brusquely. "Does Rolette know?"

"Not yet."

Hercules closed his eyes for a moment as if to shut out sight of the doctor sitting there. He wished he might as easily shut himself away from this knowledge of Jane's act. But it was like her; it lay in her generous nature to do precisely what she had done; her sympathy for the children made it mandatory in her sight, certainly. Small wonder she was so well loved by all the French-Canadians in the village!

"It should not have been permitted," he said.

"I believe Madame Rolette is a free agent," countered Foote. "I tried to dissuade her, but she wouldn't hear me."

Hercules thought of her fair skin, the beauty of her unmarred features. "Is there danger of her taking the disease?" he asked.

"I'm afraid so," answered Foote honestly. "I wish I could say there weren't—but it wouldn't be the truth. If the disease showed any signs of abating, perhaps she might with care escape it. But I'm afraid we're in for an epidemic."

"When did she come in?" asked Hercules.

"Shortly after noon."

She had had this in mind even while she plied Hercules with questions about the epidemic; he realized it now. *I know some one who can take care of them,* she had said. Of course: who but herself! "I think you'd better inform Rolette," he said.

Doctor Foote got up. "Of course, now she's in, she'll have to stay in," he said uncertainly, as if in doubt of his ability to keep her there. "I don't know what Rolette will say, but there's nothing he can do."

"Go and tell him," said Hercules. "Meanwhile, I'd like to talk to Madame Rolette."

"There's to be no contact, of course. The north window would probably be the best place; she's near it."

"I'll go right over."

He got up, thanked Foote for informing him of Jane's action, and walked toward the Pest House, which was close to the river and set a little apart from the houses near it: a gaunt, forbidding building, its appearance suggesting a use akin to that to which it had been put. A west wind was rising slowly, cooling the air a little; the quaking aspen and the cottonwoods rustled and whispered overhead; on the wind came the smell of distant rain, the water freshness combined with the fragrant distillation of the deep woods. As he approached the Pest House, the sound of life in the village receded behind him, became a distant murmuring.

The north window stood open. He went up to it and called Jane's name. In a few moments she appeared, looking doubly beautiful in the stone window-frame. She smiled at him and raised her eyebrows.

"Ah, Mistaire Dousman is a pairsistent visitor. But I am glad to see him."

He ignored this. "Jane, what are you doing?"

She answered his gravity with a prolonged gaze of patience before she said, "I have inform' Mistaire Dousman that I could not bear the thought of these poor children suffairing; so I have come myself to nurse them as long as I am able."

He was unable to answer her smile. "Jane—didn't you think of yourself? If you should catch the pox!"

"I could not think of myself when these children suffaire! How could Mistaire Dousman expec' me to! And if I catch the pox—it do not mattaire. Who am I? I have no one to miss me; by this time even Virginie and Joseph are use' to being separate' from me. When I considaire' that somewhere my own children may be sick and in need of some one to nurse them, I could not sit at home without doing something about it. So I come." She cocked her head at him and wrinkled her forehead in a slight frown. "Mistaire Dousman seem upset."

"I *am* upset. While I'm sensible of your motives, Jane, I'm dis-

tressed about this. Something may happen to you. I don't want anything to happen to you." He shook his head as if to emphasize this. "Besides, Doctor Foote tells me there's almost certain to be an epidemic; you'll be here longer than you think."

"I'll be here as long as there are these poor helpless children to suffaire. I cannot bear to think of children suffairing. Besides, I would not think to ask some one else to do something I would not do; so I come myself."

He knew that it would be futile to ask for her withdrawal now; she had committed herself; he would only offend her. "I hope that Madame will do everything she can to prevent herself from taking the disease."

"But of course," she said. "I do not wish it; I wish only to help them. But I do not think I will get it."

He would not tell her that Doctor Foote was not so optimistic.

"I'm sorry," she said, "one of them is call' me; I mus' take up my duties. Thank you for visit' me, Mistaire Dousman."

"I'll come again," he said. Just as she was withdrawing, he raised his voice and called after her tensely, "Jane, Jane—take care of yourself."

Her eyes lingered on him almost with tenderness; then she was gone. He stood for a moment looking at the Pest House with a sick feeling inside him, grimly conscious of fear for her assailing him; then he turned and hurried back to the Company's office.

He had hardly reached there before Rolette came bursting in, his eyes wide and angry, his fists clenched.

"Hercules—have you heard——"

"About Jane? Yes. I just came from there."

"She won't come out?"

"I didn't ask her. I knew she wouldn't."

Rolette took a turn about the room, grumbling savagely. "She's out of her mind! It's her damn' softness. *Sacré nom!* to expose herself like that! She doesn't use her head, only her heart!"

Hercules observed that it was a good thing people had hearts to heed.

Rolette sat down, tugging at his beard. "If she'd been with me, perhaps she wouldn't have gone."

"She would have gone in any case," said Hercules.

"Think of what the pox could do to her!" Rolette groaned. "It will leave her scarred forever."

Hercules could not deny this; he said only that there was a possibility that she might escape the disease.

"If she gets out untouched, I'll give up liquor. I swear it!"

Hercules smiled; even in the midst of the depression upon him because of Jane's impulsive action, he could not help pointing out that this vow was akin to that other in regard to Rolette's being saved from the storm on the water.

Rolette grimaced. "But I kept my promise, and by God! I'll keep this one."

"Goaded into keeping it," said Hercules, laughing. "And who will goad you into keeping this, if Jane has already been unable to persuade you? I'll tell you, Joe, you're carrying on as if this separation were just another childish prank of Jane's. But it isn't; she means it; she'll not come back to you unless you stop drinking, and nothing else you can do will change her mind. Now that you think some harm may befall her, you're ready to make sacrifices."

"I'm fond of Jane," grumbled Rolette, passing one hand through his hair. "But a man can't give up his pleasures at every whim."

"This is more than a whim. But we won't talk about it. You should have realized that Jane was quite as much in danger of other kinds living alone on that island, and needn't have waited until she went into the Pest House." He went on to justify Jane, though he did not relinquish his wish that she had not gone.

"Stop!" cried Rolette presently. *"Mille tonnerre!* By and by you'll have it that it's all my fault she went. It seems there's more harm in a glass of whiskey than even the devil contemplated!" He got up.

"What are you going to do?" asked Hercules.

"Do? I'm going to see Foote and get her out of there."

Hercules shook his head. "That will never work, Joe. Better to accept it now and hope for the best. She won't thank you for interfering on her behalf—and most likely she'll read you a lecture you'll remember."

"God damn it, a man has the right to talk, to act," shouted Rolette. "If something happens to her, the children will never permit me to forget it."

Hercules thought this a little absurd and said so. In the first place, the children were too young to think much about it—apart from Elizabeth, and she was not Jane's child. In the second, it would be some years before they came back from the East. And finally, the possibility of Jane's dying from the pox was not too strong. That should settle all the ghosts which plagued Rolette.

"After all, I'm her husband!" said Rolette. "It's my right to keep her from exposing herself so needlessly, so foolishly."

Hercules went on talking as if Rolette had said nothing. The thing which had sent Jane to the Pest House was doubtless her concern for her own children; hearing that children were without care save for that of a woman sick herself, she thought at once of her own Virginia and Joseph, she imagined them in a similar predicament, she could no longer then keep herself from following the urgent impulse to go to their assistance; this was an essential part of her great love for her son and daughter.

Rolette appreciated this, but still, he said, he would go to see Foote. He went out, still grumbling to himself, still hounded by this sudden fear come upon him for Jane's safety in the Pest House.

Left alone, Hercules could not present to himself half as hopeful a prospect for Jane as he had put to Rolette. He lowered his head to his hands and sat so for a few minutes, fighting to control the fear for her rising within him, fighting against the thought that something might happen to her, something might come to take from him even the little pleasure he knew in the innocent company of the woman he loved.

That summer was difficult for Hercules. Each time he walked to the Pest House to call Jane, he feared that she might fail to come to the window, or that she might come with her beautiful features marked by the pox coming upon her. All Rolette's storming had failed to move her, had if anything intensified her conviction that she belonged where she was. Nor was she without attention, for daily grateful mothers came to the window with food and little gifts for the children and for her, and the village was constant in praise of her courage. The epidemic spread slowly and was not checked until midsummer.

It was not until early September that the Pest House was empty,

and Jane went back to the house on the island. Hercules paid her a brief visit there on his way to the Pierneau hill along the Wisconsin two days away; he could see that her long confinement had told, in the paleness of her cheeks, her weariness, which changed to animation only when she told how the children had recovered, to sadness when she recounted the death of one. Hercules was in haste, and said he would stop on his return in five days.

He came back on the sixth day, stopped at the island, and hurried to the house. His knock was not immediately answered; he knocked again. There was a disturbing air of desertion about the house, he now noticed, and quick alarm took possession of him.

"Who is it?" It was Jane's voice rising from within.

He told her.

"Oh, Mistaire Dousman—I am sorry. You mus' not come in."

He was astonished. What was it? he wished to know. Had he in any way offended Madame?

"No, please. I do not wish it. I am unwell."

"Are you alone?"

"Jus' now. Eugenie has go for Doctaire Foote. I do not wish it, but she go regardless because she think he should come."

"So he should," said Hercules. He paused a moment before he asked, apprehensively, "Is it the pox?"

There was an almost tangible hesitation before she replied. "Since Mistaire Dousman ask, I think it is. But I do not wish M'sieu' Rolette to know of this. Please to say nothing to him."

He was swiftly conscious of a desire to walk into the house, but at this moment he heard a canoe drawn up on the beach, and, turning, saw Doctor Foote advancing along the path. "Madame will be glad to know that the doctor is coming," said Hercules. "I'll go, but I'll come back every day if Madame will permit it. If there's anything I can do, please don't hesitate to say it." He turned and went to meet Doctor Foote, whose face was lugubrious.

"Eugenie just told me," said Foote. "You haven't been inside?"

Hercules shook his head. "I'll wait for you out here, Foote," he said. "I want to know how bad it is."

Foote nodded and hurried away. Presently Eugenie came up the path, carrying supplies she had bought in the village; she was laden,

evidence of her belief that their imprisonment on the island might be a long one. He stopped her and asked whether Madame Rolette had been ill a long time.

"Two days, maybe," she said. "But long tam before she took the fevaire. Now she has the pox."

"Is she very sick?"

"*Non, grace à Dieu!*"

She went on.

He sat down at the base of an old cottonwood, his eyes fixed on the door through which Foote must emerge. He was unconscious of midges humming about his head, and did not feel the sting of a mosquito on his arm. He had dreaded this; now that it had happened, he felt sick, nauseated by the fear that Jane, weakened by her long ordeal in the Pest House, might not be able to withstand the pox. The moments until the doctor reappeared were endless, stretching in a web of mental torture from minute to minute. He could think of nothing but Jane, whose danger now was greater than it had been in the Pest House; he could not free himself from fear for her; he could only think how empty his existence would be without even the occasional sight of her he permitted himself, and he thought how unjust of destiny it would be to repay his care to withhold his feeling for her from her knowledge by demanding her life. But already, he realized, he was steeling himself for even that.

Doctor Foote came out in half an hour. He did not look too grim, thought Hercules, who asked him at once about Jane.

"I don't know, frankly, Dousman. Just at present the disease does not appear to be so serious. She's broken out, but not badly. However, her physical condition isn't too good—you might expect that after the summer she put in." He shook his head. "But one thing is certain—she has the ability to throw off the pox, if any one has, notwithstanding her condition otherwise."

"You wouldn't say then that her condition was serious?" pressed Hercules.

"My friend, the pox is always serious," countered Foote. "I think she'll want rest more than anything else. I've forbidden any kind of contact with outside until I know just where she stands."

"Will you let me know?"

"I will, if she wishes it. I've already been told that I'm not to let Rolette hear of this."

"When will you know?"

"In two or three days." He hesitated, stepping tentatively away and coming back again. "I suppose you feel you're in part responsible for this, Dousman. I don't think I'd look at it that way."

Hercules shook his head as if in denial. Doctor Foote had no knowledge of what he thought; it was better that he had none. They went together to the mainland, and parted before Hercules' office.

Hercules turned resolutely to his work, but he could not concentrate on the trade; he found it impossible to rid his mind of the specter that haunted it. He did not want to think of Jane down with the pox, but he could think of nothing else, and his mind's eye was as if fixed upon the vision of her beautiful face hideous with eruptions which would leave their marks to scar her beauty. He thought presently of Rolette, in some doubt about informing him. It was possible that Rolette might learn it if he visited the island some day soon; he himself could not tell him, since he had promised Jane he would not. Yet if anything happened to Jane, if she should be unable to withstand the ravages of the pox, he would never forgive himself for not telling Rolette while there was still time to effect a reconciliation between them.

He experienced two days of torment, refraining from making any visit to the island, in deference to the doctor's wishes. On the evening of the second day, Doctor Foote stopped in on his return from the island.

"Dousman, she's got only a very light case, I'm happy to say," he said with an air of pride, as if he had effected this miracle himself.

"That means she'll recover!"

"Not only that, but probably without any kind of scar. She did manage to build up some resistance to the disease while she nursed the sick, and for that reason has only the mildest kind of a case now. As a matter of fact, she's up and around, though I didn't advise it; still, it will probably do her no harm."

"I presume I may visit her as long as I don't enter the house?" asked Hercules.

Foote nodded. "By all means. She would enjoy that, I know. She still doesn't want her husband to learn of this until it's all over. After the hullabaloo he stirred up when she went into the Pest House, I can see her point of view."

"Well, Doctor, it can remain our secret until she's better once more." He took Foote by the arm. "Come, let's go down to Brunet's and drink on it, sir."

In a month Jane had completely recovered.

Not a day had passed but that Hercules was fully aware of her progress, and on this first day of her freedom he went joyously to sit once more in her little parlor. It was a warm October day with the sweetness of willow in the air along the river; up and down the Mississippi many craft moved—canoes, pirogues, keel-boats, and a steamboat from St. Louis; the trappers were going out for the season, some of them singing the old voyageurs' songs, no longer so often sung at the post; hearing them, he grew mildly nostalgic for Mackinac and the years of his youth there. In the mellow air smoke rode from the west—Indians burning brush for grazing land, perhaps. On the island the cottonwood and birch were golden with autumn in their leaves.

Jane was at the piano, and her voice drifted out to him. He stood listening.

> *Bird of the greenwood,*
> *Oh, why art thou here?*
> *Leaves dance not o'er thee,*
> *Flowers bloom not here;*
> *All the sweet waters——*

He pushed open the door quietly and went into the room where she sang, slipping unnoticed into a chair and listening there where he could see her, too. Her voice was as he expected it to be: soft but clear, a good voice to hear. The song she sang was evidently recent, for it bore still the marks of folding, as if it had been sent to her from the East, as most likely it had. Before the piano, Jane looked diminutive. He scrutinized her as well as he could, but saw no sign of her illness and was filled with a deep warm glowing of happiness that she had escaped unscarred. She sang the song before she was

aware of him when she turned to reach for another sheet of music.

"Oh, Mistaire Dousman—you frighten' me!" she cried. "When do you come? I do not hear your knock."

"Madame will forgive me, but I didn't knock. I heard your voice and came in to enjoy it the better."

She smiled.

"Jane, I'm glad you're well again," he said soberly. "You don't know how frightened I was."

She laughed at him, rising from the piano stool to go to another, more comfortable chair. "I was not," she said. "I pray evair' night that I get bettaire without the scars so many of those poor children had. And you see—here I am, I am bettaire, I am not scar', I am no worse off."

"Your prayers seem to have helped."

"Ah, *le bon Dieu* is vair' good," she assured him gravely. "He even keep M'sieu' Rolette from find' out until today, and then it do not mattaire any more."

"Was Rolette here?"

"He was," she said, nodding vehemently as if to emphasize his presence. "He was right here and he say, 'Now, you see what have happen'! You see what you get for doing so foolish thing! You see, Madame,' he say, 'it is punishment for going into Pest House.' He speak vair' brave, vair' strong."

"And what did Madame say?"

"Me? I only laugh at him. I think he was vair' fonny. He would wish to have know' earlier, so that he could have go to Doctaire Foote and say, 'See, did I not tell you so?' M'sieu' Rolette could not be much angry when I am no longaire ill, could he?" She cocked her head at him in that manner so typical of her, her lips faintly curved, her eyes laughing.

"No, I suppose not. But he would have been worried—as worried as I was."

"Was Mistaire Dousman worry'?" she asked. "Why?"

"I wouldn't have wished anything to happen to you," he said. "We're all very fond of you, Jane—it would have been a hard blow to bear if anything had happened to you."

She got up and walked over to him, looking at him elaborately from this side and that. "Mistaire Dousman is so serious I do not

understan' him," she said with mock concern. "Is it maybe something he has eat?"

Yes, said Hercules, grinning; it was something he had eaten—but not with his mouth.

She pondered this for some moments in perplexity; then shrugged and gave up attempting to fathom his meaning. He was content that she should not try overmuch, for he had not been subtle. She returned to Rolette.

"He have storm' all ovaire," she said. "He scold Eugenie because she say nothing. He say he will speak to Doctaire Foote, too."

"No doubt he will," agreed Hercules. "But Foote won't listen long; he's as impatient as Rolette."

"Then they should get along." She smiled. "Tell me the news, Mistaire Dousman. I have hear' vair' little of it, but what Doctaire Foote bring' to me."

He said there was very little news worth telling.

"How are your Indians? How is your business?" she asked.

He assured her that his Indians were very well; there was some kind of trouble among the Winnebagos to the north, but it was not thought important. It had not in any event interfered with the trade, which was as good as it could be expected to be, and as for the land, while there appeared to be some uncertainty among buyers in the East now, it would doubtless soon blow over and the settlers would begin coming in greater numbers than before.

"Go on," she urged, when he paused.

"No, it's you we should talk about," he answered.

"Me? Ah, but I have do nothing; I have jus' been sick, and that is nothing. You know all about what I have do, Mistaire Dousman."

"But not about what you will do. Jane, while you were sick, I thought a great deal about you—isolated here, alone, cut off from help almost."

"Not all that," she protested, shaking her head lightly. "Do I not have a visit evair' day from Mistaire Dousman? I do. So—would I have that visit if I had not be here? I do not think so. You still wish me back with M'sieu' Rolette?"

"Yes."

She sat down close to him and gazed at him with such intentness that he was almost disconcerted. "I have tell you once I do not

understan' men sometime. Now you tell me you wish me to go back to M'sieu' Rolette, no mattaire what he have do to me, and you say this as if it were truth, and yet you say you enjoy these visits with me and you know you would not visit me so much if I were with M'sieu' Rolette. Mistaire Dousman, it is two men who talk, not one; they are both in you. Which one of them mus' I believe?"

He smiled. "Madame, they're both right."

This she refused to accept. "No, that cannot be so, because one say what the othaire say to the contraire. When you say I should go back to M'sieu' Rolette, do you speak for him or for me? Do you think about M'sieu' Rolette then?"

Hercules assured her brusquely that he thought only of her own welfare; she should be aware of this, since he could hardly make it any more clear than it already was. In this regard, she would see, both of the things he had said could be right, even though they were apparently in contradiction.

She observed that he was a very good talker. "But you have not convince' me, Mistaire Dousman. M'sieu' Rolette, he drink as much as evaire, and he is so impatient—no, no, I do not agree with you. It is bettaire I stay right here where I can be alone with Eugenie and do not need to hear what he say."

He remonstrated with her anew until she stopped him, saying she wished to hear no more about this, she heard enough of such talk from M'sieu' Rolette, she hoped to be spared it from Mistaire Dousman. He acquiesced and asked about her children, thinking this an innocuous subject to discuss.

Immediately, however, she grew animated and excited. "What do you think?" she cried. "I have wish' to see my children, and M'sieu' Rolette say no, they mus' stay where they are until they have do all their learning; then they may come home. That is three years yet, and three years is long time to wait. Me, I cannot go eas' to see them; they are separate', you know, I could not see both of them therefore anyway. But he do not wish them to visit us because he say it costs too much."

"I'm afraid he's right," said Hercules. It began to seem to him that whichever way he turned in his conversation, he met with reference to the disagreement between the Rolettes. "You see," he hastened to amplify his statement, "Rolette has not so much money

that he can afford these things. You must try to understand this, Jane."

"If that is so, why do he not say so to me? He do not say in so many words he do not have the money; why not?"

"His pride, perhaps, prevents it."

Her laugh rang out. "M'sieu' Rolette use' pride like a coat, to be put on or off as occasion demand'. He is vair' clevaire. So he do not have to be ashame', because what he have is mine, and what he have not is mine, too." She shook her head abruptly. "But here we are ready to fight again. We are always ready to fight, Mistaire Dousman. How is this? Can you say?"

"We have both too much fire," he said.

"You are vair' earnest," she said, smiling. "If you really think this, I will think it, too, so that we may be in agreement."

He looked at her seeking some betrayal of her meaning, but her face was bland, her eyes were masked.

"So, now, Mistaire Dousman, let us speak of something pleasant."

"If Madame will select the subject, I will do my best to oblige."

She gazed at him with a studied smile. "Then I think we had bettaire talk about the weathaire—it is always so safe."

He could not help bursting into loud laughter, in which she joined him. Eugenie came to the threshold of the kitchen and stared at them open-mouthed; they paid no attention to her. He bent and took Jane's arm, and led her firmly but gently to the piano stool.

"Now, come, Madame," he said, "let's start over. Here it is, your song. *The Bird at Sea*. You were singing here—we'll begin again."

The year ebbed slowly away, and the next year brought panic. The trade declined sharply, the sale of land in the Wisconsin Territory came to a standstill, few settlers came west, and those who came had little or no money. From time to time Hercules went into Milwaukee; here and there among the settlers on the land he established himself as a future shipper of wheat, looking ahead to the time when Wisconsin would ship grain to eastern and perhaps foreign markets by the lake route; on rarer occasions he went out with Lapiage or Souligne to examine the trapping country. In whatever he did, he carried Jane with him; he was no longer concerned about her isolation on the island, since she had shown herself fully

capable of taking care of herself, and his fears were groundless; he withstood Rolette's grumbling, which had become habit.

He had no time to worry unduly about the panic; he was kept too busy, and, as if the financial crisis in the nation were not enough to plague the trade, runners arrived in Prairie du Chien to say that the Winnebagos, who still claimed certain lands in northern Wisconsin, were in a very ugly mood, and ready to rise up against the whites. Hercules sent at once for Thunder Walker, who came in three days.

"What is this?" Hercules demanded, telling him what he had heard.

It was true, admitted Thunder Walker. The Winnebagos who had signed the treaty only a month before, in early November, were already dissatisfied with the agreement they had made and now wished certain changes put into the treaty.

Did they make any claim of being just in their demands? asked Hercules.

Cetainly they did, asserted Thunder Walker. Little Dandy, Yellow Thunder, Spotted Eagle—all the chiefs who were yet in the Wisconsin Territory made these claims; they said they were not paid enough for relinquishing all their lands west of the Mississippi. Now the Great White Father in Washington had promised to examine their claims once more, at the full of the moon next August, eight months and three weeks away.

Rolette came in and stood listening quietly. When the Indian had finished, he broke out, "God damn it, we'll never have rest until they're all across the Mississippi, every last one of them. I always said it."

"They'll be gone in two more years or so," said Hercules quietly. He turned back to Thunder Walker. What did the Indians expect beyond having payment of some $200,000 in claims against them assumed by the government? he asked.

"More," said Thunder Walker gravely.

Hercules turned to Rolette. "Call on Street and hear what he has to say," he suggested. "I'll be kept busy here for some time. I can see that."

Thunder Walker sat down, relaxing on his crossed legs. He regarded Hercules with impassive eyes, and presently began to talk

about what a great friend of the Indians Hercules had always been, thanking him volubly and often for the aid he had sent the Winnebagos during the smallpox epidemic.

Hercules interrupted this harangue to press Thunder Walker for information about a possible uprising.

The Winnebago did not know whether or not there would be one. "Already the white men are as numerous as the stars above, and still they keep coming," he said. "It would be very foolish of the Winnebagos to fight against so many, when they themselves are so few."

Hercules agreed, but he remained unconvinced that they might not even try.

Thunder Walker asserted gravely that anything was possible.

After half an hour of this elaborately detailed conversation, it developed that Thunder Walker actually knew very little about the dissension which stirred his people now. In disgust, Hercules gave the Indian some presents and sent him away.

Rolette came in just as Thunder Walker left, and at once complained about Hercules' generosity, saying bitterly that the Indians got too much as it was without loading them up each time they came in; if Hercules continued to do this, he said, he would soon be able to spend his entire day making presents to all the Indians who would come.

Hercules waved this away. "What did Street have to offer?"

"He said we weren't to worry, most of the trouble centered about Fort Winnebago at the Portage. And I said, what did he mean we didn't have to worry? We had the trade to think about."

"How much is there to the story of the Indian chiefs gathering?"

"They had a little meeting and went home."

"To wait for spring, no doubt." He shook his head. "I thought we had this all settled half a dozen times before this; now we'll have to settle it again. However, if it's near the Portage, it will be on the agent's shoulders up there, and we can sit back and wait to learn what happened."

In this, however, he was wrong. The winter passed, the spring drew by, the summer came in. Suddenly came grotesque rumors of Indian fury in the north, and on their heels came urgent word from one of the commissioners demanding Hercules Dousman's presence

at all costs. Hercules made ready to journey northward when a second message came to say that the place of the council would be Prairie du Chien, since it was the ancient place of peace. He waited, accordingly, until the commissioners arrived, accompanied by a secretary from the office of the Secretary of War. It was this man, Major Firkin, who was anxious to see Hercules. He wasted no time in coming to the Company's office.

He introduced himself, bowing from the waist, his little eyes appraising Hercules, his thin-lipped mouth almost prim. He had come at the behest of the Secretary of War to establish contact with Mr. Dousman.

Hercules waved him to a chair, a little annoyed at his slightly pompous manner.

Firkin sat down, continuing to talk. The fact was, he explained, that the situation among the Indians was thought to be so alarming that only some one who had had long training dealing with them could be counted upon to negotiate with them. "I am proud to say to you that every one thought immediately of you, sir," he concluded, smiling frostily at Hercules.

"What is it they're afraid of?" demanded Hercules.

"The chiefs aren't to be depended on. They're ready to call the braves to the war dance. They mean to do so."

"Have you tried talking to them?"

Firkin looked at him with a very superior air. "That would be as much as our lives are worth. We'll have a council; we'll hope to have you sit on that council. You have influence; they'll listen to you."

"I'll talk to them alone first." He got up, kicking his chair back. "I'm damned sick of all this shilly-shallying. You let yourselves be bluffed by a lot of warpaint and noise; those Winnebagos don't want to fight."

"If they come, you can talk to them first."

"If they come," repeated Hercules heavily. "My dear sir, I don't propose to wait for them; I propose to go to where they are. You said near the Portage, I believe."

Firkin nodded.

"Then, good day, sir. You've done your duty; I'll do mine."

They shook hands stiffly, and Firkin walked out in a military march. Hercules called one of his engagés from the warehouse and

sent him with a message to a friendly Winnebago runner to carry on ahead of him to the meeting place of the chiefs. Then he prepared provisions for several days, packed them compactly, and rode sultrily off on Major along the military road to Fort Winnebago. He rode for hours, thoroughly vexed both at the Indians and at the incompetent handling of Indian affairs by the government. He did not diverge from the military trail until after dark, when he came opposite the great prairie of the Sacs; then he left the road to spend the night at the Pierneau house where it stood high on the hill, looking proudly down upon the tawny prairie sweeping northward.

At noon of the following day he reached Fort Winnebago, where he learned from Rausart, the agent who had replaced Pauquette, murdered four years ago, the whereabouts of the Winnebago meeting place. Rausart had information that Hercules' messenger had come through at dawn; so doubtless Hercules would find the Winnebago chieftains assembled. Hercules did not stop to take lunch; he pressed on.

The Winnebago chieftains were assembled, as Rausart had said. They sat in a semicircle at the moment of Hercules' arrival, listening to an harangue by Little Dandy, a minor Winnebago chieftain who was more outlandishly clothed than any other among them. Hercules was in no mood to wait upon any one of them. He dismounted and went directly into the semicircle, where he tapped Little Dandy on the shoulder and told him to sit down.

An ominous muttering swept the chieftains; behind them some of their braves came to their feet, hands on their weapons. Hercules ignored their anger; he outfaced them. Presently Little Dandy walked a little confusedly to his place in the circle, and the chiefs subsided, waiting for Hercules to speak. This he did, at once.

What did they mean by stirring up trouble? he demanded. The Great White Father had sent men among them to see to it that the Treaty of 1837 was carried out justly, and now it was the Indians who rebelled against it and did not wish it carried out. The commissioners were waiting, and they heard only rumors of impending war. No wise Winnebago would go to war where he would be outnumbered by almost a hundred to one. He paused and repeated this, so that it might be impressed upon them.

They were impressed. Old Spotted Eagle nodded wisely, as if he

had known this all the time. The younger chiefs remained hostile; they clearly wished the war test of strength; but they were in the minority. This was fortunate.

Hercules went on, growing more heated. They should be thankful, he said, that the government thought of them at all. The Great White Father was busy, very busy; he had thousands of wards in all his country, and he needed more time than he had. Was this the way to repay him for his efforts on their behalf? He pounded at them, cajoled, begged, scolded, hammered at them for over an hour; their mutterings subsided, they sat still as stones, listening, nodding now and then.

When he had finished, they got up one by one and made conciliatory speeches. They were sorry, said Spotted Eagle, that they had offended their old friend, Dousman. And certainly, if *he* felt that the Winnebagos were in the wrong, then they must be, because he had always befriended them in the past. They offered him the pipe to smoke.

Hercules smoked the pipe of peace and ordered them to appear at Prairie du Chien when notice reached them to do so. He promised them that he would sit on the council himself, to make certain that they were fairly dealt with. Then he took his leave of them, snatched a sandwich to eat at Rausart's, and rode into the south again to reach the Pierneau home before nightfall.

Plagued by mosquitoes rising in clouds from the undergrowth on all sides, he rode as swiftly as Major would carry him, and diminished his pace only when they had left the wooded country and rode over prairie land beyond the Barribault River. The sun was low in the west, and all the sky was aglow with the intimation of old rose soon to hold the western heavens; woodland and grassland already held early darkness among trees and blades, and the evensong of birds had begun. Before him scattered curlews and killdeers crying wildly, and overhead hawks wheeled homeward toward the hill country to north and west. Far in the south loomed the Pierneau hill, still an hour of hard riding away.

As he rode now leisurely across the prairie of the Sacs, he could not help but wonder how many times yet the Indian troubles would beset the Territory. This should be the last, he thought, because the Winnebagos now had no more land east of the Mississippi. Even if

this were last, he was convinced with an almost fatalistic belief, that there would arise new troubles from among the settlers themselves long after the Indians were gone. There would always be trouble for men to cope with; trouble lay in their natures; they could not resist it. It was something which grew weedlike with ingratitude, hatred, greed—all the lesser attributes of mankind, those attributes he had come to discover increasingly with the advent of settlers from the East. No doubt the trans-Mississippi traders were finding this out, too, he thought, thinking of the Conestogas going westward across the river at Prairie du Chien, mounting in numbers year by year.

He was a little tired now, and looked across the long grass to where the last sunlight lingered redly on the oak groves, held to the clumps of wild crabapple and made long dark shadows upon the prairie; above the setting sun, seven platelike clouds shone like liquid gold, and higher in the heavens a tall cumulus cloud burned purple and bronze on the turn of its banks.

He could not help wishing that the problems brought into his life by his affection for Jane Rolette might be solved with the same dispatch that he had dealt with the Winnebagos. He forgot the Indians even while he still thought of them; the image of Jane rose up before his mind's eye, and he rode thinking of her, of how much and how futilely he loved her, filled with a tumultuous desire that something might come about to bring them forever together. But he was not sanguine; he was too weary even to hope. He thought dispassionately: I'm thirty-eight now, I'm getting old.

The year slipped past almost unnoticed, so quietly did events come to pass now.

One afternoon in early October, Hercules encountered Jane on the street leading to the Brisbois house. She smiled in pleasure at sight of him and came directly up to him.

"Mistaire Dousman, what a plaisir it is to see you! For long time we do not see each othaire."

It was true that he had not gone to see her for months; he had not thought it right that he do so, feeling about her as he did. He made his excuses as handsomely as he could and said that surely Madame's obvious joy was not on account of this meeting, which could be nothing but trivial to her.

"Ah, no—it is not trivial. But you are right, Mistaire Dousman. I have good news. Of a sudden, M'sieu' Rolette has sen' for my Virginie and my Joseph. So now they will come home again, and I will not be alone some more."

"What brought about this change of heart?" asked Hercules.

"He have lettaires from Mistaire Crooks who say that Joseph was ill, he was not well for many weeks, and Virginie she grow much concairne' about him; so she wish to visit him, since he was not able to travel, and Mistaire Crooks he say M'sieu' Rolette have no money to spend carelessly, she mus' be stric'ly economical and make her expenses small. Then he write this to M'sieu' Rolette and he say that the rivers will soon be too low for steamboats; so they should come home at once if they come at all. But M'sieu' Rolette do not sen' for them until now, and that was in June. So they are on their way to St. Louis, and they will come up the rivaire by steamboat from there. Think of it, Mistaire Dousman—in less than two weeks, maybe, I will see my darlings again, I who have not see them for almos' ten years."

He was delighted with her joy of anticipation, but he could not help cautioning her that the children might have changed, she would no longer have them children; they were in their adolescent years now, not children any more.

"Oh, they will always be *mes enfants*," she said. "I do not think any mothaire evaire think of her children as anything else."

"I suppose that's so, Madame." He hesitated for a moment and then asked whether Rolette visited her regularly.

"He do when he is sobaire," she said. "He know I will not see him othairewise. So he stay sobaire when he visit me."

He was curious to know whether the children had been informed of the state of affairs between their parents.

"Well, no, they have not," said Jane reluctantly. "Mistaire Dousman well know that we could not say how long we would be separate', only until M'sieu' Rolette give up his drink', and he has not do this when I have expec' him to do this long time ago; so we do not say to *les enfants* that we are part' because by time they come home, we thought we might be togethaire again. But M'sieu' Rolette, he have make up his min', and I have make up my own, and they are not alike."

"It will be very difficult for the children," he said.

"I think they will come live with me," she hazarded. "Sairtainly Virginie will; so I will not be alone. But if they prefaire to live with their fathaire, why they may do so; I shall see them, too.—But I shall miss them," she added as an afterthought.

"Rolette would, too, if they were with you," he pointed out.

"Ah, but he would drink and forget it." She shook her head. "I do not wish to think about this. I want only to think of *mes enfants* coming back to me."

"Madame must eventually think about this," he said.

But she was adamant; she would not. She walked away from him saying she must visit her Aunt Brisbois, and adding that she would expect to see him at the landing place when the boat came in. "On the fourteenth of Octobaire," she said.

He looked after her, thinking fleetingly of his own Emily, about whose education his mother had only recently written him; then he turned and went back to where Rolette was at work in his office.

"Look here, Joe, forgive me—but I was just talking to Jane about the children. You know, your being apart will make it very difficult for them. Why can't you at least try to do what Jane wishes?"

Rolette looked at him steadily. He did not seem offended, thought Hercules, but as he returned the older man's stare, he was aware of the hollowness of Rolette's eyes.

"The truth is, I couldn't stop," said Rolette. "In the first place, I don't want to. In the second, I'm not well enough to bear illness without liquor. That's the long and short of it. I know the children won't like this separation, but it isn't as if we were miles apart; they can see both of us, and they can stay where they like."

"They will probably separate," said Hercules. "Virginia will almost certainly wish to go with her mother."

Rolette was listless. "Yes, I suppose so," he said. "But I have Elizabeth, too. It doesn't matter."

Hercules looked at him searchingly. "Joe, if you're not feeling well—have you seen a doctor?"

"No," answered Rolette gruffly.

"Go to see Foote," suggested Hercules.

"As long as I can be on my feet, I'll be all right," said Rolette. "And I'm a long way from being off them."

"Joe, take care of yourself," warned Hercules. "You're inclined to be reckless."

Rolette waved this away. "Some of the voyageurs' families are planning to be down at the landing place with music, to play and sing—that's in honor of Jane, for the children," he said. "Like a celebration."

"Of course, you'll be there?"

"*Sacré bleu!* Certaintly. I'm as fond of the children as Jane is, even if I don't show it as much."

The fourteenth dawned with a slow rain, but by mid-morning the sky cleared, the sun shone upon sodden leaves and glistening trees, and, as a consequence of the precipitation, the rain-washed air was sweet with the fragrance of leaves and the pungence of herbs from the bottoms along the Mississippi. Hercules came early to his office, as was his custom, but already he found Rolette there, sitting before his table with a distant look in his eyes. He turned languidly at Hercules' entrance.

"Oh, it's you, Hercules," he said. "You know, I'm in a little quandary—I don't know just what to tell the children. At this moment, I wouldn't like to tell them Jane and I are separated."

"Jane will tell them," said Hercules.

"I suppose she will." He shrugged. "But now I don't want them to know it. There's no way of preventing it."

"Unless you can compromise with Jane." He waited a moment for anything Rolette might say, but his partner said nothing. "As a matter of fact, I think the children know the situation. Though you and Jane may have written nothing, it's almost certain that Elizabeth has, I should think. You told me they corresponded regularly."

"So they did. But if they knew anything, they never wrote about the matter to either one of us."

"In any case, they'll have to know," said Hercules. "So you might as well face it. What time is the boat due?"

"I think about noon—but of course, everything depends upon the water; it's not as high as it might be."

Hercules observed that the night's rain now beginning to let up might raise the water a little. He went on to ask what had possessed Rolette to send for the children just at this time. Why not

wait until spring? He understood that Ramsay Crooks had written to suggest that the children go already last spring.

"That's quite true," admitted Rolette. "But now I got tired of hearing Jane talk about them every time I called on her and tried to reach an understanding; so I sent for them. Besides, it takes money to keep them in school."

"That much you have," said Hercules.

Rolette did not deny it. He pulled at his beard, brushed at it with the back of one hand, and looked away. He admitted presently to some desire to see them himself, as well as to a deference to Jane's wishes. In addition to this, there was the possibility that with the children around her, Jane might soften a little toward him, and forget to make demands for reform upon him.

Hercules laughed. At this moment the sun broke through the gray clouds, and a rising wind showered drops from the trees beyond the office.

Rolette brightened, gazing at the sunlight streaming across the floor. "Ah, that's a good omen," he cried.

Hercules said nothing and presently returned to his own office. There no sun shone as yet. He sat down before his work, thinking that Rolette must be contemplating Jane's return, and wishing that she might go back to him while yet at the same time hoping she would not. It would give him more easiness in his mind if she returned to her husband, but it would do little else. As it was, it was rather more difficult to see Jane than when she lived in the Rolette house. He sat looking out of the window to where the sun lay like a dye of yellow rose leaves upon the autumn grass, wishing that there might be some solution to this triangle which would please them all equally well. But there could not be.

Shortly before noon he followed Rolette to the landing place. Jane was there, in the center of a gay party of voyageurs. The French-Canadian men and women were playing their instruments and singing. The sun made doubly bright the colors of their gay clothing. Jane herself was becomingly dressed in a full skirt and bodice in blue, ornamented by a single pin at her throat, and protected by a shawl in black and gray; these three colors were repeated on her small bonnet also, so that she made a pleasant harmony of color standing there. The French-Canadian women were pressing upon

her to thank her with renewed effusiveness for her many kindnesses to them, making a ceremony of this, and she seemed to be enjoying it, though she cast anxious eyes from time to time down the Mississippi, looking for the steamboat which might come at any time. There was still no sign of smoke foretelling its approach beyond the islands.

The October air was warm as in summer; a south wind blew gently, breaking the surface of the river into small ripples. The pungence of smoke and dying foliage rode the wind; overhead from time to time flew clouds of migrating ducks and passenger pigeons; occasionally a small flock of songbirds dropped down near by and for a few moments the air was held by their voices before they were on wing again. Still in nostrils lingered the fresh odors of the morning's rain on leaves and earth.

Rolette stood off a little to one side, in conversation with Rausart, who had come down from the Portage the previous day and was now on his way back. Hercules walked slowly over to them and stood listening.

Rausart's dark face betrayed sullen anger. He was talking animatedly about the Winnebagos, saying that the government planned to move them if not this fall, certainly during the coming year. He speculated upon the effect on the trade; so many of the Winnebagos still left in Wisconsin Territory brought pelts to the post at the Portage; it was certain that the trappers employed by the Company could not balance this loss by any addition to their own harvest, since they already worked as hard as they could.

Rolette damned the government for meddling. "But on the other hand," he pointed out, "if the Indians make trouble, it disrupts the trade anyway. So perhaps it's a matter of six of one and half a dozen of the other. What do you think, Hercules?"

Hercules agreed with them. He did not like to see the Indians removed, but a man must face facts, and it was a fact that the influx of settlers made it increasingly difficult for the Indians to continue their peaceful existence on their ancestral lands. That the government had treated them shamefully did not alter that fact.

Some one down river gave a long, echoing cry. The boat was coming at last, and the first faint evidence of smoke drifted above the line of trees along the Mississippi south of Prairie du Chien.

Immediately the comparative quiet of the landing place stirred to
activity: shouts went up, voyageurs ran to their craft alongshore
and pushed out to meet the steamboat, raising their voices joyously
in song; the women around Jane fanned out away from her, and the
little band of musicians began to play with renewed vigor. Rausart
went to his canoe and made off; Rolette and Hercules walked
slowly over to where Jane stood.

She turned gay eyes on them. "I have wondaire' whethaire M'sieu'
Rolette and Mistaire Dousman chose to stan' apart."

Rolette smiled stiffly.

"Madame was so surrounded that we could not go to her until
now," said Hercules. "I suppose you're overjoyed, eh?"

She gave a quick little nod. "I am vair' happy, Mistaire Dousman.
I have not see *mes enfants* for so long; it is too long. Now I will
have them with me as long as they like to stay."

Rolette pursed his lips and looked away. Hercules flashed a quick
glance at him; he could not tell what the older man thought, but
it was evidently about the children, for he kept his eyes turned to
that place in the river where the steamboat would first appear. Below
the bend in the Mississippi, smoke rose blackly into the blue sky
above the treetops.

"There—there it come'," said Jane animatedly, looking southward
eagerly, her lips parted, eyes glistening, already rimmed with tears
of joy.

The stern-wheeler came slowly around the bend, smoke pouring
from her stacks, water spraying upward from her wheel, gleaming
in the sunlight, the white boat itself glowing against the river's blue
and the maroon and yellow of the trees on the slopes beyond. Her
decks were not crowded, though people stood here and there along
the rail. Already the first of the voyageurs had reached her; the
words of their gay songs came back over the water, sung with that
same precision which characterized the departure of the brigades
each autumn. The boat came on, voyageurs now turning to speed
ahead, some of them to fall back alongside; the steamboat's whistle
blew commandingly, twice, a deepthroated sound that echoed from
the hills on the western shore of the Mississippi and was thrown back
and forth among the islands.

Hercules glanced at Jane. She was tense now, standing with one
hand at her throat, the other clenched at her side, her eyes fixed un-

movingly upon the boat now slowly edging into the landing place, oblivious to the voyageurs coming to shore all around her. People all about her shouted and waved, but the passengers on the boat were strangely apathetic; a few of them waved and nodded, no one shouted. Hercules flashed a quick glance at Rolette; the older man was staring intently at the ship's captain; Rolette's eyes were clouded, his lips were slightly parted, he was frowning. He too had noticed something amiss.

Meanwhile, however, the steamboat came into her place and was quickly tied up. The plank went down almost directly opposite the place where Jane stood. There was, oddly, no rush of passengers to the ground; as if by common consent, they moved apart on both sides of the gangplank and one alone went down, a young man whose direct gaze immediately found and held to the Rolettes. He came stiffly down the gangplank, his elegant clothing all somber and dark, and went directly up to Jane. It was Joseph.

Jane cried out and caught him in her arms, her voice ringing with almost angry surprise. "Joseph! Joseph! You're a man now. I did not think——"

He kissed her gravely and turned to his father, clasping the older man's hand.

Jane turned from him and stood looking toward the ship along the gangplank. There was about the passengers, about the captain standing at the head of the gangplank, about the steamboat itself, an ominous air of waiting. She looked over the faces of those standing there at the railing, some of them surely meaning to disembark; then she turned to her son.

"Joseph—where's Virginie?"

In that moment a murmur stirred the passengers on the ship. Joseph turned slowly and gazed at his mother with weary eyes; the captain hurried down the gangplank, followed by another man who hopped a little absurdly to keep up with him, and came to where Jane stood still waiting for her son's answer, which did not come. The captain bowed.

"Captain Burnham, at your service, Madame Rolette."

She nodded a little uncertainly, looking questioningly to Joseph and Rolette and back again. "Yes, sair—I look' for my daughtaire. I ask' my son, but he do not say."

"Madame, I regret to be the bearer of bad news. Your daughter

took sick of a fever not far out of St. Louis. Her condition was difficult at the outset. At Galena——"

She interrupted him. "You have leave her at Galena!" she cried. "Oh, you could not do that; she will be alone." She turned to Joseph. "Joseph—you should have stay' with her there."

Abruptly the tenseness, the gravity of every one around her impressed her sharply. The color went out of her cheeks; the animation drained from her eyes; she sucked in her lips, which had begun to tremble.

"Madame, I'm sorry—Miss Rolette died at Galena yesterday. We have brought her body home for burial."

She stood looking at him as if she could not understand that this could be true. The doctor pressed forward and introduced himself, speaking rapidly to conceal his nervousness. He said he had done everything in his power to save Miss Rolette, but the fever had been too strong; it was impossible to save her; her resistance was low. She heard none of this, her eyes fixed upon the gangplank, down which two of the ship's crew now came carrying a stretcher whose burden was covered by an American flag. They came to the landing place, from which the voyageurs, understanding what had happened, had begun to edge away, leaving a wide circular open space. The stretcher was carefully lowered to the earth, and the men stood waiting for further directions.

With a stolidity which did not conceal his own grief, Rolette walked toward them, pointing to where his house stood.

Abruptly Jane ran forward, escaped Rolette's outflung arm, and came to her knees beside the stretcher, crying out in a terrible voice, "Virginie! Virginie!" She tore away the flag and exposed the young girl's face, beautiful in its repose, and knelt there gazing at it, dry sobs retching through her body, all the more terrible because of her futile attempts to stifle them.

Young Joseph ran forward, but was stopped by his father, who stood behind Jane, shaking his head. Hercules, too, came ahead, looking questioningly at Rolette, who sighed and turned away, withholding his own agony. All around them the crowd fell back and vanished, drifting by ones and twos away from the landing; all was still but the sound of passengers coming at last down the gangplank and walking into the village, and, from the opposite end

of the boat, the sound of express being unloaded. For a few moments the scene held, the warm sun falling upon the dead girl's white face and dark hair, Jane kneeling there in the dust sobbing dry-eyed, Rolette, his son, and Hercules ranged behind her, and, behind them, Captain Burnham and the ship's doctor. Then Rolette bent forward to touch Jane gently on the shoulder.

"Jane," he said quietly.

She did not seem to hear.

Rolette nodded to Hercules, and together they bent toward her, each of them taking one of her arms, and gently but firmly raising her to her feet. She did not object, only putting out her arms uncertainly toward Virginia lying there; seeing this, young Joseph came forward and drew the flag up again to cover his sister's face.

Jane stood watching the stretcher being carried away; she would have started after it, had Hercules and Rolette not held her firmly between them. At length she indicated by shrugging her arms and shoulders that she wished to be released, and Hercules stepped back. Rolette, however, held to her.

"Jane, come home," he said quietly.

She nodded slowly, her eyes still fixed upon the stretcher and its bearers ahead of them. Young Joseph came up uncertainly, his eyes asking his father whether it was intended that he go on or wait here for them.

"Go ahead and prepare Elizabeth," said Rolette shortly. The boy walked rapidly away, and Rolette turned once more to Jane. "Come now, Jane. We'll go, too."

"Yes, we'll go," she said. "My poor Virginie!" She clung to him for a moment, sobs tearing from her again; then she composed herself, turned to fix her hot eyes on the captain and the ship's doctor, and thanked them gravely before walking away on Rolette's arm.

Hercules stood looking thoughtfully after them, the picture impressing itself upon his mind: the sudden shattering of the gay web which had held the midday landing-place, the vanishing of the people who had gathered to await the steamboat, the boat itself now taking on cargo, the receding stretcher-bearers and their burden, young Joseph running before them, and now Jane and Rolette,

once more together. He felt Jane's grief like a tangible thing; though he had never himself become intimate enough with the child Virginia had been, he could yet experience a personal sorrow at her death. Knowing, too, how devoted she was to her children, he could understand that the depth of Jane's grief had not yet been revealed, and the thought that now, if at any time, she might of her own accord go back to Rolette. But he thought of this not with either dismay or hope, but with a kind of tired apathy, as if he had fought too long.

9.

The Tide at Flood

1839-1843

A WEEK after the funeral, Hercules went over to the island to call upon Jane. October had aged, a cold northeast wind tore the sienna and saffron leaves from trees, and on the island made a shower of gold from quaking aspen and birch there, spreading over path and earth a yellow carpet upon which dark, thinning autumnal shadows were flecked. The cold wind presaged winter coming. He stood on the island's shore and looked back toward the village, where the trappers were setting out for the winter in the wilderness, fewer of them, he thought, than before, always fewer. The great brigades were no more, would probably never be again at the meeting place of the rivers. Time passes, he thought dispassionately. Thinking thus, he turned toward Jane's little house, and his pulse quickened; he thought again with a warmth of affection flooding him, how he would rejoice if only he were walking now to his own home, to where his own wife waited for him, his wife in the image and person of Jane; but resolutely he put his thought down and hurried on.

She was packing, on her knees before a hamper into which she was putting clothes which Eugenie brought to her. Her face had a hollow look, but her eyes were a little more serene now; for a few days of that week just past she had looked very old, but this had passed, and now she bore the mark of her grief only in the wanness and gauntness of her beautiful features; this aspect, however, lent to her features an aspect of otherworldness, a spiritual quality which intensified her beauty. He held his breath momentarily, standing there on the threshold.

"It is M. Dousman," said Eugenie. "We have need of his strong arm."

Hercules assured them that he would be delighted to be of any help whatever.

"No, no, please, Mistaire Dousman," said Jane. "You mus' overlook my failure to rise, I am tired, I mus' pack. Sit down, please."

Eugenie went out of the room, and Jane sat back on her heels, her small body diminutive in the flowing skirts spread all around her.

"You're going back to Rolette, then?" Hercules asked.

She nodded thoughtfully, cocking her head a little to one side and looking at him with strange intentness. "You have do this, you have tell me he was ill. Now I have see this for myself. Something is wrong with him, and pairhaps that is why he is drink' so all the time." She shook her head, sighing wearily. "I do not know. I only know you were right. I have not forgive him his liquor, but if he need' me, I mus' go to him. And I think he need' me; he, too, have suffaire because of Virginie." She broke off and looked down. "I miss her vair' much, I do not know how to say it."

Hercules sympathized gently, but returned presently to Rolette. How did he seem affected? Did he complain of being ill?

"Oh, M'sieu' Rolette, he say nothing," she cried. "He is too proud to say to me he is ill. But I can tell. It is in his ches', I think."

"Does he seem to have pain?"

"Some time I think he do. He drink, and I can do nothing with him. But you know him, he will not go to bed, he will not see the doctaire, he will do nothing at all."

"Have you tried?"

"Not yet vair' hard. When I do, he will say I nag him."

He watched her while she relieved Eugenie of more clothing. When Eugenie had gone out again, he asked about Joseph. Was he staying with his father, then?

"Yes, but it will not be for long. He has write to Mistaire Sibley before he come home, and in the spring he is to go to Pembina to work in the trade. We have not know this, but he say so."

"You'll be alone again after all, then," observed Hercules.

She nodded. "Yes, vair' much alone. I do not know what Elizabeth will say now that I come home again; she is so devote' to

M'sieu' Rolette, it seem she just live for him and for no one else."

Hercules said that he had noticed this. He sat watching her for a while; she was preoccupied, her thoughts still upon the sad events which had just taken place. He was glad that she was returning to live with Rolette, and said so.

"He need' me," she said simply. "I see that now. He is not young, and now he is begin' to show his age. He do not make these long trips so often now, he is more at home; when he is so, I know he is not well."

After half an hour, he took his leave. There was a queer choking sensation that he felt; he was depressed that after all the Rolettes were together again, and yet he was happy that it was so; this paradox of emotions persisted all the way back to the mainland; he could not escape it. He knew that his satisfaction at this culmination of the separation between Rolette and Jane was due solely to his wish that both of them might be happier; but at the same time he recognized that his depression grew out of his own withheld affection for Jane, his strong and growing love for her, the control and suppression of which afforded him so much concealed distress and concern. He went through his office into Rolette's, and found his partner standing listlessly at the window. He sat on the edge of Rolette's table, swinging one leg a little.

"I've just come from Jane's house," he said. "She's packing to come back. I'm glad it's come to this at last, Joe. It's the best thing."

Rolette looked at him with weary eyes. "Maybe," he said laconically. "Me, I don't know. I'm as fond of her as I ever was, but it comes to me now more than ever, now I'm feeling my bones a little, as the saying is, I should never have married her. I was always too old for her. At first, you know how it was, I was still young, I was taken by her when I saw her sitting on the Brisbois fence one day when I passed—she was a child, then, but pretty, very beautiful. She was a child when I married her, still, and then I went away four years and came back to her; that was no way to do. We were happy enough, but something in her is still that child. Do you understand me, Hercules?"

"Yes, I understand it all quite well," said Hercules quietly.

Rolette shrugged. "Now, I don't know. I know only I should

never have married her then, I could have waited, later on, perhaps."
He shrugged again. "Once I thought time would tell—and now
time, I fear, is too short to tell. . . ."

"Have you seen a doctor, Joe?"

"No. I don't need one," said Rolette shortly. "How was it with
her packing?" he went on. "Is she almost finished?"

"I didn't notice. I watched her only, how tired she looked."

Rolette came slowly from the window and sat down at the table.
"She took Virginia's death very hard. If she could only cry—but
she couldn't, no tears came, just those terrible sobs, night and day.
Now she's resigned to it, but something went out of her. That it
should have come like that, with no warning. All along it was
Joe who had been ill. Virginia would write us and say that Joe
had been sick, and she would write Crooks, and Crooks would in
turn mention this in his letters. All the time, you see, Joe sick, Joe
unwell, and then this to come all unexpected." He shook his head.

Hercules sympathized. Nevertheless, he felt, things would be different now that Jane was returning. He himself had shared Rolette's
uneasiness of mind at Jane's living in so isolated a fashion on the
island, but he had recognized how little might be done about it.
Now that she was coming back, all would be well again.

Rolette shook his head. "It won't be the same. Now I couldn't
even stand those discussions about her clothes; if Stambaugh wrote,
I don't know what I would tell him. I'm better off now than I
was, but I don't know."

Hercules said nothing more. He slid from the table, glanced briefly
from the window, and observed that he must be getting back to
work, since he saw the priest, Mazzuchelli, coming up the road,
doubtless to see him, and returned to his own office. He was
thoughtful. Rolette did not look well, but neither did he look like a
man suffering from a grievous illness. He thought that by some
means he must induce Rolette to see Doctor Foote, lest Rolette be
suffering from some disease which might be communicated to Jane.
He began to feel a slow, insidious depression creeping over him,
something he could not escape, something deriving from his concern for Jane on the one hand and his awareness of the swift,
inexorable passage of time on the other, the years going by with
nothing in them of Jane for himself, nothing for them together. He

sat down to wait for the priest, already calculating how much money he would give him for the new stone church now being built as a result of the incessant energy of the dark-eyed Italian missionary.

The months went by, and, as slowly, Rolette's health fell away. He came unfailingly to the office, however, working sometimes among the pelts, sometimes in the Company's store. The village grew, and Hercules increased his wealth, despite the sums he gave out to all manner of charities, to the churches and their societies whose members, like Hercules, hoped vaguely for the betterment of mankind and, lacking Hercules' perception, continued to hope from one generation through the next. In this time Hercules grew close to bitterness. He resigned himself to Jane's contentment with her husband and threw himself with renewed vigor into his schemes for the years to come. Long ago, it seemed, when as a boy he had witnessed the occupation of Mackinac by the British and seen the blunders of the Americans together with the fighting methods of the British, he had believed that a man of wealth whose ideals were held untarnished within him might bring into being through his wealth a nucleus of people who would eschew the pettinesses of communal living for an existence made more harmonious and pleasant for all its members. He dispensed his wealth liberally; this was easy to do, for the western migration brought ever more and more people; his land holdings went up, his agricultural investments began to pay rich dividends; his shipping interests increased in value. But he found that nothing could change the fundamental nature of people; he found that as often as his wealth was used for social betterment, it was used for private aggrandizement; nor could he sit in judgment on any one but himself for his hope.

He turned from his dream without looking back upon it and strove to fill the empty place in his heart by new ventures. He joined with Juneau and Kilbourn in Milwaukee in a project for a canal from the Rock River to Lake Michigan, but even as the Territorial government blessed the plan he surrendered this for a mounting interest in railroads. He journeyed to St. Peters and with Sibley bought large tracts of land in that region. He spent night after night laying plans for his new home, which he was now ready to have built on the site of the old fort.

The irony inherent in all his activities lay in his constant thought of Jane; since her return to Rolette, he thought of her all the more; he could not banish her from his mind. He had thought that with her return to Rolette, he could escape her hold on him by turning to all the pursuits in which he had foreseen himself engaged years ago. But, despite his resignation to loss of her, he could not dismiss her; she haunted his thoughts, though he saw her seldom. If he left Prairie du Chien, he was always happy to come back, not so much because it was his home place as because Jane was there; often in the middle of the night while he sat at work upon his books, her image took possession of his mind's eye, he saw her with her head provocatively cocked to one side, her eyes flashing at him, her smile mocking him; there were occasions when he found it utterly impossible even to put her from his thoughts. So deep was the futility with which he looked upon Jane, that for long periods he was apparently unaware of Rolette's steady decline.

Two years passed, and another winter. Rolette had aged in this time. There were occasional days—his "bad days," as he called them—when he did not come to the office, but sent some one to inform Hercules that he would not be down. From time to time he passed his tasks to Hercules to perform; he was no longer equal to many of them. Again and again, increasingly with the passing of time, he asked more favors from his younger partner, and slowly Hercules began to appreciate the extent of Rolette's involvement in various ventures.

One morning early in spring of the third year since Jane's return to live with him, Rolette sent Eugenie to ask whether Hercules could take the day and accompany the women to the syrup camp at the brook across the Mississippi from Prairie du Chien. Many of the villagers were already in the maple groves making sugar and syrup, and Rolette's camp had been opened, but he himself could not go; he was not up to it.

"But who will stay with Rolette?" Hercules asked Eugenie.

"Elizabeth will stay. She is all tam wit' heem."

"All right. Tell Rolette, I'll meet the ladies at the landing place near his boat."

He resigned his work with a mingling of reluctance at being

too long away from it, and of pleasure at the thought of being with Jane. He went a little early to the landing place, so that he might not keep them waiting. Some one had been at the boat, since materials were already packed there: birchbark for casseaux and mococks, basswood spouts, little buckets for the maple sap, and flannel for straining it. He thought it would be one of the engagés, most likely, and so it was; while Hercules waited, he came with a few blankets, "in case of cold," he explained. It was Souligne. Marking his birdlike air, Hercules went swiftly back to that trip down the lake from Mackinac to Green Bay, so exhausting to Souligne. Sixteen years ago! he thought. Souligne showed very little aging since then, but obviously the very fact that he no longer went out regularly indicated that he was losing his usefulness. Hercules watched him dispassionately, making trivial conversation.

Presently the women came, Jane hurrying ahead of them. She was dressed to withstand either a clement early April day, or late winter weather, since she wore a crinoline dress with leg of mutton sleeves, a woollen scarf and shawl, and a fur toque darker than Souligne's coonskin cap. She came hurrying up to Hercules, carrying a long cloak of snuff-brown broadcloth.

"Oh, Mistaire Dousman, I have keep you waiting. I am so sorry."

"Madame need not distress herself. I came early on purpose not to keep you instead."

He helped her into the boat and Eugenie after her.

"Will it be a good day, do you think?" she asked him.

"I believe it will," he said, while Souligne shoved off into the Mississippi.

A light wind blew from the south, presaging even warmer weather. The river, which had broken open from beneath its winter coat earlier than usual, was filled with blocks of ice, making travel difficult, but Souligne had lost none of his deftness, and Hercules could handle a paddle as well as any voyageur. Already along the shores bluebirds and robins sang, and vesper sparrows haunted the willows, yellow with pollinating catkins now; high above ospreys wheeled over the Mississippi's shallows seeking food, and geese flew over from time to time. The air was thick and heady with the thawing fragrance of snow and ice, almost a miasma on the river, but occasionally there came also the sweetness of willow in

bloom, and the faint aroma of blossoming flowers along the shores where the snow had gone.

They reached the camping place across from the mouth of the Wisconsin, and were hailed by those who had preceded them, many of them by several days, and not a few by weeks. Several families had camps here in the maples, and remained throughout the season, day and night, without returning to the village until the sap had ceased to flow. Mococks of sugar, buckets of syrup, barrels of sap were everywhere in evidence; the camps were filled with activity— men coming in with yokes weighted by heavy buckets of sap, women tending the fire, cleaning and washing buckets, casseaux, spouts, strainers. The odor of sap and syrup held the air.

They went immediately to Rolette's camp, which two of the French-Canadian women, aware of their coming, had got ready, even to the extent of starting a fire and scouring the boiling kettle. Hercules set to work without delay, but in a little while his thoughts turned to Jane and held there. He watched her from time to time, seeing that, though she habitually chose the lightest work for herself to do, she shirked none. When Souligne and Eugenie went among the trees to wait for the casseaux to fill with sap, he went over to Jane.

"I never thought to ask, Jane. How's Joe?"

She shook her head, and made an expression of distress. "He is not well, not well at all, Mistaire Dousman. He look' forward to this trip, and now he cannot make it, you see. So he have evair' little while these bad days, and they come more often. But Elizabeth, she take' care of him vair' well."

"Does he have the doctor?"

"*Non,* he will not see him. You know how stubborn he is; I can do nothing with him. And he still drink."

"How does he get it?"

"Why, Mistaire Dousman, I pairmit him to have it, I think if it do him good, he may have it; besides, he is sick, I like it no more than evaire I did, but if something should happen to him, I would nevaire forgive myself." She looked uncertainly toward the maple groves. "Will it be long, the sap?"

He assured her that it would yet be some time before they need think about hanging the kettle. Meanwhile, he suggested, why not

walk to the top of the hill—Pike's Peak there, which Lieutenant Zebulon Pike had selected for the site of that fort built later in Prairie du Chien. The south slope was clear of snow, and the frost was apparently also out of the earth there. "We can follow that tributary of the brook; it leads to a spring on the west slope, if you like."

She looked once again toward the maples, and assented.

They walked in silence, her eyes moving constantly from stone to tree, bush to sky, and he seeing only her at his side, thinking with increasing bitterness how the years that had divided them were not yet ended, and perhaps would never be. They passed the spring and reached the level place at the top of the hill. Here the brown grass and leaves were colorful with lavender and blue windflowers. He bent and picked a few of them for Jane, putting them gravely into her hand and closing her fingers about them.

"They make the winter seem less long," he said, smiling.

She cocked her head at him. "Mistaire Dousman seem in a mood today. Pairhaps he do not feel well?"

He laughed. He felt all right, he assured her, but for a pain in his memory.

"What mannaire of pain is that?"

"Very serious," he said. "It is almost as serious as Joe's."

He turned from her and looked east across the river and the prairie. From this hilltop the meeting place of the rivers lay sharply, clearly drawn under the bright April sun: the Wisconsin meandering bluely from the northeast to become one with the broader Mississippi, the great Father of Waters driving powerfully from the north, both streams patterned with ice blocks now, and both rising slowly with their burden of thaw-water from the wilderness country through which they flowed. Between them, on the Mississippi's eastern shore and the long island there, stood Prairie du Chien, its fort this morning bright in the sun with its flag red and blue against a white cloud in the sky there. The sunlight lay summer-like upon the prairie and the eastern hills, though the aspect of winter held still to the land itself, the naked trees, only beginning to thicken with buds, the brown grassland and the undisturbed autumn fields. A few boats moved among the islands above and below Prairie du Chien. Looking upon this beautiful tawny prairie encircled by its

hills, watered by its great rivers, he went back in his thoughts to the eager anticipation and keen joy with which he had set out from Mackinac to make his home here, he thought fleetly of the magic inherent in the vision of the meeting place of the rivers, and he thought of all that had happened since then: the rise and decline of the fur trade, the growth of agriculture, the Indian affairs—and his heart's isolation in his love for Jane, who stood at his side as silently as if she followed his every thought.

"You're so still, Jane," he said quietly.

"I see that Mistaire Dousman is think'; so I do not speak," she said. "But I, too, was think'."

"Ah, what have you to be troubled about?" he said, laughing. "We all know that every one in the village has conspired to shield Madame from toil and care!"

"Yes, that is so," she agreed. "Excep' for that time M'sieu' Rolette drink so."

Between them lay the urgence of Rolette, but neither of them wished to speak of this. If Jane had any knowledge about her husband's health, she would not speak it; Hercules had the conviction, born of his weariness and growing bitterness, that anything might happen, anything but the fulfilment of his dream. What dreams a man has! he thought, thinking bitterly of his hopes for the people of Prairie du Chien, and through them, of those beyond. Beside him stood Jane, tranquil as the sunlight upon her fair skin, so near to him, and yet so far. He could still feel as if it were yesterday, the fire of her lips. He shook his head and half-closed his eyes.

"Come, Jane—we'll go down," he said.

She gave him her hand obediently, her eyes burning for a moment into his, and turned gravely with him to descend the slope.

Late that summer Hercules went to St. Louis to meet Pierre Chouteau and arrange with him for the American Fur Company to function with the Missouri Company more closely as a unit, signing a new trade agreement taking the place of that made in 1834 when Astor had sold out. On midmorning of the day after his return, Hercules was visited by Elizabeth, now a young woman whose demure manner was in no way touched upon by her forthright directness in regard to her father, for whom she bore an unwavering

attachment. She came into his office silently and stood before Hercules' desk waiting for him to speak.

He looked up and came at once to his feet. "Elizabeth—sit down. How are you? I trust the sun is not too hot for you." She sat down, smiling faintly. "I suppose you've come to tell me your father won't be down," he went on. "You know, there's no need of your making this special trip. I know he's not well."

"Yes," she said. "But this morning he wants to see you, Mr. Dousman."

He was immediately apprehensive. "Does he seem any worse to you, Elizabeth?"

"He is worse," she said quietly with a conviction grown from knowledge gained through her unflagging attention to the old man. She looked at him steadily for a long moment before she added, "Papa will die this year."

This he was unwilling to believe. He said that Rolette had been ailing for some time, with little perceptible change except his aging. It was not likely that his death would take place for a number of years. "Has he had the doctor?" he asked, rising to open the door and permit greater circulation of air from the hot summer outside. "I've told him repeatedly to have the doctor, but he doesn't want to."

"He's had the doctor," said Elizabeth.

"What does he say?"

"He says papa is very sick."

Hercules was disagreeably startled. He had accustomed himself to Rolette's indisposition to so great a degree that he had almost come to believe the older man's assertion that his trouble was nothing of importance.

Elizabeth got up quietly and began to walk toward the door.

"Just wait a moment. I'll go with you," he said.

He took his hat and stick and went to join her where she waited just beyond the threshold. On the way to the house, he plied her with questions. Was her father in any pain? It appeared that he suffered a little from time to time. Did the doctor name his ailment? No, he had not. What were the symptoms of his illness? Only a great weakness, some pain in the chest and abdominal regions, sometimes a little fever; also, Rolette had difficulty taking his breath from time to time.

The cloudless day was hot under the summer sun, so that Hercules was uncomfortable by the time they reached the Rolette house. He was refreshed, however, by the dust-free air of the house, secure behind drawn shades. Jane met him in the hall, her face white in the semi-darkness.

"Oh, Mistaire Dousman, I am so glad you have come. My poor M'sieu' Rolette is vair' sick. He say he mus' see you."

"Elizabeth was kind enough to tell me," he said.

"Elizabeth has been vair' kin' to her papa," agreed Jane.

Elizabeth, meanwhile, had gone into Rolette's bedroom and now came out again, nodding. "Papa is ready," she said. "If Mr. Dousman is."

Hercules smiled reassuringly at them both and entered the bedroom. The window here was not quite covered over, so that a shaft of light fell upon the bed and disclosed Rolette lying there. Hercules had not before noticed how thin his partner had grown; Rolette had always worn his clothes carelessly, and his beard had concealed the gauntness of his cheeks. He turned his head toward Hercules.

"*Sacré bleu!* you were long about coming," he said.

If his voice had lost some of its strength, it had lost none of its force. Hercules smiled. He sat down and explained that Elizabeth had come as directly as she could and he had delayed only a little while. "Joe, what's the matter?"

"I want to know first how the business with Chouteau went. I couldn't wait—I have the feeling it may be a long time before I come back to the office."

Hercules told him what had happened. "After all, Chouteau is a realist. He knew as well as we did that buffalo-robes were certain to go out of fashion even as the beaver hats fell before the silk hats; he has no illusions about the trade, but he thinks it's good for twenty or thirty years yet, though it'll never be what it was."

Rolette grinned. "Those were the days, eh? *Ventre Saint-gris!* When I think of those days, it makes the blood rush still." Slowly his smile faded, and he shook his head. "All gone—all those good years gone, Hercules!"

"Times change," agreed Hercules. "I miss the brigades—but I missed them as soon as I left Mackinac."

"I—I miss the woods, the wilderness, the wild country. *Sacré nom!* I miss even the Indians, damn 'em!"

Hercules laughed.

Rolette was abruptly serious once more. "Next thing I want to know—the business. If anything happens to me, will there be enough left for Jane and Elizabeth, if my share is sold? You know, I'm not young."

"Both of them could be quite well off. You needn't worry. Besides, you've felt bad before; you've been down before; you've always got up again."

"Sometime one doesn't get up again," said Rolette. "To me, it makes no great difference. I don't want to die, I don't think any one does. But I've had some good years, many of them; I've had a time to remember, I would not do anything different—unless perhaps the drinking. It was not so necessary as I thought. But you don't know what it is to have a woman nagging at you even when she thinks she's doing her best for you. You've always been a bachelor, and you'll probably stay one."

Hercules felt a faint twinge. He looked steadily down at the older man but offered nothing in reply save to say that in his opinion Rolette was still some way from dying, and there was no necessity to look for that end as yet.

Rolette laughed with something of his old vigor. "You're not the one to hesitate about facing realities, Hercules," he said. "I can tell something by the way Elizabeth looks at me; I read her mind."

"What did the doctor say?"

"He said I must have rest, I must sleep, I must take it easy, and take this medicine three times a day—what is it doctors say? Always these things. Let the machine rest and see if it won't heal itself! That's so, isn't it?"

"Yes. But did he name your trouble?"

"Not to me. Perhaps to Elizabeth."

The sunlight had crept to one of Rolette's dark hands and lay there glowing, illuminating the entire room with its brightness. Rolette's eyes gleamed, as if he had a fever; his hand lay lax; his great eyes roved the room restlessly, like those of a man imprisoned. Hercules held his cane a little tighter.

"Joe, if there's anything you want me to do, you'll say so?"

"Of course. But there's nothing now. If I pass on, then perhaps—but that time isn't yet. If you hear of me getting worse, Hercules, don't wait for me to send for you. Come at once. I'll want to see you."

This was encouraging. If Rolette did not think his illness grave enough at this time to tell Hercules what he withheld, it could not be as serious as he had at first thought. He sat talking for a while longer and then withdrew. He found Jane waiting for him. She came to him, took his hands, drew him to a chair in the parlor, that same parlor where he had sat so uneasily the first time he had come into the house—sixteen years ago now.

"Now, tell me, Mistaire Dousman—what do you think?"

He told her that Rolette was still hopeful; so was he. "If he has a mind to get up, I think he will. There's still fire in his veins, Jane."

"My poor M'sieu' Rolette!" she repeated. "I think maybe if I had stay' with him, this would not have happen'."

He brushed this aside, saying a little tartly that this was a sign of weakness he had not expected to find in her. No, Rolette's illness was nothing grown from her absence alone; it was something more. It was simply the wearing out of machinery put to far more strenuous use than that for which it was intended.

"Mistaire Dousman speak almost like the doctaire."

He smiled. "M'sieu' Rolette will be up again, I'm confident."

"Elizabeth do not think so."

"Elizabeth does not know everything."

He was none too certain, however, that he was right about Rolette's condition. He made his way back to the office and took down his books to look up his accounts, particularly in regard to the amount Rolette was in his debt. Seeing the figures, he smiled wryly at the memory of his assurance that Rolette could die easily. Thirty thousand dollars, a little over: so much Rolette owed him alone. Of course, he reflected, this was not only the sum advanced to stave off Astor's mortgage, but also included payment for Jane's dresses and other things ordered from Stambaugh by Rolette himself at occasions when he found himself unable to pay, as well as certain loans made to Rolette. If the older man died now, he would leave virtually nothing, should Hercules collect this amount. He

was hopeful, however, that Rolette would soon be on his feet again.

He did not hope in vain; within a fortnight Rolette was back at the office, ready to resume his work. He was still pale, he needed to conserve his strength, but he was on his feet, and this was better than half his battle won.

In autumn Hercules went to Milwaukee, going on horse from Prairie du Chien directly across the Wisconsin Territory toward the lake shore. Milwaukee lay to the northeast from the settlement at the meeting place of the rivers, and the way there traversed low rolling country broken by occasional hills and prairie-land into which the settlers had begun to filter. The wilderness at this time was colorful with birds; the migrating warblers came in flocks and took possession of the woods for days at a time—golden-blue prothonotaries, yellow-throated masked warblers with their sweet songs, black and crimson redstarts, gray and yellow myrtle warblers ceaselessly feeding on their southward passage. Hercules rode swiftly along, yet with an eye for bird and beast, and with even more attention for the evidence of growth: new settlements, new cabins and log houses up, the lessening in the number of Indians encountered en route. Woodland and prairie country alike were fragrant with the rich odors of foliage and earth, of blossoms starring the deep grass and riotous in watery places, along streams, ponds, sloughs, lakes—the yellow compositæ, coneflowers, sunflowers of all kinds, with the cardinal flowers' tall spikes among the reeds, the lavender of Joe-Pye weed, and the mauve of the winding ground-nut.

When he reached Milwaukee on the following day, he was astonished anew at the way in which the city had grown from its small beginnings less than a decade before, and he could understand why his holdings there had brought him so substantial an income. He paused briefly at Juneau's place to inquire about the proposed Rock River Canal, and then went on to the home of his brother, George, a new house which stood well back from the street, its three stories raised in brick behind young trees which had not long ago been set out. He rode up the path and around the house, where he came upon his brother just setting out in his carriage. George hailed him joyfully, and got out to come over to where Hercules was dismounting.

"Hercules!" he exclaimed. "I'd just written you. Mother's here, and not too well. She'll be delighted to see you."

Hercules observed quietly that he would be as pleased to see her. "Did she bring Emily along?"

"No, she's at home with father."

Hercules nodded. "I'll go right in, then."

"No, wait a bit. She's sleeping just now. Walk around with me, I want you to get a good look at the new house. Fred can take your horse." He called to a stable boy to take both Hercules' horse and the carriage in which he had been about to ride away.

Hercules put a hand on his brother's arm. "Don't let me keep you from business, George. Make that a cardinal rule."

George shook his head. "No danger. That can wait. After all, I see you less often. Come along."

They walked slowly around the house, George talking animatedly about various details of its construction.

"You've really done yourself proud, George," said Hercules. "I hope you can pay for all of it."

"I can handle it," said George confidently.

"Good. If you need help, of course, you know . . ."

George laughed. "I can never understand, Hercules, how one so essentially prodigal with wealth as you can yet amass so much of it. You give it away right and left, you make loans I would be dubious about, you subscribe to every charity . . ." He shook his head. "I can't understand it."

Hercules replied gently that charities were investments, too. Besides, he made no careless loans; rather outright gifts than carelessly secured loans. In addition to this, his investments had been good. Indeed, next year he too would build a house. He added quietly that it would be larger than George's.

"You, a house? And larger than mine?" exclaimed George in amazement. "What in the world will you do in it? Get yourself lost, eh?" He stopped suddenly and held to Hercules' arm. "Or—say, are you getting married, Hercules?"

"I don't know that I'll get married," Hercules said. "I have no plans for marriage at present."

George made a rapid calculation. "Forty-two—you'll soon be beyond it, Hercules. Your first wife hardly counted; you had her so

short a time." He went on in this vein until Hercules thought it expedient to change the subject.

"How's Marthe, George?"

"Fine, fine. Just now she's off somewhere in the city. But she'll be back in time for dinner, never fear."

"And that land of ours in the south part, George?"

George clenched his fists in sudden, spontaneous elation. "My dear brother, you never did a wiser thing than to invest in it. It will pay you a hundredfold, mark my words. I say to you not to sell yet; hang on; in ten years you can be a rich man simply by disposing of those lots."

Hercules smiled at such enthusiasm. "I'm already a rich man, George," he said. He stopped suddenly and waved toward the house, where, at a window, his mother sat. "She's up now," he said. "I'll go in and see her."

They went together to the second floor, where his mother's room was, George to stay only for a few moments before taking his leave to continue on the business, on his way to which Hercules had caught him. Hercules was left alone with his mother. He went over, kissed her, and sat down near her, now thinking how long it had been since he had seen her. But she was frail now; she looked more than her age. Her hair had grown white, and her face had thinned, too. But her smile was unchanged.

"If I had dreamed you might be here, I'd have come sooner," he said. "And now I find you unwell, like an invalid in a chair."

She nodded. "I *am* an invalid, Hercules." She looked him up and down, talking desultorily about her illness. "You look well, my boy. You look very well. We all know you've succeeded. Do you know what Drew used to say about you, Hercules? I've heard him so many times talking to your father. You know, Drew's gone now, too."

"I liked Drew," said Hercules.

"He used to sit there and say, 'Aye, ye can make up yer mind, Dousman; that boy 'll have a bright journey through his life. Ye mark my words.'" She imitated him perfectly, even to the burr of his dialect.

Hercules laughed. "But a man's success from the outside is never the same to him on the inside."

"You're rich," said his mother. "Your father and I never were."

"And never needed to be. You were happy, you are happy. I'm as restless as Rolette used to be, except that my restlessness doesn't take the form his did."

She smiled. "We've always been happy—but he worried me, with his going into the wild country so often."

He could not help thinking of her thirty years ago, thinking of that evening when she stood in the doorway looking anxiously for Michael Dousman, who came only to warn of capture by the British. She had the same look in her eyes now; she gazed not at him, but through him, looking back into the same years to which his mind's eye had turned. For a brief moment this shell of memory held.

She talked about her sons with increasing animation. "John does so well; he is such a good doctor, and so kind—I think sometimes he is too generous. George and Talbot are so well established in their businesses. But you, Hercules—you've done better than any of them; we've always been proud of you."

He smiled, but ignored this. "How's Emily?" he asked quietly.

"She's a good girl, Hercules. "But now she wants to go to her father. I didn't know what to promise her."

He nodded. "Next year I'm building a house, too, a large house. I'll have a place for her then."

"She's a pretty girl, too," his mother went on reflectively. "She might well make a good marriage."

"She shall, if she's a mind to it. And she'll have a handsome dowry. I've planned for that."

"But you'll not marry her off just to be free of her?" asked his mother anxiously.

"You know I wouldn't," he chided her gently. "She shall have her own choice, and if she decides not to be married, she shall not."

"We'll not like to lose her, but after all she's no longer a child. Still, it will be some time before she'll be thinking of marriage." She sighed tiredly. "Hercules, you'll be here for a while?"

He assured her that he would.

"Then I'll sleep a little again. I heard your voice and got up."

He left her, thinking still about those early years on Mackinac, caught in a web of time in which he knew time past as well as time

present, a fusion common to all men from time to time throughout the experience of living, and he thought, how different things are now! Drew's words about him coiled about the core of discontentment at his heart.

He returned to Prairie du Chien at night ten days later, going, as usual, directly to the Company's office. There he found Lapiage awaiting him, the voyageur dozing on the stoop where he sat. He was almost upon Lapiage's rotund body before he saw him and stopped. Lapiage came to, blinking.

"Dousman!" he exclaimed. "I've been waiting for you since God knows when. You're to go to Rolette's right away, no matter what time you get in."

"What's the matter? Is Joe down again?"

"He is. Bad. Three days now," said Lapiage shortly. "He's been asking for you—we sent to Milwaukee."

"I got no message."

He wanted to ask about Rolette's illness, but he would not take the time. Tired as he was, he rode on over to Rolette's. However, Lapiage ran alongside, explaining that the old man had collapsed in his office after a cold rainy day which he had spent at work. They had taken him right home, and the doctor said he was in a bad way.

Yellow lights burned throughout the Rolette house. Some one came out and rode away just as Hercules came up, but he could not determine who it was. He flung himself from his horse and ran up the verandah, throwing open the door and hurrying into the parlor. Jane was pacing the floor; she turned, startled at his entrance, gave a cry of relief, and came toward him.

"Oh, Mistaire Dousman—please to go in right away. M'sieu' Rolette, he call' for you so often. It wring my heart that I cannot bring you when he want you. But he still live', he wish to speak to you."

He held her hands for a moment and looked into her eyes. "How is he, Jane?"

She shook her head. "He is not good. The doctaire say he has the lung fevaire; there is nothing to do but hope. He has no strength lef', all that wondairful strength is gone from his body!"

He went into the bedroom, held in a yellow half-light shed by

guarded lamps. Elizabeth rose silently from the bedside and went out to join Jane. Rolette lay on his back, breathing with difficulty, his eyes closed, his lips parted. Across his forehead beads of perspiration made a crown of light, holding the reflection from the walls beyond the lamps. Hot in the room was the cloying odor of sickness, of medicines. Hercules sat down in the place where Elizabeth had been.

"Joe," he said softly.

Rolette turned his head slowly; his eyes opened to narrow slits. Presently he saw Hercules bending above him.

"Joe, it's Hercules," he said.

"Damn it, Hercules, where've you been?"

"I've been in Milwaukee. Just got back. Save your strength, Joe."

"No good. None to save." He paused and took a deep breath. "Hercules, there's something I want you to do." He was shaken abruptly by a fit of weak coughing. Hercules bent over him, steadying his shoulders. For a few moments more the old man lay breathing, his weakness obviously greater than he cared to admit.

"Take it easy, Joe. We've got all night."

"Jane and Elizabeth," the older man gasped.

"Do you want them?"

"No, no—only you. Hercules, take care of them. Watch over them. They don't know the world, either one of them. It needs some one . . ." The coughing set upon him again, a horrible futile retching.

"Go easy, Joe. There's no hurry."

"A dead man can't talk," said Rolette with something of his old vehemence. *"Sacré bleu!* Answer me."

"Joe, I'll do anything I can for you."

"About Jane and Elizabeth . . ."

"Yes, Joe. I'll take care of them. Don't fear."

The older man's head rolled from side to side. "I tried to be a good husband to her—but I was too old." He closed his eyes and made futile mutterings which came incoherently from between his dry lips.

Hercules stood for a minute, waiting until Rolette spoke clearly again.

"My debts," mumbled the old man.

"Don't worry about them, Joe."

Rolette groaned and sank back a little into the bed. He said nothing more. Hercules went silently into the hall and on to the parlor, where Jane and Elizabeth sat. Both of them looked up apprehensively at his entrance.

"I think he'll sleep now," he said. He glanced from one to the other of them, seeing how exhausted both of them were. "You look tired, both of you."

"We have not sleep vair' much," admitted Jane.

"Some one must be with father," said Elizabeth, slipping noiselessly from the room.

Impulsively Jane came over to Hercules, clung to his lapels and lowered her head to his shoulder. She began to weep softly, stifling her sobs, her exhaustion making itself manifest. He held her to him briefly before he led her to a chair, where she sat tensely staring at the wall opposite.

"What shall I do without him, Mistaire Dousman? M'sieu' Rolette was a good man in his way. If he die now, I will be alone, but for Elizabeth."

Hercules said quietly that there was no need to think of this, since Rolette was not yet dead, and that in any case Madame Rolette need not concern herself. Her immediate need at the moment was sleep. "If Madame and Elizabeth will sleep, I'll watch at Joe's bedside."

"I do not know that I can sleep," she said.

"Nonsense. Of course you can. You will do neither yourself nor Joe any good exhausting yourself like this."

She consented finally to rest, and he returned to the bedroom to take Elizabeth's place. Rolette still slept, deep in the bed. His breathing was irregular, deep, uncertain, so that often it came so labored as to make an imperative groaning sound. Hercules moved his chair next to the window so that he might look out, turning from time to time to watch for any change in Rolette's condition.

At dawn Elizabeth came silently in, touched Hercules on the shoulder, and woke him from a shallow doze to tell him she was ready to take her turn once more. Hercules let himself out of the house. His horse still stood where he had left it; he mounted and rode thoughtfully to his own little house where he went immediately to his bedroom and cast himself upon the bed, fully clothed, to get what sleep he could before going to the office.

At midday, when he went to his desk, he dispatched messages to

Sibley, to Chouteau, and to young Joseph Rolette at Pembina, to notify them of Rolette's imminent death. Then he got at Rolette's accounts and began to put them in order against the inevitable day when a reckoning must be made. He worked at this most of the day. During the dusk hour, he walked over to Rolette's and inquired about him.

There was no change, said Jane. "But I know he will not live. I feel it," she cried. "Oh, my poor M'sieu' Rolette!"

While he had watched in the night, Hercules had noticed a bottle of whiskey and a glass on the medicine table. He asked about this. How had it come there? Why was it there?

"It was I who put it there. Whenevaire M'sieu' Rolette take sick, his pain is so much less with the whiskey that I have not the heart to say he mus' not have it. Do I do wrong, Mistaire Dousman?"

"No, I think not." He asked about Elizabeth.

"She take it vair' hard. She live for her fathaire; she see no one else; she is devote' to him." Her forehead wrinkled, her mouth drew down a little; she shrugged. "I do not know what we will do, she and I, when he is go from us."

He said presently that he would return to share the waking hours with Rolette in the night, and went back to his office, deep in a confusion of thoughts about Jane and the years before her.

In the second night after Hercules' return from Milwaukee, Rolette died.

Hercules wasted no time in taking hold of Rolette's affairs. He made public no word of the older man's debt to him, but summoned all his known creditors to meet him at the Company's office one evening and persuaded them to accept only partial cash payment for the amounts due them, the remainder in land or Company goods. In this way he saved money for Jane and Elizabeth; that it was at his own expense made no difference, since he had now more money than he knew what to do with.

All that winter he worked to straighten out Rolette's tangled affairs. He called on Jane from time to time to discuss with her the settling of the estate, saying nothing about the sum Rolette owed him, having already crossed this from his own books, and salving his business conscience by reminding himself that the land he had

taken from Rolette in return for some of the money loaned him had paid him enough to cover the entire amount of Rolette's indebtedness to him.

When he had finished in the spring, he brought to Jane his plans for the house on the mound where once the old fort had stood. He had decided to build not squarely on the fort, but a little south of it, so that only a portion of his new house would actually rest above the fort's foundations. He had spared nothing in these plans; he had spaced even the trees which he wished to dot his estate, and before the building of the house was begun he had ordered many trees brought to Prairie du Chien and planted. The house would be set in the middle of a ten-acre plot of land; it would face to the east, a broad brick walk leading down to the gates. A verandah would almost circle the house. To the south he would in time have ponds; angling away from the house on the north he would erect a series of lesser buildings—immediately near the house, an ice-house and his office; behind this, a wine cellar; beyond this, a carriage shed and stables; and eastward, a laundry. On the west, a long slope of vineyard and lawn would sweep to the shore of the Mississippi. Two stories with an attic, of brick and stone and wood brought in for panelling, stair treads, framing—he had planned even the servants' quarters in the minutest detail. A white picket fence would surround the entire estate.

She made little suggestions from time to time, most of which he incorporated into his plans. When presently the building was started, Hercules brought her to watch the workmen one afternoon. Already the summer had begun; some of the trees he had put in were leafed out; some were just beginning to put forth new leaves to replace the buds which had fallen off as a result of transplanting. There was an aspect of spring still among the pale-green trees. Of the house, only the beginning of the framework was rising now; the foundation was in, and workmen pounded and sawed, hastening to complete the house before winter.

"Oh, but it is big," said Jane. "It is too big for Mistaire Dousman. What will he do in a house so big all alone?"

"I hope not always to be alone," he said soberly, looking directly at her.

She asked about Emily.

"She'll come as soon as the house is finished. Since my mother died last winter, she's been like a woman at Mackinac, helping father. And there'll be servants, of course." He shrugged. "Perhaps even your Eugenie."

She drew herself up in startled surprise. "Mistaire Dousman know vair' well that Eugenie will not leave me."

"Indeed I do," he replied, smiling impishly now.

She caught his smile and answered with her eyes. Turning, she looked critically over the great framework rising so rapidly before them.

"If you have any changes to suggest, Jane, suggest them now. It would be unwise to make them after the house is finished."

"I have say so much already," she answered. "I do not wish to say more. Besides, there is nothing more to say. I like it, I like all your plans."

"I hope you'll find yourself able to subscribe to all of them in the future," said Hercules matter-of-factly.

"Mistaire Dousman has always seem' so sure of himself," she answered, glancing at him with sly mockery from the corners of her eyes.

He was not disturbed.

As summer and autumn waned toward winter, the house neared completion. In early November, sitting in his old office, where always the aura of years past held to the atmosphere, Hercules wrote a long letter to his father. He wrote of many things, as in that first letter he had written to his father from this place. *I have achieved one goal, and foresee that I may soon achieve another. My new home is almost completed; it is so close to being done that I already think of it as finished. I suppose Emily might be sent on in the spring, if you do not yourself need her with you. I would like her here; besides, she should be sent perhaps to Florissant in the south for some further education. I am the owner of the most pretentious home in the Territory of Wisconsin; it has about it an air of grace such as I would never have dreamed possible; and it is said not without basis, that I am the wealthiest man in the entire Northwest Territory. I believe it is true. This is despite all the sums I have given away for one cause or another. Yet I am not at peace with myself, I am not as happy as I might be. I remember how once you*

said to me, You are young, my boy! And indeed, I was, was I not!
And before mother died, she told me what Drew had said. May he
rest in peace; I, too, was fond of him, but did he know, I wonder,
that the gleaming of a bright journey might conceal the bitterest dis-
appointment and dissatisfaction with one's self? Perhaps not. He was
a simple soul who had only the beginnings of knowledge about his
fellowmen; he did not ever come to know the full depths of duplicity
and meanness of which men are capable. I was once naïve enough
to think that a man of wealth and power might do much for his
fellowmen. I have wealth, but I have rejected power; I learned in
time that I was wrong, even with the best intentions a man can have.

Late in that month the house was completed, ready for occupation.
Hercules had ordered furniture from Stambaugh; some of it had
arrived from St. Louis; still more had come down the Fox-Wisconsin
waterway; Sibley had sent some hand-carved pieces from his own
new home. Before he was ready to move in, Hercules took Jane
through the house one autumn evening, from room to room, coming
at last to the verandah looking westward, where the sun had vanished behind the hills, though its red light still lay upon the treetops
there and in the east bathed the stones of the little hilltop cemetery
where her Uncle Michael Brisbois now lay in a high place at last
free of the Mississippi's annual flood waters.

Both of them were silent, looking into the west, across the Mississippi to the vast country beyond the prairie where the village stood.
They were sober now, their examination of the new house having
brought home to them more than anything else the changes which
had taken place in the past decade, making them sharply conscious
of time fleetly passing. They talked desultorily about the house now
as a feat accomplished.

"It is even more beautiful than my own," she said thoughtfully.
"I would nevaire have think a house could be bettaire."

He took her hands and drew her close to him. "Jane, will you
share it with me?"

"M'sieu' Rolette," she murmured.

"I know—it's little more than a year," he said. "But tell me now.
You must know I've loved you for a long time, Jane."

"Yes, I have know you have been vair' fond of me," she admitted.

He searched her eyes, appraising him as calmly now. There was nothing of the mockery so familiar to her; her gaze was steady, her lips firm.

"Jane," he said gently, urgently.

"Yes, Hercules," she answered steadily. "I, too, have learned to love you."

For an eternal moment their eyes held; then she came into his arms, and he took her mouth and through this ecstasy rose a great conviction of security against the years to come, a warmth of happiness flooding him, overpowering an emotion which she shared in all its fullness.

She drew gently back. "In one year more, Hercules, I will come to share this with you."

He smiled to conceal his first immediate disappointment. "After waiting seventeen years, I can wait one more, surely," he said.

"And I know," she went on quietly, "that Mistaire Dousman will make me as happy as I can be." She smiled, and once again came that familiar glint of mockery he knew and loved. "But there is one thing I hope—that Mistaire Dousman will not forget to make those han'some speeches he make so well after I am his wife."

He laughed, and with the sudden warm conviction that the world lay at his feet, he drew her unresistingly back into his arms, and so held her, while there flowered up within him a feeling of such peace and contentment as he had never known before, a withdrawal from the world outside into a country of his own, where now his spirit's restlessness might find its haven in Jane, toward whom its ceaseless striving had always been directed. The moment was endless, washing down the years behind, the years before.

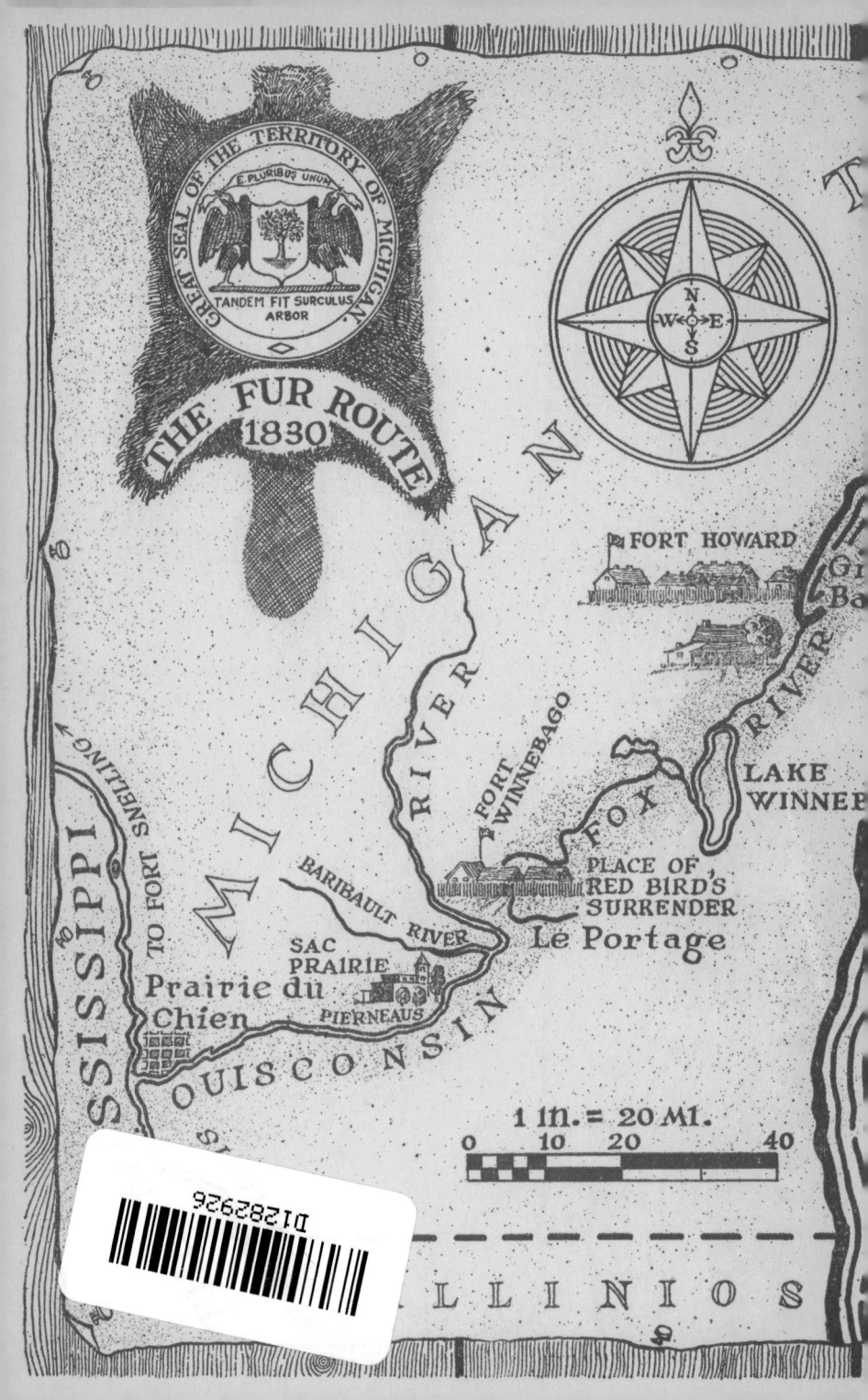